CAUGHT IN PASSION'S FLAME

His hands cupped her chin, lifting her head toward him. Bending over her, he kept one hand on her neck while the other slid slowly downward, his fingers grazing the ruffled bodice of her dress, then slipping lower.

Complete panic washed over her, a panic issuing as much from her own desire as from his seductive touch. "Let me go," she cried and pulled herself up out of the chair. "I must go back." The wine glass tumbled to the floor, spilling the garnet liquid.

She got to the door with her hand on the latch before he caught her. He pushed it shut and pressed against her, turning her body to face him.

Claire threw up her hand, but he caught it and pressed her arm against the door. His lips were hard, almost bruising, against her face, moving across her cheek, her neck, her chin until they locked against her lips.

His body was a flame and she was caught in its heat. It went searing through her and set her afire . . .

SIZZLING ROMANCE
from Zebra Books

REBEL PLEASURE   (1672, $3.95)
by Mary Martin

Union agent Jason Woods knew Christina was a brazen flirt, but his dangerous mission had no room for a clinging vixen. Then he caressed every luscious contour of her body and realized he could never go too far with this confederate tigress.

PASSION'S PARADISE   (1618, $3.75)
by Sonya T. Pelton

Angel was certain that Captain Ty would treat her only as a slave. She plotted to use her body to trick the handsome devil into freeing her, but before she knew what happened to her resolve, she was planning to keep him by her side forever.

TEXAS TIGRESS   (1714, $3.95)
by Sonya T. Pelton

As the bold ranger swaggered back into town, Tanya couldn't stop the flush of desire that scorched her from head to toe. But all she could think of was how to break his heart like he had shattered hers—and show him only love could tame a wild TEXAS TIGRESS.

WILD EMBRACE   (1713, $3.95)
by Myra Rowe

Marisa was a young innocent, but she had to follow Nicholas into the Louisiana wilderness to spend all of her days by his side and her nights in his bed. . . . He didn't want her as his bride until she surrendered to his WILD EMBRACE.

TENDER TORMENT   (1550, $3.95)
by Joyce Myrus

From their first meeting, Caitlin knew Quinn would be a fearsome enemy, a powerful ally and a magnificent lover. Together they'd risk danger and defy convention by stealing away to his isolated Canadian castle to share the magic of the Northern lights.

RAPTURE'S
SPLENDOR
ASHLEY SNOW

ZEBRA BOOKS
KENSINGTON PUBLISHING CORP.

ZEBRA BOOKS

are published by

Kensington Publishing Corp.
475 Park Avenue South
New York, NY 10016

First printing: February 1987

Printed in the United States of America

One

All the way across the moor Pastor Donovan's words echoed in Claire's mind, blinding her to the first signs of spring in the stark hills around her.

"Why not go after Alan, then? In my mind 'twould be the best thing for all the Montcrieffs."

Yes, it would be the best thing—the best thing for Pastor Donovan. In one stroke it would rid him of the two most vexing problems in his parish—Alyce Dawes and Tom Montcrieff. Particularly Alyce.

Claire had waited a long moment before answering.

"Alan has been gone nearly two years now. I wouldn't even know where to find him."

She could still see how the pastor had shuffled a little as he pulled at his beard, obviously hedging yet too intrigued with the possibility of getting rid of her family to back down.

"His aunt told me only a few weeks back that he was near New Netherland somewhere. She'd know right enough where to find him. She's goin' there herself in just a month."

It was all Claire could do to keep the disgust she felt for this ineffectual clergyman out of her voice.

"You know Esther Varn would never send me to

Alan. She doesn't want to see him marry me — or any other lass for that matter. She's made no secret of the fact that she hopes her Daniel will remain his heir."

"All the same, the two of you are spoken for, are you not?"

"You know we are. You heard our pledge yourself."

" 'Twas so long ago I barely remember. When did you hear from him last?"

"It was before last Twelfth Night. Not a word since. Perhaps he's gone and married some other girl by now."

Pastor Donovan shook his head, setting his velvet cap bobbing.

"I doubt that. Alan's got a rare stubbornness about him. And as I recall he was quite taken with you."

Claire clenched her fists as she strode along the steep path up the side of the gorse-covered hill. Her answer to that comment still had the power to bring tears smarting behind her eyes.

"He loved me. I know he did. But he's been gone so long."

"All the same," the pastor had gone on hurriedly as though her feelings embarrassed him, "he's the one to cast your cares upon. The Laird MacDairmid canna' help Tom keep his farm and, if he is helpless, how can you expect me to do anything? Alan is your best answer, there's no doubt."

Your best answer! She furiously kicked a stone on the path and hurt her toe. These selfish people, the laird and the pastor both, were going to stand by and watch Angus Varn steal her father's land, and their only solution was to urge the Montcrieffs to leave Ben Brogain and emigrate to a world full of strangers, leaving them in peace. If Angus had his way, it would mean there was no justice left in Scotland, yet

6

every day she felt less able to prevent it. As if Tom Montcrieff had not endured enough suffering already.

Claire felt a sudden stab of pain in her foot as her weight came down on a large pebble that had worked its way into her shoe. Furiously she tried to shake it free, hopping forward a few more steps, but it was too firmly lodged and too irritating to walk on. Plopping down on a nearby boulder, she removed her shoe and realized that she was breathing very hard in spite of the fact that she had taken this path effortlessly many times before.

It was the rage within her that made her breathless. Leaning back against the rock wall behind her, her shoe in her hand, she sat quietly for a moment gazing out over the vista of moorland and blue sky, her anger gradually replaced by a keening sadness.

She must do something to help her father save his farm. That the land was not valuable enough to be the cause of all this distress no one knew better than Claire herself. Along with her father and her younger brother, Jamie, she had struggled for years to wrest a decent living from it. Not even the sheep seemed able to do more than subsist on its stubborn, rocky surface. Yet it was all they had, and the thought that Angus Varn, their avaricious neighbor, might steal it from them was too infuriating and unfair to be borne. He wanted it for years but now it was as though, through some mysterious circumstance, the Montcrieffs had been rendered vulnerable and helpless. Angus had stepped up the pressure, and it looked as though he was going to succeed at last and Claire could do nothing to stop him.

This would not have happened in those long-ago days before her mother died when they lived in the cottage on the grounds of the MacDairmid's great house. Tom Montcrieff had been the laird's chief steward then and life had been comfortable and good. Then, without any warning, he had been put off, thrown this miserable farm as a sop, her mother had died, and the laird had degenerated into a drunken, ineffectual shadow of the man he had been. He sat up there now with his manor crumbling around him, allowing one son to ruin his tenants with his cruelty and greed and the other son to waste his life in debauchery and violence. Sometimes it seemed to Claire that the fortunes of the Montcrieffs and the MacDairmids had gone downhill together. At least the MacDairmids, no matter how degenerate they grew, still retained their landed estates. Who was going to help the Montcrieffs keep what was rightly theirs?

Almost unbidden a phrase she had heard whispered for years crept into her consciousness:

"It was taking in that foundling that turned the fortunes of Tom Montcrieff. He should have known better than to tempt fate and the Devil that way. Better that Alyce Dawes should have died a babe than be brought up to ruin those who nursed her."

"Rubbish!" Claire said aloud. "Foolish, superstitious nonsense!"

Sitting up quickly, she slipped her shoe back over her dainty foot, stood up, and smoothed down her skirts. She had spent more time that she had intended walking into Ben Brogain, and, if she did not get home soon, supper would be late. Enough of this wasteful wool-gathering. It wasn't going to solve anything. She would think of some way to outwit Angus Varn though right now she did not have a clue what it would be. Mentally she totaled her assets as she began her stride back over the hill. She was healthy, she was clever, and she was the prettiest girl

8

in the village. She could say this without vanity, knowing the truth of it. Her long, wavy ash-blond hair, her eyes blue as cornflowers, her full figure and her complexion alive with the bloom of youth and good health — had they not all made her the target of amorous young men as far away as Loch Tay. Because she was known to be betrothed to Alan, they kept their distance and respected her virtue. Yet as time passed by and Alan's memory grew ever dimmer, surely they would soon begin to see her as fair game once again.

Once more Claire felt tears smarting behind her eyes. If only Alan had not gone away. They would have been married by now, and she would probably have one or two little children pulling at her skirts. Alan could have protected her father from the Varns for he and Angus were related. And he would have protected her. She could have depended on him to shoulder the cares of her family instead of having to bear them herself, almost completely alone since Jamie was so young. But Alan had left Scotland and now her youth was passing relentlessly by, leaving her with only memories, hopes, and longings. Perhaps Pastor Donovan was right, and they should go to the New Netherland.

New Netherland! No, that was the wrong name. It had been an English province now for nearly twenty-eight years and was called New York. Both names evoked a magic though, an enchantment born of that word "new." A fresh wild country, new people, a new beginning — it woke something deep inside that whispered tantalizingly of adventure.

She was so absorbed in her thoughts that she failed to hear the soft clatter of a horse on the path ahead. Suddenly there was a huge shadow across her path, and she looked up to see a man on a fine chestnut

9

stallion blocking her way not two rods off. Claire stopped suddenly, catching her breath.

The fine horse and distinctive tartan told her immediately she was looking at one of the MacDairmids. Her first glance at the handsome cloak and gleaming leather boots led her to expect to see Edgar, the eldest son, looking arrogantly down on her. But Edgar was dark and had a trim black beard. This young man, with his square chin, clean-shaven and strong, his neat shoulder-length hair, his laughing eyes and half-mocking smile, was certainly not the scowling Edgar. Claire's heart gave a start as she realized she was looking into the gray eyes of Fall MacDairmid, Edgar's younger brother and a man with the reputation for ruthless satisfaction of his appetites.

Fall MacDairmid had been away from Ben Brogain so often that Claire knew him only by reputation — a reputation that could reduce the elders of the kirk session to babbling hysteria. "Irresponsible," "lecherous," "wanton," and "anti-Christ" were only a few of the epithets hurled at him in sermons that detailed the failings of the MacDairmids in general. It was immediately obvious to her why — he was handsome in a daredevil kind of way and his ready smile was full of mischief. It took her only a moment to realize that he was giving her the same close scrutiny she was giving him, though it was obvious he did not recognize her.

Leaning one hand on his saddle, he grinned down at her.

"Well? And who have we here?"

The amused mockery in his voice caused Claire some misgiving. Summoning all her dignity, she put up her chin.

"Please, sir. Allow me to pass."

"And are you in such a hurry, my pretty lass?"

10

"Aye, I am." Claire answered, glancing to the side in the hope of going around him if he refused to move. As if he had read her mind, he slipped one leg over the saddle and slid off his horse. Taking a quick step back, Claire bumped up against the boulder.

"Can you not take a moment to become better acquainted? I hadn't hoped to stumble on such a beauty in this barren place."

As he walked toward her, she found herself noticing again how very handsome he was. Not nearly as dark as his brother, he had a square, strong face with deceptively shapely lips and deeply set eyes fringed by thick brown lashes. The mocking self-assurance in his attitude blatantly suggested that she should be as happy to have run across him as he was to have stumbled on her. Claire tried to step back again, moving edgily around the rock that blocked her path.

"I know who you are," she said, trying to keep the nervousness from showing.

"You do? How convenient. I wish I might have the same honor."

"I am the daughter of Tom Montcrieff."

That stopped him, but only for a moment.

"You are old Tom's daughter? Odd's life, but you've grown up to be bonny. I'd no idea he had such a vision hidden away in that little farm of his. I can see I ought to have spent more time in Ben Brogain."

"I have not been hidden away, sir, as you would certainly know had you kept up my father's acquaintance. He is expecting me at home any moment now, and I would be greatly pleased if you would allow me to go on my way."

"Why, so I shall, after we have had time to get to know one another better." He stepped closer, pressing her back against the sharp edges of the boulder, and leaned on one hand near her head. Claire found she

11

was closed in, and her heart gave another nervous leap.

"What is your name, Tom Montcrieff's daughter?"

"Claire," she murmured as she attempted to break away.

"You are a very beautiful lass, Claire Montcrieff." Reaching out, he lightly ran a finger down her neck. In spite of her concern Claire felt a delightful shudder course through her body.

"If you want to know anything about me, you should speak to my father," she said defiantly.

He laughed. "A girl of spirit. I like that. However, since your father is not at hand, I must ask my questions of you. Are you promised? Married? Have you given your heart to someone?"

A desperate hope rose to the surface. "Aye, I am promised. And have been for two years."

She thought she noticed a hesitation in his manner. "Two years? Do you mean your betrothed has allowed a bonny girl like you to wait on him two whole years? Whatever for? Is he a sapskull?"

Angrily Claire tried again to break away from his confining arms. "It was not his choice," she said defensively. "He had to go to America."

Immediately she realized her mistake. He laughed and moved closer, pinning her to the boulder.

"He went to America, leaving you here for two years. He must be a sapskull. I would never be so foolish."

Very slowly his free hand slid up to her chin, lifting her face. His lips were only a few inches away. Her treacherous body gave another shudder even as Claire fought to evade his lips, her outrage growing.

"Sir, if you were a gentleman, you would not force yourself on me like this," she snapped between clenched teeth.

Fall stepped back slightly, dropping his hand.

"Force? Why should there be a question of force? It's a lovely day, we are quite alone, and you are a bonny girl. Why cannot we simply enjoy each other's company?"

"You may be used to girls who—"

She got no farther as he moved quickly forward, gently dropping his mouth on hers, moving his lips sensuously, then wandering on to lightly kiss her cheek, her neck, the lobes of her ears.

"Let me go—" Claire stammered, even as her body began to come alive with a heat she had never known before.

"Do you really wish me to," he whispered, his hands slipping down her shoulders to her back. She felt the delicious drift of his fingers on her body, stroking and sliding, his firm, hard body pressed against her own. Her mind was whirling. Until a few moments before she had not set eyes on this man for years and now, here she was writhing under his insistent fondling. Before she knew what was happening, he had slid her down the rock to the grass and was kneeling over her, his hand working at the laces of her bodice.

"No!" Claire cried as Fall pulled them free and thrust his hand deep inside her shift to close around her firm breast and taut nipple. He slipped down to lie half over her, his hands busily engaging her body. Claire pushed against him, still protesting, as he slid his hand up under her skirt, smoothly stroking her thighs until he found that secret place she had never even touched herself. She went limp, unable to fight, swept away in such an engulfing wave of desire that she was almost oblivious to where she was.

"Don't—please—" she cried as she felt his fingers thrust deep within, knowing what would come next.

13

Her overwhelming rush of desire was suddenly throttled by the cold voice of reason. Was she to lose her maidenhood like this, in the space of a few moments with a man who—for all that he was gentry—she barely knew? What if he got her with child, leaving her unmarried and alone? The disgrace and scandal would be certain to finish off the Montcrieffs. In a burst of outrage and fury she flailed against him with her fists.

"Let me go! Stop!"

Her fury only enflamed him all the more. He clasped her tightly, murmuring:

"Be easy, my lass. It's a pleasure. Enjoy—"

"Claire! Claire, where are you?"

The distant voice broke in on them both at the same time—a girl's voice coming up the path. In a few minutes she would be upon them. Muttering a curse, Fall rolled over while Claire scrambled to her feet, yanking down her skirts and pulling the laces of her bodice taut.

"Claire," the girl called again, nearer now than before. Claire recognized her sister's voice and, hastily tying up the laces on her bodice, shouted back:

"Over here, Alyce."

"Alyce?" Fall muttered, looking at her with a strange expression. "The foundling Alyce?"

It was obvious to Claire that, though he might not have know of *her* existence, he was familiar enough with Tom's ward.

"Yes, Alyce the foundling," she answered bitterly, glaring as Fall scrambled to his feet and moved away from her.

"The witch?" he asked, looking up expectantly.

"She's not a witch," Claire snapped, "though I wish she was. I'd have her call down such spells on you to make you suffer the rest of your days."

He had backed away, leaving the spot on the path where only a moment before he had been so engrossed on her seduction. The expression in his eyes sat strangely on him, it was so incongruous with the strength and daring he had exuded before Alyce appeared. Yet, Claire thought, why should she be surprised? Fear of witches was a way of life, from Pastor Donovan down to the lowliest shepherd. Why should the laird's family be immune?

At that moment Alyce bounded round the rocks to see Claire standing, still tying her laces. She glanced quickly from Claire to the young man standing on the path scrutinizing her. Shrinking back, she hastily drew up her plaid shawl over her head, covering one side of her face. Glaring at Fall, Claire ran to her and took her arm.

"It was good of you to come to meet me, Alyce. Come along now. We must be getting home."

Alyce looked up at her, wondering. "That man—"

"He's no one. Fall MacDairmid, the laird's son. I happened on him."

Alyce's gentle eyes darkened. "Are you all right?"

Slipping an arm around her shoulders, Claire hurried off with her foster sister down the path toward Tom's farm.

"I'm quite all right. Now, let's get home or Papa will be complaining that his supper is late."

Without a backward look, she half-ran down the hillside, keeping Alyce's hand tightly clasped in her own. They had covered almost half the distance down to the level plain where the moor flattened out before Claire allowed her pace to slacken. Alyce, whose legs were not as long, had been hurrying to keep up and when Claire's long strides slowed she gratefully slackened her own. Glancing around the barren heath, she made certain they were completely alone, then

15

dropped her plaid shawl back around her shoulders.

"I followed a curlew this morning," she said in her quiet way as though she was sharing a secret. "It had such a *poolly-woolly* cry as if I was too close to its nest. I wish you might have been there too, Claire."

Claire looked thoughtfully at her foster sister walking quietly along beside her. In the bright sunlight of the afternoon the red-wine-colored stain that covered most of one side of Alyce's face looked hardly more than a pink flush. It was strange how the mark could change hue, at times darkening almost to a rust, at other times so light as to seem more a blemish than a birthmark.

"Alyce, why did you come looking for me just now?"

Alyce glanced at her warily, her large, fawnlike eyes narrowing with caution.

"I only thought to meet you and walk back with you from the village."

"Tell me the truth. Did you hear one of your voices?"

Alyce stared doggedly at her feet as she scuffed along the path. "In a way. I was sitting under my tree and it told me—"

"Alyce! How many times have I explained to you that a tree cannot talk?"

"It was like a voice then. A voice in my head that made me think you might be in some kind of danger. So, I thought perhaps it would be wise to go and see."

Claire made a soft, clucking sound with her tongue.

"Did I do right, Claire?" Alyce asked timidly. Impulsively Claire laid her arm around the girl's thin shoulders and hugged her.

"Yes, love, you did. In fact, I was very glad to see you. I did not relish the thought of losing my

16

maidenhood to a chance encounter with a rake like Fall MacDairmid."

"I'm glad I did right."

"But, Alyce, you must not tell anyone else that a voice told you to go and meet me. Remember that, please. No one at all."

"Oh, I won't. I promise. I never talk about my voices to anyone but you, Claire. You know that."

"That's a good girl. And please, try not to spend so much of your time beneath that rowan tree."

"But it is my friend. I love it so—"

"Yes, but rowan trees—oh, what's the use. Just believe me, dear, when I tell you it is not wise."

Alyce smiled shyly up at her. "But it was wise today."

Claire's scowl faded under Alyce's childlike pleasure. "Little minx! Yes, today it was wise indeed. Come now, we'd better hurry, or Papa will be out here searching for us both."

The house that Tom Montcrieff had inherited along with his farm was substantial compared to many of the crofters' huts scattered around the moors surrounding Ben Brogain. Fashioned of stone with a steep thatched roof, it had the luxury of a separate room off the main kitchen-parlor. A narrow loft stretching along the rear of the main room served Tom and his son, Jamie, as sleeping quarters while Claire and Alyce shared a bed in the extra room. Though the day had been warm, by the time Claire pulled her dress over her shift and slipped between the coarse wool covers, the evening air had a brisk nip to it. Alyce, who was already in bed, snuggled up against her, both girls glad for the warmth of each other's bodies.

17

"Claire," Alyce whispered, "Angus Varn came over this morning."

"He did? Papa didn't mention it."

"He roared at Papa something fierce. And after he left, Papa brought out the whisky jug. That was why he wasn't himself tonight."

Claire groaned. "I might have known. That is always Papa's answer to every problem. Yet, poor man, he is vexed beyond what most men have to endure. Angus Varn is a neighbor that would drive any man to drink. You didn't say anything to him, did you?"

"Oh, no. I stayed out of sight in the byre, just as you told me. Did I do right?"

"Yes, love. You did. I'll talk to Angus tomorrow though I dread the thought of it."

"Claire, do you think we will ever have our dream come true?"

"Of course we will. Someday. We'll have all the things we talk about—a fine house, servants to wait on us hand and foot, pretty clothes—"

"And you will have a strong husband and children of your very own, who will call me 'Aunt Alyce.' "

"What about children for you?"

"I would be happy just to have friends who would make merry with me."

"You shall have thousands of friends, and we will give such entertainments as to make people come from miles around."

"And can I tell them about my voices?"

"Well—perhaps it would be better to keep that our secret."

Alyce's face grew serious. "Perhaps it would. You know better about those things than I."

Kissing her lightly on the forehead, Claire said; "Go to sleep, little one. We can talk about dreams tomorrow."

"I will. Only—do you suppose, when our dreams come true, we might find a way to make my mark go away so that people would not be afraid of me anymore? I should like that so much."

"My dear little Alyce, why not? We'll make it the most important part of the dream."

Claire hugged the young girl fiercely and watched as Alyce turned on her side and snuggled into her pillow. Lying on her back, staring up at the heavy beams in the ceiling, Claire fought down her anger that such a gentle creature could be so hurt by something that was not her fault. "The touch of the Devil," they called her birthmark in the village and looked constantly for clues to prove that Satan himself had named her for his own and was using her to work his evil ways. Even Fall MacDairmid had watched her with caution. His hot desire had calmed considerably when he saw Alyce approaching on the path. "The witch?" he had asked as he stepped away.

At the thought of Fall her body began to tingle and Claire found herself stretching and smiling with pleasure. Mentally she chided these emotions that allowed lustful passion to overcome pride and outrage.

And yet, the memory of his hands and lips on her body awoke such a longing as to be almost overwhelming. Not since the brief, furtive moments she had spent alone with Alan had she known this kind of delicious longing. All the time he had been gone she had pushed down these feelings, not daring to let them rise to the surface, not only because of the guilt they brought on but more because of the pain they gave her when they went unsatisfied.

And now this forceful man had caused them all to come flooding back, stronger than ever before. How could she feel this way about a man who so arrogantly assumed she wanted him as much as he wanted her? And after only a chance first meeting?

True, he was handsome in a roguish kind of way and exuded such masculine strength as to make lesser girls swoon with desire. Yet how foolish to allow herself to be swept away by these shallow characteristics.

Plumping over, she pulled the covers around her chin, listening to Alyce's quiet breathing on the other side of the bed.

Fall MacDairmid! He was a selfish, vain brute, and she would force herself to remember it!

Two

For two days Claire brooded over her ambiguous feelings for Fall MacDairmid until she finally convinced herself that he was nothing but a degenerate brute like his father. Then, gradually she became so absorbed in the problems of the farm that he slipped to the back of her mind altogether. Right after two of the new lambs were discovered missing, a bag of their precious barley flour hoarded from the previous autumn was found split open with its contents scattered on the storeroom floor. Claire and Alyce spent most of one day unsuccessfully looking for the lambs. When they returned home to find the flour ruined, Claire became more convinced than ever that these incidents were deliberate and that Angus Varn was behind them. The following morning Jamie sought her out to tell her he had found their old sheepdog, Mungo, dead in a gully on the moor. Though the dog was nearly fourteen years old, the fact that it was found lying beside the carcass of a long-dead quail suggested it had not died from natural causes.

"How did he look, Jamie? As though he had gone to sleep?"

The boy, who was only ten, could not keep the tears from running down his cheeks even though he was as much angry as he was grief-stricken.

"Nay, he looked more like he'd eaten something poisoned. His eyes were open and his mouth wasn't right. I'd have carried him home but he was too heavy."

"It's all right, Jamie. Don't cry. We would have had to get a new dog soon anyway since Mungo was too old to have gone on much longer. But I'll wager it wasn't old age that killed him. Angus Varn had a hand in this just as he did with the lambs and the barley flour."

"But why would he poison old Mungo, Claire? Why would anyone do such a mean thing?"

"Because he's a black-hearted old miser, that's why, and he wants to drive us from this glen. Well, that settles it. If Papa won't face up to him, I shall have to."

"You're going over there?"

"Yes, right now while I am still furious with him."

"Then let me come with you. I'll hit him right in the nose for doing such a black deed."

Claire smiled at him as she swung her shawl around her shoulders. "No, you stay here. I need you to watch the sheep and make sure no more lambs are lost."

Jamie looked up at her, the tears still glistening on his lashes. In coloring and features he was a younger version of Claire herself, both of them resembling their mother more than their dark-complexioned father.

"I'd rather go with you."

She gave him a brief hug. "No. You're needed more here. Don't tell Papa where I've gone. If he asks about me, just say I didn't mention where I was going but that I'd be back soon."

She left him still pleading to be taken along and set off down the narrow path that wound around the hillside for half a mile until it reached the substantial gate that opened onto Angus Varn's house and barns. Claire moved with firm purpose, buoyed by her rage even though she was uncertain what she was going to say when she finally stood face to face with Angus. He had always been a bad neighbor but lately he seemed to have decided that Tom was not going to be able to hold onto his land much longer and his avaricious hostility had grown worse every day. His first offer had been made at a ridiculously low price and with much flattery and fawning. Once it had been turned down with no hint of acceptance at any price, Angus had grown determined he would get this adjoining piece of land by any means possible. How he could so arrogantly assume the Montcrieffs would sell to him was more than Claire could understand, though it would not surprise her to know that there was someone behind him, someone egging him on who would share in the profits.

As Claire pushed open the worn gate, she saw a woman sitting in Angus's yard working at a flax wheel. The woman glanced up as Claire walked toward the house, her narrow eyes scowling.

Esther Varn, Claire thought, recognizing Alan's aunt who was married to Angus's brother, Lace Varn. She had forgotten that Esther and her family were staying here until they left for New York, and it did not raise her spirits any to know that she would have to contend with this difficult, unlikable old woman as well as with Angus.

"Good day, Mistress Varn," she said stiffly. "I'm looking for Angus. Is he here?"

Esther raised her hand to her eyes as though

shielding them from the bright sunlight behind Claire.

"He's round by the barn," she answered without any hint of polite greeting. Her hostility toward Claire was strong enough to be almost felt, but her tiny little eyes betrayed a curiosity stronger than her dislike. She laid aside her wheel and rose to follow Claire.

"I'm obliged," Claire said and set off toward the barn very conscious of Esther's tripping steps behind her. Ahead she saw Angus wielding a pitchfork near a haystack, his heavy body surprisingly agile. Beside him worked his younger brother, Lace, much smaller and thinner. A young boy, very hefty with a shock of yellow hair, stood on the other side of the rick, desolately plying a rake. Claire went purposefully forward, undaunted by the thought that she was going to have to deal with Angus's entire family.

Varn saw her coming and leaned on his pitchfork as though he had been expecting her. Pulling off his cap, he wiped an arm across his brow and scowled at Claire as she approached.

"Angus Varn," she said, her voice sharp with anger, "I wish to have a word with you."

" 'Twould be more seemly if it was your pa come to speak to me."

"I can speak for my father."

"Very well, then. Say what you've a mind to so I can get back to my work."

"Our old dog was poisoned last night."

"What's that to do with me?"

"Two of our lambs are missing and a sack of flour was destroyed. All of these things happened within the space of a few days and after the last time my father refused to sell out to you."

"Who's the pretty lady?" the boy said, drawn to the voices. Glancing over at him, Claire recognized Dan-

24

iel, Esther's slow-witted son. He had grown so since the last time she had seen him that she had not known him at first. Angus ignored him and stared defiantly at Claire.

"What is it you're saying? That I'm to blame? If that's what you mean, come straight out with it."

Claire's eyes blazed. "Yes. I believe you are."

Lace Varn stepped up to his brother's elbow. "Who is this lass to accuse you of such things? I never heard the like."

"What can you expect of a drunkard's family," his wife answered in a loud half-whisper. Claire glared at her but turned back to Angus without answering. Her business was with him though the mocking half-smile on his thick lips was not encouraging.

"Your lambs probably wandered over a crevice because that dog of yours was too old to watch them properly. A fox got into your flour like one got into mine once or twice. That quail your dog ate was no doubt spoiled and he was too aged to know any better. You got no cause to come round blaming your ill luck on me."

Claire looked from one sneering face to the other. They were all in this together.

"How did you know Mungo ate a quail's carcass? I said he was poisoned. I never said how."

Angus's eyes darkened and he looked quickly away. "Matter of fact, I saw him dead before you did," he answered. "Happened on the body early this morning."

He was lying and Claire knew it. Angrily she yanked the ends of her shawl across her chest.

"We will never sell our farm to you, Angus Varn, and you may as well accept that fact. I'd rather give it to the pastor for a glebe than let you steal it from us. Your harassment will never change our minds, so you might as well give up trying."

"Seems to me that's for your pa to say."

"I speak for my father and for the rest of the family. If you don't leave us in peace, I'll find some way to make you."

There was no sneer on Angus's face now. "Are you threatening me?" he said softly.

Claire stepped back, realizing just in time that she was running the risk of having Alyce dragged into this dispute.

"No, I'm not. I only mean that we intend to protect ourselves even if we have to appeal to the kirk sessions or the laird to do it. I hope it will not come to that."

She was aware at once of a subtle change in Angus's manner. Once again his lips settled into that mocking half-smile as though he dared her to follow through on her words. Snapping his cap back on his head, he said briskly:

"I've work to do. Good day to you, Mistress Montcrieff."

Feeling like a dismissed servant, Claire turned and walked from the yard with all the dignity she could summon. Behind her she heard Daniel Varn giggling over something his mother said in low accents. Slamming the gate behind her, Claire hurried down the path to her home, filled with dismay. She had done nothing to help her father and probably had made everything worse by openly accusing Angus. It was obvious the man was not afraid of anything the laird or the sessions might do, and once again the thought came that there was some power here she could not identify. No matter how she searched her mind, she could think of no way to stop him.

By the time Claire reached home, the afternoon had grown lowery with dark, blustery clouds weeping a slow drizzle. It lasted the rest of the day, always more threatening of a storm than actually becoming one, and by evening it had blown over, leaving the air refreshingly cool. After supper all four Montcrieffs, as was customary, moved outside to enjoy the air, Jamie and Alyce playing with a leather ball under the tall rowan tree and Claire and her father sitting on a bench against the house. Claire searched through a sewing basket, intent on making use of the light as long as possible, while Tom smoked his clay pipe, quietly meditating.

It was Claire's first opportunity to speak to her father alone, and she was grateful that he was more sober than usual so late in the day. She studied his worn, lined face and, summoning her courage, plunged in.

"I went to see Angus Varn today, Papa."

Tom looked up quickly, his eyes full of questions. When he made no comment, she went on.

"I came right out and told him that I believed he was behind all the trouble we've been having. And I'm right, I'm certain of it. He knew that Mungo had eaten the carcass of a quail though I never mentioned it."

"He didn't admit to poisoning Mungo, did he?"

"No, of course not. He told me that he had come across the dog's body before Jamie found it, but I know he was lying. I could see it in his eyes. It was as though he was laughing at me the whole time I was accusing him. Esther and Lace were there too, hanging on every word. They were laughing as well."

"I'm not surprised—a chit of a lass like yourself facing up to a man like Angus. It was brave of you, Claire, but hopeless. You ought to have let me go."

"I thought to spare you, Papa. I know you're not well and—"

"I'm well enough to stand up to a bully like Angus Varn!" Tom said with a rare show of spirit.

Claire concentrated on her sewing, knowing full well that, had she asked her father to accuse his neighbor, he would have found some excuse not to.

"It's just that I did not know what else to do, Papa. Angus seems determined to force us out of Brogain. If the laird won't help or Pastor Donovan, then there is no one else to turn to. With the Earl of Perth in jail and his brother in France, there is no one to curb the greed of Covenanters like Angus. And I'm afraid—"

"It won't come to that," Tom said quickly, laying a hand on her arm. "How do you know the pastor won't help? Did you speak to him as well?"

"Yes. Several days ago. He believes we should sell the farm to Angus and go to New York to find Alan."

"Aye, he'd like that. 'Twould satisfy Angus and rid him of one more problem. He's one of the few ministers in Scotland that's managed to hold onto his living through Episcopacy and Presbyters alike. He'll not let the Montcrieffs disturb his peace."

Claire looked up to see Alyce darting around the grass chasing Jamie. The musical cascade of her laughter echoed back to where they sat. It was a lovely sound and one they did not hear often enough.

"Perhaps we ought to think about emigrating, Papa. I admit at first the idea seemed preposterous, but the more I think on it, the more attractive it grows. America is a new country and perhaps there would be new ways of thinking there. I'm told land is easy to obtain—good land, not worn out with centuries of tilling like ours seems to be. And people may not be so set in their ways as here. Alan would take good care of us, I know he would."

28

Tom sucked thoughtfully on his pipe, his heavy brows creased to a straight line above his steel-gray eyes.

"I was never that sure of Alan myself," he murmured.

"The last letter I had from him said he wanted me to come. You know it did, for you read it to me."

"It goes against my spirit, Claire, to let Angus cheat me this way. He was always a vain, bullying man, and, now he's an elder on the sessions, he thinks he's God's appointed prophet."

Claire laid her sewing in her lap and faced her father squarely. "It's no good trying to pretend he won't have his way. You know what he'll try once everything else has failed. He'll accuse Alyce and then—"

Tom squirmed on his seat. "Now that is not necessarily true. It's only old women who were accused of witchcraft, those who have no one to stand by them."

"None of those old women had so visible a mark."

"There haven't been near so many trials lately as there used to be. I can remember as a boy there was a hanging all the time. That's slowed considerably."

"Only because the King's Advocate doesn't take as much notice of them now, but you know that hasn't stopped the accusations. Look at old Goody Masterson. She wasn't tried and hanged but she died in prison of poverty and cold. We can't risk that, Papa."

Tom stared out at the hill before his house where the small boy and the older girl romped under the rowan tree. In his silence Claire's spirits went plummeting and she found herself gripping her needle.

"I'll go along tomorrow and have a word with the laird," Tom finally said. "After all, he hasn't evicted us yet. Maybe he could speak to Angus. It's worth a try."

It was on the tip of Claire's tongue to tell her father how little Angus had been impressed with her own threat of going to Morgan MacDairmid, but she said nothing. At least Tom would be making an effort to do something, and he knew Morgan well from his years as chief steward. Perhaps this time it would do some good.

She picked up her sewing and plied her needle through the coarse cloth, hoping her despair was not too evident to her father.

"I'd be grateful, Papa, if you would, for it seems to me there is nothing else left to try."

The next morning Tom washed his face, clipped his beard, put on clean linen, brushed his worn serge coat, fortified himself with a large tankard of ale, then set off for the stone house on the hill overlooking the village of Brogain. The manor was an ancient structure that had once been a castle but that had been slightly modernized by an enterprising Mac-Dairmid in the service of old King James. His descendents, not nearly as ambitious as their great-grandfather, had allowed it to drift back into crumbling neglect. Even Tom was surprised at the sorry state of the stables and outbuildings as he made his way round to the rear entry. As he had hoped, old Meg, the MacDairmid's ancient nurse, now a kind of derelict dependent, met him at the door. It had been nearly a year since he had last seen her, and in that time she had grown more cronelike than ever. The hairs on her upper lip were longer and thicker, and her faded, perpetually watery eyes were even more blind. She hobbled back to a bench beside the gaping stone hearth after showing not the slightest surprise at seeing Tom standing outside the door.

"Come in, Tom Montcrieff," she motioned with a clawlike hand as she eased herself down. "Come and sit, if you've a mind."

"Good day to you, Meg," Tom answered as he entered the kitchen, raising his voice so she could hear. "I cannot sit with you now as I've come to see the laird."

"What did ye say?" she cried, leaning toward him. "You know I don't hear so well anymore. Speak up then."

Tom drew in a breath to give her a yell when footsteps on the inner stairwell caused him to hesitate. Looking up, he was relieved to see Robbie, a footman from his own days as steward, bearing a tray into the kitchen. Robbie greeted him warmly, remembering how Tom had been the one who had first brought him into the MacDairmids' service. Setting down the tray, he went to a cupboard and brought out a small bottle of aqua vitae and, over all of Tom's protestations, poured them both a glass. When Meg spotted the bottle, she tottered to the table and the three of them sat reminiscing for a moment before they got around to Tom's reason for coming.

"Not that ye have to have a reason," Rob said. "We don't see enough of you, Tom Montcrieff. And you not living more than five miles away."

Tom shook his head. "I don't like to come here," he said, glancing at Meg who nodded seriously. "I'll tell you truthfully, Robbie, I'd not of come today but that it's so important. I owe it to Claire to give a try."

"Is Claire in trouble?"

"No, no. No more than we all of us are. Angus Varn is trying to drive me off my land, and there's no one to stop him but Morgan MacDairmid. That's why I need to see him."

Rob lifted the bottle and refilled Tom's glass. "It's

31

not much help you'll be getting from him, I fear. To begin with he's not here. He's gone down to Kinross and won't be back until the day after tomorrow. But I have to tell ye, Tom, that, even if he was here, he wouldn't help you."

Meg, whose hearing had suddenly suffered a vast improvement, leaned over and tapped Tom's arm with a curved, bony finger.

"It's not the laird you'll be needin' to see, Tom. It's that black-hearted son of his. And you'll not move him, not if you read him the Gospel itself!"

Tom looked a question at Robbie. "Morgan Mac-Dairmid knows what's owed me. He wouldn't stand by and see me robbed of what he himself settled on me when I left his service."

"No, he wouldn't," Robbie answered gently. "But old Meg's right. It's not the laird that's behind Angus's villainy. It's Edgar."

"Edgar MacDairmid has no quarrel with me, nor I with him. I don't understand."

"He don't need a quarrel," Meg answered, leaning into Tom's face and lowering her voice to a loud whisper. "He as avaricious as any English king. He'd steal the *pittane silver* off his dead mother's eyes with never a qualm. Mark me, Tom Montcrieff, it's Edgar that's pushin' Angus to take your land, sure as my name is Auld Meg."

Again Tom looked to Robbie as if for confirmation of the old hag's words. Robbie nodded gravely. "You'd do well to watch yourself, Tom. Edgar and the sessions evicted Georgie Talbot just last fortnight. Sent him off with no certificate of good behavior so he won't be able to rent another farm anywhere in the midlands."

"But why? What had he done?"

"They said there was a whole list of things, from

stealin' his neighbor's pigs to sittin' in front of his door of a Sabbath talkin' to his wife. What it really was, Edgar wanted his farm to give to a Covenanter from Lothian who done him a favor. If I were you, I'd walk very careful."

"The Kirk Sessions has nothing against me," Tom scoffed. "I keep their discipline as well as the next man."

"All the same, you'd do best to give them nothin' to accuse you of. Do you go regular to service twice of a Sunday?"

"You know well that I do."

"Do you stay indoors and quiet between times? Do you denounce all prelacy and rituals?"

"Aye."

"Do you read family prayers every day?"

Tom hesitated. "Well—"

"Don't be lax for that's all they'll need. Edgar has them in his pocket."

"But it doesn't make any sense. If the MacDairmid wanted my farm, why not evict me? He could have done it anytime but he hasn't."

"Morgan never would. We both know that. But his son, that's another matter. And, sad to say, the more the old laird wallows in drink, the more his elder son takes control. If he hasn't evicted you yet, it must be because he knows it would be the last straw for his father. But that can't last much longer. The laird has the look of death about him even now."

"Aye," Meg interrupted. "He stopped carin' about livin' long ago when his pretty Elizabeth died."

"His health is poor," Robbie went on, "and the worse it gets, the more his son goes about freely taking anything he wants. He'll have Angus in his pocket too once he gets your land, and it'll be well worth it to him."

33

"But if I spoke to Morgan," Tom said, despondency in every tone. "If I explained what is happening, surely he'd help me put a stop to it."

"I don't know. Sometimes it's as though he doesn't have the strength to stand up to his elder son."

"Or is afraid of him," Meg added, "as well he might be."

With a quick motion Tom swallowed the last of the searing aqua vitae. "What about his other son, Mac-Fall? Is there no hope from that quarter?"

Rob laughed bitterly as he stuck the stopper in the neck of the bottle. "He'd be no help a'tall. He's only just returned from France, and he's at odds with Edgar same as you are. When he was livin' here, there was nothin' but fightin' and quarreling' all the time between the three of them. 'Tis sad indeed to see what the MacDairmids have become. When I remember the laird as he was when I first came into his service—"

"You needn't be reminding me," Tom said, standing up and reaching for his hat. "It seems as though Morgan's fortunes and mine were both struck down at the same time. I suppose the good God has a purpose in all this, but I'd be obliged if He'd let me know what it is."

"Don't speak blasphemy!" Robbie cried in genuine alarm. Tom smiled and clapped him on the shoulder.

"Not blasphemy, Robbie—just a gentle chiding. The kirk wouldn't approve, but I'm certain the Lord takes my meaning."

" 'Twas the devil's work—" Meg intoned, clawing absently at the table with her long fingernails. "Not the Lord's. The devil's."

Tom turned from her in disgust. "I thank you, Robbie, both for your advice and your drink. I'll come back, maybe, in another two days and have a

34

try at speaking with Morgan. At least I know better who's behind all this."

"I wish you good fortune, Tom Montcrieff," Robbie said, opening the door. The bright sunlight spilled into the gloom of the dark kitchen with an eye-searing glitter. Tom couldn't answer him. He nodded gravely, then quickly stepped outside to hurry back to his home.

Three

Sir Francis Murray's country house at Shear was a grand place as befitted one of the shrewdest merchant traders in Scotland. His town house in Perth was a narrow structure of black stone whose front door was reached by a row of steep stairs leading directly off the road. Its small-paned windows looked out across St. John's Street to the ancient church opposite, though on this gloomy afternoon with the fog blowing in from the Tay, little could be seen even of the traffic in the street. Fall MacDairmid, who had lived for a time as a child with Murray's family, stared through the opaque window panes at the gray day and wished he were inland riding those crested hills.

Behind him he could hear the tough crackling of parchment as Murray spread out a map on a massive oak table covered with a Turkish carpet. The carpet, the furnishings, even the quality of the white claret in the glass Fall held in his hand all bespoke the success of the network of Murray ships that plied the waters between Scotland and the Continent these many years. The young man might have found himself envying this enterprising gentleman his fortune if Murray of Shear had not been almost like a father to him. Indeed in many ways Sir Francis was more of a father than his own since Morgan MacDairmid had never excelled at that relationship. Fall smiled cynically to himself at the thought. As far as he could tell, Morgan had never excelled at anything except the amount of wine and brandy he was increasingly able to consume.

"Come. Look here, Fall," Sir Francis said behind him. Turning, Fall walked to the table and set down his glass to peer at the map over Murray's shoulder. The older man's finger skimmed the surface of the parchment, mesmerizing Fall's attention by the play of light on a large emerald he wore.

"We sail from Leith," Murray went on, concentrating on the map, "then to Portsmouth where the bulk of the passengers are taken on. From there it's only a matter of weeks across to the coast of America unless we hit bad weather. Five at the most."

"You're very easy with your 'we' considering it's 'I' you're talking about," Fall quipped. Murray looked up, smiling at him above his trim beard. "I consider all my ships part of myself," he said, "and this one more than most."

"Where exactly is this New York?" Fall asked, looking back at the map.

"Here, at the mouth of what I'm told is a truly remarkable natural harbor. It was a Dutch colony until twenty-eight years ago, but by now the transition to English rule is complete."

"The English are customarily efficient at transitions, particularly when it is to their way of life."

"In this case, it was effected without bloodshed or reprisals. Most of the wealthy merchants in the town are of Dutch descent. This fellow I'm working with, Frederick Philipse, came originally from Friesland but he considers himself Dutch. He arrived in New

York—New Amsterdam it was called then—forty years ago, married a rich widow, and built one of the tidiest fortunes in the colonies."

Fall balanced one hip on the edge of the table, rested one hand on his knee and picked up his glass with the other.

"At the risk of pointing out the obvious, I wonder that you have not remembered that our English friends have imposed restrictions that prevent Scotland from trading with their valuable colonies. Or is this something else you have succeeded in circumventing?"

Sir Francis gave a brittle laugh and rolled up the map. Settling in a chair opposite Fall, he crossed his legs and tapped the edge of the scroll lightly against his knee.

"Don't be facetious, Fall. I know very well that the Navigation Act prohibits Scotland from trading with the merchants in the colonies. That is why I cannot approach Philipse openly, but we need this trade. Since the French began refusing our shipments of herring and woolen cloth, our economic exports have fallen off drastically. We see the ports at Glasgow and the Clyde expanding while shipping of the Forth and even the Tay has subsided to only a shadow of what it used to be. My own company is so heavily mortgaged that I must have this trade or face bankruptcy."

"And I was just thinking how rich you are."

Sir Francis shrugged. "I once was, before revolution and "Dutch William's" Continental wars interrupted the flow of trade. If I can come to an agreement with Frederick Philipse, it will be to his benefit as well as mine. We might be able to use the Hague or the French Indies as a middle ground. However, I need someone I can trust to go to New York and make the arrangements. Needless to say it

38

must be done in strictest secrecy."

Fall turned the glass, admiring the play of light on its ruby surface. "Diplomacy, secrecy, even trustworthiness have never been my strong points. You need someone like William Kincaid or MacGregor's son, Robert. You know what I am."

Absently Sir Francis smoothed the curls of his elaborate periwig before answering. His eyes had a glimmer of humor in them for all the penetrating manner with which he scrutinized Fall.

"I admit you've spent most of your twenty-odd years, Fall MacDairmid, trying to convince the world that you're a wastrel—a womanizing, useless rake. But I'm unconvinced. I saw something in you better than that when you were just a lad, living with my Janet and me because you received nothing but neglect in that pile of stone your father calls home. And I still see it. Perhaps I believe, if you agree to go, that you won't fail me. Perhaps it's just that I think it will do you good to have something useful to accomplish for a change. Whatever it is, I'm asking you to do me this favor."

In spite of himself, Fall felt a hot flush on his cheek at Murray's words. Affection was something he tried very hard not to allow himself to feel, but Sir Francis had a way of conjuring it up even when Fall would have preferred he didn't.

"And who will I be making this journey with?" he asked quickly.

"Does that really matter?"

"Indeed it does. I won't spend the better part of three weeks on the same ship with a Robertson or a MacDermont. One of us would be overboard before we reached Portsmouth."

"Pshaw!" Murray exclaimed. "These endless quarrels! You young lads have nothing better to amuse yourselves with than hating each other. That's a great part of your trouble."

"Nevertheless —"

"You needn't worry. There are no MacDermonts or Robertsons scheduled to sail. Only a group of emigrants — failed farmers and their kin, tradesmen, and a few artisans. As to the English contingent, I don't know. Probably a group of Covenanters."

"God's blood, not more religious fanatics! One of the few reasons I might consider leaving Scotland would be to escape from these endless religious feuds and now you're asking me to set myself right down in the middle of them. And on a small boat, too."

"Seventy tons' burden. That's not so small. What say you, Fall?"

Fall stared toward the window, then slowly shook his head.

"I canna' do it, sir," he said, lapsing into a country brogue. "I appreciate the honor you do me, asking me to take on such an important task, but responsibility is something I have spent most of my life trying to avoid."

"Call it an adventure then. A great adventure."

"Your adventure might mean a stretched neck at the end of an English rope, should they discover what I was about."

"I cannot believe the man who followed Lord Melfort to France out of a sense of loyalty is afraid of an English rope. Besides, they wouldn't go that far."

"I wouldn't be too sure of that. No. I'm sorry, Sir Francis, but I canna' see myself doing this. Nor am I anxious to leave Brogain completely in Edgar's hands. What inheritance I have would surely be absorbed into his by the time I returned."

Murray studied the younger man as he rubbed a finger along his broad chin. The emerald danced in the gray light from the windows.

"I accept 'no' for your answer now, but think on it a while. There are nearly two weeks yet before the *Selkirk* is due to sail from Leith."

"I'm not likely to change my mind," Fall said, standing up and draping his cloak over his arm.

Sir Francis nodded. "We'll see. I'll ask you again before the time comes."

By the time Fall hurried down Francis Murray's stone steps to St. John's Street, a light drizzle had begun to seep out of the fog. It had not discouraged traffic on the busy roadway, and Fall soon found himself obliged to step over beggars, dodge hurrying apprentices, and circumvent vendors carrying their trays. The street was raucous with the cries of street sellers and the never-ceasing clatter of horses. Housewives leaned from windows above, shouting conversations back and forth, ragged children, chasing pigs and stray dogs, darted among the pedestrians, which included men of business, young gentlemen like himself, and even a few women in mantles and hoods carrying baskets. A scrawny fellow, whose black robe and velvet cap proclaimed him a clergyman, thrust a pamphlet in Fall's face, exhorting him to renounce the evils of prelacy or doom his soul to hell. Fall thrust the man's arm away and hurried on. As he rounded a corner, he saw a familiar figure on the opposite side of the street and waved a greeting to Will Straton, the sheriff of the town, followed by a burly bailiff. The sheriff stared back at him in shocked surprise, and Fall moved on thinking that his return was not as well known as he had presumed.

As the drizzle grew stronger, Fall pulled his hat down around his eyes and settled his cloak around his shoulders. Lowering his head against the rain, he turned without looking ahead into the narrow alley where his horse was stabled and promptly collided with another young man just emerging from the lane. Knocked back against the wall, Fall was about to snap at the man to look where he was going when he recognized the thick lips and coarse features of Donald Robertson, one of the despised clan who had been at enmity with the MacDairmids for generations. His mild reprimand died on his lips.

"God's blood," he muttered, "I might have known. Only a Robertson would blunder like a clumsy ox into a man without looking."

Under his plaid cap, Donald's eyes grew alive as he recognized Fall. Recovering his balance quickly, he slipped a hand furtively inside his short jacket and smiled in anticipation.

"So, the whoreson MacDairmid has come slinkin' back to Scotland. Where are your Papist friends, Jacobite? Sulking behind Louis Roi's satin skirts?"

Through the gray gloom of the fog Fall caught the glint of the dirk Donald whipped out from under his coat. Snatching off his cloak, Fall swung it quickly around his arm as his own knife flashed in response. The feud between the Robertsons and the MacDairmids went so far back its origins were lost in antiquity. Neither man, however, needed a reason to justify their rivalry. Dislike on both sides had grown over many confrontations into full-blown hatred, fueled by pride and the need to never lose face. Like many of their friends, both loved a fight, which was more a means to vent rage and frustration than to avenge old wrongs. Now both men stood, knees slightly bent, bodies poised to spring, moving in a formal, half-circle dance around each other in the narrow street. Behind them a merchant in a round hat and two

42

apprentices, whose noses had sensed a fight almost before it began, hurried to form the first of a fascinated ring of spectators that began to grow as more passers-by were drawn like flies to a pot of honey. Fall, his blood up, smiled in anticipation as he moved warily around his opponent, watching for his chance. A distraction behind him—the call of an apprentice to come see the excitement—of a second and he sprang, his knife whipping the air. Donald jumped quickly back, then slashed downward, and ripped the sleeve of Fall's coat. A gash showing blood through the tear brought a laugh of satisfaction to his lips. Furious, Fall lunged again, grappling with his opponent as he struggled to break his grip and thrust his dagger forward toward Donald's stomach.

Suddenly he was grabbed roughly from behind. A burly arm caught him around the throat, yanking him backward so that his boots slipped on the wet street and he was half-supported, half-strangled in the viselike grip of his unknown assailant. His dirk was knocked savagely from his hand and fell clattering to the ground. In a rage, Fall saw that opposite him Donald, too, was struggling, locked in the thick arms of Sheriff Straton.

"Bloody fools," Will shouted, glaring at Fall. "If you want to kill each other, do it on your own ground, not mine."

"Take your hands off me," Fall cried, fighting to get away from Sheriff Straton's huge bailiff. "You've no right—"

"I've every right. Be grateful I don't clap you both in gaol." Releasing his man, the sheriff shoved him with a well-placed boot in the backside towards the broad thoroughfare at the end of the alley. "Go home, Donald Robertson. If I hear that you cause any trouble in Perth tonight, I promise you it will be the inside of a prison ye'll see before morning."

Donald glared murderously back at him and then at Fall. "Ye'd better thank your stars, Fall MacDairmid, that the sheriff came along to keep you from lying here a dead man, for it's certain that's what you'd be now if he hadn't."

Fall lunged at him against the strong, restraining arms of the bailiff.

"Be off now," Will cried, shoving Donald a second time toward the wall of gaping spectators. He disappeared around the corner, followed by most of the disappointed crowd. The sheriff, in an abrupt change of mood, reached down and picked up Fall's dagger.

"Put this away, lad, where it belongs."

"Why did you interfere?" Fall said, finally shaking off the bailiff. "It was no concern of yours."

"The peace of this town is my concern. And though you may not be aware of the fact, there are a number of other Robertsons wandering the streets of Perth this night. All they have to hear was that you'd taken on a fight with their Donald and you'd have had the whole bloody clan on ye're back. I've no wish to see you dead for nothing, Fall MacDairmid."

Sheathing his knife, Fall inched his sleeve away from the wound on his arm and saw it was only a scratch.

"All the same—" he muttered, pressing the cloth against the nearly dried incision.

The sheriff, clapping a hand on his shoulder, spoke in a much more kindly tone.

"Aye, I know you'd like nothing better than a brawny brawl and I came along and spoiled it for you. But there'll be plenty of others. Come and have a drink with me. I was glad to see you'd come home for I want to speak to you about another matter completely."

"What matter?" Fall said glaring at the bailiff who was trying to hand him his hat.

"Come along down to the Green Man, just at the end of the lane here. We can have our talk and wet our throats at the same time."

Will Straton set off down the narrow alley with Fall following, not unaware that he was being led in the opposite direction from that which Donald had taken. However, by this time his curiosity was greater than his pique at missing an opportunity to cut up a Robertson and he went along. When they stepped inside the tavern it was as though night had suddenly come down like a curtain. The dark wood, low ceilings, tiny shuttered windows, and narrow room all conspired to create a murky dimness in which a few candles glimmered like fireflies. The room was crowded with men in Monmouth caps and smocks, drinking at the long table in the center, and gentlemen in feathered hats and lace collars sitting in the booths on the side. A slatternly woman with long strands of hair dangling like straw from under her grimy cap moved listlessly around the center table carrying a tray. Will led Fall toward one of the booths after hailing the burly tapster on a platform near the door.

They were hardly in their places before the woman appeared with two glasses of ale. This was quickly followed by a trencher bearing a half a loaf of bread, several dried herring, and a fair-sized piece of cheese.

"They must know you well here," Fall quipped, digging his dagger into the cheese.

"I'm well known in most of the taverns of Perth. I have to be. Too many seamen about."

Will studied Fall as he chewed absently on a slab of bread and cheese, marveling at the resiliency of youth in men who could be fighting for their lives one moment and hungrily devouring their dinner the next.

He deftly sliced a section of herring and slapped it on a chunk of bread.

"I'm grateful for this chance to speak with you, Fall, for I've been concerned for some time at the way things were going with your family. You've been away too long."

"The pleasures of Paris held me longer than I planned," Fall answered. "And home's not so bonny a place that I longed much to see it again."

"That may be. But while you were enjoying yourself on the Continent, there were things going on at home that maybe you ought to have been aware of."

Fall poised his knife to cut into the cheese again. He hesitated only a moment, glancing up sharply at Will.

"What things?"

"Your father, the laird, is more and more indifferent to what is happening in his own house while your brother, Edgar, sets about grasping everything in sight. He has evicted tenants, hounded debtors, even had people thrown into gaol to get his hands on their property. He claims he is implementing the discipline of the sessions, but the truth is he is lining his own pockets at the expense of others."

Fall went back to slicing the cheese. "I have no control over my brother. I never did have. I hate him almost more than Donald Robertson, and he has the same 'affection' for me."

"For God's sake, man, somebody in the MacDairmid family has to stop Edgar. By encouraging Covenanters he's turned his barony into a minor kingdom, expelling anyone who doesn't meet the standards of the presbyters or whose land he covets. And he won't stop with the small holdings around Brogain. He'll go

46

after his neighbors next. And with that ardent Presbyterian, Crawford, as president of the Privy Council, he just might succeed. We'll have the same kind of bloody feuds that the Campbells have brought on in the Highlands."

"It's none of my concern. It's between my father and his heir."

The sheriff stayed Fall's hand, leaning over the table to speak more urgently. "Listen, Fall, you know that the only power and freedom a man has in this country depends on his landholdings. Edgar has begun to prey on any of the landed gentry who have even a suspicion of Jacobite leanings, and, with the Covenanters and Kirk's Sessions behind him, he's succeeding past his own expectations."

Fall gave a bitter laugh. "That's almost humorous. Edgar is probably the most completely irreligious man I've ever known."

"It's not the religion in him that likes the repressive and punitive discipline of the kirk. God's bones, Fall, doesn't the description I've given you of the men he's gone after tell you anything?"

"What do you mean?"

"Jacobite leanings, nonattendance at church, irresponsible landlords, debts not paid. Do I have to spell it out for you?"

Fall's eyes narrowed as he began to understand. "He wouldn't —"

Will Straton sat back. "He already has. Did you think you could go adventuring in France with the papists of Perth and remain untouched? The moment you left with Lord Melfort, Edgar saw to it that your lands were confiscated. Then he paid the fines, back rents, and 'cess' taxes himself and petitioned Crawford to have your holdings made over to him. I myself saw the affidavit."

"But I've taken the Oath of Allegiance. That was why I was in Edinburgh last week."

"It may be too late, Fall. Your brother has a nose for vulnerable estates. Quietly and methodically he has set about enlarging his own wealth at the expense of anyone whose debts or loyalty to James Stuart left them open to censure."

"But he couldn't do that to me. My father would not allow it."

"Have you seen your father recently?"

"No. I was home only briefly before going back to Edinburgh, and he and Edgar were both away at the time."

"Morgan is old, Fall, and very sick. Worn out with grieving and drink. I don't think he can stand up to Edgar even though in his heart he may wish to."

The food forgotten, Fall laid his knife on the table, looking thoughtfully into the darkness.

"Perhaps, since I've taken the oath, the council will refuse to go along."

"I wouldn't put too much hope in that. Crawford needs men like Edgar. Your brother has sworn to help restore the Conventicles and purge the sessions of any ministers with questionable leanings. I agree with you that there is not a drop of true belief in his whole body but it's his way of buying allegiance."

Pushing the trencher away, Fall slipped the dirk inside his coat. "Perhaps I have been away too long," he said bitterly. "I'm obliged to you, Will. I'll set off for Ben Brogain this very night."

Will Straton laid a hand on his arm as Fall started to rise. "Edgar is no hothead like Donald Robertson, Fall. He knows the law well and he'll use it for his own means. Everything will be done legally, and yet you'll still find yourself robbed of everything you own."

"Aye. He's a serpent."

"My advice to you, Fall MacDairmid, is to walk very, very carefully. I know it's not your nature to do so but this time you would be wise to make the effort."

Fall gave him a long searching look and then, without answering, turned and made his way through the crowded room to the door.

Though he had at first intended to ride straight for Brogain, the fact that the rain was growing heavier and he could not reach home before dark finally decided Fall against so hasty a trip. Bedding down in the stable later for the short night, he was up at the first hint of dawn a few hours later, cantering out of the town and through the narrow wynds that led westward.

He found himself uncommonly reflective as he rode toward his old home. Apart from one year's study at a university, he had little to show for a life that, up until now, had been built around the principle of instant gratification. Early on he had decided there was little enough to enjoy in this world and had made up his mind that, whatever his feelings, satisfying them was his one goal. It had earned him the contempt of his relatives, the enmity of several other young men and several outraged fathers, and the adoring devotion of a number of beautiful young women between Inverness and Paris. But what had he really to show for it? All along somewhere at the back of his mind was the thought that someday he would return to those meager holdings left him by his grandfather and set up his household. A wife, an heir or two, the usual satisfactory quarrels with his neighbors and rival clans — these were his aims in life now, albeit distant, and accepted without enthusiasm because there was nothing better to be had. Now he saw even that slipping away through the machinations of his brother and the indifference of his father. Something about it galled him in his deepest self where nothing had ever touched him before. He would not allow it. Not even if he had to destroy Edgar to save what was rightfully his.

But how? Where Edgar was devious and crafty, he was inclined to confront the issue head on. That would never work in this case. He must beat Edgar at his own game — no easy prospect since his brother had a clever way of always making things work to his own ends.

Fall turned over scheme after scheme in his mind, coming up with nothing that seemed satisfactory beyond running his brother through with a sword. Finally, he allowed his horse his head and sat easily back in the saddle, enjoying the beauty of the countryside around him — the loch still as glass, its surface mirroring the steeply rising hills that surrounded it; the blue sky, very clear today after the fog of the night before; the cries of the larks and gulls, the distant bleating of sheep, the dim barking of a dog down the glen.

As he rounded a boulder, he came on the spot where a few days before he had come across Claire returning from the village. It was the first time he had thought of her since that encounter. A lovely girl, he thought, smiling to himself. Too bad that fey sister of hers had come along. Having once seduced her, she would certainly have been ready to come back for more, and that would have afforded him a very pleasant dalliance in contrast to his usual dismal visits to Ben Brogain. Perhaps he ought to stop by old Tom's farmhouse someday though he knew from experience that fathers in general did not look kindly on him. But Claire was a girl worth having. She had responded to him hotly even as she pushed him away in righteous indignation. It would not take much to bring her around as long as he could avoid the marked foundling she called sister.

Having made up his mind to seek Claire out once all this unpleasantness was over, Fall promptly forgot her as his horse picked his way down the steep hillside and into the village that lay clustered below the hill on which the MacDairmids' tower house sat. A few people in the street looked up as he rode by, nodding to him. Pastor Donovan gravely touched his hat. Old Mother Dickerson bobbed him a curtsy, and Joseph, the smithy, interrupted the pounding of his anvil long enough to call a greeting. Though there were was no fond gentility in their manner, neither was there the active dislike that Edgar MacDairmid usually met when he walked through the village. Fall had seen it often enough to be keenly aware of the difference, and it made him all the more angry at the way his brother was using these people to make himself rich. Edgar had no concern for their well-being. He would push them aside in a minute if they had something he wanted. Wasn't that what he was doing to his own brother?

Fall was so absorbed in his thoughts that it caught him by complete surprise when his horse suddenly shied, dancing up on his front hooves and whinnying with nervous fear. A young boy had come dashing precipitously out from the dark shadows of a narrow slit that lay between two houses, both of which faced the street. Fall pulled up on the reins, struggling to bring his mount under control as the boy stepped hurriedly back, flat against one of the stone houses, staring up at the surprised rider with round eyes in a white face.

"Why don't you watch where you're going, you young rogue?" Fall snapped. Gently he stroked the lathered neck of his horse, trying to calm the animal. "You might have unseated me and been hurt yourself."

"I'm sorry, sir. I dinna' see you," the child cried. "I dinna' expect—"

"Jamie!"

The girl's voice was heard before she appeared, darting from the shadows between the houses toward the child. "What's wrong? Are you all right?" She stopped, looking up at the huge horse that all but filled the narrow lane and gasped.

It took Fall a moment to recognize Claire. When he did, he leaned forward, assessing her with surprised delight.

"Well, well. The lady of the moor. Good morrow, mistress. I presume this urchin belongs to you."

Claire could feel the blood drain from her face only to feel it come rushing back again as she recognized the younger MacDairmid staring down at her. She recovered quickly.

"He is my brother," she murmured.

"Then you should teach him not to go running out unexpectedly into narrow lanes right under the hooves of nervous horses. He could have been trampled."

Claire stepped up beside her brother. "But he wasn't."

"And I could have been thrown."

Her look all but said she would have liked to have seen it.

"But you weren't," she answered coolly. "Come along, Jamie."

The boy pressed against her. "I didn't mean to,

Claire."

She laid a hand on his shoulder and turned him back toward the narrow tunnel between the houses. "It doesn't matter. Come. We must be getting home."

"Wait a moment," Fall called as they both melted into the dark shadows. For a moment he contemplated going after them, but the space was too narrow for his horse and he was loath to dismount this close to home.

"Cheeky girl!" he muttered and kicked his mount to continue up the steep lane toward the manor house at the top.

By the time Fall left his horse in the stable and walked into the big hall of the house, he had worked himself up into such a fury over Claire's rudeness and Edgar's veniality that he wanted nothing so much as to fly at his brother's throat. Shoving Robbie aside, he angrily asked after his father and was told he was in the small room off the upstairs hall they still called the solar. Fall took the stairs two at a time, threw open the door, and announced to the man hunched over a table in the center of the room that he wanted a very important word with him.

Morgan MacDairmid looked up, trying to focus his bleary eyes on the son he seldom saw and thought about even less. Morgan had been a big man in his youth, but by now all his strength had turned to flab, heightened by the red blotches on his complexion, the scars of his addiction to drink.

"I'd forgotten ye'd returned from France," he said as though he hadn't heard anything Fall said. "Where have ye been?"

"In Perth. Where I heard some disturbing news."

"News? What news? When was there ever anything worth telling in Perth."

In disgust Fall reached out and pulled a squat green

53

bottle away from Morgan's trembling hands. "You'll oblige me for a few moments by keeping sober long enough to tell me what my brother is about. Sheriff Will Straton told me he has sworn out an affidavit to have my inheritance written over to his possession. And with your agreement."

"You'll keep a civil tongue in your head," Morgan said with a burst of his old fiery temper. "Robbie—hey—come here. Go find Edgar and send him here to me. Tell him his prodigal brother's come, and we're going to kill the fatted calf."

Robbie, who had quietly followed Fall up the stairs and was now standing outside the open door, took off in a flash while Fall stormed across the room and slammed the door.

"Must we let the whole house know our private quarrels? See here, Papa, I want you to tell me what Edgar's up to before I face him. Is this true?"

"Haven't you learned yet that we have no 'private' quarrels in this house? Whatever we do here is talked about in the village and all the farms around it." He turned up his glass, noting that it was empty. "Yes, it's true. Edgar swore out the paper and I signed it."

Fall leaned his hands on the table and bent to look into his father's face.

"But why? Why would you agree to such a thing? Why would you sit by and watch him rob me?"

"Because Edgar always gets his way," Morgan said, scowling at his son. "And because I'm tired. Too tired to fight him. This would never have happened if ye had stayed home and hadn't followed Melfort to France. Or if ye'd come back sooner. Ye weren't home to protect yourself, and so why should I make myself ill trying to help ye. I can't do it."

"This is no home to me. It never has been. You were always gone in drink. A brother who lies in wait like a serpent to strike me when I least suspect it. There's more to the world than that."

"Then ye should have stayed with Melfort. Fight the Pretender's battles against Dutch William. Win glory. Come home a hero. Instead you waste your youth and my money on England's quarrels, squandering it on foolish kings and loose women. If you want the inheritance your grandfather left you, then ye've got to take some responsibility for it."

Fall kept silent for a moment, taking a long look at his father's ravaged face. For the first time he realized Morgan MacDairmid had the look of death about him. It was in the gray cast under the flushed skin, the eyes not quite seeing the world about him, the sag of his shoulders, the trembling of his hands. There was just enough truth in his father's accusation to make the furious retort he longed to make die on his lips.

At that moment the door opened and Edgar entered. One look at that smug, black face and all Fall's rage came rushing back. Edgar was everything his father was not—self-assured, arrogant, completely in control. He was also expensively dressed in severe black velvet with a shining jewel carefully placed on the fall of lace at his throat.

"So, the prodigal has returned," he said, contempt in every syllable.

"You bastard! Did you think I would stand by and let you steal what's mine as you've stolen from everyone else?"

Edgar sauntered around the table, looking disdainfully down at his father's bowed head, then back at Fall.

"Who told you?"

"The sheriff of Perth."

"A pity. I had hoped you would not learn of it until

after it was a fait accompli. I didn't count on the possibility that you might actually return to Scotland."

He reached out to the bottle Fall had pushed away from his father and slid it back across the table to rest in front of Morgan. With trembling fingers, Morgan removed the stopper and poured his cup half full.

"You'll have a dram with me, Fall?"

"Father, can't you leave that alone long enough to help me stop this man?"

"Ye canna' stop Edgar. Edgar always has his way. Ye may as well give in gracefully."

Fall looked up into his brother's dark eyes. "Never."

"He's right, you know," Edgar said without a trace of emotion. "It has all but been done already. It only requires the approval of the Privy Council, and they won't withhold that from a sworn Covenanter. It is too important for them to have men like me in the right places."

"The Council cannot truly believe you are a Covenanter. Your Presbyterianism sits even lighter on you than my papacy does on me."

"That may be true but it signifies nothing. It is politics, not religion, that is at stake here. You made a great error, little brother, when you so rashly threw in your lot with the Earl of Perth and his brother. They changed their religion when it was politic to suit Jamie Stuart. He lost, they lost, and now, you have lost as well."

"I owed allegiance to Melfort."

"Very noble of you but unfortunately you didn't pick the winning side. The Earl of Perth languishes in gaol at Kirkcaldy, and his brother is in exile in France where you, need I point out, should have also stayed."

"While you stole my patrimony!"

Edgar shrugged. "I am merely taking advantage of the times. Your oath of allegiance to Dutch William comes too late in the day, Fall. Even now, if you could come up with the fines, rents, and taxes that I have paid for your land, I would see to it that you could not persuade the council to return it to you. My good friend, the Earl of Crawford, would back me completely. Besides, it is a substantial sum — some thirty hundred merks."

Fall gave a bitter laugh. "You know I have no way of raising that amount. Unless —"

He looked down at his father slumped over the table. There would be no help there for it was obvious Edgar controlled the purse strings in this house. Mentally he calculated the men he knew who might be in the position to help him. There was only one — Sir Francis Murray and hadn't he already said he was in tight straits financially. Fall's rage at his brother boiled swiftly to the surface. With a cry of fury he lunged suddenly across the table and gripped Edgar by the front of his velvet doublet, his knife poised above his throat.

"Damn you, I'll have your blood before I let you rob me of my living."

Edgar smiled thinly without a trace of fear.

"That is your answer to every problem, isn't it, brother? A claymore or a dirk. Bombast and violence. Go ahead if you dare, and sink your dagger in my throat. But you should know that I instructed Robbie to call two other servants and wait outside, listening to everything we say. If you kill me in cold blood, they will tell the sheriff of it. The courts do not look any more leniently on murder than they do on irresponsible ownership of land."

Raising his head, Morgan turned furiously on them both.

"I'm still the master here," he yelled, glaring at Edgar. "Aye, for all you'd like it, the glen still belongs to me, and it will until the day I die. Let him go, McFall. This creature is still your brother, for all his evil ways. I won't have the blood of kin spilt in my house."

"Bah!" Fall spat in Edgar's face. "You're not worth hanging for though I admit I would enjoy killing you." He stepped back, sheathing his knife and studying his brother across the width of the table.

Giving Morgan a look that was both contemptuous and guarded, Edgar moved to lean on the wide window ledge, folding his arms across his chest.

Fall noted his brother had changed. He had always been calculating and crafty but now his selfishness and greed were beginning to show. His long face and thin, sharp nose appeared aristocratic and elegant until one noted the set of narrow lips and the cold assessment of the eyes. Not even his finely cut, expensive clothes could disguise the singleminded severity of his tall, long-limbed figure. His dark, angry eyes said all too clearly how frustrating it was that the real wealth of Ben Brogain had to wait on the useless life of a drunken father.

Fall asked, "Why? Why do you want my pittance? You are the heir. You will have it all someday. Isn't that enough?"

Edgar brushed at a crumb on his velvet sleeve. In his cold look there lay all the resentment of years of watching his attractive younger brother excel him in every field.

"I could say it was because I detest you, but that is only part of it. This chaos in Scotland, brought about by deposed kings and religious fanatics, has now left the way open for those of us among the landed gentry who have the nerve for it to achieve a power we've

58

never had before. The great houses are divided in their loyalties and the English king, William, doesn't really know which of them to trust. With all this infighting and confusion I intend to build myself a fortune. With a firm foothold in the Protestant party I will be a very wealthy man someday."

Fall sneered, "A minister of the Crown, perhaps. Even a peer."

Again Edgar shrugged. "It is not outside the realm of possibility."

"And with all your wealth you cannot even allow me the small living left me by our grandfather."

"Why should I? You left Scotland with King James' friends. Your lands were confiscated. They would have gone to someone in any case. Why not me? This way we keep it in the family."

His narrow smile at his little joke enraged Fall all over again. "Family," he spat the word. "You don't know the meaning of it. You've left me, your own brother, in unlanded penury."

Edgar smiled in satisfaction. "Then go build your own fortune. There is chaos enough out there. Any man clever enough can profit from it."

"As long as he has no principles."

"I never noticed that principles were something in which you particularly excelled," Edgar said, walking to the door. Opening it, he motioned with his hand as there was a soft scuffling of the men who had been standing outside.

"I must admit I'm grateful to a merciful God for one thing," Edgar went on, "that He provided me with a brother who has none of my own ambitions. You are simply a nuisance and I intend to be done with you. Go make your own way. You'll get nothing from me."

"I'd starve before I'd ask."

"I've no doubt you will—if you don't earn a hangman's noose from some violent quarrel first."

Fall turned in desperation to his father. The old man glanced up at him, then slid his arms down the table, and laid his head on them.

"Go away, both of you," he murmured. "Leave me in peace."

"I'll go," Fall said bitterly, turning back to his brother. "But I'll come back. I'll return with that fortune, and I'll drive you out of this glen. You'll be the one to slink away with nothing but the coat on your back. I make this promise to you, Edgar MacDairmid. I'll ruin you as you've ruined me or die in the attempt."

Edgar's sardonic grin was his only answer. With one last look at his father's bowed head, Fall pushed by his brother and strode out of the room, sending the servants in the hall scurrying. He did not even remember going down the stairs. The huge oak front door slammed behind him and he stood for a moment on the stone threshold, fighting down his rage.

Mounting his weary horse, he rode out of the village, never looking back. He was halfway to Perth when he remembered Sir Francis Murray's ship, the *Selkirk*.

Four

Ordinarily Claire looked forward to market day in the nearby town of Drummond as a welcome break from the monotony of her life on the farm, but recently so many unpleasant events had piled one on top of another that she waited for its approach with a mixture of two parts trepidation and one part anticipation. She could not shake the feeling that something more dire than ever lay just over the horizon waiting to fall upon her and her family, and, had this been an ordinary time, she would have stayed away from the town completely. As luck would have it, however, they had processed some excellent wool the previous autumn, and she and Alyce had found a field of wild arthemisia growing in the glen that made a strong yellow dye that, mixed with blue, produced a vivid and unusual green. Between them they had accumulated a stock of knitted caps and scarfs that ought to fetch a good price at the fair, and since hard money was now more precious to the Montcrieffs than ever before, she forced down her fears and made plans to go.

No one else in the family shared her concern. Jamie was ecstatic, running around to hitch up the small pony to the cart, too excited to keep still more than a moment at a time. Alyce hummed to herself as she tied up the knitted garments and imagined the awed faces of the buyers as they inspected the quality of their work. Even Tom was scrubbed and combed and—more importantly—sober as he took up the reins and slapped the pony's back, jarring him into motion. Claire knew why, of course. The ancient pony cart was Tom's only remaining symbol of his former status as the laird's steward. The road would be filled with crofters and shepherds walking to Crieff, but the Montcrieffs would jog past them in a cart, a symbol to all of the prosperity they had enjoyed in better days.

By the time they neared the old town even Claire's fears were fading before the excitement and novelty of market day. They found a stable for the pony near a modest tavern just inside the town gate and then walked up the High Gait to the square, which was already filled with people milling about beneath the banners that fluttered over the booths. Drummond was usually a gray town, but on market day it exploded into colorful life. The strident cries of vendors hawking their wares could be heard above the din of excited voices, the bleating of sheep herds stumbling along together, even an occasional thump of a drum and lively squeak of a fiddle. The air was filled with the heady aroma of pastries carried on trays through the crowd and a roasting pig rotating on an outdoor spit beside the largest tavern.

In spite of the recent rumors that there was pox in the town, Claire was surprised to discover that the music she heard came from a small group of mummers who were traveling from the great fair at Aberdeen to the next one to be held in Edinburgh. They had brought with them a gypsy fortuneteller, a dancing bear, and a group of acrobats, all of them taking advantage of the opportunity to earn a few coins on their way to the city. At once Jamie went bounding off to seek out the acrobats while Tom immediately slipped away to the nearest tavern. Claire, with a word to Alyce to stay close by, went in search of a merchant to whom they might sell their goods. After helping Alyce to arrange her shawl over her face so as to cast her mark in shadow, she pushed her way through the crowd, conscious of her sister close behind.

From previous experience, Claire knew that Tam MacCleary, the wool craftsman who kept a booth at the market, would give her just as little as he could get away with for her work. "Auld Tam," as he was known, had a shrewd way of knowing just where the limit lay between sending a disgruntled housewife off to seek another buyer and allowing him to hand over as little as possible. Claire knew that these caps were well made and of an unusually lovely color, and she knew too that her family needed money as never before. She haggled with Tam for nearly half an hour before they struck a bargain by which he agreed to pay her something for the caps and also allow her a small portion of whatever was sold that day. Amid cries of how he was being run into the almshouse by her hard-nosed ways, she left him, determined to enjoy the rest of the day. It was only then, looking around, that she realized Alyce was gone.

At first she was not much concerned. There seemed such a contagious, congenial feeling among the people milling about the square that her sense of unease was soon laid to rest. She wandered about, catching sight of Jamie staring in fascination at the gyrations of two acrobats, enjoying the movements of the mummers, wondering how long it would be before the pastor of the kirk and the members of his flock sailed in to shut them down, and nibbling on a meat pastie as she looked over trays of trinkets and ribbons she could not afford to buy. Her pleasant mood was shaken once when she caught sight of Esther Varn, her odious son in tow, standing at the next booth. Esther looked up to catch Claire's eye on her, and her narrow face froze in its accustomed scowl. Claire noted clearly enough how the woman's little eyes scanned the area round her, looking for Alyce, no doubt, and for the first time she was glad her sister had slipped away.

And yet it might be wise to find the girl. She nodded a barely polite greeting to Esther, who frowned back, and wandered off, looking now in earnest for Alyce. The drum before the mummer's tent was pounding away, signaling some dramatic turn in the story, and Claire moved up to the front, searching the crowd that stared raptly at the performers. Some of them, Covenanters, no doubt, openly registered their disapproval. Others were so caught up in the unfolding story taking place on the slapdash stage that their faces had a frozen, almost stunned expression. Claire soon saw that Alyce was not among the spectators and was about to turn away when her eye was caught by a man staring at the stage on the other side of the crowd. He was an imposing figure, his more than six feet of height elongated to gigantic proportions by his old-fashioned, sugar loaf hat. But it was the face that held her—thin, swarthy, old but with an ageless ferocity that was most striking in the eyes that burned like two pieces of anthracite in his skull. Long wisps of white hair straggled from under his hat to sprawl over a wide white collar. There was something about the man that was impressive yet at the same time alarming, and Claire found herself touched once more by an increasing sense of anxiety as she hurried away from the mummer's booth. Really, she ought to find Alyce.

Yet, once away from the disturbing stranger, her anxiety eased again. She ambled back as far as the tavern where a wooden bench stood invitingly empty in the sunshine, propped against the ancient stone wall. Settling on the bench, Claire leaned back, lifting her face to the warm sunlight, her eyes closed. The noises around her merged into a comfortable, indistinct blur, and for a moment she almost dozed off. She was pulled back to reality by the strong, undefined sense of someone staring at her. Opening her eyes, she saw two men standing only a few feet away, pausing as they were about the enter the tavern door. One was an older gentleman in an elaborate periwig and a wide lace collar. The other, a quizzical half-smile on his wide lips, his eyes devouring her with a look Claire could not quite define—part delight, part anger, part unadulterated mischief—was Fall MacDairmid.

In two bounds Fall was in front of her. "So, we meet again. And without all the interfering siblings around."

Jumping to her feet, Claire grabbed up the shawl that had slipped down around her waist and yanked it over her shoulders, crossing the ends over her breasts. She tried to dart away but had taken no more than two steps before he was standing in front of her again, barring her path.

"Oh, no, mistress. I won't allow you to slip off again until we've become properly acquainted."

"I suspect I know what 'becoming acquainted' means to you, sir, and I want no part of it," Claire snapped.

"I don't believe you," he answered, smiling down into her face. It was such a rakish, attractive smile that Claire had to force herself to remember how arrogant and overbearing he was.

"No, I don't believe you at all," he repeated. "Your words say 'no' but your eyes and your body—and a lovely, luscious body it is, to be sure—tell me something different."

There was just enough truth in what he said to infuriate Claire even further. "You arrogant rake! You see only what you want to see. Please allow me to leave."

For answer he moved closer, forcing her back. "I was hoping to come across you again, but I never expected to be so lucky here in old Drummond. You wouldn't run off a third time, would you, just when we've finally found each other once more?" His hands moved easily to her shoulders, pressing her against the wall.

"My father is waiting for me," Claire snapped, furious at the cavalier way he assumed she should be flattered with his attention.

"Old Tom? Oh, but old Tom won't mind waiting a while. Tom is partial to the MacDairmids. After all, he's been dependent on them long enough."

The cold stones of the tavern bit into her back. With his finger, Fall traced a light pattern down her throat, tickling her sensitive skin and gently easing away the edges of her shawl until one end fell over her shoulder. Bending his head he brushed her neck

66

lightly with his lips. Above his head Claire caught a glimpse of his companion standing, watching them, his arms folded across his chest in patient resignation with Fall's dalliance. It was the look on the man's face that brought her anger to a head. A look of disapproval—not directed at Fall but at her. That look said all too clearly that he assumed she was what Fall MacDairmid's conduct proclaimed her to be—a wanton.

Summoning all her strength, she tried to shove the persistent Fall away. He only laughed and pushed against her, pinning her to the wall.

"Let me go," Claire hissed, trying not to create too obvious a scene.

"Come now," Fall murmured, searching out the soft delicacy of the hollow of her throat. "You know you enjoy it."

To Claire's horror, her treacherous body began to respond to the seductive tickling of his lips on her skin. She felt a warmth deep down beginning to spread and her body slackened. Fall felt it too and anticipating a victory of some sort, he slid his hand up her bodice and cupped her full breast, gently lifting it closer to his wandering lips.

Claire stiffened. This simply would not do. She was not a wanton and this cocksure—an appropriate metaphor if ever there was one—arrogant young man was not going to make her into one for his amusement. Squirming and twisting, she managed to force her body sideways so she was no longer pinned flat against the wall. Then, using the leverage she had gained, she pulled back her fist and socked Fall against the side of his head.

Her blow caught him off guard and knocked him away long enough for her to dart out of his grasp.

Fall swore softly.

"I told you to let me go," Claire cried. "I won't be treated this way, not by you nor any other man. And I don't say 'gentleman' for certainly that is not what you are."

"And you are no lady. You wouldn't know a gentleman if you fell over one."

"I know well enough when there is not one around," she spat at him, her blue eyes blazing. Throwing her shawl over her head she caught the ends under her chin and draped them around her neck like a wimple. Fall saw her face, a pale oval against the dark plaid, the shapely lips pursed with anger, her eyes glaring at him, slate blue like Loch Tay on a lowery afternoon, the honey-colored arched brows knitted in a frown, two bright spots of color vivid against the creamy hue of her cheeks. Once again he was struck with how simply beautiful this girl was. He felt it in the leap of his heart, in the sudden warmth of his loins, in his enjoyment of her despite her rebuffs.

"I'll take payment for this someday," he murmured and started toward her again. He was stopped by a strong hand gripping his shoulder.

"I think we had better be going along," Francis Murray said, giving Claire a look that was not without a glimmer of admiration. "We have more important matters to face. Pray, excuse us, mistress."

Fall's glance back at Claire promised that he was not finished with her yet, but he allowed his companion to lead him back toward the tavern door. Though Claire had no idea who Sir Francis was, the kind smile he bestowed on her made her feel infinitely better about herself than his first glance had done. She let her shawl fall back around her shoulders and turned on her heel to make for the crowded marketplace. Perhaps it would be better after all to find Alyce and Jamie so that it would not appear she was alone and available. Oh, she mused, if only Alan were here. He would never allow her to be so mistreated and set upon, not even by an arrogant peer like Fall MacDairmid. Alan would have made him pay for treating her so shabbily.

She had barely joined the stream of people in the square before she spied Jamie running after a wizened little man leading a lethargic bear by an enormous chain around its neck. In a few strides Claire grabbed her brother by his collar, spinning him around.

"Where are you going?" she cried as he strained against her.

"To watch the bear dance. Come with me, Claire. It's something to see!"

"I want you to stay with me, Jamie."

"Then you come too."

"No. We need to find Alyce. Do you know where she is?"

Jamie groaned and pulled away from her. "Please, Claire. I've never seen a dancing bear. Alyce is down at the other end near the gate listening to the storyteller. Can't I go, please?"

"What storyteller? Where?"

"By the sheep pen. Please, can't I go?"

He was half out of her grasp, dancing away from her. "Oh, all right," she said, relenting. "But come and find us directly it's done."

"I will," Jamie called as he was swallowed by the milling crowd. Claire sighed, then turned, and started back toward the entrance to the square where she remembered seeing the animal pens. She had to push her way through clumps of people clustered around every booth. Two young men barred her way with a more than friendly comment but she darted around both, not even deigning to answer. Once or twice she felt a hand on her waist, and one lusty young shepherd even made so bold as to slide his fingers up the wide curve of her breast, tickling her nipple. She slapped his hand away, giving him a look that she hoped would part his hair, then hurried on. By the time she reached the sheep pen she had eyes only for Alyce's dark-green plaid.

There was a man sitting on the fence dressed in a bright scarlet waistcoat and wearing a blue cap perched jauntily on his head. On the ground in front of him sat a group of people, mostly children, listening enthralled as he spun them a story of ancient Highlands chiefs and ghostly half-men, half-seals, called selkies. Claire spotted Alyce at once sitting to the side, holding a young child on her lap. Her face was half-covered by the shadow of her shawl but what could be seen of it was fastened on the storyteller in rapt attention. Edging up beside her, Claire noticed with some concern that the child in Alyce's lap looked lethargic and flushed, with two bright spots of color on each cheek. She reached out to gently tap Alyce on the shoulder.

"Come, dear. It's time to go."

"Oh, Claire, I can't leave yet. This baby's mother asked me to watch her for a while, and we are both enjoying the story so much."

"Where did the mother go?" Claire asked. "Can't you give the child to someone else?"

"I don't know where she went. The baby was fretful and crying so I offered to hold her. The mother seemed grateful."

Claire looked around, hoping to see some sign of the child's parent. "I really think you should leave her, Alyce. For one thing, she doesn't look well. I don't want you to get something from her."

Gently Alyce smoothed the child's soft hair away from her warm forehead. She had an affinity for young children and was infinitely more comfortable with them than with adults. They were very direct about her birthmark. They asked her about it right away and then did not seem bothered about it any more.

"I hate to leave her alone," Alyce said. Picking up the child, she stood and moved away from the group listening to the storyteller. "At least let me take her," Claire started to say, reaching for the child. She had no more than touched the baby when it began to cry and snuggled against Alyce's shoulder.

"There's her mother now," Alyce cried and Claire saw a thin young woman in a dirty cap and shabby dress making her way through the crowd. Just behind her, keeping a close watch on all that was going on, came Esther Varn. All the vague sense of unease Claire had felt up until now began to boil up in acute dread.

"My poor little bairn," the mother said as she took the child from Alyce's arms. "She isn't herself today a'tall. Perhaps I ought to have kept her home."

"Yes, perhaps you should have," Claire said with some bitterness.

"I thank you for watching her for me," the woman said to Alyce and started to turn away. She was abruptly stopped by Esther who had moved up behind her.

"Did you willingly give your child over to that girl's care?" Esther asked in a voice filled with doom. The

71

surprised young woman nodded and Esther bent into her face. "I can only believe you did not know what you were doing. You had better keep a close watch on your babe, for the devil will be after her now for certain."

"Why, what do you mean?" the mother stammered, looking back at Claire. Grabbing Alyce's arm, Claire began to drag her away.

"Don't you run from the truth!" Esther's voice thundered. "You poor benighted woman, didn't you see that this girl has the devil's mark upon her? You might as well have put your child directly into his cloven hooves."

The blood drained from the woman's face. Her peasant features were transformed into a mask of numbed terror. "I don't know what you're talking about," she cried. "She seemed like such a pleasant girl, and my Jennie liked her right from the start."

"The devil's blandishment!" Esther cried. Alyce shrank behind Claire as the group listening to the storyteller began to shift their attention to the commotion on the edge of the crowd. Even the voice of the storyteller droned to a halt, interrupted by all the excitement.

"Don't try to hide your blemish," Esther cried, conscious now of how she had the group's attention. Reaching out quickly, she yanked the shawl away from Alyce's face, revealing her bright-red birthmark. There was a gasp from the crowd. Moving quickly, Claire threw the shawl back over her sister's head and, with one arm around her shoulder, half-pushed, half-dragged her into the knots of people gathering around them. In a few steps she was swallowed by a moving body of people swelling around the dancing bear that, led by the chain, wobbled along after its keeper. They had collected a mini-group of their own, sweeping around the square with the animal and its keeper at the nucleus. It afforded Claire the chance she needed to disappear into the confusion of the crowd as it was carried along. Behind her she could hear the laments of the mother punctuated by Esther's frustrated cries for someone to stop her. She would have preferred to stand her ground and tell Esther Varn just what she thought of her, but it was wiser to get Alyce away for now.

Once they were outside the orbit of the storyteller, no one paid them any mind, and Claire was able to get her sister to the opposite side of the square where they slipped toward the town gate and the tavern stable where the pony waited. She had already made up her mind that they would find a darkened corner in the stable and wait out the rest of the day when she saw Tom hurrying toward them. At first glance Claire feared he was gone in his cups. Then she realized he was cold sober. It was the look on his face that was both alarming and distressful.

He took her arm and pulled her away from the stall where Alyce stood smoothing the pony's mane and feeding it some hay.

"You must go and find Jamie at once," Tom said. "We have to go home, right away."

"What's the matter, Papa?"

"It's the witchfinder. He's here. I never thought to see him ever again. Dear God, it's been thirty years at least since the last time. I thought he was dead—*had* to be dead by now. Then I saw him today—still looking just as he did when I was a boy."

"The witchfinder?"

"Aye. I only saw him twice. The last time was a'fore your mother and I was married. Three women they

73

hung then, at Perth. I'll never forget him, standing there with the money in his hand, the look in his eyes like the devil himself."

Claire felt the blood drain from her face. "Does he wear an old-fashioned, tall hat?"

"That's the one. Evil man. Evil!"

"I saw him too but I had no idea . . ." Mentally she weighed the choice — waiting the day out for a portion of their sales on the caps against the danger of having this terrible man discover Alyce in the crowd. Especially after Esther had already made such a scene about her. There was really no choice at all.

"You stay here with Alyce and harness the pony," she said softly. "I'll go and find Jamie. The sooner we get home, the better."

It began to rain as the pony cart pulled away from the old town. It rained on the Montcrieffs all the way home and continued to rain for two days afterward. Claire lived in dread the whole two days that one of her family might come down with a cold or even some worse sickness carried back from Drummond. She told herself it was the fear of illness that caused the nagging sense of unease that lay like a pall over her every step. Yet she knew in her heart it was more than that. Esther's mean little scene, the frightful image of the old witchfinder, even the insulting way Fall Mac-Dairmid had treated her, all contributed to her malaise. She went around those two days expecting some unknown blow to fall, and, at the end of them, it did indeed.

The clouds broke on the evening of the second day, allowing the suggestion of pale color in the sky to remind them there was still a sun somewhere up there.

The tight yellow gorse of the glen was touched with rose, the clouds etched with lavender and rimmed with gold. Claire stood at the door of the house, not even noticing the spectacular sunset as she watched three black figures, like dark, elongated birds of prey, trudging up the slope toward her. Somehow she knew that, whatever they were coming for, it was not going to be pleasant.

Alyce was sitting under the rowan tree carding some wool. Her back was to the fields and she did not see the three visitors approaching. They were nearly on her before she turned. All four stood frozen, the three men staring at the girl and the girl visibly shrinking under their hostile glare. Circling away from the tree in order to avoid coming close to her, the three men continued up to the door where Claire waited.

She recognized them at once — Pastor Donovan, Angus Varn, and Jess McClure, the blacksmith. Of them all, only Jess removed his cap and nodded to Claire with a hint of embarrassment. The pastor drew himself up and stared down his thin nose at Claire.

"We've come to see Tom Montcrieff," he said, and Claire mentally wondered how it was that the clergyman managed to make every utterance, no matter how banal, sound so ponderous. "Please to tell him we are here."

"He's not to home," Claire answered. "He went up to the manor house." He was actually probably falling over a table at the Golden Boar by now but they ought to know that. If they didn't, she was not going to be the one to tell them.

"Then we will speak with you, Claire Montcrieff," the pastor answered. The three men stood glancing at one another as though each was waiting for the other

75

to begin.

"Won't you come in," Claire asked none too politely, "and have a drop of something? I haven't much to offer you but—"

"No, thank you," the clergyman interrupted her. "We've not come for a social visit."

"Then why are you here?" Behind the men she could see Alyce edging toward the house, keeping well back but trying to listen.

"We have come to tell you, Mistress Montcrieff, that the bairn yon marked girl"—he nodded imperceptibly in Alyce's direction—"was holdin' and fondlin' on market day died that self-same night."

"Died!" The word choked in her throat.

"Stricken and died, that very same day. Under the circumstances we've no choice but to call a meeting of the kirk and hold an inquiry into the cause and meaning of the child's death."

"Why should there be an inquiry?" Claire went bravely on. "The child was ill when my sister offered to care for it. I could see that myself. Her forehead was burning up, she was whimpering and lethargic."

"And did you see this before the girl took her in her arms?"

"Well, no. But—"

Angus Varn, taking courage from the pastor's words, leaned toward Claire. "There's none to say but that the child was as well and hale as you or I until she was taken up by that witch!"

"Alyce is not a witch! This is absurd. Jess McClure," Claire said, turning to the only one of them who might be sympathetic. "Tell them that Alyce is a gentle, good girl. As unlike the old women you people call witches as anyone could be."

"They are not always old women," the pastor

intoned. "The devil can use anyone for his tricks. Men, children—"

"But not Alyce. She would never harm anyone."

"She bears the devil's mark!" Angus cried.

"She does not!"

"Enough, mistress," the pastor said. "We've no more to say for now. You tell Tom Montcrieff to come to the kirk tomorrow at noon of the day to face the council—and bring that poor, benighted creature with him."

"You are making a mistake," Claire cried as the pastor and Angus turned their backs and stalked down the hill. Jess McClure waited a moment until they were gone, then laid a hand on Claire's arm.

"Ye'd better do as they say, Miss Claire. It might have been worse. There was talk of clappin' poor Alyce in gaol right away, but they decided it would be more Christian to wait until the inquiry."

Fighting back her tears, Claire was unmoved by his half-hearted kindness. "Christian! They don't know the meaning of the word. They'll hound that poor child to her grave and for something she has no control over at all. She didn't ask to be born with that terrible mark."

Jess lowered his voice as he saw Alyce hanging back near the tree. "But it's there, all the same. Who knows how it came to be there? Or why?"

Claire turned on him angrily. "I know this much, Jess McClure. There is nothing of the devil in a girl as sweet and kind as Alyce. There is more of him in those who accuse a pure child of evil ways."

The blacksmith had a kind heart and he felt Claire's grief keenly. Yet there was so much that was mysterious about the world. So many dangers, so many invisible forces whose powers were beyond

77

comprehension and control, so much that could not be explained.

"Things are not always what they seem, Miss Claire," he said lamely.

Deliberately Claire walked over to Alyce and laid an arm across her shoulders. "You go back, Jess McClure, and tell the council that we will be there to answer their absurd charges. The Lord will protect us, especially Alyce. You tell them that!"

He nodded and, without looking directly at Alyce Dawes, he hurried after the pastor and Angus Varn. Claire watched him go, thinking that, as bad as this confrontation was, now she must somehow find a way to explain the charges to Alyce. And that was going to be infinitely more terrible.

Five

Although it was still light outside, the interior of the Brogain kirk was cast in deep shadow. The darkness was little helped by the narrow slits in the stone walls that served as windows and was even more enhanced by the stones themselves, old, dank, splotched with green mold, and forbidding in their frigid austerity. Claire, over her father's objections, had insisted that she be allowed to attend the inquiry and stood quietly behind Tom, studying the people facing them from behind a long table with a heavy heart. There were no friendly faces now, not even the qualified kindness of Jess McClure. Pastor Donovan sat in the center, flanked on one side by Angus Varn, Sally Carne, the smug wife of a well-to-do farmer from the other side of the glen, and Timothy Sprague, the wheelwright, who was also one of the deacons. On the pastor's other side sat a second deacon and a scowling widow, Mistress Leary—a woman who, but for her ample marriage portion, might have been accused of witchcraft herself. A chair beside the widow stood ominously empty. Alyce stood next to Tom, her slight body drawn inward and swathed in the voluminous folds of her plaid. Claire thought she detected the slightest twitching of the girl's shoulders, and she moved closer, laying an arm gently around her sister's waist to steady her.

When the door off the sacristy opened and a tall figure emerged from the gloom, Claire's worst fears were confirmed. She was not even surprised to recognize the witchfinder, still wearing his tall, old-fashioned hat, his thin face all the more frightening for the dark shadows cast upon it by the dim church light. Claire glanced at her father and saw Tom's face go white.

The pastor began by explaining in careful detail that this was only an inquiry, not a formal accusation. Yet the crimes ranged against Alyce were formidable. Every chance happening in which she might have figured was brought against her. The principal crime was, of course, the death of the child in Drummond after she had held and fondled it, but there were other, more suspicious charges as well. Little Robbie Ivy, sick of a fever after playing a game with Alyce near the town well one afternoon three years ago. Old Mrs. Leary, claiming she saw a spirit in the likeness of a kitten that was similar to an animal known to be fond of Alyce, explained how the kitten had jumped on her shoulder, nibbled at her ear, and promptly made her sick near to death. That she recovered at all was due only to the prayers of Pastor Donovan, who himself could testify to the mysterious nature of her sudden illness.

"Alyce never had a kitten," Claire spoke up defiantly. The truth was she had never allowed her to have one because of the threat of having it labeled a familiar.

"She was seen petting this kitten in the village," the old woman cried, bending over the table toward Claire. "I saw her myself."

"Pray, Mistress, but that does not seem to me to constitute the most unprejudiced of witnesses," Claire quipped. The hostility that flickered over the faces of the people ranged against her warned her too late that flippancy might not be the best approach to this business.

"There is more," the pastor continued. "One of Malcolm Dabney's gloves disappeared last winter and was later found buried, but not before that gentleman himself was in torment, his insides rotting away just as his glove rotted in the ground. There was no doubt at all that a terrible spell had been cast upon him."

"You have no way of connecting Alyce with that glove. She never saw it. She doesn't even know Master Dabney."

"What about the dog, Mungo?" Deacon Sprague spoke up. "Was he not her familiar and did he not suffer a mysterious death?"

Claire started to speak but Tom stopped her with a raised hand. In a fierce, but level voice he answered: "Mungo was a working dog who herded our flock of sheep as anyone in this town can testify. He was never with Alyce except in the evening from time to time. That hardly makes him a familiar."

"Well, she must have some familiar," the Widow Leary answered stubbornly. "They all do. She just keeps hers well hid."

"Perhaps her familiar is that rowan tree," the deacon added. "She's more than fond of it. Always sitting under it, she is, and I hear that it even talks to her."

"That is not true! Rowan trees protect against witches." Claire cried and realized too late that her reaction was overstrong. It would be better to laugh at such ridiculous accusations. Then she caught a glimpse of the witchfinder out of the corner of her eye. He was sitting silently with his

81

chin in his hand as his quick little eyes studied the three people standing before him. Claire's blood turned cold. There was really no chance at all that Alyce was going to be let off. She could see it clearly.

Once more Tom spoke up with a dignified, level voice that seemed to make an impression on the judges.

"Pastor Donovan, we all know that this poor child was born with a terrible mark on her face, but is that her fault? It was none of her doing, and had she the opportunity, she would gladly be free of it and of all these wicked charges people are so quick to bring against her. Alyce is a good, kind girl who never harmed a soul. She has absolutely no meanness in her and these foolish accusations have no justification at all. The babe that mother at Drummond handed over to her was already sick. Is it Alyce's fault that it died later? As for talking trees and rotting gloves and kittens — they are all nothing but fancies, and there is not a shred of evidence to connect them with this poor girl. In your heart — your Christian heart — you know that is so."

The clergyman cast his eyes downward for an instant, and Tom saw that he had gained a small advantage. He pressed on.

"I know you want to do your duty and what is right, but would you want to make an innocent child suffer wrongly? Think, sir, what if you are making a terrible mistake? What if there is really no basis for these accusations? Take away her mark, and does this lovely girl look like the old crones who have been hanged as witches?"

"The devil can use all manner of disguises," the Widow Leary cried, seeing that Tom's level words were having an effect. "It's not always poor old women whom he uses."

The pastor nodded. "Widow Leary has a point. But Tom, your words too are well said. We want no miscarriage of justice here. That is why we have invited our learned friend to join us." He leaned toward the end of the table and the witchfinder gave him a grave nod. "However, there must be one test that will help us form our conclusions. The girl must be stripped and searched for the devil's teats."

Claire's heart fell. She knew it would do no good to object; in fact, it would be taken as evidence of guilt. Yet for Alyce to undergo such an indignity made her sick to her stomach. And what if they should happen on some small mole or birthmark? As far as she knew, there was none on the girl's body; yet anything, even the smallest mole or freckle, might easily be construed as one.

"The good Widow Leary will undertake this search," the pastor added.

"I ask that I be present too," Claire spoke up. "Alyce is my sister, and I would like to give her comfort during this ordeal."

"She is not your sister, Mistress," Deacon Sprague said, "except in the loosest form of the word. She is a foundling as is well known in the village, and all the more reason to suspect her origin."

"I'll vouch for her origin," Tom said quickly. "I've had her in my home since she was a tiny babe, and there never was a sweeter child anywhere. She has been nothing but a blessing to me and my family."

"Yet you found her lying by the side of the road, did you not? Who's to say how she came to be there? Why could not a spirit have taken flesh and deliberately been laid in your path, knowing you would have a soft heart and take it home to raise?"

Tom threw the deacon a scathing look. "Timothy Sprague, I may be soft in the heart, but you are even softer in the head if you really believe such a hare-brained story as that."

"Enough." the pastor said. "Widow Leary, you will take the girl into the sacristy and search her. Look you well for any sign of a teat upon which a familiar or a spirit might take suck. And because we are not mean-spirited people but good Christians trying to rid the world of evil, we will allow the Mistress Montcrieff to accompany you."

For the first time Alyce threw Claire a look that was fraught with panic and horror. "Don't be afraid, dearest," Claire whispered, concerned that the girl might go into hysterics, which would make her cause even worse. "I'll be with you. It will be all right."

For the rest of her life Claire would remember the next twenty minutes as among the most horrible she had ever lived through. Alyce's embarrassment and shame, the victim she had suddenly become, was horrible enough. Even worse was the way the widow went over every inch of the girl's skin, half-slavering and half-determined to find something, some blemish, no matter how small, that she could use as proof of Satan's hand. Never had Claire been so thankful for Alyce's pure, unspoiled fair body. Nowhere on her pale skin was there even the slightest suggestion of a mark. When the three of them moved back into the nave to face the council, the widow was tight-lipped with disappointment. Claire's only desire was to leave this place, to carry her distraught sister back to the sanctuary of their bedroom and hide her from these evil people. But this she was not yet allowed to do. There was more to be endured.

After countless whisperings back and forth among the group at the table and several furtive, soft questions directed to the grotesque figure at the end, Pastor Donovan finally stood and announced that they were free to go for the moment. To Claire's surprise, Tom did not move.

"And what of the charges?" he asked sullenly.

"This council will examine them privately. You will have our decision by morning next. I advise you, however, Tom Montcrieff, to confine this person to your home until our judgment is reached. We allow you this in place of putting her directly in gaol out of sensibility to your former station."

Tom's lips folded into a thin, tight line that only grudgingly opened to allow a curt "thanks to ye," to the council. Then, hurriedly before they could change their collective minds, he rushed his daughters from the church. In the gathering dusk of evening the three of them almost ran back to their house as though every shadow hid some new accuser. Once home they bolted the door, poked up the fire, and sat dejectedly at the table before the hearth. Alyce cried into Claire's shoulder, her tears a mixture of chagrin, fear, and distress that she had brought such a calamity on her family. After much soothing and some hot tea infused with rosemary leaves, Claire was able to put her to bed and watch her fall into a fitful sleep. Then, totally unable to sleep herself, she went back to sit with her father in the kitchen.

They were still there, silently studying the flames, when a soft knock at the door brought them both sharply alert.

"Who—" Claire started to say, but Tom laid a finger on his lips, warning her to be silent. Quietly he moved to the window and peered through its clouded surface to see who was standing outside. Claire heard him give a sharp intake of breath and sat transfixed as he carefully raised the wooden latch.

A stranger slipped inside the room swathed in a wide plaid and with a velvet hat pulled down over his face so as to throw his face in shadow. When the light fell on his face, Claire came to her feet, staring in disbelief.

She had not seen Edgar MacDairmid many times, but one could not easily forget that narrow face, neatly trimmed black beard, and those small, penetrating eyes. The expensive clothes and the large cairngorm that twinkled in the firelight would have been enough to proclaim his exalted station. He looked her over with barely a moment's interest and turned directly to Tom.

"I'll have a word with you, Tom Montcrieff," he said, more as an order than a request.

Tom pulled a chair away from the table and offered it to his visitor. "Is there anything you would like to drink, Mister Edgar? Claire, bring the whisky I was saving—"

Edgar raised a jeweled hand. "No. Don't bother, mistress. I've come on business and the sooner settled, the better. Perhaps you had better leave us though."

Having made the required polite gesture, Tom shook his head and sat down opposite Edgar. "Whatever you have to say to me can be spoken in front of Claire."

Edgar threw her a dark glance and for just that second Claire caught a resemblance to his brother. It was something about the eyes, something that was mischief in Fall and meanness in Edgar.

"Very well," he said grudgingly. "It's nothing to me."

The two men sat facing each other while Claire faded back near the stone fireplace, half-hidden in the shadows. Edgar laid his arm easily along the planks of the table, a thin half-smile on his lips.

"I know about your problems," he began. "I know

86

the council is at this moment trying to decide what to do with the foundling you've been caring for."

Tom's eyes burned into the man's impassive face but he did not answer.

"I have come to propose a solution to you," Edgar went on quietly. "One that will be to your advantage and to mine as well."

Tom's look flicked up to catch his daughter's staring at him from the shadows. "Does the laird know ye've come here?" he asked.

"No. Why should he? He's beyond caring about anyone's problems, even yours. No one knows I'm here since it seemed to me this was a matter better conducted in private."

"I'm not interested," Tom began but Claire stopped him by stepping forward to lay a hand lightly on his shoulder. Ordinarily she would have been grateful to see her father heave this man out of their door, but right now their situation was desperate, and help in any form was worth examining.

"What is it you propose?" she asked Edgar. His cold eyes glanced briefly up at her, and then he went on speaking to Tom.

"I believe you know as well as I that the council will convict that girl in there of witchcraft."

"We don't know that."

"It's a foregone conclusion. Even if all of them were convinced of her innocence, that fossil from another age they call the witchfinder will never allow them to let her off. There's money in it for him if she's caught and hanged."

"It couldn't happen," Claire cried. "God wouldn't allow such an injustice."

"My dear girl, we both know that a just God has allowed many an old crone whose only crime was senility to be hanged as a witch and has never, so far as I know, lifted a heavenly finger to help. I cannot see Him intervening on behalf of this one child, no matter how pure. She will certainly be convicted and executed."

"I thought that madness was behind us," Tom muttered.

"Not quite yet. However, I have a solution. Leave Ben Brogain. Find a home somewhere far from here, and take the foundling with you."

Claire waited for her father to answer, but Tom only continued to stare at his fingers gripped together on the table.

"We don't have the money for such a change," she said finally. "We would be strangers wherever we went and unwelcome."

"I'll see that you have the money and a letter of good conduct as well."

Tom lifted his head. "I've lived here in this glen all my life. Why should I leave it? What about my farm?"

"Of course you shall sell it to me. I'll give you enough for it to see you safely away. You can take your beloved foundling out of danger, and I shall have the land I've wanted for a long time now. If you leave before morning, you will also escape the long arm of the kirk. I guarantee they will not pursue you."

Tom sat in silence, still staring sullenly at his hands. With a careless gesture Edgar threw a small velvet pouch on the table, that gave a soft clink as it landed. Edgar sat back, certain of the effect.

"What's that? Thirty pieces of silver?"

The half-smile on Edgar's face turned to an angry grimace. "I don't have to listen to this," he snapped and started to rise.

"No, wait!" Laying both her hands on her father's

shoulders, Claire stood behind him, forcing Edgar to deal with her. "We accept your offer."

"Just a minute, daughter—"

"We have no choice, Papa. No choice."

Tom looked from one to the other, his daughter, distraught but resolute, and Edgar, smug and satisfied. Fury welled within him. He wanted to take the arrogant coxcomb by the throat and choke him until the life was forced from his evil body. Yet just as quickly as it had come, his anger receded into a hopeless despair. He did not want to fight Edgar and Claire both. He did not have the strength for it. In a strange way it was even a relief to let Claire make the decision for him. He needed a drink—that hot, seering inner fortification that kept him going. That was all he wanted now.

Claire knew both from instinct and past experience the stages her father was undergoing. She kept her fingers lightly touching his thin shoulders as she addressed Edgar. The man seemed at last to realize that Tom was useless and, if he wanted anything settled, it was going to have to be through her.

"It will be difficult for us to get our things together and leave Brogain by morning. Can't we have a little more time?"

"Take all the time you want, mistress. Only know that as sure as the sun rises, those committeemen from the kirk will be at your door to fetch Alyce Dawes to gaol."

"If you can guarantee they won't pursue us, then surely you ought to be able to hold them off for a day or two."

"It is quite impossible. I don't want to get involved. The thing has gone too far and touches too many people. No, you must either accept my offer as it is or reject it. Either way, it is nothing to me."

"I don't believe you. In fact, it would not surprise me to learn that you and your brother are behind this whole thing. You've wanted this farm back for a long time."

"Bah!" Edgar spat the word, rising to throw his plaid over his arm. "Father and daughter, you are both stiff-necked and obstinate. Yes, I want this farm, but I could easily take it and give you nothing for it. No help and no money. Let the girl be hanged."

"Then why have you offered to help us? Why do you want us to leave?" Realizing he was moving to the door, Claire darted across the room to stand with her back against it, blocking his way. "Why do you want us to move to another glen?"

Edgar gave a brittle laugh. "I don't care what you do, mistress. Now please allow me to leave."

Claire notice that the velvet bag still lay on the table. He had not picked it up even though he seemed to be withdrawing his offer.

"Very well," she said quickly. "I don't understand your reasons but we will accept your terms. Alyce must not be harmed, and, if that means we must all leave Ben Brogain, then that is what we shall do."

"As you choose," Edgar said lightly, but there was no disguising the satisfaction in his face. "Just make sure you are gone before dawn. Your only hope is that when they arrive here they find an empty house."

Claire nodded and moved away from the door. Edgar paused long enough to throw her an oblique look before slipping through the door and closing it behind him. With a sudden movement Claire threw the latch and turned to her father.

"Get Jamie and Alyce up, Papa. We've got a lot to do in the next few hours."

Tom stood white-faced behind the table. "I can't believe I heard my own ears. I can't believe my own daughter agreed to that snake's—"

"Please, Papa," Claire cried, leaning across the table to stare into her father's face. "Listen to me. We have to leave this glen. It's Alyce's only hope. We're not moving to some other town to be hounded again as we have been in the past. We have Edgar's money now, and we're going to use it to make a real beginning—in America."

"America! What in God's name are you talking about?"

"Don't you see. It's a new country without all these old prejudices. Alyce will be safe there. And I can find Alan. He wants me to come to him, he told me so in his last letter."

"But that was months ago. You don't know what you're proposing. It's thousands of miles across an ocean, and what will we find at the other end, assuming we even get there?"

Even as he spoke, Tom reached for the whisky bottle. This was all too much for him. His clouded mind cried for the narcotic of alcohol, to throw up a screen between him and all this confusion and pain. Abruptly Claire grabbed his hand away.

"Papa, you're going to stay sober tonight if I have to pour this bottle on the ground. We have too much to do."

Tom stepped back, amazed at the fierce determination on his daughter's face. "But Claire, we don't have a way to get to America. I canna go—"

"There is a ship leaving Leith within the next two days. I heard of it in the village. Some of the townsfolk have been planning to take it for weeks now. I intend to get us aboard that ship somehow, Papa, but I need your help. Now please rouse Jamie and Alyce. We have to start putting together what we can take with us."

He stood for a moment as though thinking over her words, wavering between fighting her or giving in. Then, with a shrug, he shuffled toward the loft. Claire was relieved to see that her father had given up the fight, for she did not know if she had the strength to wear him down, no matter how resolute she sounded. She felt heavy and filled with a terrible ache over the impossibility of taking everything they needed in so short a time. But she was even more overwhelmed by the unbearable thought that in a few hours they would be leaving this place she had always called home forever, never to see it again. Perhaps it was best to cut away quickly and cleanly, not carrying too much of the past with you. Perhaps, once it was over, she would be grateful.

She hurried across the room, threw open the lid of a heavy oak clothespress, and began spilling the contents around her on the floor. How long until dawn? Four, five hours of darkness in which to sort, bundle, and load all the accumulation of a lifetime — everything and anything they might need to start a new life in a strange, unknown world.

Six

"I'm sorry, mistress, but I have a full complement of passengers. There is no way I can make room for four more." Though the master of the *Selkirk*, Jonathan Mendel, looked a gruff man with a bushy white beard that spilled over his dark coat, his voice was kind and he seemed sincerely distressed that he could not make room for them.

Claire struggled to hide her disappointment so that it would not be too obvious, but she wasn't going to give up so easily.

"That cannot be true," she answered as calmly as possible. She did not want the man to think he had a hysterical female on his hands as that would certainly hurt their chances of getting aboard. It was bad enough that it was she and not her father trying to arrange this passage.

"I saw the passengers on the upper deck when you were speaking to them, and there were not nearly enough people to fill this vessel. We have the money if that is what's worrying you, and we need to get aboard this ship."

"No, no. It is not the money. You see, we've been promised enough passengers waiting at Plymouth to more than fill the ship. I cannot be responsible for more."

"But suppose there aren't that many people waiting at Plymouth? After all, there might be many reasons some of them would have to change their minds at the last minute. If you had a few extra passengers on board, then you wouldn't be short any passengers. Please, Master Mendel, we have to make this journey."

The captain pulled off his hat and threaded his thick fingers through his shock of white hair. What, he wondered, would make so likely a lass so eager to leave Scotland. Yet he was moved by Claire's pleading. He had a daughter only a little younger who was very dear to him though he saw little of her, and Claire reminded him poignantly of that girl. Yet he was master of this ship and he must put practicality ahead of sentiment.

"No, no, my girl. I cannot do it. That's my last word. However, there will be another ship bound for New York within a month or two. She's the *Glasgow Lass* and she's larger than our *Selkirk*. You should not have any trouble getting put on her manifest if you try right away."

Knowing she was not going to be able to change his mind, Claire turned from him. "I thank you for your advice," she murmured and walked across the deck and down the gangplank to where Alyce and Jamie waited. Alyce, seeing the despairing look on her face, knew she had not had a satisfying talk with the captain.

"He wouldn't take us on?"

"No. He has a full set of passengers, or he will, once they reach Plymouth."

"What will we do, Claire? We won't have to go

back to Ben Brogain, will we?" Her eyes were large saucers, stark against her pale skin. The panic alive in them moved Claire's heart. She shook her head.

"Don't worry about that, dear. We'll never go back to Ben Brogain. Not while I have life left in my body." She looked up at the high sides of the *Selkirk* gently straining against her mooring ropes. "We're going to get aboard this vessel somehow. I'm determined that we will."

The nightmare of the trip from Ben Brogain was already fading into a memory best forgotten. The furtive haste, the loved belongings left behind, the hurried trek across the moors in the cold morning mist with an eye ever on the road behind them fearing to see horses following—it was all so horrible that she wanted nothing so much as to block it from her mind forever. At least Edgar MacDairmid had been as good as his word, and they had slipped away unnoticed— just about the only good thing that could be said for him.

Jamie slumped against one of the thick piers and threw a pebble into the water, knocking some floating garbage. "I don't see why we had to leave home anyway. Why did we have to sell the pony? Why can't we go back?"

"It is not our home any longer, Jamie. It belongs to Edgar MacDairmid now. We're going to find a new home—a better one. One you will come to like just as much as the old one."

"But if we can't go back and we can't get aboard this ship, how are we going to find a new home? I don't want to stay here. I don't like Leith."

Claire understood that his anger came more from loss and confusion than from actual homesickness. She studied the ship as it creaked in the water, undulating on the gentle flow of the current. Surprisingly there were not too many sailors about. A few of the passengers setting out for or returning from ventures into the town, moved down or up the gangway. With a little luck she might be able to slip aboard and discover for herself some way of getting around the master's ultimatum.

Absently she squeezed Jamie's shoulder. "Don't worry. We're not going to stay in Leith, Jamie. We're going to get to America if we have to swim there!"

Claire got her chance early the next morning. The *Selkirk* was to lift anchor later that day, and she noticed that most of the passengers spent their last night ashore. The crew also took advantage of their last shore leave to carouse in the sleazy dockside taverns, leaving a sleepy and inattentive watch on the ship. Claire was easily able to slip up the gangway, keeping to the shadows. When she saw that the hatch was open, she made her way down it silently and furtively.

The orlop deck lay below the passenger one and was designed to hold cargo and stores of water and food for the long voyage. Though most of the cargo was to be picked up in England, the deck was already half-filled with barrels and kegs, stacked bales and boxes with a long empty space down the center. Claire had brought a candle stub and flint with her, and, once she made certain no one was about, she lit it, crawled down the last of the steep steps, and searched out a corner where she and her family might hide until the ship was well underway. The orlap was an eerie place — dark, damp, and heavy with the assorted odors of stored foodstuffs. Faint scurryings that accompanied the slow movement of her tiny flame suggested there were rats living down there as well. Claire shuddered, wondering if perhaps they might not do better to wait for the *Glasgow Lass*. Then her resolution hardened. They were going to New York to make a new life, and, if this was the only way to do it, then so be it.

She slipped to one end of the deck where a small partition separated a section from the rest. The floor here was raised and seemed dryer than the other part. She was just thinking how this might be her best answer when she heard movement on the deck above. There was a soft, almost furtive whispering followed by the scuffling of feet. A second louder whisper gave directions. She looked about frantically and noticed a tall stack of bales just outside the waist-high partition. Blowing out her candle she slipped behind the bales, crowding into a tiny, pitch-dark space.

It was only dark for a moment. A light appeared in the hatch opening, and the dim, scattered light of a pierced lantern enabled her to make out figures moving down the hatchway steps. Two men carrying something large and dark between them were soon followed by two more. As they moved toward the raised platform, a fifth man slid easily down and followed them, holding the lantern high. His cloak collar and hat hid his face, but Claire recognized Fall MacDairmid nonetheless and, shrinking back into her narrow cave, dislodged one of the bales. It wavered and thumped for a second before stabilizing. All five men froze. Terrified, Claire could hear Fall's step as he waved the lantern along the wall of bales, walking up the deck and back again.

"What was it?" one of the sailors whispered loudly.

"It was nothing," Fall answered. "We must have

disturbed the rats. Hurry now. There is still a lot to bring down!"

From her vantage point behind the narrow slit between the stacked bales, Claire could just see one of the men lifting a section of the floor. To her surprise he jumped down into a space where no space should have been, only the ship's ballast. The burdens that had been carried down were handed to him and stored out of sight. Then the four sailors moved back up the stairs, only to reappear shortly afterward with more. This was repeated until Claire wondered how there could be space enough for all the hidden cargo they were stashing away. She hardly dared to breathe the whole time, and finally with great relief she heard one of them mutter, "that's the last of it, sir." Her body was cramped in the small space, yet she dared not move.

The wooden planks were replaced and the opening was closed. The men had reached the steps when she heard Fall say, "You men go ashore. I'm just going to have a last look." There was a soft clink of coins as he handed a bag to one of the men.

"You needn't worry, sir," the sailor whispered. "Those English deputy inspectors wouldn't find that false floor in a hundred years. By the time we reach Plymouth, it'll be covered with legitimate cargo, and Drummond made it fit so well you'd never know it could be moved."

"All the same," Fall said guardedly, "I'd like to check it for myself. Up with you, now, and remember—not a word to anyone of this."

The only answer Claire could make out was the quiet sound of the men's boots on the steps. After they were gone, she heard Fall walk over to the raised partition, inspect the floor, walk to the stairs and look up the hatchway, move back to the partition, and hang the lantern on a hook on the low wall.

"All right, Mistress Montcrieff. You can come out now," he said loudly.

Claire was overcome with chagrin. She was so sure she had been unnoticed.

"I knew you were there the whole time," he went on. "I did not want to embarrass you in front of my men."

Drawing herself up, Claire stepped out into the small circle of light. Across from her Fall stood leaning against the wall, his arms folded across his chest, the suggestion of a smile playing about the corners of his lips. Claire decided to take the offensive.

"So. You add smuggling to your other sins," she said sarcastically.

"And you, spying to yours. I must say, you do turn up in the most amazing places. This is perhaps the last place I expected to see you. What are you doing here anyway?"

"That's none of your business."

"Let me see," he said, rubbing a finger along the edge of his lower lip. "Why would a beautiful girl be skulking around the cargo deck of a ship in the early hours of the morning unless—of course! You're going to stow aboard."

Claire's eyes flashed, knowing the look on her face told him how right he was. "Not just me. My whole family."

"But why? Why not go to the master and buy passage? I assume you can afford to."

So he knew about Edgar's thirty pieces of silver, Claire thought bitterly. Well, she had suspected the two of them were in this together all along. "I tried but there is no room. Too many people are scheduled to board in Plymouth," she muttered, not even looking at the infuriating Fall.

"And you thought, if you got aboard secretly after we were under sail, he would have to let you stay. What idiocy! Don't you know there are twenty towns between here and England where he could have you put ashore, not to mention Plymouth itself. Besides, Captain Mendel doesn't look kindly on being coerced against his will."

Her face fell. "But he's got to take us. There must be a way. We have got to leave Scotland and go to New York." There was a note of desperation in her voice. "You could talk to him. You're in charge of the passengers. You could make him take us!"

"Why should I?"

"He might be very interested to know about this cargo you were hiding tonight. I don't know why you're doing it, but I do know it is very uncommon to bring cargo aboard at this hour. Why? Something you don't want the master or the English to know about?"

"A good try, mistress, but blackmail does not suit you. The master already knows about this cargo. And it is not mine. I'm merely handling it for a friend."

"That doesn't make you any the less guilty."

She saw him reach impatiently for the lantern, and a fierce desperation washed over her. If he ruined this chance, there would be no other to get aboard the *Selkirk*. They would be forced to stay in Scotland for many more weeks, perhaps even months, living in a seaport town and running the risk of persecution against Alyce. They had to sail. She gritted her teeth and caught his arm as he reached the steep steps.

"Wait!"

Fall turned. The dim lamplight bronzed her hair, which had fallen about her shoulders. The delicate bones of her face were shadowed, her full, slightly open lips in stark relief. She was so beautiful that the urge that swelled up in him was almost painful.

"Wait," Claire went on. "You—you like me, don't you?"

"I'm not sure I understand what you mean," he answered though his eyes said he knew exactly what she was talking about.

Claire moved her shoulders suggestively. "If you did like me, well, I might not be so—so distant to someone who did me a good turn."

Fall had one foot on the first step. He removed it and turned to face her.

"Let me understand you, mistress. If I talk Captain Mendel into adding you to the passenger list—"

"Me and my family. Tom, Alyce, and Jamie."

"All right. The four of you to the passenger list, then you'll—"

Claire stepped quickly up and laid her fingers over his lips. "I am only saying that I might look kindly on someone who did me such a great favor. No more."

It was enough. Her very closeness was intoxicating. He slipped an arm around her waist and pulled her against him. The promise of a long voyage with this enticing body in his arms made his head whirl.

Fall dropped his lips hard against hers. She forced herself to respond. Then, as his tongue sought her lips, thrusting between them into the sweet moistness beyond, a rush of flame consumed her. Her arms slid around his neck, and for a moment she gave herself up completely to the exquisite delight of melding against his hard body.

Then she remembered: don't give too much—just

the promise of more to come. She pulled away, gasping for breath and trying to appear nonchalant at the same time.

"You surprise me, mistress. I thought you more innocent, more virginal. This is better."

His words masked his true feelings. Actually there was a tinge of disappointment deep down underneath his searing excitement at her promise. He really had assumed she was a virgin, a sweet maiden, and it came as something of a shock to realize she knew so much about the world. Still, the idea of sharing his narrow bed with this luscious body made a voyage that he had begun to dread suddenly appear enticing. He did not even have to think about it.

"I'll speak to Captain Mendel. He'll do what I ask. Can you have your family ready to be on board in two hours?"

"Yes, yes. I can."

"Good." He kissed her again, lightly brushing her lips. "Until later then."

He was halfway up the steps when he stopped again, leaning down. "And not a word to anyone about this cargo. That's got to be part of the bargain."

Claire nodded and turned away as he disappeared. Her heart was thundering so loudly she could barely breathe. What had she done! Promised her body to this rake, this infamous rogue who had all but driven her family from their home. For all she knew he could even have been behind the terrible rumors that threatened Alyce. And she had as much as promised to give her body to his horrible lusts!

Yet she had succeeded in getting them aboard the ship, she rationalized as she gradually calmed down. They would sail on the *Selkirk* to America and that was all that mattered.

She smoothed her skirts and stuffed her hair under her cap, looking up at the empty hatch. Fall Mac-Dairmid was a blackguard. No need to worry about making good on a pledge to such a man. Besides, it was a long way to America. Just let him try to collect on her promise!

"I think the last passenger is coming aboard."

Jeanne Kinross, standing beside Claire at the ship's rail, shielded her eyes with her hand and squinted at the shore where a longboat was pulling away from the stone quay. "And it's high time too, don't you think? Here we are already in the channel. You'd think people would be more considerate."

Jeanne went on chattering as Claire mentally tuned her out. She had already determined that Jeanne was a chatterbox who enjoyed the sound of her own voice. But she had good eyesight, Claire thought, for all she herself could make out were the shadow forms of two people seated in the stern beyond the sailors pulling at the oars. The huge round hat of one of them told her it was a woman.

Turning her back to the shore, Claire looked anxiously around the deck for Alyce and spotted her sitting next to Tom on the quarter deck, her back to the rest of the ship as she watched the seagulls playing on the water. The girl's hood was around her head as it had been continually since they came aboard. Absently Alyce leaned against her father, who laid his arm around her thin shoulders. Claire was gratified to see it for she had been half-afraid that Tom might harbor some kind of grudge against his foster child for being at the center of the plot that lost them their home. She had underestimated her father, she realized. He had every bit as much affection for Alyce as she did herself.

It still seemed a miracle that they were here aboard the *Selkirk* and that this very day, within the hour, the sailors said, they were to slip anchor and sail away. Deliberately she forced herself not to turn and gaze once more at the shoreline. She would allow herself a last look at Scotland when they were under way and not before.

"Ho, Claire." She recognized her brother's voice before she saw him fling himself down the fo'c's'le steps. "I met a sailor, Mister Drummond, the ship's carpenter. He's going to teach me to carve! Isn't that the best! He says, if we can find the right piece of wood, we'll carve a ship just like this one. Imagine, Claire! What fun!"

Jamie's eyes were brimming with excitement as they had been since he had first stepped on the deck of the ship. This was a high adventure for one of them at least, Claire thought. "That's lovely, Jamie, but you must not run around the deck so wildly. You'll get in the way of the sailors, or you might knock down one of the other passengers. Please try to settle down."

Jamie's eyes automatically shunted to the other side of the deck where Esther Varn and her son, Daniel, were sitting with their backs to the other passengers. At least the boy knew who to watch out for. He nodded to his sister and took off again at a slightly slower pace than before though still not sedate enough to suit Claire. She too was trying to be very careful to avoid trouble with the Varns. It was unfortunate that they had booked passage on this ship long before the Montcrieffs were forced to join, but there was nothing she could do about that. She had made up her mind at the first sight of them on the quay that her family would stay clear of that family as much as possible.

The rest of the passengers seemed pleasant enough. In fact, she had been surprised at the friendly way they all accepted an enforced closeness with perfect strangers. The Menzies, Anne and Ranald, strolled around the limited space on the waist with their four-year-old son, Clifford, bobbing behind. There was one other family, the Spattles, who were also from the Brogain area, but she did not know them well. They seemed friendly enough however. The most pleasant surprise had been the girl chattering beside her, Jeanne Kinross and her brother, Ned. Jeanne was a pretty brunette with sharp green eyes and pouty lips that could suddenly flame into a vivacious smile.

Her brother, though similar in coloring, was as different from his sister as could be. A more dour, sober young man Claire had never seen. It probably came from the circumstances of his life, which had brought the siblings aboard this ship. At his father's recent death, he found he was left with nothing but debts. Having a sister to care for and being penniless, he had made a sudden decision to try his luck in the New World. Jeanne had carelessly confided these intimate details with the same ease she might have used in discussing last night's dinner, but it had given Claire some insight into the young man. She could see that Ned was a worrier. Having made a decision of such importance, he did not set it aside and get on with it but rather chewed endlessly over whether or not it had been wise. The lines of concern never lifted from his long, narrow face.

The crew, with one exception, seemed as pleasant as the passengers. Claire already knew four of them by name—Drummond, the carpenter, Carne, a mate, Davie, another mate, and young Hawkins, the captain's boy. They were rough and worldly-wise, as one might expect seasoned sailors to be, but they were kind to her and to Jamie, and she liked them for it. The only crewman she did not like so far was the first mate, Jimmy Cole, not for any reason he had given her, but simply for that uneasy feeling she had gotten when she had caught him staring at her several times. She recognized that hungry look—it could not have been more obvious had he licked his lips as his eyes swept her up and down. She would avoid him just as she planned to avoid the Varns.

The Varns! If only they had not been aboard. Otherwise, she could have been completely at ease and happy to be leaving the place of so much fear and pain. But here they were, and the only thing she could be grateful for was that so far they had not said so much as a word to any of her family. Esther had given Claire a long bitter look when she had met her on the quay as they were waiting to board and had then looked deliberately away. Lace Varn, his pinched face screwed in a malignant grimace, had mumbled under his breath while behind him his odious son, Daniel, giggled like the imbecile he was. None of them had forced a confrontation, and Claire could only hope that would hold true throughout the voyage as well. For her part, at least, she would make certain that her family stayed out of their way. They had made their berths in the passenger hold as far from the Varns as possible, and on deck they would keep their distance. It was a small ship, true, but where one was determined to avoid a fight, one could do it.

A thumping against the side of the ship announced

that the longboat had pulled up next to the rope ladder. Claire turned and walked across the deck to the far side, keeping as far away from the Varns as possible while Jeanne reluctantly followed her. When a man's feathered hat appeared through the opening in the rail, Claire recognized before she saw him clamber aboard that Fall MacDairmid had joined the ship. Beside her she heard Jeanne Kinross give a quick little gasp, followed by a high-pitched soft giggle.

"Oh, cor," Jeanne breathed low. "Now ain't he a beauty!"

Sweeping off his hat Fall made the ladies an elaborate bow.

"Good morning, Miss Montcrieff," he said with just the slightest hint of sarcasm in his voice.

"Mister MacDairmid," Claire acknowledged through tight lips.

"I am Mistress Kinross," Jeanne said, smiling brilliantly at Fall and dipping her skirts. Fall nodded to her before turning back to Claire.

"I trust you are settled in."

"Very comfortably, thank you," Claire answered, unable to meet the promise in his very direct gaze.

Captain Mendel stepped up abruptly and laid a hand on Fall's arm. "Come along to my cabin, Fall," he said, pulling him away. "We've a deal of papers to sift through before the tide begins to turn."

Reluctantly Fall pulled his eyes away from Claire's flaming cheeks and tight lips. He caught a glimpse of Claire's family at the other end of the ship before following the ship's master to his quarters.

"Oh, my goodness," Jeanne breathed. "Do you know that gentleman?"

"Yes I do, to my sorrow."

107

"Then you must introduce me, oh, please, Claire. Just think! To be sharing a voyage with the likes of him. How exciting! I never hoped—"

Claire looked at her as if she had lost her wits. "You don't want to have anything to do with him! He's a rake and a liar. Believe me, it will be best if you leave him strictly alone."

Jeanne cocked her pretty head at Claire. "Methinks the maiden doth protest too much. Now, Claire, if you're not interested, you must stand aside for someone who is."

"Oh, don't be so silly!" Claire snapped. There was a loud thumping across the deck as the second passenger climbed aboard. Claire was almost afraid to see who would appear above the railing. She half-expected to see Edgar MacDairmid, and that would have been enough to set her jumping over the side. Then she heard a woman's voice, complaining loudly. At least it wasn't Edgar.

"I'll never make it! Oh! Be careful where you push, you rogue. Turn your eyes, you rascally knave! I'll not have the likes of you peering up my petticoats."

The longboat swayed and thumped against the side of the ship, and Claire would have sworn the *Selkirk* listed a little at the weight coming up the ladder. By the time a feathered hat with a tall crown came bobbing up between the railings, she was staring with fascination. Under the hat came a round face, heavily rouged, a perky mouth constantly moving, and two round chins, followed by a hefty form swaddled in ruffles and petticoats. Bravely hoisting the ample lady at the other end of the ladder stood an embattled sailor, fighting with one hand to hold his precarious perch while pushing and shoving with the other until with a loud thump the woman came wallowing over

108

the ship's edge and onto the deck.

"You miserable cur of a jackanapes!" she cried, stumbling to her feet and grabbing her sunshade to pound on the poor fellow's head as he scrambled back down the ladder. Claire thought she heard him mutter an oath or two at the woman, but it was hard to catch them over the length of scathing insults she hurled at the man and his mates in the boat.

With a few oaths of their own, the sailors pushed away from the ship and began to row back to shore. Turning to the deck, the woman in the feathered hat put two hands under her ample breasts and shook her body back into its accustomed proportions. She caught Claire and Jeanne watching her, Claire with a sympathetic smile on her lips and Jeanne, eyes still round with the accumulation of curses she had just heard. The frown melted from the woman's features, and the rose lips parted in a broad smile.

"Well, what can you expect from sailors, I always say," she said, cheerfully. "Pardon, ladies, for my uncouth language. I rather lost me head just then." She put out a chubby hand. "Nelly Nelligan," she said. "From Dunbar. The *Widow* Nelligan."

"So pleased to meet you, Mrs. Nelligan," Claire said. "I'm Claire Montcrieff and this is Jeanne Kinross."

"And we're all goin' to the New World," Nelly answered, her hands on her hips as she surveyed the rest of the deck. "My, my, but such a worm-eaten vessel I never seed before. We'll be lucky to make it to Portsmouth, much less across the Atlantic. My dear old Davy used to say 'there's nothin' better anywhere in the world, Nell, old girl, than right here in Scotland. No, you'll niver find a better land.' God rest his soul, he'd be some surprised right now if he could see his old girl picking up lock, stock, and barrel to sail halfway across the world to a strange country."

"My brother says the *Selkirk* is seaworthy enough," Jeanne said, looking with some concern at the rigging above her head.

"Oh, I suppose we'll make it all right," Nell added hurriedly. "I was just running my mouth a little. Davy always said I had a bad habit of running my mouth. And you, Mistress Claire. Are you going to New York to get yourself a husband?"

Claire laughed. "In a way you might say so. I have a fiancé there waiting for me."

"Oh, you lucky girl. You've already done your work. Well, Nelly Nelligan is going to the New World to find a husband, and she don't care who knows it. Not that anybody could replace dear old Davy, but, since the Lord saw fit to call him, I think I got a right to look for a replacement. Yes, mistress, it's the promised land, all right, with wealthy gentlemen standing on every corner just waiting for a wifely woman to walk by. And I'm going to latch onto one of them, or my name's not Nelly Nelligan!"

Claire smiled at the strange figure before her, one plump hand clutching her large hat against the slight wind, her skirt clinging to her ample hips, her round stomach thrust forward. In spite of the rather comic figure Mistress Nell presented and the unguarded way her tongue rambled on, Claire could not help but like her. She had a sparkle in her little gray eyes and a shapely mouth that seemed to fall naturally into a warm smile. And she was certainly honest about her motives. That was a welcome contrast to the man who had just disappeared inside the master's cabin.

"Now, Mistress Jeannie," Nell went on, "why don't you show me where I'm to berth before this here wind

110

carries me over the side. No doubt it'll be damp and close and crawling with fleas, but what more can you expect on a boat this size? My Davy always said you got to make the best of a bad situation. It don't gain nobody nothin' to fret about it."

Jeanne threw Claire a look that pled to be released, but it did her little good. "Yes, Jeanne," Claire said, pushing the girl lightly toward the hatchway. "Why don't you show the Widow Nelligan to the hold? She can put up at our end if she likes. There are still a number of empty berths there."

"That sounds neighborly, it does indeed. Thank you, Mistress Claire. Come along then, Jeannie."

"I *hate* to be called 'Jeannie,' " the girl whispered to Claire, but she reluctantly followed. Claire watched them leave, smiling to herself, then climbed to the quarter deck to join Alyce and her father. She wanted quiet to think and try to handle the seething emotions that filled her. Some of them were the result of the sudden increased activity on deck that suggested they were about to get under way. To be honest, though, some of them focused on Fall MacDairmid and the knowing, expectant way he had looked at her. She was torn between the dread of what she had promised on the one hand and the ruthless determination to suppress such foolishness on the other. After all, she owed him nothing. The fact that he had gotten them aboard did little to undo his other sins. He was a rake, a seducer, and a liar. He was above her in station, and his intentions were to use her and then throw her aside. She must not give in to the siren call of a strong physical attraction that would only end in damaging her life.

Yet it would be so much easier to be strong if only he did not have such an unsettling effect on her. The

111

memory of that kiss on the orlap deck was enough to set her blood tingling and send waves of heat through her body. She must not give in to this. She must be resolute and strong and keep her distance. She must—and she would.

Inside the captain's cabin Fall was struggling with some of the same demons. He was excited by the promise of sharing this voyage with Claire, and yet he could not easily forget how hostile she had been at other times. She was a girl that needed taming in a body that cried out for loving. The idea of both excited him.

"I'm grateful to you for adding that family to your roster," Fall said, attempting to sound matter-of-fact. Captain Mendel was pouring over a sheaf of papers, trying to concentrate on the figures while at the same time being acutely conscious that the tide was almost right for departure.

"What family?" he answered absently.

"The Montcrieffs. Old Tom and his children."

"Oh, them. It was only as a favor to you, Fall, and I can only hope we don't regret it when we reach Plymouth."

"All the same, I'm grateful."

"Look here, Fall. This cargo worries me no end. It is all accounted for and all stowed away, but I've no assurances at all that it won't be sniffed out by the English inspectors. Especially if they suspect we're hiding anything."

"Why should they suspect? Who knows about it? You, me, Sir Francis—"

"And the men who loaded it. While I tried to get the most reliable of my crew, yet there is no accounting for what they'll say when they're in their cups."

"They seemed trustworthy enough when it was smuggled aboard this morning. Aren't your crew generally reliable?"

"I think so. All except my first mate, Mister Cole. He's a shifty bastard."

"It is as well hidden as I could make it — below the orlap with the food and water casks above it. Those inspectors will have to work to find it."

"But if any suspicion should reach their ears that we are carrying contraband to New York —"

"It won't. Sir Francis has been extremely circumspect about this. His whole future is at stake. And I certainly have not spoken to anyone. Bribe your sailors well. There is almost nothing even an honest man won't do to fill his pockets with gold." He picked up the sheaf of papers and ran a finger down the lists. "And it is all here?"

"Every bale, barrel, and keg."

"Then that's all that matters. Come now, Captain Mendel, you are about to transport a group of adventurers to the New World as settlers. The bulk of your cargo comes aboard at Portsmouth sent by English merchants to America. All perfectly legal."

"And how do I explain you?"

"I too am a prospective settler. If I become quickly disillusioned with America and return home, who can question it? All of us are not pioneers, you know."

Taking the papers from Fall's hand, Mendel rolled them up and tied them with a leather thong. "Sir Francis has paid me a pretty amount for this, but, all the same, I'll be relieved when we leave England behind. And I'll trust you to keep these well hidden," he added, handing the roll to Fall.

"You can count on that. After all, I'm not anxious

113

to end up in an English gaol either."

"I'd better get above now. The tide's right and I want to get this ship underway. Oh, and by the way, I'm counting on you to keep this group of paupers and religious fanatics in order. Keep them from quarreling with each other and out from under the feet of my crew, and we'll have a decent crossing."

"Religious fanatics?"

"They're to board at Portsmouth. A great group of Moravians."

"I see. I'll establish it as a rule from the beginning that any scolds and rascals will be heaved over the side at once."

Captain Mendel gave Fall a long, serious look. "I think you have much to learn about leadership," he said, shaking his head. Clapping on his hat, he stepped from the cabin. Fall could hear him shouting orders outside as he gathered up the secret cargo manifest, the list of passengers, and the papers Sir Francis had given him and made for his tiny cabin off the captain's quarters. At least he had privacy and solitude, even if it was the most cramped conditions of his life. The thought of enduring such close, uncomfortable quarters for the weeks it would take to cross the ocean was dismaying until he recalled Claire's promise on the orlap deck earlier. As he deposited the secret manifest in a hidden compartment of his chest, then laid the rest of the papers in a more obvious box inside, his eye fell on the narrow bunk, very tidy and plain. He smiled to himself. He had several weeks ahead to entice that lovely girl underneath those covers and teach her a lesson in humility and ecstasy. And, by God, he was going to enjoy doing it.

With the wind snapping the sails, the *Selkirk* moved sluggishly in the water, turning her bow toward the open sea. Claire was fascinated and not a little impressed with the way the ship's master barked out incomprehensible phrases that sent the crew scurrying up the masts or pulling at the sheets without so much as a question. Every man seemed to know his job and turn to it with an enthusiasm and proficiency like none she had ever seen on a farm.

She stood with her arm around Alyce's thin shoulders, watching the low shoreline melt into a gray mist and found that, curiously, she was not as sad to see the last of Scotland as she had expected to be. The anticipation and excitement she felt over the new opportunities that lay ahead more than made up for what lay behind. The hope of safety and a quiet life for her poor sister made all else fade into insignificance.

Turning southward, the ship followed the narrow strip of land for a long distance. Claire grew weary of squinting at it and left Alyce with their father to go down to the passengers' hold to lie down. She climbed down the ladderlike hatchway steps, made her way to the far end where the Montcrieffs' bunks were piled with their belongings. It was time to stow those bundles away, she thought and began sorting them to stuff into the corners and under the bunks. As she worked, she grew conscious of distant screams before it finally dawned on her they sounded familiar. Jamie! She'd know that high-pitched howl anywhere.

Throwing down the clothing in her hand, she hurried to the hatch. In the hold one deck below she could see her brother at the foot of the steps, straining against a figure that was holding him and beating his back with a switch, screaming at the top of his lungs all the while.

"Stop that! What do you think you're doing!" Claire yelled and scurried down the steps. She recognized the round hat and sallow face of Mister Cole, the first mate, before she touched the orlap floor. Throwing herself at the man, she tried to catch the arm that was flailing Jamie's shoulders and got a sharp cut on her own. With that, the man recognized her and stopped, still grasping a squirming Jamie by the collar.

"Beg your pardon, miss," the first mate said, "but you shouldn't of interfered."

Claire yanked her brother away from the man's tight grasp. "What are you doing? You've no right to beat my brother. I'll discipline him if he's done anything wrong."

"Done anythin' wrong—I should say he has. Stealin' the stores he was. We can't have that, miss. Why, if he was a seaman, he'd be at the mast for lashes for what he done."

"Stealing! I don't believe it."

The first mate stepped back, his anger giving way to interest as he realized he had stumbled into a confrontation with Mistress Montcrieff. "Ask any man aboard this ship. He'll tell you that the stores is the most precious thing we got. Got to carry us across an ocean, they do, and for one person to help himself at the expense of all, there's no worser crime. Can't have it, miss."

Claire looked down at her brother's tear-stained face. "Did you break into the stores, Jamie?" she asked, knowing from the guilty look on his face that he had.

"Well, yes, but Daniel told me it was all right."

"Daniel?"

"Yes. Didn't you, Daniel?"

For the first time Claire noticed Daniel Varn's lumpy body standing in the shadows behind Mister Cole. He was smiling his idiot smile as though the whole scene was for his enjoyment, but he shook his head all the same.

"Didn't do it. Didn't do naught," he mumbled, still giggling.

"You did too! You did. You told me—"

Again Daniel giggled and rubbed his arm across his thick lips. "Didn't. Didn't do naught."

Grasping her brother by the shoulders, Claire pulled him against her. She felt a sudden revulsion at both the Varn boy's idiocy and at the way First Mate Jimmy Cole stared at her, his eyes full of an interest that had nothing to do with the boys. He fastened on the hint of cleavage where her kerchief crossed and leaned into her face.

"Don't get yourself upset, miss. It's a bad thing to do, no saying it's not, but boys will always be into mischief. I'll see it's not brought to the master's attention, if you like. Do it for you, miss, and that's a fact."

"You needn't bother," Claire said, straining back away from the sailor's foul breath. "I'll see that Jamie doesn't touch the stores again, not for any reason."

"Oh, but I'm glad to watch out for you, miss. It's a long voyage we have ahead of us, and I can make it more pleasant for you if you'll allow me to. No question on that score."

Yes, and no doubt he would expect her to make it more pleasant for him as well, Claire thought bitterly. She looked up to see Daniel Varn eyeing them both, his tiny eyes alive with interest, and shoved Jamie

117

toward the ladder. Daniel was too stupid to understand ordinary things, but he had a talent for grasping subterfuge anywhere he spotted it. "Come alone, Jamie," she snapped. "Get above at once, and I never want to see you down here again."

Reluctantly she followed her brother above, holding her skirts tightly as both Cole and Daniel pressed against the ladder to look up at her.

"Scum!" she muttered, then took out her annoyance by twisting her brother's ear.

"Ow!" Jamie yanked himself out of her grasp and rubbed his ear lobe. "It wasn't my fault, truly, Claire. Daniel said I was a coward if I didn't. He dared me to."

"Then it most certainly was your fault for paying any attention to that terrible boy. You stay away from him, Jamie, and that's an order. He's bad. He knew it was wrong to go into the ship's stores, and he only dared you to get you into trouble. Pay no attention to anything he says, and stay completely away from him."

"That's hard to do, Claire. I mean, the ship's not that big."

"You have to do it, so find a way. Those Varns will harm us any way they can, and our only hope to get through this time with them is to stay clear of them all. Now, let me look at your back," she said, softening. "Did that first mate hurt you?"

"No, not so much."

Claire was relieved to see that, though the red welts on Jamie's shoulders were angry, the skin had not been broken. She straightened his shirt and then looked down at his tousled hair and freckled cheeks, her heart softening. "You'll be all right. Go ahead now up on deck and play. But stay away from the

Varns!"

Jamie took off at once, calling back, "I will." She sat for a few moments after he was gone, thinking over the whole scene. It was troubling that Daniel had so easily maneuvered Jamie into creating a fracas and before they had even left Scotland behind. It did not speak well for the rest of the voyage, and she would have to be ever vigilant and alert if she was going to foil any more such attempts. The thought of leaving Scotland reminded her that her last glimpse of her country was slipping by, and, straightening her kerchief and skirts, she climbed up the hatch to step back out on deck. The air was more misty than ever but a dim outline of gray land was just discernible off the rail. It was lower than before, almost a pencil line now, with thin streaks of green showing through the gray mist. Leaning against the ship's rail, she pulled her shawl across her breast and watched as it faded into the horizon.

Her last glimpse of Scotland. Suddenly she realized that she was leaving behind all that was familiar and known. The thought brought tears smarting hotly behind her eyes.

"Do you weep for the motherland?" said a voice beside her.

Turning sharply, Claire saw Fall McDairmid beside her with his hands on the railing. He was staring at the disappearing shore. His coat had been removed, and he stood in wide shirt sleeves and long waistcoat, the wind playing about his hair.

"This is the second time I've sailed from Scotland's shores, and neither time has it bothered me over much," he said.

"Yes, but you'll be coming back," Claire said softly. "It's not likely that we ever will."

119

He looked down at her, his eyes unexpectedly kind. "Perhaps you will. Life has a strange way of working itself out. Sometimes we get what we least expect. For example, a fortnight ago I never thought I'd be standing on the deck of the *Selkirk* bound for America."

Claire stared off into the mist. "It cannot be more of a surprise to you than it is to me and my family."

Leaning back against the rail, Fall folded his arms across his chest and studied her. "Why are you here, Mistress Montcrieff? You said you had a fiancé in New York, but you gave no indication that you were about to be off to join him. What prompted your sudden departure?"

There was a hint of amused irony in his voice. He's making fun of me, Claire thought, watching the mischief dance in his dark eyes. The rogue! The arrogant, supercilious, wretched rogue.

"You know well enough what brought us here. You and your kind! What you want you must have, no matter who is hurt in the bargain. What chance do people like my father or me have against your greed and your lusts? None. I hope you're satisfied with what you've done!"

The hint of amusement in Fall's eyes immediately darkened to suppressed anger. His smile turned grim.

"You make it sound as though I had a hand in bringing you here. While I admit it pleases me to think we shall be thrown together, yet, I assure you, seeing you on the orlap deck last night was just as great a surprise to me as seeing me was to you."

"How like a MacDairmid to deny guilt. Take your pleasure, indulge your greed, then pretend it is no more than your due!"

In a sudden fierce gesture, Fall reached out and

120

grabbed her hand, crushing her fingers.

"You go too far, mistress."

Claire grimaced in pain, but her sudden fury was too great. She would die before she begged him to release her.

"Take your hands off me!"

"Oh, no, Mistress Montcrieff. Don't pretend you hate me to touch you when it is written in your eyes that you long for my hands on your body. You can't know how I look forward to the fulfillment of your promise."

"You arrogant, conceited—"

Grasping her shoulders, he pulled her violently to him, pressing her against his hard body. Claire strained away, looking around desperately for her family. They were hidden from the other passengers by the cabin wall. His arm around her waist was like a steel vise. His mocking face was so close she could feel the warmth of his breath on her cheek. Vainly she struggled against him, beating her fists on his shoulders.

Though Fall still felt the sting of her bitter words, his blood warmed at the feel of her softness, her round curves in his arms. There was a tinge of power in what he felt. She was weak while he was extremely strong. What a satisfaction it would be when she finally lay satiated in his arms.

"Yes, a MacDairmid takes his pleasure where he will. But contrary to what you think, I had no part in getting you aboard to 'satisfy my lust' as you so delicately put it. I won't deny how much I look forward to that pleasure though, since we will be forced into sharing such close quarters."

She was on the verge of snapping, "Never!" when she recalled her bogus promise. Gritting her teeth she managed to mutter, "It is a long way to New York. Anything can happen."

Though her words were suggestive, her eyes spat flame at him. Abruptly he let her go, stepping back while Claire struggled to regain her balance. With an angry gesture she pulled her shawl up around her head. Fall's quizzical look said too clearly that he was beginning to wonder if he had made a bad bargain. Quickly she turned away, hoping he would not sense her disgust.

"I must see to my family," she mumbled and ran up the steps to the quarter deck where Jamie and Alyce sat quietly with her father, watching the fading horizon. The tears were hot behind her eyes, yet she dare not give way to them.

How she hated the whole despicable clan MacDairmid! She stared out at the long stretch of rolling water. She was turning her back on Scotland now too and, for the first time, welcoming the unknown land that waited far ahead. Whatever it held, it had to be better than what they were leaving.

Seven

Only the day before, they saw the last of the land birds. Claire felt there was a strange silence without them — only the monotonous sighing of the sea and the sloughing of the wind in the sails to break the stillness. Now and then a group of children would dart about the deck in some quiet game, but even they were subdued. They had already learned to stay out of the way of the sailors and to keep their high spirits under a tight rein, the less to disturb their Bible-studying elders.

Claire sat leaning against the cabin bulkhead mending a petticoat for Alyce and stopping often to enjoy the warm feel of the sun on her face. Never before had she experienced such prolonged sunshine or the leisure to sit and enjoy it. It was fast becoming one of the most pleasant experiences of the trip.

How many days now since they left Plymouth? She had almost lost track, there was such a sameness to each one. Drummond, the ship's carpenter, had assured her it would be like this until they hit their first spell of bad weather and then she would be longing for the slow comfort of these days.

Shaking herself out of her lethargic reverie, Claire opened her eyes to look around the deck. It was much more crowded now that they had taken on the passengers at Plymouth. The additional cargo, also put aboard there, carried the ship lower in the water. The monotonous undulating waves seemed at times to roll right up to the ship's rail.

Far down at the other end Pastor Doggett, a stern-faced man dressed in black, sat surrounded by the members of his congregation and read from his large Bible, as was his custom. Beside him sat his quiet little wife, her severe black dress relieved only by a white collar and cap, holding her baby in her lap. They were a friendly enough group but very serious and pious and not a little inclined to keep to themselves. Claire suspected they considered the rest of the passengers heathens and not to be trusted.

Across from their group sat the one passenger they obviously considered to be the biggest heathen of all—a small, wiry man, with a sallow face and a shock of grayish hair, named Caleb Browne. Caleb had made no secret of the fact that he came from the stews of London and had nothing but contempt for pious folk, who in turn looked down their noses at him. It amused Claire to see that Caleb was, as usual, deep in the middle of a conversation with the Widow Nelligan. Though Nellie spoke disparagingly of Caleb when he was not around, Claire suspected she had her eye on him. He seldom ventured above the deck without her singling him out for some question or other—to his evident dismay. Claire chuckled to herself. She liked Caleb. He was witty and worldly and had a sly twinkle in his crinkled gray eyes. Somehow he always found a way to escape the widow's clutches without bruising her feelings in the least.

Nearer to where she sat, but not so close she could overhear what they were saying, Ned Kinross stood deep in a studied conversation with Fall MacDairmid. Beyond them the Varns and the Spattles sat together, saying little but watching the others with eyes that missed nothing. Jeanne Kinross stood beside her brother. Claire had a clear observation of the adoration on the girl's face as she looked up at Fall. Now and then she would break into her brother's conversation, her eyes sparkling and alive with interest. Though Fall seemed to be paying her little mind, Claire recognized the small flirtatious stance of Jeanne's shoulders and the way she now and then lightly laid her fingers on his sleeve.

Well, so much the better, she thought. Jeanne was a willing lamb offering herself to the wolf, and she would be consumed like the mouthful she was and then spit out. Perhaps she ought to be warned of the kind of man she was seeking to entice, but Claire was not going to be the one to tell her. It was none of her concern. Although Jeanne and Ned Kinross were pleasant enough companions, she was not going to involve herself in any business that meant associating with Fall MacDairmid. Bad enough she had to share the living quarters of a small ship with him.

"And where is that quiet little sister of yours this lovely morning?" said a voice beside her. Claire looked up quickly to see that Caleb Browne had somehow detached himself from the Widow Nelligan and had joined her on the bench against the cabin wall.

"Alyce? She's below, I think, helping Jamie with his lessons."

"Now that's a shame. This is too pretty a morning

125

to waste in a dark hold. You ought to make her come up more."

For a moment Claire wondered if Caleb was only making conversation to get away from Nellie, but there was such a genuine kindness in his voice she dismissed that idea at once. It was so unusual for anyone to speak kindly of Alyce that her heart warmed to the man more than ever.

"She feels—uncomfortable, I think, since the deck is so much more crowded. I've asked her to come up, but she wants to be below, and I must honor her feelings."

"Tush, tush. You're only coddling her because of her mark. You mustn't, you know. Better that she should face the world with a stern courage. It'll get her through more tight spots than anything else. I know. I've been around folks all my life who've had to take life by the tail or be stomped on by the world. You do her no favor by trying to protect her too much."

"I've thought of that myself many times. But you don't know, Mister Browne. There have been so many difficulties—"

Caleb's gray eyes took on a amused twinkle. "Let the good Widow Nelligan call me 'Mister Browne.' You, my dear, must call me Caleb. It's what I'm accustomed to."

"All right then, Caleb. And I'm Claire. I'm grateful for your interest in Alyce. She hasn't had many friends in her life, saving her family."

"I only had a few words with her once so far, but she seems a gentle, timid creature, and I've always had a soft place for such as them. As for her mark, well now, I've seen worse than hers in London town. Some you wouldn't believe. Them poor souls never let it stop them 'cause there weren't nobody to protect

126

and coddle them like a loving family would. I can't help but think maybe they was better off for it."

"Perhaps you aren't aware of all the — complications."

" 'Tis true, Mistress Claire, that you come from a small village in Scotland and I from the streets of a great city. Yet there's not much I ain't learned in my years in London. Not much. Excepting, maybe, how to escape the clutches of an amorous widow on a small ship!"

Claire giggled at the mischief in Caleb's eyes.

"You may have to spend more time in the hold yourself," she said, smiling.

"I tried that already. It don't work. She chases me down there too."

"Excuse me, Mistress Montcrieff."

Claire looked up to see the first mate, Jimmy Cole, grinning down at her.

"Sorry to interrupt, mistress, but Master Mendel wants to see you in his cabin."

Claire had gone out of her way to avoid this unpleasant man, and it gave her a strange feeling to have him leering down at her so closely, even to deliver a message.

"He wants to see me? Are you certain it is not my father?"

"No, miss. He said it very clear. 'Ask Mistress Montcrieff to come to my cabin.' 'Not the one with the mark?' I says, just to make clear who he meant. He swipes me one and says, 'no, you blockhead. Her sister. It's her sister I wants!' The master has a fierce temper at times when his patience is tried, as you'll see, miss."

"My heavens, I hope I haven't tried his patience," Claire mumbled more to herself than the others. Caleb, eyeing the first mate with a knowing look, picked up Claire's sewing basket and handed it to her. "I'll go with you if you want, mistress."

"No," Claire said, dumping her mending in the basket and trying to recall if her father had awakened from his drink-induced drugged sleep of the night before. Probably not. "I'll go. Master Mendel has always been most pleasant to me, and I cannot think of any reason for him to change."

"Shall I accompany you there, miss?" Cole asked as Claire rose, leaning toward her as though he had lost his balance and brushing against her. She pulled quickly back.

"That won't be necessary, thank you. I know how to find the cabin."

She was off across the deck quickly. Behind her she missed the interested way Fall MacDairmid watched her disappear up the stairs and the way Jeanne's eyes darkened as she watched him watching Claire. Even if she had seen them, Claire was too intent on what the captain might want with her to care. She knocked lightly on the cabin door and when she heard his gruff "enter," she squared her shoulders and walked inside. It was a surprisingly pleasant room compared to the dark passengers' hold. Light streamed from a sloping window and fell on a plank table in the center, a large desk against a wall, and a curtained enclosed bed opposite. Captain Mendel sat at the desk with a turkey quill in his hand, writing in a ledger. He rose at once and, offering her a chair, sat down opposite her. His manner was brisk, but Claire sensed at once that it was not antagonistic, and inwardly she began to feel relieved.

"I called you in today, Mistress Montcrieff, because I want to share something with you. I try to run a good, tight ship. I've learned from many crossings that one of the best ways to accomplish this is to nip any little disturbance in the bud at once."

"If you are referring to that little escapade with Jamie, sir, I can assure you that it will never happen again. He was put up to it by one of the older boys and—"

Captain Mendel waved a hand, cutting her off. "No, no. That was nothing so bad. Something like that almost always happens when we first set out and is only a problem if it begins to occur with any regularity. Your brother does not seem to be a wicked boy, and I've noticed you have a firm hand with him."

"He's not wicked at all. He's a good boy but perhaps a little too easily led."

The captain nodded absently, stroking his chin with a plump hand. "Actually, it is not of your brother that I wish to speak."

A familiar coldness began to creep through Claire's chest.

"If it's my father's drinking—" she began hurriedly, almost as if to ward off what she knew must come.

"No, it is not your father. He'll sober up when the whisky runs out. It's your little sister of whom I wish to speak."

"Oh, dear."

Captain Mendel gave her a searching look. "I can see you are accustomed to conversations like this. Well, I suppose it must be inevitable."

"What has Alyce done?"

"Done? She has done nothing. She is a quiet creature who never bothers a soul. Why, one would hardly know she's aboard, she's so timid and retiring. It's not anything she's done that bothers me. It's the talk about her that others do."

"What talk?" She had to ask even though she could answer it herself.

"I suspect you know how it goes, mistress. There

129

are those who see your sister's unfortunate mark as a sign of Satan's possession—"

Claire sprang forward in her chair.

"Sir, I assure you nothing could be farther from the truth."

"Oh, you don't have to convince me. I'm not such a believer in that kind of thing that it would ever worry me. I've noticed that most of the time the motives that drive people to make accusations of this sort have little to do with religion and much to do with human greed and hate. What worries me, however, is to have such talk on my ship. It can cause harm. Much harm."

Claire gripped her hands in her lap. "Master Mendel, my poor sister has been dogged by this malicious kind of rumor since the day she was born. Must we continually be running from it? I had hoped to escape all this in leaving Scotland. I believe I know who is behind these accusations, and they indeed have little to do with true religion. Yet my family always seems to be powerless to stop them."

"I'm convinced it is not the Puritans we took on at Plymouth. They are a pious group to be sure but not mean-spirited."

"No. I believe it is the Varns. They knew us in Brogain. Indeed, it was partly because of them that we were forced to leave. How unfortunate they should be on this voyage!"

In an impulsive gesture Captain Mendel reached out and gave Claire's hand a friendly pat. "Well, my dear, you are not entirely powerless while you are on my ship. I cannot afford to have this kind of talk stirring up my passengers. I'll have Master MacDairmid put in a word with Master Varn and see if we can't put a stop to it at once."

Claire gave a bitter laugh. "With all due respect, sir,

I do not think it is Master Varn who spreads these rumors though no doubt he has a hand in them. Mistress Varn bears a bitter grudge toward us, and she is no stranger to gossip."

"Then Master Varn will simply have to keep a tighter hold over his wife's tongue. I shall have MacDairmid speak to him. A ship is rather like a little kingdom, and, while I am 'king,' I will not be troubled by a gossip."

"I would be grateful to you, sir, if you could stop all this. Alyce doesn't deserve it."

"Don't give the matter any further thought."

The captain rose and ushered Claire to the door with a fatherly officiousness. She thanked him again, keeping up a brave front until the door closed behind her. Then she leaned against it in the dark hallway, aware all at once of how she was trembling inside.

Not again! Not here where she had hoped they would be freed forever from this terrible fear. It wasn't fair. Were they never to have peace? Was Alyce never to be allowed the open and happy life she deserved?

"What's the matter, mistress? You look a trifle pale."

Claire's eyes flew open. Fall MacDairmid loomed over her, his body filling most of the space in the passageway and blocking her path to the door.

"You followed me," she cried angrily, more annoyed that he should see her distressed like this than that he might have actually come after her. Yet even that was infuriating. He was always turning up where he wasn't wanted.

"Not at all. I admit I saw you leave, but I was about to go back to my cabin anyway."

"Did you listen at the door too? You know all about the things the captain told me, don't you? It would not surprise me to know that you were the one spreading these terrible rumors."

Though the light was dim in the narrow passageway Claire could see that her words hit home.

"I know something of it, yes. Naturally Captain Mendel would confide in me since I am the person responsible for this assorted batch of emigrants. As for spreading rumors—that is not my way, as you would know if you got off your high horse long enough to look."

"I don't believe you. Why should I when it was your family that drove us out?"

Fall sighed with exasperation. "Mistress Montcrieff, I am *not* my family. In fact—oh, what's the use. The truth is you and your father ought to have left this foundling behind. She is going to be nothing but trouble to you no matter where you go."

Claire shrank away from him as much as she could in the confining space he left her. "What a selfish, wicked idea! How typical of a MacDairmid!"

"You can malign the MacDairmids all you wish, Claire Montcrieff, and I'll not disagree with you. However, this MacDairmid has learned from past experience that there are times when one ought to think of one's self and one's own skin. If there is a millstone about your neck you have a right to cut it loose before it pulls you under with it."

"Alyce is not a 'millstone'!"

"Well, she is trouble and you cannot deny that. She is going to be trouble wherever she is. She bears the brand of trouble."

"Only because people are so mean and insensitive and stupid that they cannot see past the mark on her skin to the person she is underneath."

Claire was dimly aware even as she spoke that she was being backed against the wall. Fall loomed over her, his lean face indistinct in the gloom of the passageway. There was a pleasant, faintly masculine odor about him that set her blood stirring. Against her will her body began to respond to his maleness, her skin tingling as though it was pricked by a mass of tiny needles. She had to fight to keep her fury strong. As though sensing this, Fall leaned closer to her, speaking in a quiet, conciliatory voice.

"Come now, let us agree not to fight. I only meant that, as you were going to a new land to make a new life, it might have been better to leave behind all the aspects of the old one that caused you such difficulty."

"I would never leave Alyce."

"That is to your credit. And since she is here, we must see that she is protected. But enough of the foundling." Casually he reached out and lightly ran a finger along Claire's arm. "There are better things to discuss."

Quickly Claire shoved him back. Moving hurriedly, she pushed past him, their two bodies crowded against each other in the narrow passage. She almost made it, but he recovered and grabbed her, slipping an arm around her waist and cupping her breast with the other.

"Come now, Claire. A little kiss to seal our bargain." Crushing her to him, he forced his lips against hers, brutally at first, then easing a little to taste sensuously of her mouth. Claire felt her body slacken, but she quickly forced down that treacherous excitement.

"Let me go," she snapped when at last he released her lips.

To her surprise he stepped back, and she leaned against the wall, trying to hide her breathlessness.

"Yes, I will let you go for now, but we have a

rendezvous to keep, my girl. I want you, and you want me, much as you try to pretend you don't. I can feel the yearning in your body, but I want you to come willingly."

"Never!"

He laughed, tracing his finger lightly down her cheek, along the smooth curve of her neck and down to the swell of her breasts above the linen modesty piece tucked into her bodice. "What was it you said— 'it is a long way to New York. Anything can happen.'"

"Oh, you are impossible!" She saw the way was clear and ran quickly to the door. Without even being aware of how she got there, she found herself on the waist deck, the air off the water cool on her flushed cheeks. Looking up she saw several pairs of interested eyes focused upon her and, throwing her shawl over her head, made her way to the most isolated spot she could find, a pile of ropes and rigging on the quarter deck. Once there, she made certain no one was paying her any mind and then allowed the tears of frustration, rage, and confusion to stream down her face. It was difficult to sort them out even in her own mind. They were part grief over Alyce's persecution, part anger at Fall MacDairmid, Esther Varn, and even herself for enjoying in the smallest degree the feel of his hands on her body. And they were part frustration that she could not, must not allow herself to be carried along by his enticements, even though a part of her wished to be possessed by him more than anything in the world.

What a dreadful thought. Seduced by a rake. Unfaithful to a betrothed. Giving her precious maidenhead to a man who made no secret of the fact that he wanted her only for his own pleasure. What was she thinking of!

"Forgive me, Miss Claire," said a voice suddenly, and Claire looked up to see Caleb Browne bending over her. Quickly she wiped at her eyes.

"If there's something wrong—" Caleb asked very gently.

"No, no. I just caught a cinder in my eye."

Quietly Caleb sat down beside her. "My dear, you'll have to go some to get a cinder out here in the middle of the ocean. In the middle of Blackfriars maybe, but not here."

Claire laughed. "I suppose not. I won't try to deceive you, Mister Browne. I've had a distressing talk with Captain Mendel but I will be over it soon."

"I'm sorry to hear that, Miss Claire. Is it anything you can tell me about? I'm not one to pass on confidences. I can keep a problem to myself if that worries you. Sometimes it helps to get it off your chest, so to speak."

Claire studied his thin, sallow face. He had small crinkly eyes and a wide mouth that lifted at the corners and bespoke generosity. She decided she could trust him.

"It's my sister, Alyce," she said very softly. "The poor girl has suffered all her life from that terrible birthmark. I thought we were leaving all that behind us, but the master told me there are people on the ship whispering that it is the devil's brand and it marks her as a witch."

Caleb shook his head, making a clucking sound with his tongue. "I guessed as much. Poor little tyke."

"There's no truth at all in it, Caleb. A witch is a mean, vindictive old woman. Alyce is the sweetest, gentlest, kindest person I've ever known. She doesn't deserve this."

"Life was never fair, mistress, as I'm sure you know.

135

Did the master say he was going to do anything to stop this evil talk?"

"Yes. He thinks he knows who's behind it and he intends to speak with them."

"He's a forceful man. No doubt it will go a long way to squelch the rumors. Mayhap there's something more that can be done too. Your sister ought to be out more. She should be on deck, mingling with the others, letting them get to know her. Familiarity would do more to protect her than all of the captain's efforts."

"I agree with you, but I've never been able to convince her. She is so terribly shy and self-conscious about her appearance. And now, she is terribly afraid too."

"Well, we shall just have to see what we can do." He reached out and squeezed Claire's hand. "You keep encouraging her, Miss Claire, and I'll have a go at it too. I think your little sister just needs a friend. A friend who is familiar with the ways of the world and whom it takes considerable much to make afraid."

"Would you, Caleb? I'd be so grateful."

"It'll be my pleasure. And mayhap it'll keep that widow from roaring down on me everytime I stick my nose above decks. Come now. Dry your tears and let's go and find little Alyce. It's time she took a turn around the deck."

It took Caleb three days to make good on his promise to Claire. He began by setting up a game of checkers in the darkened passengers' quarters, near enough to draw Alyce's curiosity. As the light from the lantern threw dancing shadows on the dark wood, he got both girls to giggling with his antics and anecdotes. He promised Alyce that he would teach her backgammon, then lured her on deck by declaring that it was impossible to teach anything in the dim light of the lower deck. By the third day she was spending most of her time outside, her marred face shadowed by her plaid.

The sound of her laughter became a frequent thing and it gave Claire such happiness to hear it that her heart swelled with gratitude toward Caleb. He was such a storyteller and gamester that before long they had collected children as a hen collects her brood. Claire happened to be standing nearby the first time one of them asked Alyce matter-of-factly how she 'got that thing on her face.' Claire held her breath, fearing that everything that Caleb had accomplished would be undone. Then she heard him answer the child in such a casual way that the whole subject was passed over and forgotten. From that moment on Alyce was as comfortable around Caleb and the younger children as she had always been around her own family.

It seemed to her too that there was a subtle change in the attitude of the adults toward her sister. Now and then one or two of them would smile a greeting or even speak a kind word to her. Claire could not be certain that Captain Mendel had been able to squash the gossip about Alyce, but she suspected he had done something, to judge by the difference in attitude toward her sister.

The only confirmation she had for this change was in a brief conversation between Lace Varn and his wife, which she happened to overhear. She was descending the hatchway stairs one morning, assuming everyone was above on the upper decks. As she stepped down into the darkened interior, she heard whisperings at the other end. Before they noticed she was there, she caught a few angry phrases.

"It isn't right. I'm a Christian woman—"

She recognized Esther's voice immediately.

"You're a scold and a shrew and you'll keep your tongue quiet in your head. I won't have my peace ruined by . . ." Lace's voice ebbed away, his words becoming undistinguishable.

"You've no right to talk to me that way!"

"Who's got a better right! You're nothing but a burden and a trial. You can't even give me a decent heir. A dimwit, an idiot like all the Moreheads!"

There was a strange kind of sob in Esther's voice. "How can you speak so of your only son?"

"Hold your tongue, woman."

Embarrassed, Claire hurriedly moved to the far end of the hold where her family had their bunks. While she had not meant to listen in on family secrets, perhaps she understood better now why Esther Varn was so hateful to others. In fact this was the first time Claire had ever suspected Esther might not always be in absolute control of those around her. It was almost enough to make her feel sorry for Esther to hear the way her husband talked about their son—even if he did have justification for it. And, after all, he was Angus Varn's brother. Why should his lack of character even be surprising?

The following day she drew cooking duty with Esther and was even more surprised at the way the woman acted toward her in their enforced companionship. Not that she could be considered friendly— that would be expecting too much. Yet she did seem less hostile than usual. To Claire's surprise, while they were waiting for the stew to simmer, she even attempted to make a civil conversation.

"I suppose you are going to New York to meet my nephew, Alan," Esther said, more as a comment than a question.

Claire looked over at her, a little surprised. This was the first time Esther had mentioned anything not related to the chores they were working on. Claire distrusted her so she hardly knew how to answer.

"I hope to see him."

In the dim light Esther's face looked more hawkish than ever — her tight cheeks under her starched severe cap, her thin lips slightly unsymmetrical in the way one side turned farther downward than the other, her long nose, her narrow, sharp chin. Esther glanced up suddenly and, catching Claire studying her, returned the gaze with one of her own. She has fine eyes, Claire thought. They were possibly her only good feature. Her eyes were slanted upward at the ends and very dark but burning, like banked coals. Though she had always thought of Esther as a contemporary of her father's, she realized with a small shock that the woman was probably only ten years older than herself.

"He has written to you then?" Esther asked in clipped accents.

Claire looked away. "He has written but not for some time now. He asked me to come to America some day so we could be married. I was not able to send him word before we left, so he may not be expecting me quite so soon."

Esther gave a little sigh as though this news pleased her.

"Aren't you going there to join him?" Claire asked.

The woman shrugged. "I suppose we will eventually. If we can find him. He doesn't live in the town anymore, or maybe you know that."

"Yes, I do know that. I don't know where he is now."

"Nor I. But, knowing Alan, he won't have gone too

139

far from the town."

With that Esther's lips closed and she made no more conversation. Claire was tempted to ask her more about Alan but on reflection decided that would not be wise. She knew how Esther opposed her proposed marriage, and it seemed foolish to push this tentative peace between them too far. She would be satisfied just to have it maintained during the rest of the voyage. It was too bad, though, that Esther could not tell her where to find Alan.

Her feeling of satisfied complacency lasted until late the following morning when the passengers on the deck were drawn below by the sound of shouting. Crowding into the hold, Claire fought her way to the center of the group where two men were grappling on the floor. Bending over them, Fall MacDairmid was struggling to grab one of them by his collar and pull him off the other. Several of the men in the group, enjoying the fight, were egging them on while some of the others, primarily Pastor Doggett, made half-hearted attempts to help Fall break it up. Claire was horrified to recognize one of the men on the floor as her father. When they rolled away toward the middle of the room, she saw that, where her orderly beds had been, there now lay only a jumble of clothes and belongings tossed about haphazardly.

Fall managed to wedge himself between the two men long enough to throw one of them to the side where the clergyman and one of his congregation pinned him down. Reaching down, Fall yanked Tom Montcrieff to his feet.

"What's this all about?" he demanded while Tom stood, breathing heavily and glaring about him. His shirt was pulled away from his breeches and his hair was disheveled. There was a long tear in one sleeve, Claire noted. That was going to be hard to mend.

Tom pointed a hand at the man the pastor was holding against the far wall. At first Claire did not recognize him. Then she remembered his name—Jock Spattle, the farmer from Loch Tay.

"That bastard stole one of my bottles," Tom exclaimed.

"You're a liar! I did no such thing."

Tom threw himself at the man but Fall held him back. "Ye did too. I had five left and there's nought but three now. And I saw it on your bed hid beneath the covers."

"It was given to me. That was my blackjack, give to me afore I left Leith. You're a lyin' bastard yourself, Tom Montcrieff."

"Stop it!" Fall yelled. "Both of you. We'll get this matter cleared up and without fist fights."

"I want what's mine!" Tom shouted back. "It's near gone now. I won't have two bottle lost through thievin'."

With a sudden move Fall twisted Tom's arm around behind his back and held him in a painful iron grip. "Now, you listen to me, Tom Montcrieff," he snapped. "If that blackjack is yours, we'll see you get it back. In the meantime I won't have the two of you battling it out like this. This is too small a ship. We'll settle these matters in a decent, fair way like gentlemen."

"Bah!" Jock Spattle cried and Tom spat at him over Fall's shoulder. His arm was gripped tighter and he yelled in pain.

"Now are you going to cooperate," Fall said, "or do I have to throw the both of you into the orlap deck? And you'll get nothing to drink there but water—and that foul—until I say so."

"Please, Papa," Claire whispered in her father's ear. "Please behave."

Tom seemed to come to his senses, glaring around for the first time at the gawking spectators that surrounded him.

"All right," he muttered. "We'll leave this matter to the laird, Jock Spattle. But I want justice!"

Jock lunged at him but was held back. "I want justice as well."

Pastor Doggett shook his head without releasing his hold on Jock. "This is what spirituous liquors brings men to. If I had my way, Mister MacDairmid, you could pour the contents of all four bottles into the sea."

"You keep your notions to yourself, Pastor," Tom cried.

He was echoed by Jock, "You don't have any say in this matter. This is between the laird and Tom and myself."

"Jock is right," Fall said, releasing Tom and straightening his own coat. "Come along. The three of us will go up to my cabin right now and settle this." He looked around. "But I give fair warning to all you people. I won't have these brawls. If there's a disagreement, come to me. You can fight all you want once we reach New York, but not before!"

Claire watched as they led the others up the hatch and onto the deck. She was left looking at the mess of clothes and objects tossed around her, and she was feeling a little sick at heart, both that her father would cause so much disturbance and at the thought that he still had four bottles of whisky left. She had hoped it was nearly gone.

Listlessly she began picking up shirts, petticoats, and other assorted articles Tom had strewn around in his search for the missing bottles. He had even upturned one of Alyce's boxes though why he should suspect the girl of hiding his whisky was impossible to fathom.

Claire bent over the cot straightening Alyce's clothes that had been laid so neatly in her box. As she felt among them, her hand brushed something unfamiliar, something she had never expected to find. With a sudden rush she climbed on the bunk and began tearing the folded garments away from one corner. It was dark in the end of the bed and, with a rush, she yanked the portmanteau onto the floor and under the lamp where she could see.

The light fell in a copper prisim on a spray of tiny clustered leaves, on red berries with a perfect star at each stem-end, on the long, wandlike branches of wood.

A rowan tree plant! Small, in a neat little pot, but alive and growing in the dark, hidden from the sun. She must have secretly brought it with her. And berries and strips of wood. The leaves were withered and brown. And so many of them.

Why? Why would she do such a stupid, deceitful thing? If Esther Varn should see these . . .

Frantically Claire looked around, thanking the Lord there was no one nearby. She threw the plants back in the box and covered them over, not even caring if she destroyed the tiny tree in the process. Then, when she was sure they were well hidden, she went up on deck and found Alyce playing with two of Pastor Doggett's children. Thankfully, for once, Caleb was not around.

Sending the children away, she drew Alyce behind the cabin wall where they were alone.

"How could you bring that rowan plant on this ship!" she cried, trying to keep her voice as low as possible but unable to disguise her distress.

Alyce's eyes grew large in her small face. "You found it? I thought —"

143

"You thought it was well hidden. That makes it all the more terrible. You hid it from me. How could you, Alyce? You know how damaging it would be if anyone found out."

"But Claire, it's for protection. If I have the branches surely no one will think . . ." Her voice trailed off. "Besides," she went on. "It was only because I loved the tree so much. I wanted something of it in this new land. Everything will be strange and different. It was like having a friend with me. Is that so terrible?"

Claire gripped her sister by the shoulders, trying to suppress the urge to shake her violently.

"Yes, it's terrible. You know what they say about rowan trees. Every one associates them with witches, Alyce. Witches! They make them into charms against curses . . ."

Alyce began to cry, tiny whimpering sounds. "But I wouldn't do that. I only wanted something with me that I loved. Truly, that's all."

Claire was all at once filled with remorse and removed her hands. It was so frustrating trying to make poor Alyce conscious of the dangers of this attachment. Perhaps she should have warned her about the master's words, but she had so wanted her to believe that they had found safety and peace at last. She pulled her sister to her and hugged her.

"It's all right, Alyce. Don't cry. You can keep the plant and the berries and the leaves, but we must throw the branches overboard sometime when no one can see us. They'll die anyway eventually, and it's too dangerous for you if they are found. Agreed?"

Alyce nodded against her sister's shoulder.

"And, Alyce, please try not to play with the children too much. I know you enjoy them but, if they should take sick or something like that—which could easily happen on a long voyage—it might not be good for you."

"What about Caleb?" Alyce muttered.

"Caleb is all right. I don't think any illness would dare touch him."

Looking up at her Alyce tried to smile. "He's a nice friend."

Smoothing the feathery hair away from her sister's face, Claire kissed her lightly on the forehead. "Yes, he is. A better friend than any rowan tree!"

Eight

Two nights passed before Claire found enough privacy to slip up on deck with the rowan branches hidden under her cloak. Once there she had to wait for an opportunity to be alone near the ship's rail, for Mister Cole, the first mate — not to mention several of the other sailors — considered a pretty girl standing and looking wistfully out to sea an invitation to wander over and chat. By pretending she had a bad headache and only wanted fresh air, she managed to discourage most of her would-be comforters though Cole was so extremely persistent that it took a curt dismissal to keep him at bay.

She felt fortunate that, when she finally found the opportunity to be by herself, it turned out to be a dark night with little moonlight. Even then, the wind had picked up so strongly that she was afraid for a moment it was going to carry the thin slivers of wood back onto the deck. Instead they veered downward and landed lightly on the water. The last glimpse Claire had of them was a sudden shimmer of white on the surface of the dark, rolling waves, like miniature whitecaps. She returned to the closeness of her bed more relieved than at any time since the morning she

146

had discovered the wands in Alyce's box. She never saw Fall watching her from the poop deck above. After she had left, he stepped down to the rail and peered over to see what she had thrown into the sea. All he could make out were a few sticks gyrating wildly on the turbulent water. What on earth could be in her mind, he wondered.

Claire was wakened the following morning by the angry tossing of the ship. Though she sensed it was daylight, the passengers' quarters had a twilight cast to them. The precarious lanterns threw an eerie glow against the dark wood as they bounced on their chains. There was a pungent unpleasant smell Claire recognized immediately as vomit—her first experience with seasickness. The hold was usually full, with people lying on their cots or huddled near the stove in their cloaks. Stepping out of the bunk, Claire was surprised to feel the dampness of the planks as though the sea was seeping in through the side walls.

Claire dressed with one hand, using the other to cling to the nearest object while the ship careened back and forth. She made her way above and stepped onto the deck to a black sky huddled down over a furious, nasty sea. She hung tightly to the mast while the crew raced around her, lashing down everything movable. The wind was so high pitched and whining that she could barely make out the voice that called to her from above on the fo'c'sle. Looking up, she saw Captain Mendel bending down toward her.

"Best you keep below, Mistress Montcrieff," he shouted. "We're in for a spell of bad weather."

"What is it?" Claire called back, frantically pulling her long hair away from her face where the wind had blown it.

"Oh, just a little storm. Have to expect them, you

147

know. We've had exceptionally fine weather up until now. But we can't expect the gods to smile forever."

Claire looked out at the heaving sea. "Are we in any danger?"

"I should guess not. The *Selkirk*'s a fine trim ship, and she's weathered worse than this many times. However, you'll all be safer if you stay below." He didn't add that they would also be out of the way of the harassed sailors, but Claire could determine that herself. "I'll send Mister MacDairmid along after a while to calm down the passengers," the captain added.

Fine lot of good he'll be, Claire thought as she made her way back to the hatch. He's probably hanging over his own bed right now.

Yet several hours later when Fall came easily down the narrow hatchway steps, she was almost disappointed to see how fit he looked. He had a scarlet camlet cloak thrown over his coat, and his high boots thumped loudly on the plank floor as he walked the length of the room, looking over the huddled passengers. The low ceiling grazed the top of his head, and from time to time he had to reach up and grab hold of one of the timbers to steady himself against the roll of the ship.

"Captain Mendel says we've a storm to get through," he said, speaking loudly enough for all to hear. "It means a few changes in the way we live but I'm sure you can all handle it. None of you look too done in by the weather."

As if in protest to his casual words, the ship gave a sudden lurch to one side, sending every movable object sliding in that direction. A child screamed at the far end and a baby began to cry. Jeanne Kinross, whose bunk was near the hatch, picked up one of the

148

children.

"You don't know what's it's like down here, sir," she said tentatively.

"Jeanne's right," Lace Varn added, stepping nearer to Fall. "It's hard without no air to breathe or no light to see by."

"You can't let in air and light without letting in the sea as well," Fall answered patiently.

"The sea's already in." Claire recognized Ranald Menzies' voice, as petulant as Lace's had been. "Look at the floor. Lay your hand on it. Everything's wet through."

"It may be damp, but that's nothing compared to what you'll get if the ship really begins to leak. Come now. You knew we couldn't have pleasant weather the whole voyage. This had to happen."

"But what about the stove?" This came from Pastor Doggett's little wife. "My children are already chilled through. They need something hot."

"We can't risk it until the storm lets up."

There was a muddled protest of voices. "But that could be for days!" "You can't expect us to do without cooking." "We'll all have the ague down here."

Fall sighed. "Nonetheless, you'll have to make do without the stove until this blows over. You don't want the ship to catch fire, do you?"

"But my babe is already chilled through and has a little fever with it," Matilda Doggett cried. Her husband laid an arm around her shoulder. "Be strong, wife," he said in his best clerical tone. "The laird's right. We cannot risk a fire in a storm. We'll have to make some sacrifice until God sees fit to restore a calm sea."

Lace Varn's pinched features flashed in the swing-

149

ing glow of the lantern.

"It's easy for the laird to say that. He'll be above where there's light and warmth."

"There's no fire in the galley, Lace, as you might know if you thought about it before complaining."

"That may be, but at least it's not stinking and wet."

Fall turned away from Varn in disgust and walked to the far end of the hold where Claire sat with Alyce and Jamie, one on either side, huddled against her. He paused long enough to look down into her upturned eyes, a burning look that set her skin tingling. Then he turned away. At the other end another baby began to wail.

"Look, I know this is going to be unpleasant for all of you, but it simply has to be borne. It will pass and, with any luck, we'll have the pleasant conditions we had before this storm. Meanwhile, I want you to stay here below and take care of yourselves as best you can. We'll ration the food because there is only so much that doesn't need cooking. The water will be as precious as before and that too must be used with care. I want to know immediately if anyone, child or man, comes down with a sickness. Is there anyone here who is accustomed to tending the sick? A midwife or an herb woman?"

One of the women from Doggett's congregation stepped forward. Claire struggled to remember her name. She was a tiny thing with a round face and tight, gray hair peeking from under the rim of her plain white cap.

"I've had some experience, sir. I mixed my own potions and was often called on by the people in my village to tend sickbed."

Fall peered down at her. "What is your name, mistress?"

"Merchant, sir. Charity Merchant, from Somerset."

"Well, Mistress Merchant, we shall be in need of your 'charity.' And grateful for it indeed."

Claire could not keep a smile from hovering on her lips at his small pun.

"See that you ask this woman to help you, any of you who come down with illness. And Mistress Merchant, you will please inform me at once if there is sickness here that seems to be spreading."

Charity Merchant bobbed her head up and down. "Oh, I will, sir. I will indeed."

Pulling his scarlet cape around him, Fall went back up through the hatch and closed it after him. The darkness seemed to close in around the huddled groups of people as they lay back on their beds or separated into small groups. At the other end Claire could hear the muffled prayers of Pastor Doggett's congregation, petitioning for better weather. Would God heed them, she wondered. Did God send this horrible storm, or did Satan perhaps? Was it some kind of punishment for . . .

Nonsense. A few twigs floating on the sea. Superstitious folly to make any more of it than that!

"Humph!" Lace Varn snorted, moving back to his wife's side. "Easy for him to talk of staying below. He's up there dry and warm and swilling his good wine."

"He's the laird," Claire heard Esther mutter. "He's got a right."

"What've we got?" Lace went on, his voice rising. "Nothing but sour water and sea water. Not even a drop of good whisky though there's some of us that

151

do."

Claire could feel the hairs on her neck rising. Her father, stretched out on the bed beside her with his arms under his head, stared into the wall, pretending to pay no mind. She could tell by the firming of the lines around his mouth that he had heard Lace all too well.

"Come on then, Tom Montcrieff," Lace went on, walking toward their bunks. "We all know you're hoarding a dram or two. Be a good neighbor and share with the rest. There's nothing else going to help us bear this wretched place."

"Mind your business, Lace, and leave me be," Tom muttered.

Lace snapped like an angry animal. "Just like a Montcrieff! Selfish! Greedy! You'll swill it all, and let the rest of us be damned."

With a sudden motion Tom sat up, swinging his legs over the edge of the bed.

"Mind your tongue, Lace Varn! I brought that whisky aboard with me and I'm making it last as long as I can. You've got no claim on it nor on anything else that's mine. Be satisfied with the one you've already had."

Lace made a lunge at Tom but was stopped by Ned Kinross who heaved himself in front and gripped him by the shoulders.

"Are you accusing me of taking your blackjack? First Spattle, now me. Make up your mind, Tom Montcrieff."

"It was one of you," Tom cried, jumping to his feet. "If not one, then the other."

"You don't call me a thief. You got no proof!"

"I don't need it."

"Stop it!" Ned cried and was helped by three

152

members of the pastor's congregation, who jumped to his aid and pulled the two angry combatants apart.

"You heard what MacDairmid said," Ned went on in a calmer voice. "We're going to have a hard enough time living through this storm. We'll only make it ten times worse fighting among ourselves. For God's sake, put your differences aside, at least for the time being."

"Then make him share that blackjack," Lace said sullenly.

"You lay a finger on one of those bottles and I'll cut it off with my own dirk," Tom muttered.

Ned glared at them both. "Keep your whisky, Tom, but keep it put up. It's hard on the others to see you drinking it. As for you, Lace Varn, the whisky belongs to Tom. It's his by right to do what he wants with. If he doesn't want to share it, well, that's his right too."

Pastor Doggett, his Bible still in his hand, had stepped up to help separate the men. Shaking his head he muttered, "I told MacDairmid he ought to pour that devil's brew into the sea!"

Alyce nestled her head closer against Claire's shoulder. "Is this what it's going to be like until the storm blows over?" she whispered into her sister's ear.

"It will probably get worse. We're all so close here—almost on top of each other. And with everything shut up and no heat or hot food—"

"Excuse me, Mistress Montcrieff."

At the polite hushed voice, Claire looked up quickly. Matilda Doggett was standing before her, peering down with her soft, nearsighted eyes, a child whimpering against her breast.

"I'm so sorry but—"

"That's quite all right, Mrs. Doggett. Is there

153

something I can help you with?"

"Well, not you exactly. That is, I was wondering if your little sister would mind giving me a hand. I've three little ones, you know, and they are all so cross and frightened. I would welcome another pair of hands with them, and your sister has such a kind, understanding way about her. The children like her."

Claire heard Alyce's quick intake of breath. "It really would be better if—" she started, but Alyce was quickly on her feet, her eyes peering out of the dark shroud of her shawl.

"I would be very happy to help you, Mrs. Doggett," she said. "Poor little Andrew. Look how fussy and unhappy he is. Shall I sing him a little song?"

"That would be lovely," Matilda answered, handing the baby to Alyce. He went into her outstretched arms without a murmur while Matilda reached down to lift her three-year-old Jonah, who was clinging to her skirts and crying.

"I really would prefer—" Claire tried to protest, abut Alyce was already crooning to the baby that nestled contentedly under her chin. Filled with an unreasoning panic, she laid a hand on Alyce's arm as Matilda started back toward the other end of the hold. Alyce about to follow, turned to look back at her sister.

"It'll be all right, Claire. You'll see."

"I wish you wouldn't," Claire hissed, trying not to let the people close around them hear her.

"But it's so boring just to sit for long hours. I really would rather take care of the little ones. I won't hurt them, truly I won't,"

"I know that. It's you I'm concerned about."

Claire was all at once aware the Caleb Brown had appeared beside Alyce. "Now then, you look like a

154

lady who could use some help," he said cheerfully. "What do you say we have a little game? We can get a few of those other little ones who are disturbing the rest of the good wives with their tears and amuse them for a while."

Alyce gave the child in her arms a steadying heave. "That would be just the thing to take their mind off the storm, Caleb," she said. "Thank you for thinking of it."

"It might even take our minds off it," Caleb answered, giving Claire a barely perceptible wink. He led Alyce off, leaving Claire to watch them, grateful but still uneasy. It was going to take a lot of undoing before she would easily accept Alyce's care of young children without fear, but it would come eventually.

It seemed to Claire as if the storm would never end. For three days the passengers were tossed from side to side within the ship in a monotonous movement that was part terror, part struggle to stay upright. The dampness, cold, and stink of the place was almost more than she could bear. Nearly everyone who could sit up was huddled in small groups while most of the passengers were groaning on their beds, sickened by the constant upheaval and motion. Claire was one of the few who never seemed to lose her equilibrium and was never taken by seasickness. Thus she was one of the few on whom the whole burden of caring for the others evolved. Tom and Jamie lay together on Tom's bed, clinging to each other and wishing they could die and get it over with. Alyce, who like Claire was not seasick, spent most of her time trying to comfort the children and help Mrs. Merchant with those who were truly growing ill. Though tempers were short, everyone was too absorbed in his or her misery to be quarrelsome as though each person had turned inward, trying to block out any other concern and using what strength remaining in the effort to endure.

By the afternoon of the third day Claire thought she sensed the motion of the ship was easing slightly as though the storm might be wearing itself out. The thought gave her hope, and she set about trying to administer a thin, cold gruel to those who could keep food down with more briskness than at any time since the storm began. Then Mistress Merchant took her aside.

"One of the children is ill with the fever," the lady whispered to Claire. "It thought it might be coming on, but I hoped I was wrong. Now I'm certain."

Claire glanced at the dark beds near the end of the room where most of the young children lay. "How bad is it?"

"Bad. Came on quick with great force. It's little Robbie Menzies. He was none too strong anyway, and now he's got no strength to fight it with. His fever's mortal high."

"Dear Lord," she breathed. Though it was not unexpected, she had hoped they would be spared this sort of sickness. Once one child caught the fever, it was certain to spread.

"The thing is," Charity Merchant went on, "Mister MacDairmid wanted to be told if sickness took hold down here. I think he ought to know about it."

"We haven't seen him since the day the storm started. Why should he care?"

"Well, mayhap he had plenty above to keep him busy. Anyway mistress, I think he ought to be told."

"Then you go and tell him," Claire almost snapped. Until Fall MacDairmid was mentioned, she had not

156

realized how annoyed she was that he had shown so little interest in their welfare. Had he been seasick too, she wondered. That might explain his absence. Yet it would have been more politic of him at least to send someone down to inquire about them.

"I can't, mistress." Her voice rose on a wave of panic. "I can't go up there. I wouldn't know where to go and besides, I'm a-feered." Mistress Merchant grabbed for the hatchway steps as the boat gave a lurch. "Those big waves, all that wind — I couldn't stand it. I might be washed overboard and — oh, dear."

"All right, Mistress Merchant. You won't have to go. I'll send someone to tell him."

"Oh, miss, please don't send someone like that Lace fellow who'll only make matters worse. We need Jesuit's bark, and some hot food. If only he'd see that we got something hot, it would help to break the sickness. I know it would."

"Well, there aren't very many of us who are able to go above. You needn't worry about Mister Varn. He can't even stand up. I'll find someone."

"Oh, please, miss. Won't you go yourself? He likes you, I could tell. There's no one here who could get him to do more for us than you."

Claire almost laughed. But giving the lady her assurance that she would take care of the matter, she turned to finding someone else. It was ludicrous to think that Fall MacDairmid would pay any of them any mind, much less her.

Yet it was very soon apparent to her that there was no one else to send. The people who were not bedridden were either too weak or too afraid to go above to face a MacDairmid. Telling herself that she was not afraid, Claire threw her cloak about her shoulders and climbed the hatchway stairs. She had to struggle against the cover, which felt as though three men were trying to force it down against her efforts to raise it. It finally opened with a lurch as though an unseen hand had pulled it from her grasp. She stepped up into a blast of cold rain and wind on her face. One glimpse around told her no one was there. With her hood whipping about her face and her cloak caught by the cold fingers of the wind, she climbed up and shoved the cover shut once more.

Fall MacDairmid gripped his fingers around the neck of the squat green bottle and lifted it unsteadily to his lips. He knew from long experience that he was not a sloppy drunk. How often had he watched his friends slide under the table or grow maudlin and bleary-eyed while he himself had maintained both his dignity and his composure. Those who knew him well could detect a slight alteration in his appearance that grew more pronounced as the night wore on — a slight narrowing of the eyes as he struggled to focus, a small wobble in the step, or the merest indication of a tongue that had come unhinged and refused to wrap itself around the customary burr in his speech. He considered it a talent, this ability to disguise his drunkenness. At least it had been a talent when he was in places where polite company and the maintenance of his wits mattered.

But that was before the *Selkirk*. What did it matter now when he was surrounded by rude men like that First Mate Cole or the sailors with their baggy trousers and greasy pigtails? Or even a master who cared more for his compass and glass than for wit or conversation? What did it matter when he was saddled with a bunch of quarrelsome commoners and their mealy-mouthed women and eternally crying children? When he ached for the softness of a woman and the only one worth having turned her soft luminous eyes from his face everytime he came near her?

He groaned and set the bottle on the table with a thump. The *Selkirk* gave another of her endless lurches, and the bottle began to slide toward the end of the table. Fall grabbed for it. God, how he hated this ship and everything about her! The eternal pitch and wallow of the cabin, the damp and cold that made his bones ache, the boredom and salt smell, the dampness that made every stitch on his body cling with a chilly glue.

He was suddenly conscious of a pounding on his door—a pounding that had been there for several minutes. Pulling himself straight up in his chair, Fall whisked the bottle off the table and into a wine cellarette below and yelled somewhat more loudly than he had intended, "Enter."

It was one of those greasy seamen, standing in the dim light, his wet hair plastered to his rustic face.

"Captain want to see you in his cabin, sir," the man said. Fall staggered to his feet, gripping the edge of the table for support as the room shifted on its axis. What now! One more foolish complaint from the miserable passenger deck? He reached for his coat but couldn't find it in its accustomed spot and so decided to ignore it. Holding onto the walls he made his way to the door and down the narrow passage to the captain's quarters while the sailor disappeared in the opposite direction.

Claire entered the low passageway just after the sailor had left. She inched her way down the dark

159

passage to a spot where a dim slit of light filtered through a half-open doorway. When she knocked lightly on Fall's door, it swung completely open, revealing the empty room. Thinking he might be asleep on the bunk, she stepped quietly inside. The bed was deep in shadow, and she had to bend close to make out the fact that it was empty. She looked around the room with some disgust. It was neat enough in spite of the constant tilting, but it smelled unpleasantly of fish oil from the lamp and heady wine fumes. An empty glass on the table had over-turned. Fall's coat was hanging on a peg near the empty bed and, when a sudden lurch threw her against it, she caught the faint odor of the man himself. Something within her stirred but she reso-lutely fought it down. Automatically she reached out to right the empty glass.

Fall's suspicions proved to be correct. The captain was worried about sickness in the passenger deck and wanted him to go down and check in the morning.

He made it back to his cabin and was standing in front of his door when it gently swung open before his hand. He had grown accustomed to the dim light over the last three days, but now he strained to see the figure standing just beyond the doorway, staring back at him from behind his table. A vision of a beautiful girl, *his* beautiful girl, standing there with her cloak clinging to her body and her lovely hair in golden spirals about her face. He leaned against the door-frame. The gods had heard his cry. There she was, a gift from heaven.

The light that was so dim to Fall was bright enough to Claire to illuminate clearly the tall figure standing in the doorway and looking at her as though she was a spirit. The lamp's wavy shadows heightened the lean planes of his face and tinged the waves of his hair. He wore his waistcoat over his shirt with the full sleeves pushed up from his wrists, revealing the blond hairs of his arms. Her heart gave a leap, which she quickly forced down. She was here on business, after all, and this was a man who for three days had not bothered to see how the people below were getting on, even though they were in his charge.

"Excuse me," Claire said icily. "I'm sorry to bother you but —"

Fall stepped into the room just as the ship pitched wildly. He grabbed for the table's edge to keep his balance while Claire steadied herself against the other side.

"It is no bother at all. So, you've come to me at last. At last you keep your side of the bargain." He managed to get around the table and extend a hand to her, which she edged away from.

"You don't understand. It is just a word I'd be having with you, no more. You said we should let you know if there was sickness in our quarters."

Fall stood very straight, his head moving ever so slightly as he struggled to focus his wandering eyes. "Sickness? Did I? Oh, yes, I remember. You have sickness down there?"

"Yes, we do. One of the young children."

He waved one hand as the other gripped the table's edge. "Oh, that's not so terrible then. Children always get sick. It's to be expected."

Claire's eyes narrowed as she studied him. This was not the man she was accustomed to seeing, yet she could not immediately identify what was different. The callousness with which he dismissed the illness of

161

a child was of a piece with what she had come to expect from the MacDairmids.

"With all respect, sir," she said, levelly, "a child's sickness usually means it will spread to others. Already some of the other children are weakening and many of the adults as well. It's so damp and cold down there, and we live so closely—"

"Please, Miss Montcrieff—Claire—won't you take a seat? I have some fine Canary here in my cellarette. If you're cold and wet, it surely must go a long way toward making you feel better."

Canary! Claire could have licked her lips just thinking of its good warmth and fruity taste. "No, thank you, sir. It wouldn't be right."

"Why not?" He had edged around the table now and stood close to her. She moved away from him, realizing too late that he was between her and the door.

"The others, sir. They've all had to do with stale water and cold food. I wouldn't feel right enjoying something like Canary when they—"

"Nonsense. They are not here, are they? What harm is it for you to enjoy a small pleasure when the opportunity is offered?" Stepping very carefully, he moved to Claire's side and laid his hand on her arm. She moved back, stumbled against the black, ornate chair that was bolted to the floor, and sank down into it.

"Ah, that's better," Fall said. He reached under the table, rummaged around and brought out a narrow-stemmed glass and the green bottle. First pulling out the cork with his teeth, he filled the glass and handed it to her. The motion of the ship caused some of it to slop over the rim onto the table where it trickled in a narrow stream, and glimmered in the shadows.

"I shouldn't have come here," Claire muttered, her fingers curving around the glass stem. "I really ought to get back."

Fall stood beside her chair. "No, no. First drink your wine. It's very good, you know, and will improve your spirits immeasurably."

Claire took a satisfying sip and looked up at the man standing beside her. It was something in his eyes that was different. He smiled and suddenly she realized what it was.

He was drunk! Intoxicated. Not in the revolting slobbering manner of her father when he had had too much whisky, but drunk nonetheless. She set the glass on the table and gripped the arms of the chair. "I really ought to get back."

Fall moved around behind her. The high back of the chair was not so tall that he couldn't reach over it and lay his hands on her shoulders. "In time. In time," he murmured. "First tell me what you came for. Everything."

"We need Jesuit's bark," Claire said as her eyes darted about the small cabin. "And hot food. A little warm soup would help more than anything. And perhaps — a little — "

Fall's fingers moved lightly, sensuously, over her shoulders and up her neck, sending a shock of warmth through her body. He traced the line of her ear lobe and up and around her ear, caressing the sensitive skin behind her ears and lightly wandering back again down her neck. Tensely gripping the arms of the chair, Claire tried not to let her treacherous body be seduced into a warm contentment. Though she could not see him, she knew he had leaned down over her, and she felt his lips lightly brush the top of her head.

163

"Everything—" he murmured.

"You are not listening to anything I've said," Claire said with a sudden officiousness. "Really, this is quite impossible. We can discuss it some other time."

His hands cupped her chin, lifting her head toward him. Bending over her, he kept one hand on her neck while the other slid slowly downward, his fingers grazing the ruffled bodice of her dress, then slipping beneath to the softness of her breast.

Complete panic washed over her, a panic issuing as much from her own desire as from his seductive touch. "Let me go," she cried and pulled herself out of the chair. "I must go back." The wine glass tumbled to the floor, spilling the garnet liquid.

She got to the door with her hand on the latch before he caught her. He pushed it shut and pressed against her, turning her body to face him. "You can't know," he murmured, his lips tracing her cheek, "how much I've longed—"

Claire threw up her hand, but he caught it and pressed her arm against the door. His lips were hard, almost bruising, against her face, moving across her cheek, her neck, her chin until they locked against her lips.

Claire opened her mouth to cry out, and his mouth caught hers while it was open. He burrowed against her soft flesh, his tongue flicking again and again as it sought the warmth inside. His body was a flame and she was caught in its heat. It went searing through her and set her afire. The force of his hard body against her, the undulating movement of his hips pressing her into the wood of the door. He was all power and maleness, and she was his victim and his joy, all at once.

"No, no," she cried even as her body went soft and

pliant in his arms. His need for her was a growing, all-consuming thing that carried him beyond light enticements. He tore away the shoulder of her dress and pushed the fabric down her arm until his hand was filled with the soft fullness of her breast. Lifting it free, he bent and closed his lips around the erect nipple, sucking and drinking frantically. Claire gasped. She had no strength in her body at all and would have fallen except for his hard body pressing her against the door. Together they slid toward the floor, his arms still around her, pressing her against him.

"Sweet Lord," she cried, her body one long flame.

"You're beautiful," Fall breathed as he lifted his head to take in the fullness of her white breasts. Frantically he pushed her bodice away and pulled at the laces of her skirt. Claire felt them fall away as his searching, probing hands swept skillfully over her thighs and buttocks, raising her to heights of sensation she had never dreamed existed. She was not even aware of her own hands reaching to untie his shirt, sliding down his hips and toward the bulging firmness that was obvious against his tight breeches. With no concern for modesty or patience, he helped her, tearing away the confining clothes before thrusting his hips against her, flesh against flesh. Hers was all pearl and cream, his tanned and firm. Her skin had the touch of eiderdown, his the strength and solidity of a strong young tree.

The swaying lamp danced above them, throwing shadows on the patterned rug and the writhing bodies below. Dimly she saw the tufts of dark hair that swept from his chest, narrowing to the flatness of his stomach to emerge in a thickness at the groin. With a faint sense of surprise and amazement, she noticed

165

the thick shaft that protruded from that darkness, and timidly she reached out to enclose it in her hand. Then Fall, burying his face in the fountain of her breasts, caught one firm nipple between his teeth lightly and, pulling and drawing from it, drove her into such a frenzy of desire that everything else ceased to be. She was conscious of the cool air on her skin as her clothes were thrown aside, but even that passed as, under his kneading fingers and moist lips, she was quickened to such heights of desire as she never knew existed. His hands slid up her thighs and between her legs, and all else was forgotten but the heavenly sensation. With practiced efficiency he swiveled a long shafted finger into that secret part of her, never before approached except once long ago on the moors of Ben Brogain. Now there was no Alyce to call out and save her, but she didn't want to be saved. She wanted nothing but that perfect completion, that hot fullness inside her. His finger moved to massage the moist waiting lips between her legs, searching and finding that marvelous source of ecstasy no one had touched before and fondling it until Claire was crying in wild, whimpering need, "take me, take me . . ."

His arms were tight about her, his body pressed her into the floor, his movements were wild, gyrating, thrusting his hot, hard maleness into her, pushing rhythmically . . .

She was all sensation. Surroundings, place, time — all ceased while two bodies merged fully and completely into one throbbing whole. Claire did not begin to come back to reality until she felt Fall go slack above her. With a cry he slumped down, breathing heavily against her neck, and she could feel the wild pounding of his heart on her bare breasts.

Neither of them spoke as she gradually came to

realize where she was and what had happened. There was a sharp pain somewhere on her body and a moistness below her hips on the rug.

As Fall's hard breathing subsided, he turned and nuzzled Claire's neck, murmuring so softly she could barely hear him, "my dear, my dear." She strained away from him but his arms tightened around her. "I knew it," he went on quietly. "From the very first. I wanted you, needed you, and I knew."

The hot tears spilled from her eyes and ran in streams down her cheeks onto the rug. "Damn you," she muttered.

He pulled abruptly back and looked down at her. "Damn you," she repeated, wiping her arm across her eyes. "I should have known better than to come here alone. I should have realized you'd do something like this."

Releasing her, Fall rolled over, sat up, and began straightening his disarranged clothes. "Correct me if I'm wrong," he said with irony dripping in his voice, "but I was under the impression you wanted it as much as I did. I don't recall screams of protest or angry demands to keep my hands off. On the contrary—"

Claire scrambled to her knees, pulling her bodice up over her white breasts. "You did it on purpose. You got me so worked up I could think of nothing else. And it was all for your own satisfaction. You're nothing but a—a blackguard!"

"That's true, but I don't think it's entirely relevant in this case. Yes, I wanted you from the first, but you wanted me as well. And I seem to recall you indicated a willingness in return for a certain favor."

"I don't deny it, but some of us don't give in to every unprincipled lust that enters our heads. I told you I was promised to Alan Morehead. What will he think on our wedding night when he discovers I am not a virgin? Did that difficulty ever cross your mind?"

Reaching for the bottle under the table, Fall had a sudden realization. She was a virgin! His wine-sotted mind could barely recall, he had been so carried away. Yet he knew he hadn't expected that. He tried to cover up. "Remind him of the *droit de Seigneur.*"

"Oh! You're impossible! That's just the kind of cavalier statement I would expect from a MacDairmid." Her tears were more from anger than from any feeling of regret at the loss of her virginity. "Take what you want, no matter the cost to anyone else. Selfish, greedy—"

Fall took a long swig from the bottle and glared at her across the table. "You enjoyed it as much as I did."

"I didn't! I hated the whole thing!"

"I don't believe you."

"And even if I did . . . I came up here after three days crowded in a dark, leaky hole with a hundred other suffering bodies, cold, hungry, wet. I came to you to get medicine and aid. And what did you do! Offer me a glass of wine and a warm body. How did you expect me to react? It was all part of your plan to satisfy your own lust."

"You're very free with your insults, miss," he snapped, suppressing the urge to shake her. He was not so angry as to fail to appreciate how enticing she looked standing there in the flickering shadows of the lantern, one hand holding together the bodice of her dress over the swell of her breasts, her cheeks tinged with angry spots, her eyes alight with feeling, and the tears glistening like moonbeams. Her hair fell around

168

her face, more lovely in disarray than when she had it carefully combed.

"You were very free with me, sir," Claire reminded him. "I should have expected no more. I blame myself to some extent. What can one expect from a man who sits in his warm cabin swilling wine while the people he's supposed to care for lie in sickness and misery below? I have always heard you were nothing but a worthless rake, Fall MacDairmid, and now I know it for myself."

"You had better count yourself fortunate you're a woman. I would never take this kind of talk from a man. Not any man."

"Oh, why don't you run me through as you would a gentleman who only spoke the truth to your face? Be done with it since you've already ruined me."

"For God's sake, miss. You are making a melodramatic tragedy out of what was only—"

"Of course you'd see it that way. What do you know of my life or my feelings? Bah! You MacDairmids are all alike."

Glancing down, Fall saw her cloak lying in a heap on the floor. He grabbed it up and threw it across the table at her.

"Go on then. Go back to your leaky hold and the squalor, and spend your time cursing the MacDairmids. Leave me in peace."

Claire threw the cloak about her shoulders, crossing the fold in front over her dress. "I'll leave you right enough. You can sit here and drink yourself into oblivion like your father before you. The next time we need help of any kind, we'll go to Captain Mendel. He at least is a gentleman."

Yanking open the door, she stalked out and slammed it behind her. Fall stood, glaring after her

169

until the door closed. Then in a furious thrust he threw the bottle across the room against the door.

"Damned little hellcat!"

Claire stopped in the narrow passage for a moment, leaning against the door, struggling to calm her pounding heart. She was such a churning mass of emotions that she could barely sort them out—fury, regret, shame, and somewhere, buried underneath, so buried she would hardly allow herself to look at it, a tiny joy of ecstasy and fulfillment. She would remember how that felt later in the darkness of her bed. For now, she must concentrate on the facts of the matter. A selfish, inconsiderate rogue had seduced and tricked her into giving up her virginity. That was what mattered most.

There was a slight movement at the darkened end of the passageway. Claire recognized too late the flurry of cold air that had rushed in as it opened. She looked down to where a shadowed form stood watching her.

First Mate Jimmy Cole. How long had he been there? Could he have seen her come out of Fall's cabin? She pulled herself up, throwing her hood over her head and bunching her cloak up in front over her torn bodice as she started toward the door.

"Good evening, Mister Cole," she said formally.

He snatched off his hat, his tiny dark eyes glued to her face, a thin enigmatic smile on his lips. "Evenin', Mistress Montcrieff." The passage was so narrow that the two of them could not stand abreast. Claire stopped while he stood blocking her way to the door. Did the arrogant man intend her to squeeze by him?

"Seems strange to see you above decks, mistress.

170

It's been a while."

"Yes. We are forced to stay below until the storm subsides. I only came up to see Mister MacDairmid about some medicine and hot food."

"Don't suppose none of us will get anything hot till this nor'wester blows over. Shouldn't be too much longer, though. I seen 'em afore and three days is about all they run. Came up to see the master myself. Got a loose sheet on the mainmast. Have to watch those things, you know, in bad weather."

"Of course." Still he stood while Claire waited. "Would you please let me pass?" she finally said.

"Oh, of course, ma'am. Sorry," he said, flattening himself against the wall. Reluctantly Claire squeezed past, unable to prevent rubbing against him. Though she tried not to look at him, she caught a glimpse of white spittle on his smiling lips, and her stomach turned over.

She hurried past him as quickly as she could and ran out of the door onto the deck. The cold wind and air seemed almost refreshing as though they might wash away the lingering bad effects of the last few minutes. She stayed there savoring them for a few moments before they finally drove her below.

Nine

Cautiously Caleb Browne lifted his head through the open hatch just far enough so that his eyes could sweep around the upper deck. The black stockings of the men and the blue indigo skirts of the women were scattered among the coils of rope, the rows of belaying pins, and assorted chests and kegs that littered the space between the fo'c'sle at one end and the quarter deck at the other. Satisfied that none of the women's skirts looked wide enough to belong to the Widow Nelligan, he eased himself up out of the hatch and onto the deck, then scrambled quickly over to one side where the back of the cabin wall gave him some privacy. A small group of people stood near him, but one glance was enough to satisfy him that they belonged to the pastor's congregation and were more interested in their psalters than in his movements. Several of the Scots grouped across the deck—he recognized the Varns and the Menzies—huddled together, their voices murmuring their usual complaints. They seemed uninterested in him as well.

The weather, still reminiscent of the recent storm, kept many below deck, and only those who were desperate for fresh air or not bothered by the chill in

172

the still strong wind had ventured up from below. Still, there were enough people to cause Caleb some concern about escaping the widow's prying eyes.

It was a wonder to him how that woman managed to sniff him out no matter where he tried to hide. Below deck he could barely making a move without finding her beside him, ready to beg some favor, making calf's eyes at him, forcing him to listen to long, drawn-out tales about her "Jimmy."

"Blast the woman!" he muttered. "She's as persistent as a terrier at a rat's hole."

But not today. Today he was going to find a quiet spot where he could be alone if it turned out to be hanging over the side and clinging to the halyards. A man could only take so much!

One quick look told him the deck was clear. He darted out to the ladder and climbed up nimbly for a man his age. There were people there too but not so many since the wind was stronger up here. Avoiding a group of Portsmouth merchants, he stepped quickly behind a stack of bales lashed to the deck where he knew there was a small space tucked behind the burlap wall. Often before he had huddled there to read out of the wind, enjoying the privacy and quiet. Now it drew him like a beacon. He moved so fast that he almost propelled himself on top of someone who was already sitting there. He managed to catch himself before landing in Claire's lap and made as if to turn away.

"Oh, Miss Claire. I didn't see you. So sorry," he mumbled, trying to hide his disappointment.

"Please, Caleb, please don't go," Claire cried, scrunching down into the corner. "There is room for both of us if you would like to join me."

Caleb did not give her time to change her mind. "You're certain you don't mind?" he said as he scrambled down beside her.

"Of course not. I have to warn you though that the wind is strong even here, and it's not really all that comfortable."

"That doesn't matter a'tall," he said, pulling up his knees and clasping his arms around them. "It just feels good to get away from that lower deck and into the air. I don't mind the wind."

"I feel the same way. The weather has not turned yet, but at least it is not raining or blowing up a gale."

"And at least that Widow Nelligan won't find me for a while."

Claire chuckled. "Does she bother you so much? I thought perhaps you liked it."

"Like it! Why, Miss Claire, would you like a slathering, man-hungry wolf at your heels all the time? I tell you, she has her eye on me, that woman. It's driving me crazy. Why won't she accept the fact that Caleb Browne is not the marrying kind? My only hope is that, when we reach New York, she finds a husband right off so I can get some peace."

Claire smiled thinly. "Someone should have a word with her. She has a good heart, you know. Her help was invaluable during the storm when everyone else was so sick."

"Humph! Let her tend the sick then and leave the well alone. Speaking of the sick, you are not looking so fit yourself these last few days. Forgive me, I don't mean to be nosy, but I could not help but notice how peaked you've grown. Is there something bothering you? I've a good ear for listening, should you ever need someone to talk to."

Claire hurriedly pulled the ends of her plaid around her shoulders and murmured, "No, nothing is wrong. Nothing at all. It's just the effect of being cooped up below deck for so long. We are all of us

174

changed."

"None more than you, dear girl. But if you don't care to talk about it, that's your choice."

Claire stared out at the dark, brooding ocean without answering. Caleb at length coughed and settled into his confined nest. "The storm accomplished one good thing anyway."

"Oh? What was that?"

"Haven't you noticed how your Scottish laird has changed for the better? I was beginning to wonder if he had forgotten his responsibilities. Now he seems genuinely concerned about our welfare."

"I hadn't noticed," Claire snapped in a way that made Caleb give her a sharp glance.

"I was impressed with him when we started out. 'Twas he who suggested that I make friends with Alyce and try to draw her out. And 'twas he, as well, who put the curb on Mrs. Varn's evil tongue. But perhaps you knew that."

Claire managed to curb her surprise, but her anger at Fall was not mollified. He had probably had some ulterior motive anyway.

"I'm sure it doesn't matter to me one way or the other."

"I'm sure," Caleb answered and turned away so Claire could not see his smile.

"Well, well," a sudden booming voice came from above them. "So that's where you have got to. What a tidy little hideaway you two have discovered."

"Oh, no," Caleb groaned, recognizing the widow's dulcet tones. "Now how did she . . ."

Claire looked up to see Nellie Nelligan's wide ruffled cap bending over the bales, her mild little eyes peering down at them.

"Good morrow, Nell," she said politely. "Would you like to join us?" Caleb gave her a quick jab with his elbow on her arm, which she ignored, knowing it would be useless to try to discourage the widow once they were discovered. Hitching up her ample skirts, Nell came flouncing over the bales and squirmed down near them, filling up all the space. There was not room to sit so she half-crouched over the two of them.

"I was just saying to myself, I was, now what if someone was to be good enough to help me bring all that bedding above and give it a good airing. How nice that would be for everyone."

"I wonder who 'someone' is," Caleb muttered.

Nell caught at her cap, which threatened to blow away in the wind. "Everything is mildewed after that storm. I declare, I feel mildewed myself. Otherwise why come up into this wind and wet, save that it's so nice to escape that crowded lower deck?"

"I imagine Caleb here would be happy to help you, Nell," Claire said mischievously.

"Oh yes. Caleb this, Caleb that! Who else would she be dragging out to do her bidding?"

"Well now, I don't know as I'd want any help from any quarter as did not willingly volunteer. Nell Nelligan was never one to need favors. Why, when my Jimmy was alive, I had only to cock one eyebrow to have him running to do my bidding."

"I'll just bet," Caleb muttered, and Claire poked him with her elbow.

" 'Course it would be nice to get that bedding aired."

"Then ask one of the Covenanters to do it," Caleb said snappishly. "They're always looking for ways to carry out their Christian duty. Pick on them for a change."

Nell smoothed down her skirts. "Why, Mister Browne, I don't know what you mean. One would

176

think that I was asking you to help me, which I am most definitely not. Nothing was farther from my mind, if you must know. I wouldn't even want your help since you are so obviously unwilling to offer it."

Looking back and forth between the two of them, Claire found herself smiling broadly for the first time in several days. The heavy cloud that had lain on her heart since the evening in Fall's cabin began to lift ever so slightly, and she began to realize that life had continued to move on in its customary course even while she was so caught up in her own concerns.

Any why not? No great catastrophic event had intervened in her life. She was no longer a virgin, true, but, if one had to lose one's virginity outside of marriage, one could do worse than be swept away by the powerful forces that had carried her to the floor in Fall's cabin. And there were even worse men. She shuddered to think of that Jimmy Cole. Suppose he had caught her unawares with no one around.

Of course, she was going to have a difficult time explaining things to Alan when they were married. But then, she did not know for certain that she would even see Alan once they arrived in New York. He might have given up on her and married someone else, or she might never be able to find where he had moved.

As if to strengthen her more hopeful mood, the sun broke briefly through the heavy clouds, bathing them for a few moments in its warmth and light. Claire tuned out Nell's still protesting voice and tipped her head back to enjoy its full strength. Caleb was right in one respect. Fall MacDairmid had made some effort to meet his responsibilities as master. He had visited the lower deck three times, taking time to talk with several of the passengers. He had sent down medicine and ale and had seen that they were allowed to light fires and cook some warm food once the ship eased its wild gyrations. Claire had carefully avoided even looking in his direction, had deliberately turned her back on him when he had moved to her end of the hold, but she had not been unaware of him. In fact, the way her body came alive when he appeared, the swell of resentment, anger, and—God forbid, but it was true—excitement he aroused in her just by walking close by was too disturbing to ignore. She wished . . .

A sudden loud blast shook her out of her reverie. The ship shuddered and threw the three of them to one side.

"What was that?" Nell cried, untangling herself from the jumble in the confined space.

"I don't know."

"I do." Caleb answered as he nimbly scrambled up and around the bales. "Unless I miss my guess, that was a cannon shot."

"A cannon! Out here? But why?"

Caleb was already on the deck. Claire tried to follow but was pushed aside immediately by sailors running back and forth, calling out orders and climbing the masts, intent on some activity she could not understand. Another blast from the intruder's guns sent a shudder through the ship, and Claire grabbed at a halyard to steady herself.

"What's happening?" she cried to the ship's carpenter as he raced by her.

"Pirates, ma'am," he shouted back. "Best you get below quickly."

Behind her Nell gave a piercing scream. Even Claire felt the blood drain from her face. Pirates were the scourge of the ocean, and all the frightening tales she had ever heard about pillage and rape and kidnapping came crowding back. A shot from the pirate

178

vessel hit the water not ten feet away and showered her with sea foam. She hurried Nell down the ladder into the darkness of the lower deck to wait with the other passengers apprehensively while the boards above them groaned and thudded with the feet of the crew. More cannon fire sent the ship heaving and shaking. Each shot brought on a howl of screams from terrified passengers, who expected at any moment to see a ball come crashing through the side of the ship, showering death and sea water in its wake.

When the guns suddenly fell silent, that stillness was more oppressive than the firing had been. The people in the dark hold looked at one another, wondering what would happen next. The thumping and clanking above them grew more ominous.

"Oh, Claire," Alyce cried, snuggling up against her. "I'm afraid. What will happen to us?"

Claire stroked her head. "It will be all right," she said, but she didn't believe it herself. Beside her Jamie crouched near his father, trying to appear brave but very white about the lips. Claire gave his shoulder a squeeze. "Keep your tongue in your mouth, Jamie," she warned. "No matter what happens, don't say anything or do anything to call attention to yourself."

The boy nodded as the hatch was thrown open and two grotesque figures came clambering down the steps. They took one look around, then motioned to the passengers to go above, like a herd of cattle. They climbed to the upper deck and huddled close together, casting apprehensive glances at the crew.

Claire saw Fall right away. He had tried to put up a fight and was trussed to the mast, his arms tied behind and his head forced up by a rope around his neck. His eyes were black pools of burning hatred. Beside him Captain Mendel stood, unarmed but free. The sailors and mates of the vessel were grouped behind him, angry and defeated. The ship must have been taken and boarded as easily as a toy.

Claire cast a cautious look at the men who were parading on the deck, shoving the passengers together and smiling with the satisfaction of victors. They were not so different from the ordinary sailors she was accustomed to seeing except they were scruffier and harder looking, and they brandished long pistols with a threatening air that made her feel they would shoot anyone with no more compunction than they would have when stepping on an insect. And they were rude. They shoved the men and laid their hands on the women, yanking them forward to peer into their faces, running their hands along their shoulders and down their breasts. The Covenanter women were horrified. They cringed and twittered like helpless birds while their husbands looked on with hard, stony faces, afraid to protest.

Beyond the men who were so rudely inspecting the passengers stood three men—two swarthy figures in long coats and tricorn hats with plumes and a third, standing behind them, in a coat embroidered with gold and a long fringed scarf around his waist. His large hat was pulled down to shade his face, but the wide, square chin and thin lips filled Claire with foreboding. Those hidden eyes promised to be as hard as flint.

At a signal from his ringed fingers, several pirates went scurrying down below to search the cargo area while their companions above continued to inspect the passengers. After a few minutes the first group came back up, carrying the ship's stores and cargo and exulting in their find.

"It's not enough," the pirate quartermaster muttered. "Look again. There's got to be more."

One of the men put a knife to Captain Mendel's

throat. "Mayhap the master can tell us where it's hid," he muttered while Mendel shrank back.

"I told you, we're a merchant vessel carrying new settlers to the colonies. My cargo was severely curtailed with so many passengers."

"All the same, you wouldn't have made the trip without it's being worthwhile. I say we search the hold again." He looked questioningly at the three men on the quarter deck, and the square-chinned one with his hat pulled down gave a barely perceptible nod. Half the men crowding the deck disappeared down the hatch a second time while the other half turned their full attention on the passengers.

"What do you intend to do with us?" Mendel asked, obviously putting as brave a front on it as possible.

The quartermaster dug his knife in Mendel's throat, raising a spot of bright crimson blood. "We'll take the ship, the cargo, and the women," he said, smiling evilly. Claire's heart sank at his words. Studying him covertly over Alyce's head, she decided she had never seen a more disgusting example of humanity. His clothes were dirty, his long beard was braided to give it a frightening effect, several teeth were missing, and his skin was pocked and scarred to the point that one could not tell where one mark started and the next left off. His gun strap and wide sash held seven pistols and a wicked-looking cudgel, but his knife was obviously his favorite form of intimidation. The other men around him were scarcely any better, and the slavering manner with which they walked up and down yanking the young girls out of line to run their fingers over their white faces and necks made her seriously consider throwing herself over the side. She glanced above the pirates' heads to meet Fall's eyes intently fastened on her own. He squirmed in his ropes and instantly the quartermaster was at his side, his knife pricking the MacDairmid throat.

"One more move from you and it'll be the end, my fine young gentleman. If my knife don't slit your throat, I'll give you to the boatswain. He's a fierce man with the flat of a broadsword, he is. I seen him beat a man to death with one 'afore you could blink y'er eye."

"Colly!" said a voice from the quarter deck. One of the men in the fancy coats stepped to the rail as the quartermaster turned from Fall. "The captain says we'll not keep this ship. It's too small and not in good enough condition. Tell the sailors that any who wants to, can join up with us. And start the transfer of all cargo and stores."

The quartermaster glared up at the man on the deck above him. "Why not take the ship? She floats, don't she? We can find some use for her."

"The captain says 'no.' We've already spread our crew thin, and we can't afford to siphon off any more men."

"I don't like it," Colly answered and was encouraged by an angry murmuring from the men behind him.

"It's the captain's decision. See that it's done."

Captain Mendel, taking courage in hand, stepped forward to address the man on the deck. "Surely you won't take all our stores. How will we survive until we reach New York? We've nearly ninety people on this ship."

The three men murmured among themselves and then the speaker leaned over the rail once more.

"We'll leave you just enough to reach the New World. You're not so far that you'll need much. But we take all the wines, ale, and liquor. And such of the women as are wanted."

A sharp wail went up from the line of passengers, and Claire recognized Matilda Doggett's high-pitched voice. The fear among them all was like a live thing: eyes large, rounded, and deep pools on white faces; arms clinging, bodies pressed against the men they loved and had never expected to leave. Even Nell Nelligan, she noticed, had two angry spots on her plump cheeks, and her lips were pursed into a thin narrow line.

Claire's arms tightened around Alyce's shoulders, and the girl buried her face in her neck. Next to her she saw Caleb Browne slip his hands around Jamie's shoulders and pull him close. Her father stood looking around almost as though he hadn't yet realized what was happening. What would she do if they tried to carry her off? If they carried Alyce off?

The crew began carrying everything they could find from the hold. While the terrified passengers watched, they made trip after trip until Claire felt there could not be anything left. They were wasteful and careless with precious stores, breaking open kegs of wine to slosh it on each other and the deck, throwing what wouldn't fit into the longboat overboard where it bobbed away on the waves, passing around food, taking what they wanted and then heaving the rest overboard. There was a kind of forced hilarity among them that alternated with threatening gestures toward the ship's passengers and crew.

And then, at a sign from the silent man above, they began the process of leaving the ship, still arguing about whether to carry it off as a prize or to burn it to the waterline.

"Any crewman of this vessel who wants to throw in his lot with us, now's the time to step forward," came the voice from the upper deck. To Claire's surprise three men scurried over to the rope ladder that would deposit them on the longboat waiting below. Two of them she barely remembered, but the third was the first mate, Jimmy Cole. He stopped beside her for a moment, giving her a leering smile that made her skin crawl. "Now, over the side the rest of you," the man above ordered.

"What about the women?" the quartermaster cried. "I get the first choice. Nobody wants to argue with that, do he?" he added, glaring around at the others, his knife flashing in the sunlight.

"Go on then and be quick about it. The captain wants to get under way."

The line of passengers shrank before him as the grinning pirate began his perusal. Twice he stopped, pulling out one of the women to yank her chin up, turning another around to appraise her proportions. When he stopped before Jeanne Kinross, she turned her head against her brother's shoulder, and the pirate looked for a moment as if he could not decide whether or not to bother with her. Then he moved on, coming to a stop in front of Claire and Alyce.

Claire's chin went up and she met his eyes with a ferocity in her own. She would not allow this miserable excuse for a human being to intimidate her.

"Oh, and here's a feisty one," the quartermaster said, giggling. "An' good and solid too. I like a woman I can get my hands around."

Reaching out he ran his hand over Claire's shoulder and down her arm. His touch was cold and clammy, like a snake crawling down her arm.

"Take your hands off me!" she snapped, feeling as though she had nothing more to lose now by protesting.

"Come on, Colly," the boatswain yelled. "Give the rest of us a chance. Make up your mind."

"All in good time," Colly answered, never taking his eyes off Claire's face. "You'll get your turn but I get the first pick. And maybe you're it, lass. Bonny and with spirit too. Couldn't do no better."

There was a ripple of masculine laughter around Claire as she shrank back from the man's touch. His fingers gripped her arm, pulling her toward him. Alyce gave a muffled cry and clung to her tighter than before. For the first time Colly looked down at the pale eye that peered at him from behind the swath of her hood. It was the first time he had noticed her.

"And what's here? Another such as yourself, maybe? Sister, perhaps? How about that, mates? Mayhap I'll get two for the price of one."

"No!" Claire cried. "I'll go with you if I must, but leave her alone."

The pirates' voices erupted around her, complaining that Colly was taking too much time, keeping the best for himself unfairly, and, finally, becoming intrigued by the mystery of the girl in the hood.

"And why shouldn't I? Maybe she's even better than you, my girl. She looks very pretty, what I can see of her."

He reached out and grabbed Alyce's shoulder, yanking her away from Claire. The girl gave a terrified scream, and Claire grabbed for her, crying, "Leave her alone. She's just a child."

Yanking Claire's arms away, Colly pulled Alyce out of the line, and gripped an arm around her neck while two of his mates moved to restrain Caleb, Jamie, and Tom, who had all tried with Claire to save the girl.

"Come on, sweetie, let's have a look. Nothin' to be afraid of," Colly murmured evilly as he gripped Alyce's writhing body and reached to yank her shawl away from her face. With his hand forcing her chin up, he turned her around to face him.

His words died on his lips as he stared at the birthmark that covered half her face. It was dark, blood red with her fear, terror, and horror. With a sudden cry he dropped his hands from her, shrinking away and leaving Alyce to sink to the deck. Quickly Claire moved forward to grab her and pulled her shivering body close.

There was so much she wanted to say, but her words were frozen by the abject terror on the face of the pirate. He stared at the girl with his mouth open, flecks of spittle on the edges of his lips trickling down the growth of stubble on his chin. Whatever fear Claire had felt before was pale in comparison to that on Colly's face now. He dug at the throat of his shirt with thin fingers. "Touched!" he murmured. "The devil's touch!"

Bewildered by the pirate's reaction, Claire looked around to see that the same reaction was reflected among the others of the crew. They had lost interest in the women and were muttering among themselves. Several sidled toward the open rail to the rope ladder.

Colly seemed to collect his wits at last. He went bounding up the steps to the quarterdeck, spoke softly with the captain, then returned to lead the others to the ladder and off the ship. Claire watched in amazement, almost afraid to believe they were leaving as they hurried off the deck. When the last crew member was over the side, the three gentlemen came down, their boots thudding. The man who had done the talking previously paused beside Captain Mendel to speak to him briefly. Then they too went over the side to the longboats below.

It wasn't until the people on the deck could actually see the longboats pulling away that they began to believe they were safe. Several of the men hurried to the rail to watch, just to make certain the pirates were returning to their vessel. Captain Mendel motioned to one of his crew to release Fall and then spoke aloud to the entire group.

"My friends, it seems that pirates are a more superstitious lot than we realized. We can thank this poor girl with her unfortunate mark for our deliverance. It seems that a sign such as hers is an omen of a bewitched ship, and they wanted nothing to do with it. It's only too unfortunate that they did not see her before they took the stores, or we might have been spared those too. As it is, I fear we will have to undergo severe rationing in using what we have left if we are to make it to New York."

Some of the women began to cry tears of relief and fury at the same time. The Covenanters began to raise a prayer together, their pious voices in counterpoint to the barked orders to the crew to raise sail and get the ship underway and out of sight of the pirates as quickly as possible. Claire felt her knees give way, and she hurriedly sought a barrel to sit on. Even the men, she noticed, were glad to sit a moment and adjust to a relief that they were still afraid to accept.

Caleb and Nell were at Alyce's shoulder almost at once.

"Poor lass," Nell said, laying an arm around Alyce. "That was a near scare. She looks near to faint. Maybe I'd better take her below."

Claire nodded gratefully and watched as Nell led a still shivering Alyce away. Even Caleb seemed subdued as he sank down next to her.

"Why?" she asked the older man. "Why did they let us off so easily?"

Caleb ran his fingers nervously through his thinning hair. He was more shaken than he cared to admit. Piracy was not one of the possible pitfalls he

187

had considered before taking this voyage. Oh, he knew well enough it could happen, but it had seemed a remote possibility at best. Then too, he had little of value to lose to thieves. It had never crossed his mind that he might care so much about the welfare of two Scottish sisters and the horror of a life they might have had to face.

"Like Master Mendel said, pirates are a superstitious lot. They probably felt that the whole ship would be tainted by Alyce and her mark, and none would want to risk bringing such an omen aboard their own vessel."

"But what about the rest of us? Why didn't they take some of the other women as they threatened to do?"

"For fear you'd be tainted as well. Just thank the fates that you were spared, my girl, whatever the reason. You can be thankful for another thing as well. I doubt our men would have stood by quietly while their womenfolk were being hauled away by such scurvy louts as those. There would have been bloodshed a 'plenty before it was over."

Claire gave an involuntary shudder. "At least for once, Alyce's disfigurement worked to her benefit. And ours."

Gently Caleb laid a comforting hand on her arm. "And it will again. It's a new country we're going to, with new ways of seeing things. Maybe this is an omen of the future."

Claire fought down a second shudder as the image of Colly's gross features flashed through her mind. "I pray so, Caleb. I pray so."

By evening of that same day the *Selkirk* had left the pirates' ship far behind. On every side stretched an endless gray ocean, its horizon merging with the deepening somber hues of the sky. The little ship drove forward with the thrust of a still strong wind, her bow dipping and rising with the undulating swells like a helpless toy.

Claire pulled her hood over her damp hair and stood by the rail, her face to the cool spray. She had fled the closeness of the passenger deck, still too disturbed by the events of that morning to be able to rest. Even now her eyes nervously searched for any sign of a second sail on the horizon. She was so intent on her thoughts that she failed to hear the footsteps approaching behind her. When Fall spoke, she jumped as if struck, looking wildly around.

"I beg your pardon, mistress. I didn't mean to frighten you."

"You didn't. Well, perhaps you did a little." Claire ducked her head, hiding under her hood.

He leaned easily against the rail, folding his arms across his chest and studying her. "You have every right to be nervous after what happened this morning. I suspect it will be several days before any of us breathe easily again. Damned vagabonds! Thieves!"

His face was stark in the waning light. Claire wondered briefly why he should be so angry at the loss of their cargo. He did not share with her the fact that more than half of Sir Francis Murphy's contraband had been carried away with the *Selkirk*'s official cargo. Only the fact that one third of it had been more carefully hidden than the rest prevented the loss of the entire manifest.

"How is your sister?" he asked, surprising her with the kindness in his tone of voice.

"Still shaken but all right. She hardly knows whether to be flattered or insulted by the way they shrank from her."

Claire turned away. She was all at once intensely conscious of the fact that these were the first words she had exchanged with Fall since the evening in his cabin when he had all but raped her. No, that was not fair. She would be honest with herself even though she preferred to blame him. The truth was that she had been a willing partner, swept along by the passion of the moment. To think of it now, here in the open air, made her cheeks flame.

As if Fall could read her transparent thoughts, he coughed, moving slightly away.

"Are you comfortable down on the lower deck now?"

"More than before, thank you. The medicine and candles you sent helped. And, of course, the improved weather makes a great difference."

"Of course."

The air between them was like a live thing, yet both felt stiffly imprisoned by elements they could not control.

"The master plans to speak to the entire group tomorrow morning," Fall commented absently. "We've been taking a careful account of what those thieves left us, and we are facing some severe losses. He wants to make it clear to everyone just how little food and water they'll get and how they must make it last."

"But aren't we close to New York?"

"Not as close as he thought. The storm blew us off course somewhat, and he's not certain how long we'll have to make do with what's left."

"Why did they tie you to the mast?"

Fall shrugged. "I was all for giving them a good fight, but Captain Mendel thought our best defense was to go along quietly. I tried to do it his way but, the first time one of them laid a hand on me roughly,

I lost my sense of discretion and began laying about with my sword. I suppose I was fortunate they didn't run me though and throw what was left of me over the side. Mendel thinks so, anyway."

Claire could not take her eyes off his lean face. The waning light cast crevices on his long cheeks and set his lips in stark relief. His dark brows creased as he stared into the distance, still smarting under his failure and his treatment at the hands of men for whom he felt only contempt.

"It was brave of you," Claire murmured.

"Much good it did. Had it not been for your sister, I would have stood there trussed like an ox for roasting while you women were carried off."

"It was no disgrace," she added softly.

For the first time their eyes met.

"I should not have wished to see you lost," he said very quietly. Then he coughed again. "I should not wish to see any woman lost that way."

"I must go below. Papa and Jamie will be wondering where I am, and Alyce doesn't like me to be out of her sight very long."

"Yes, of course. Good evening, then."

She nodded and hurried away to the hatch. She was acutely aware that she had just exchanged her first pleasant conversation with Fall MacDairmid. It both satisfied and distressed her. The odd happiness it evoked was dangerous. Better that she remember how he had bullied and bothered her and, finally, taken her as lightly as he would a glass of wine. Attractive he might be, but for her he was a dangerous and disturbing intruder in her life.

The next morning, after a careful examination of the cargo hold, the master of the ship called together the passengers and crew. He stood before them with a gravely preoccupied countenance.

191

"Our situation is more precarious than I had thought," he began. "The stores are severely depleted and part of what is left has been harmed by weevils. As to drink, there is little left save the water casks and none too many of them. Those pirates thought we were near the New World, but I've no assurance that that is true. We were blown off course by the storm, and right now I've no way of knowing if, when we do come ashore, it will be in New York province.

"Under the circumstances, it will be necessary to go on strict rations. One-half stores of food and drink for the time being, to be reduced to one-third if we do not sight land soon. Mister MacDairmid, I must ask you to be responsible for the passengers' portions. Second mate Roberts, for the crew.

"I regret this necessity, my friends, but we have no alternative. God willing we will soon reach our destination, and these difficulties will seem a mere trifling inconvenience."

Silently the group dispersed in small clusters, mumbling among themselves on the quarterdeck, eyeing the master with covert glances that were more annoyed than sympathetic.

Within a week half rations were reduced to one-third. With still no sight of land on the horizon and stores dwindling every day, dissension and misery spread among the passengers and crew alike.

Gnawing stomachs and endless sea gave rise to short tempers. Arguments were fierce and frequent. Claire had thought during the storm that nothing would be so wonderful as a calm sea. Now she found that the constantly undulating sea, always shifting yet always the same, was almost as hard to bear. The monotony of the same faces, the same voices, the never-ending creak of the timbers and the whistling of the wind, the sharp snap of the sails — all preyed on her mind until she thought she must discover something new or different or die of ennui. The fact that there was so little food and the poor quality of what there was, riddled as it was by weevils and damp from sea air, only added to her misery.

Two weeks of this had passed when the master called the passengers and crew together again on the upper deck. His face was graver even than before when he had first announced the restrictions.

"There is a thief among us," he exclaimed without any preliminaries. "Someone has been breaking into the stores and stealing to satisfy his own gluttony at the expense of all the rest. I don't know who this rogue is, but I promise you that, whoever he is, he will be caught and punished. If he is a member of my crew," he said, scowling at the seamen arranged behind the passengers, "he will receive the full measure called for by the law of the sea. But even if he is one of you," and he swung a threatening arc with his hand along the ranks of the civilians ranged before him, "I promise you he will also be punished. Let this be a warning to whoever is at fault. He is nothing more than a thief and will be punished as such. I hope this warning will prove sufficient."

To the shortness of tempers now was added suspicion and resentment. The passengers examined each other with silent accusing eyes and with faces that seemed ready to pounce at the least provocation. Claire was more concerned than anyone for she recalled only too well how Jamie had been caught once before dipping his fingers into the cask of beef and, though she tried to assure herself he could not be guilty of doing so now, there remained a nagging inner voice that said he might be. Small boys can bear hunger far less easily than adults, and everyone on the ship now lived with hunger. In spite of her belief that he would never act so badly, she decided to watch him closely. She even went so far as to ask him if he was the thief. He protested with tears in his eyes that he would never do such a thing, yet still she could not quite believe him. If he was guilty, it was absolutely vital that she discover it before someone else did.

For three days she shadowed him, trying not to be obvious but keeping him always in her sight. His movements during that time were so innocent that she began to think she was just a suspicious and overly concerned sister. Then, early one morning she woke in her bed while it was still dark. She turned on her side and saw that Jamie was not in his bunk. Instantly she was wide awake. Slipping easily out of her bed, she wrapped a shawl around the dress she had not removed the night before. In her stockinged feet she moved silently to the hatch. Her heart turned over as she realized it was open just enough that someone below could force it. Holding her breath, she knelt and peered below. She could sense rather than actually see a shadow moving around below. Easing down slowly, she took the first two steps and was able to squint down into the hold.

Someone was moving about. She could not make out who it was until he moved closer, and she realized it was much too large to be Jamie. Filled with a horrible fascination, she crouched frozen, squinting into the darkness. The thief was very, very quiet, and she had to strain to catch the slightest sound. But the sounds were there: a faint scrape of a wooden lid against a barrel rim, the almost noiseless chomp of teeth on tough dried meat, a tiny grunt followed by another, and then, so low as to be almost imperceptible, a soft giggle. The hairs on Claire's neck came alive. Daniel Varn! Of course! Had it not been Daniel who had talked Jamie into stealing in the first place?

Daniel, who did not have enough sense to realize the harm he was causing himself and others by his thievery. Daniel, who could not comprehend the severity of Captain Mendel's warning.

I should have guessed, she thought as she inched her way back up the stairs and slipped noiselessly back into her bed. A few moments later she heard Jamie coming down from above, not furtively as a criminal but openly and noisily.

"Where were you?" she whispered.

"I just went up to piss," he answered in a loud whisper.

"Oh. All right then. Go to sleep."

The next morning she knew what she had to do. It was not easy to knock on the door to Fall's cabin. At his brisk response she lifted the latch and walked boldly in, careful to keep the door open behind her.

"I must talk with you," she said.

He was sitting in a chair across the tiny room and he looked up at her with a mixture of surprise and curiosity in his eyes. And something more—anticipation, hope, Claire thought.

"Nothing like that," she snapped. "It's about the thief. I know who he is."

"Do you?" Suspicion replaced hope.

"Yes. And it's not Jamie or anyone else in my family. It's Daniel Varn, Esther's dim-witted son."

"How do you know that?"

"I woke early this morning to find Jamie gone. I went looking for him and found the hatch open. I admit I was suspicious—he's only a small boy—but it was Daniel I saw. He had the lid of one of the casks in his hand and his other arm was deep inside. I even heard him chewing. It's Daniel right enough. He would be the obvious one, if you think about it, for he doesn't know enough to realize how wrong it is to

195

take food when we're all hungry. He can't think beyond his own cravings."

Fall laid the quill in his hand carefully down on the table. "Daniel Varn. Very well, it must be handled and it will be."

There was something in his tone that she didn't like. "Must you make a public example of him? Can't you just speak quietly to his parents?"

Fall leaned forward in his chair and drummed his fingers on the carpeted top in annoyance. "No. He's all but a grown man and he's a thief. He must be made to pay for it. How else will he learn right from wrong? And what other way can we prevent others from following his example? For the good of all he must receive the full and proper punishment."

"But he doesn't have his full senses. Surely that should make the circumstances different."

Fall looked her up and down, almost angrily. "A starving urchin in Edinburgh who steals a loaf of bread to appease his hunger is nevertheless hanged for his crime. I'm responsible for these people. It's up to me to make it clear that the welfare of all is more important than mercy to one."

She had her hand on the latch and have moved to go through the open door when she turned back. "Couldn't you please handle it quietly, Fall?"

"Why should I?"

"I don't quite know how to say this, but everything that happens to the Varns seems to resound in some terrible way on my family."

"Nonsense. You're imagining things."

Anger swelled in her. His words were a match to tinder. "I know what I'm talking about," she exclaimed. "It's happened before. In fact, several times before. It's as though in some fateful way their fortunes are mixed up with ours and always to our

196

detriment."

His face hardened. "I can't do anything about that. I'm in charge of these people and I must handle this in my own way. If he's guilty, he must pay the price."

She had to bite her lip to keep the words from tumbling out; can't you do it for me? But she would never ask anything so personal of this man. It would be an unthinkable breach of her pride.

She turned and left the room.

Later that afternoon when the passengers were once again summoned onto the deck, Claire went with a heavy heart. Fall stood near the mainmast, holding Daniel by the collar.

"Our thief has been found," he announced as the others gathered around him. "Daniel Varn here has been caught with his hand in the cask. You've been called to witness his punishment."

Daniel stood with his collar up around his chin, his fat lips spread in an idiot smile but his clouded, pale eyes glancing around warily.

"Didn't do it. Didn't do nothin'," he blubbered.

Beyond him Claire glimpsed his parents, Esther looking guiltily and apprehensively around, anger in her eyes, her fingers twisting nervously; Lace, hopping to either side, mumbling with a growing hysteria.

"You accusin' my boy," he cried. "You accusin' my son?"

"I am," Fall answered.

"I'm his pa. If he deserves punishment, I'm the one to give it."

"Not in this instance. What he did affects us all and we all have a stake in seeing justice done."

"He didn't do it!" Esther shrieked. "He's not a thief. You can't accuse him and whip him without proof."

"He was seen stealing," Fall answered levelly.

"By whom? Who accuses him?" Lace cried, his eyes searching the crowd.

Fall glanced quickly at Claire, then looked away. "It doesn't matter who saw him. It's true."

"Didn't do it. Didn't do nothin'," Daniel blubbered again, and there was a murmuring in the crowd that seemed to Claire to be more sympathetic than accusatory. The faces around her reflected a pity and concern over Daniel's plight. It was almost as though they all shared in his guilt and had nothing but distaste for a public whipping.

Sensing this, Fall gave a brusque order to one of the crew who stepped forward to grab Daniel's hands and tie them around the mast. The boy was big for his age and very strong. He began to cry hysterically, straining and fighting against the struggles of the crewman to tie him down.

"No! No! Not my fault. I didn't do nothin' wrong."

"Be still, damn you," the sailor cursed as he struggled with Daniel's flailing arms.

"He didn't do it," Esther Varn cried, tugging the ropes apart as fast as the sailor tied them. "He's not a thief."

"He is. He was caught with his hand in the cask."

"But he's a half-wit," screamed a voice from the crowd.

Lace Varn turned on the faceless voice, his face growing black with rage. "He ain't a half-wit! He might not of knowed what he was doing but he ain't a half-wit!"

Fall stepped forward to grab Daniel by the shoulder and spin him around to face the mast.

"I was made to do it!" the boy screamed. Yanking one arm free, he pointed straight at Alyce. "The witch made me do it. It was her. She cast a spell on me and made me steal."

The murmuring among the passengers rose on a wave of sound.

"That's absurd," Fall snapped. "Proceed."

But Lace had seen his chance. Jumping up to his son, he grabbed Daniel's hands away from the sailor who was still trying to tie them down. "It's not absurd. Can you say she didn't cast a spell? Look at what she done to them pirates. One minute they were ready to carry off the womenfolk and the next they was marchin' away as docile as lambs. How can you deny she can cast spells?"

Claire stifled a small groan. Almost automatically she and Jamie and Tom formed a phalanx around Alyce.

"That girl has nothing to do with this," Fall said furiously. All around him the cries of the passengers rose. Some of them, Claire felt, were simply concerned not to watch a public whipping. Others looked as though they were enjoying the excitement.

Lace jumped up and down near his son. "Can you prove she didn't call up a spell?" he demanded.

"I won't be sidetracked. We're here to deal with this boy's punishment, and that's what we are going to proceed with."

"You can't do it," Lace yelled. "It's her fault. She's a witch!"

Claire began to tremble with a fear like none she had ever known. "You're lying, Lace Varn." Tom cried. "You know this girl is not a witch." His voice was drowned out by others.

"It was a spell the way she got rid of them pirates."

"If she's really a witch, she ought to be thrown over the side."

"Maybe that's why we've had all this trouble."

"Those pirates were superstitious. Are we that

simple?"

Claire recognized Caleb's reedy voice and saw that he had joined the protective phalanx around Alyce.

"Throw her overboard!" a voice cried and was taken up by several others. A hand grabbed for Alyce and Claire tore it away.

"Fall," she cried, pleading at him with her eyes.

In an instant Fall had his sword out and was flailing with the flat edge to clear the area around the mast. The passengers fell back.

"Take her below," he snapped to Claire, then turned furiously on the others. "This girl is not our concern. We will proceed with the punishment, and the first man who tries to interfere will lose an arm!"

A roar went up around him. Claire got a glimpse of one of the sailors jumping to tie Daniel's arms as she pushed Alyce toward the hatch and hurried her below. Daniel began to wail loud animal cries of fear and pain even though he had not yet been struck. Putting their hands over their ears to block out the terrible cries, the two girls huddled down in the darkness of their beds. The noise above was horrible — the obscene thud of the cat on Daniel's back, the cries and wails of the spectators, the hysterical wailing of Daniel and his mother.

Alyce whimpered and shook with fear, and Claire pulled her close and tried to block out the noise from above. What would happen next? Would they come for Alyce after they had finished with Daniel? Over and over the terrible cries pounded in her ears — throw her overboard! Over the side with the witch!

Then she realized the crowd had grown quiet and the thudding had stopped. Only Daniel's bellowing was still audible. Leaving a cringing Alyce in the corner, she moved to the hatch and looked up. Far above, in the bowl of the crow's nest one of the seamen was gesturing and yelling. With a bound of her heart she caught his words: "Land! Land off the starboard bow!"

Racing up the stairs, Claire saw that the people on the deck had moved in a body to the starboard rail to stare at a thin, misty streak of gray on the horizon. As she stepped onto the deck, she met Fall who was still standing beside the mainmast.

"Is it . . . ?" she asked.

He turned and looked at her, his eyes full of relief.

"Yes. It really is. The New World."

"New York?"

He smiled and laid an arm around her shoulders.

"I don't know, but most certainly it is the New World."

Ten

New York was like no town Claire had ever seen. She stood on the quarter deck of the *Selkirk* as the ship glided smoothly through the harbor, marveling at the wide aspect of the surrounding hills and wooded islands. The harbor itself was a wonder. There was water on three sides of the town, the rivers on the east and west mingling inperceptibly with the broad sweep of the bay. Around the coast ships clustered in a forest of masts, more ships than she had ever seen at one time, even in Plymouth. She strained to make out details of the town as though that would impart some knowledge of the vast and exciting country that lay beyond. The houses sat comfortably in rows, their strange roofs gabled in steps — a Dutch pattern, Caleb pointed out. They were built mostly of brick, not the dark-stained stone of Scotland. They were a bright cheerful yellow that looked both cozy and sturdy. At one end the tall cupola of a meeting hall jutted upward and just in front of that a stone fort squatted on the spur of land nearest the water. On one side beside the river an old mill warehouse jutted its rectangular form against a background of silvery water. The bustle and activity around the wharf was astonishing to one more accustomed to the sedate trade of a country legally prohibited from many forms of barter.

"It don't look like much, do it?" said a voice beside her. She looked up into Nell Nelligan's face.

"I was just thinking the opposite. It seems fresh and bonny to me, even from ship deck."

"Well, after Edinburgh and Glasgow, it's pretty poor but that don't really matter. It's got a fine assortment of people and I know the first thing I intend to do. I'm going to find me a room where I can throw my box, then I'm going out to find a corner and just stand there waiting until the first gentleman comes along looking for a wife."

"Humph! Likely to have a long wait," Caleb mumbled on Claire's other side.

Nell peered around her. "So you may say. I know better."

"What's the first thing you're going to do, Caleb?" Claire asked.

"Oh, don't know really. Haven't given the matter much thought. I suppose the first thing's to find a place to live."

His practical comment took some of the enthusiasm out of Claire's spirit. "I suppose that's what we must do too. I have been so intent on just getting here that I really haven't thought much about how we'll manage now that we've arrived."

"You have some money put by, don't you, dearie?" Nell asked kindly.

"A little," Claire answered. "But it won't last forever. We'll have to devise some way to get a living. Papa's never done anything beyond farming, except when he was a steward. But we'll manage, I'm sure."

Nell gave her a motherly pat on the shoulder. "You're a good strong girl, Claire. I know you'll

203

manage just fine."

Claire smiled her gratitude and then pushed down her concern. It was true that she had really not thought beyond the trip itself, and now a whole new host of problems faced her and her family. The first thing was to go ashore and find rooms somewhere until they could get straightened away. She'd go at it first thing after they were docked.

With a strange pang she remembered Alan. It would soon be time to write to him and tell them they were here. But write where? She didn't even know where he was. She was not even certain she wanted to know.

But that was nonsense. Hadn't she come all this way to marry Alan? Nothing that had happened since they had left Scotland must deter her from that. It was necessary to the safety and health of all her family to find him and settle with him as quickly as possible.

Yet a little later when she told her father of her plans to look for rooms, she was surprised to hear him say that he was the one to take care of that important task.

"I'm your pa and the head of this family, my girl," Tom declared with an unusual determination. "I'm the one to work this out. You've carried the burden of our care for too long. Now it's time I took over."

Claire could only gape open-mouthed at her father in this unaccustomed role. The fact that he had been forced to do without his hard whisky for two weeks must have cleared his brain and restored some of his old authority. While she was anxious to get ashore and see something of the town, yet she would not for the world say or do anything to discourage this "new" father. What a relief it would be if he actually did take over the burden of the family. If he supported, housed, and fed them, she would be free to look for Alan.

"Try to be careful, Papa," was her only answer. "We may have to make our money last for quite a while."

"I know. You don't have to be tellin' me how to handle money."

Once the ship docked, the passengers crowded the deck with their boxes and bags, hurrying to disembark. Claire got Alyce and Jamie to help her tie up their belongings and take them on deck, then she sat watching the busy activity on the wharf and waiting for Tom, who had gone off, to return.

Nell, in a huge straw bonnet that shadowed her broad face, gave her a kiss and promised that Claire would be the first visitor in her new kitchen. Then with a flurry of shawls, sunshades, and boxes, she was gone. Caleb lingered longer, saying that he wanted to be sure the Montcrieffs were "good settled" before striking out on his own.

"But surely we'll see you again," Claire exclaimed. "It doesn't seem so large a town that we would never meet."

"Never fear that," he answered. "One reason I'm waiting is to see where your pa found you a place. Maybe it'll have room for me as well. Or, if not, perhaps they'll be a place nearby. Friends are too dear to part from forever. Besides, I have a feeling we shall all be needing each other in this strange place."

Claire gave his hand a squeeze. "Thank you, Caleb. That means more to me than I can say."

"I'm doin' it for your little sister, too," Caleb said rather brusquely. "That little girl needs us all."

Glancing over his shoulder, Claire spied Fall Mac-Dairmid staring at her from across the deck. He gave her a nod, indicating he would like to speak with her. Excusing herself she left Caleb's side and walked over to him, sternly fighting down the tiny excitement his request had awakened.

He was fully dressed in a long frock coat elaborately braided with silver thread, with a braided tricorn hat on his head. He looked handsome and fine, so much the elegant gentleman that it was difficult for Claire to force herself to remember how he had treated her in his cabin.

"Aren't you going ashore?" he said rather strangely.

"My father has gone ahead to get a place for us to stay. We're waiting for him."

"Oh, I see. And isn't your friend — who is it, Alan Morehead — meeting you?"

Claire looked quickly away. "No, not right away. I have to let him know we've arrived."

"Oh. Then you'll be getting married soon. I suppose I should wish you happy."

"Thank you," she said in clipped accents. He stood rigidly, looking out at the town.

"You know that if you have any difficulties, you can call on me?"

"No. I did not know. Thank you. That is very kind of you." She hesitated, almost embarrassed. "Where will you be staying?"

"Don't know yet, but I should not be hard to locate. It's not that large a town."

Claire had a mental image of herself scurrying through the streets of New York searching for this man. Not if she lay starving in the gutter!

"Will you be sailing on the *Selkirk* when she returns to Scotland?"

"That is my plan, as soon as I can get things worked out. What about you? Do you think you can be happy here?"

She looked up at him, startled. "Happy?" Then she caught back all the things she wanted to say. How happiness was not what she had come all this way for, nor did she expect it. Security as the wife of a responsible man, perhaps. Freedom from the fear that poor Alyce might be tormented into a gallow's noose. A small home of her own, possibly, somewhere safe from greedy peers and sanctimonious neighbors. Somewhere where every soul in the village did not know every detail of your life, even up to what you had that morning for breakfast. But happy? It had never occurred to her that she might find that.

Claire stood inwardly fighting with her demons while Fall watched her, his eyes burning into her white features. Then, impulsively, he grabbed her arm and pulled her through the door to the empty cabin behind them.

"God's blood! I won't let you go like this." His arms were tight around her as Claire strained back against them. With one hand he held her head rigid and sought her lips, drinking of their sweetness. "I want to see you again," he said when he finally released her. Burying his head in the nape of her neck, his hands roamed anxiously up her arms, over her shoulders, and down to cup her breasts.

"No!" Claire cried, pulling away from him. "I'm not your mistress. I won't be."

"But you want me every bit as much as I want you. You know you do. There's something here we can't control. A fire if you will. You can't let it end like this."

Lifting her arm she crooked it against his body as a barrier. "That fire is nothing but your lust."

"And yours."

"I'm promised to Alan Morehead, and I intend to marry him if he still wants me. Let me alone, please, Fall. Let me alone."

Her level words seemed to have an effect. Dropping his hands he took a step back.

"Very well, Claire, if that is so important to you. But promise me you will search me out if you are in need."

"How could I do that? I could never ask a favor of you because you would always want more than I could give in return."

He looked away, rubbing a finger over his wide lower lip. "There's some truth in that. It's rather hard for me not to seek satisfaction where I want it since that's been the way I've always lived."

"I refuse to be one of your 'light 'o loves.' You might as well accept that fact now."

He thought over her words for a moment. "Very well, then. I told you once before I would not force myself on you. I say it again. I won't force you, I promise, but I don't wish you to suffer in this town for the lack of a friend."

"I have friends," Claire snapped.

"Oh, yes. Friends like that fluttery widow or that sallow little rascal from the stews of London. Or dour Ned Kinross and his sister who has nothing but fluff in her head."

"You are very hard on good people."

Fall clamped his hat back on his head. "Perhaps I am. But the hard truth is none of those folk are in a position to help you if you need it, while I am."

He moved away from her and she straightened her bodice, trying to hide her confusion of anger and excitement.

"All the same, I prefer to turn to them."

Captain Mendel's voice was heard calling Fall from the upper deck. He gave Claire a long look, then abruptly tipped up her chin, and kissed her lips lightly.

"Till we meet again, Mistress Montcrieff," he said and was through the door.

It was another hour before Tom came back to the ship full of excitement over the rooms he had hired for them. Gathering up his family, he herded them off the *Selkirk* and across the wharf where they started up a wide dirt throughfare called Broad Way.

Claire looked around in wonder at the neat houses and shops. None of the houses were higher than two or three stories, with gable ends fronting the street and whitewashed stoops in front of every one. It was getting on toward evening and people were sitting on these steps, the men smoking long clay pipes with their legs stretched out in front of them, the women in broad petticoats with baskets of yarn in their laps. Children ran around the street, dodging carts and the occasional rider and horse, laughing at the antics of dogs and pigs who scrambled among them.

Alyce sidled up to her and whispered: "They all look so — so healthy." Claire noted for the first time how true her observation was. Even the dogs looked fat and robust. The children were smiling, miniature versions of their rotund parents.

"It's so clean," Alyce whispered. "Did you ever see streets so clean?"

"Caleb told me on the ship that the Dutch are famous for washing and scrubbing. This used to be a Dutch town. Perhaps that accounts for it."

"I like it," she answered, "whatever the reason."

Suddenly Alyce gave a startled cry as she saw an apparition on the other side of the wide street. Gripping Claire's arm she pointed.

"Look, Claire. What is that?"

Claire was a little startled herself at the creature in

bare feet, wrapped in a blanket and with an assortment of feathers and shells dangling from his thin neck, but she tried to hide it for Alyce's sake. "I think he's an Indian," she whispered. "Don't point, Alyce. They'll know we're new arrivals."

"But aren't they savage? Don't they kill with their long knives and — ?"

"Hush, child. He isn't going about threatening anyone with a knife is he? Isn't he striding down the street just as unconcerned as we are? You'll have to get used to things like this."

Jamie, who had been skipping ahead of them, spied the Indian and slipped back, listening to Claire's reassuring words. "How much farther do we have to go, Papa? Will any of them be living near us?"

"Not so far," Tom answered.

They walked on in silence, taking in all the strangeness of the street scene around them. Much of it seemed friendly and pleasant. The people on their stoops called to one another, laughing and jesting in a language Claire did not recognize. An occasional group was even singing together. It seemed a good omen for their arrival.

Tom ushered them to the next corner, then turned up a side street, much narrower than the one they had just left and slightly quieter. A few doors up, he stopped.

"Here is the place," he said proudly. "Our new home."

An unlit tin lantern hung from an elaborate iron fixture beside a door whose glass panes reflected the flickering firelight from inside. Claire was filled with both wonder and trepidation at the sight of warm paneled room, into which Tom led them. Gleaming pewter dishes lined the shelves along the walls. A soft

210

congenial humming came from the shadowed figures scattered about the room, and the warm odor of fresh bread mingled with the soft clatter of wooden trenchers on the wide plank tables.

The bedroom to which a neatly dressed landlord escorted them was even more welcoming. It was small but very private. Among its wonders were two beds built right into the wall like cupboards, piled high with feather mattresses and with doors that could open and close.

"Papa, can we afford all this?" Claire whispered, gathering her courage to speak the dreaded question. "How much was it?"

"Three stivers a night," Tom answered gruffly as he bustled around the room opening doors and inspecting the furniture.

"Papa, please be still a moment and talk to me about this. How much is a stiver worth?"

Reluctantly Tom faced his daughter. She recognized all too well the stubborn lines that set around his lips. "The landlord told me that it's equivalent to about one shilling. That's not so dear that we cannot manage it."

"One shilling! Papa, how can you say that? Our money must last us for a long time. At least until we can find a way to supplement it. And we have no idea when that's going to be."

"We can afford it. I'll get work soon and maybe Jamie as well. We've just endured a miserable voyage, living like the poorest peasants in a hovel for nearly two months and it's time we enjoyed some of the good things of this life. I intend for us to have them."

Claire folded her arms across her chest and glared at her father. "Jamie must go to school, papa. And it isn't prudent for us to use our money for 'the good things' as you call them. We may need it later for

211

necessities."

Near her elbow both Jamie and Alyce had stopped inspecting the room and were listening intently to their conversation. "I don't mind going to work, Claire," Jamie said with an air of importance. "I'm old enough."

"You're old enough to be apprenticed, that's true," Claire answered, taking a seat in a dark heavy oak chair with a frayed embroidered pillow. "But that's a hard life. Mister Drummond, the *Selkirk*'s carpenter, told me there are better opportunities for you to go to school here in New York than there ever would have been in Ben Brogain. I think we should take advantage of them."

"Can't we discuss this later?" Tom snapped. "It's been a difficult day, and I'm all for a good meal and a comfortable bed. I feel as though the floor is still shifting around under my feet."

Claire looked around the attractive room, so comfortable and cozy. Perhaps her father had a point. It was almost worth three shillings to be in such a place, at least for one or two nights.

"Very well. We'll stay here for now, but we must face this issue tomorrow. Agreed?"

Tom shrugged his thin shoulders and threw open the lid to one of the portmanteaus the porter had already brought up.

"Here, Alyce. Be a good girl and shake out my old liveried coat. It smells of salt air and it's as crumpled as though I'd slept in it. I won't have these burghers thinking Tom Montcrieff doesn't know how to dress."

"Why, Papa," Alyce said in amazement. "You haven't worn this old coat in years. Wasn't this your steward's dress coat?"

Tom smoothed down the faded scarlet brocade and the worn silver braid. "That was in Scotland. This is

212

New York."

By the next day Claire's optimistic hopes of forcing her father to be realistic about their housing problem had begun to fade. Tom had already made several acquaintances among the men who spent much of their days in the taprooms downstairs and every time she approached him he was "too busy" to talk with her. Attired in his old coat with a frayed lace jabot at his throat, he spent most of those first afternoons in the town nursing a tankard of ale as he regaled his new friends with tales of the voyage or sallying forth, arm in arm with them, to visit the more entertaining sections of the city.

After three days of this Claire was beginning to grow very concerned. As their stack of hard silver diminished and her father became more drawn into the circle of his friends—men who, to her, seemed extravagant and wastrel—she began to be seriously worried over their future. It seemed to her that Tom had suddenly metamorphosed into an entirely new creature from the man she had always known. That he was happier was evident to anyone with eyes to see. He was full of enthusiasm and verve as he described the places he had visited to his children in the evening—the fresh-water pond, the rope walk, the race track in the woods beyond the old wall, the stores, and taverns. It worried Claire to learn that there were many more grog shops in New York besides the one where they were staying.

Of more concern to her was the fact that he was drinking too much again. Not even the neatness he took with his dress now or the camaraderie he enjoyed with his new friends could still her concern over that. It was not yet as bad as it had been in Ben

Brogain but neither was it as little as on their last days on the *Selkirk*. Tom seemed to have adopted the attitudes of a far wealthier man, the man he had once been when he had been Morgan MacDairmid's chief steward. He wouldn't hear of Jamie becoming apprenticed or even consider allowing Alyce to market her caps and scarves again. As for Claire's suggestion that she seek some kind of occupation, he was horrified at the thought.

"None of the Montcrieff women ever worked for their pay and none ever will!" he declared vehemently.

Claire studied their dwindling supply of coins and made up her mind she had to do something before there was nothing left at all. The first step was to find a less expensive place to live.

And then Caleb Browne stopped by to see how they were getting on. Tom was out for the afternoon so Claire was able to sit in the tavern parlor and speak frankly with her old friend.

"I've just the answer," he said brightly. "The place where I'm staying has rooms to let for one-third of what you're paying here. Of course, they're not so grand . . ."

"That doesn't matter. If they're clean and if there's a bed for each of us, I care nothing for these luxuries."

"It's clean enough. It's run by a Dutch hausfrau, a widow. She's rather partial to me, if I do say so myself. She'll take you in if I ask her."

Claire winked at him. "Caleb, you must have a way with widows."

"Humph! If you are referring to that blowsy Nelligan woman, you don't need to credit me for that. She'd be after anything in breeches. I wonder if she's found a husband yet? Haven't seen naught of any wedding notice in the broadsheet."

214

"I never thought to look. If you really mean what you say, Caleb, let's go round there right now and settle the matter. The sooner we're out of this expensive place, the better."

"And what about your pa?" Caleb asked as he reached for his hat.

"He won't like it but that's neither here nor there. I can handle Papa."

An hour later Claire returned and ordered Jamie and Alyce to help her pack up their belongings. While the little house on Marketfield Street was suitable enough for her, she knew it was going to look too shabby and cramped and be too near the wharf to please her father's new notions of grandeur. The sooner she got them moved and situated in spite of Tom's objections, the better for them all.

During the time Claire was struggling to balance the Montcrieff fortunes with their living space, Fall was squaring his shoulders to shore himself up for his first appointment with Frederick Philipse, the merchant prince of the colonies. It was common knowledge that Philipse had originally obtained his wealth by marrying the widow of the owner of a substantial trading fleet. That he had taken his wife's wealth and built upon it until he was one of, if not the, richest man in the colonies, suggested to Fall that Frederick had a few uncommon gifts of his own.

The Philipse house was grand by New York standards but only comfortable compared to the palatial town houses of London. Fall was received politely by a serving girl in a spotless starched apron and cap and ushered into a room that was utilitarian for the most part but that had small signs of wealth carelessly scattered about—books, bound in rich leather and embossed with gold lettering, strewn around on tables and chairs; an ornate silver inkwell; exquisite Delft pottery; and a huge leather globe in an intricately carved wooden frame. That was something not even Sir Francis Murray could afford, Fall thought.

The plump, rather squat man who came striding in a few moments later looked more like a Dutch burger than a merchant prince. His clothes were rather old-fashioned in cut but made of the finest velvet and brocade. His little eyes were shrewd as they appraised Fall with a level gaze that suggested he saw a great deal more than he pretended. His accent, Fall noticed with surprise, was more Frisian than Dutch. He had heard both often enough during his days in exile on the Continent to recognize them at once.

After taking a seat in a heavy, black oak chair, which Philipse motioned to him, Fall handed Frederick a roll of foolscap.

"You'll find my letter of introduction from Sir Francis there," he said, watching as Philipse spread the parchment on a table covered with an exquisite Turkey carpet. "I regret that the cargo list was so depleted. I've carefully marked what was lost."

"Ah yes. The pirates. You were fortunate they only got part of the cargo. Master Mandell lost all of his goods, I fear."

"I only wish to God I had hidden the rest as carefully as the part they missed. But at least we saved some of the finest pieces. They should give you an indication of the kind of goods Sir Francis can supply."

Philipse ran a plump finger down the list. Then with a brisk snap, he rolled up the parchment.

"Can I offer you a glass of madeira, Mister Mac-Dairmid?"

"Thank you," Fall said, taken slightly aback at the

sudden shift of conversation. Philipse poured two glasses of wine from a beautiful cut-glass decanter, then took the chair opposite Fall. He crossed his legs and held the glass up, running a finger around the rim. Fall sipped at the wine and waited.

"I wonder if Sir Francis realizes that the English have assigned a second customs inspector to our port. They felt the increase in illegal trade seemed to warrant it."

"Oh? No, I don't think he did."

"They are growing very cautious these days. Fines can be prohibitive if one is caught breaking the importation laws. After all, they make the rules. I am a former member of the governor's council, you know. I must be circumspect."

"Come now, Mister Philipse," Fall said impatiently. "Let us not mince words. We both know that your ships call at every port in the known world. It is difficult to believe that you do not deal in illegal trade, and not merely with Scotland either, out of fear of England's repressive laws. You could not be the successful man you are if you let a little thing like import laws deter you."

Philipse chuckled softly. "I was hoping you'd reply something to that effect. As a matter of fact, the English love to sit in Parliament and pass laws that are supposed to make men halfway across the world tremble in their shoes. In reality we are too far from London for their prohibitive laws to be strictly enforced. Although one must play the game, of course."

"Of course. It's a pity Scotland is not farther away. We might not be in the depression we are in now if we were."

"I shall be in touch with Sir Francis. I have an agent in Scotland . . ."

One eyebrow on Fall's expressionless face inched upward at this.

"Oh yes," Philipse added, noticing it. "As you so wisely put it, I should not be the successful man I am had I not covered all possible sources of trade. My agent shall contact him, quietly of course, and we shall work out the particulars."

"Will you be sending back payment for this manifest with me? I realize it isn't much but—"

"Oh, it's far more than you think. We have recovered nearly all the entire cargo with the exception of the two casks of excellent madeira those very undisciplined gentlemen broke into."

At the open surprise on Fall's face Philipse chuckled again.

"My dear boy, don't you know that half the pirates on the Atlantic are based right here in our town of New York?"

A dark suspicion began to grow in Fall's eyes. Seeing it, Frederick actually laughed out loud.

"No, no, no, no. Those men were not in my employ if that is what you are thinking. Though I have often been accused of trafficking with pirates, so far I have not felt the need to do so. However, it never hurts to have friends among their captains. In this case that gentleman was one William Kidd who lives only down the street and whom I have often met socially. He did not realize your cargo was meant for me or he would have ordered it left alone."

Fall shook his head. "This is indeed a 'New World.' It's going to take some getting used to."

"Why sail home again right away? Stay on for a while and see something of this country. It has much to offer a young, virile gentleman like yourself. I have extensive holdings up Hudson's River which my son, Adolph, would be happy to show you. It's good rich land of uncommon beauty."

"But Sir Francis will be expecting me," Fall said without enthusiasm.

"My agent shall see that he gets his payment for this shipload. Somehow I don't think he'll be surprised if you do not hurry back. New York often has that effect on young men."

Fall studied the liquid in his wine glass absently, his thoughts running over Philipse's intriguing offer. After all, what was there for him back in Scotland? A venal brother who was already stealing him blind. A drunken father who cared little about the fate of his second son. A poor land with small opportunity. No ties, no woman who tugged at his heart.

To his surprise the lovely face that entered his mind belonged not to any well-born damsel in Scotland, but to the enticing, beautiful daughter of Tom Montcrieff. Quickly he made up his mind.

"I am grateful for your offer, Mister Philipse. And I shall take you up on it. I will stay here in New York, at least for a while longer."

Eleven

The next day Fall was summoned by Adolph Philipse to his father's house on Whitehall Street. Dressed in his best coat and finest lace, Fall set out to walk the short distance, feeling more like a man about town than he had felt since leaving Scotland. Several pink-cheeked damsels on the street threw admiring glances his way. There were more men than women in the town of New York — a fact that one good look around made evident — but there were not so many who had the air and the look of a gentleman only just arrived from Europe. He had not had a woman since that night in his cabin with Claire, he suddenly remembered. Once this interview with Adolph was over and their plans made for the trip north, he must set about rectifying this situation. He looked up to see one of the serving girls sweeping a spotlessly scrubbed stoop and staring at him with a provocative little smile on her face. With a practiced glance Fall took in the pink, plump cheeks, the creamy complexion, the white-blond hair whose tendrils peeked from under her starched cap, the full breasts, barely covered by her skimpy modesty piece, the smiling eyes that both admired and invited at the same time.

He paused and swept off his hat. "Good morning mistress."

The girl giggled, blushed, and answered him in a Dutch jargon, which was incomprehensible. Smiling broadly, Fall decided to step closer and find out her name. Then his eyes fell on two startled pedestrians who had stopped beyond the stoop and were staring at him.

Claire Montcrieff! And her blemished sister, hiding her face under a large hat as usual.

Instantly the serving girl was forgotten as Fall advanced on Claire, his hat still in his hand.

"Mistress Montcrieff," he said politely. "How pleasant to see you again."

Claire's eyes went from the handsome cavalier before her to the disappointed, buxom servant on the stoop, who had gone listlessly back to plying her broom. The cad, she thought. If she had not happened along at just that moment, he would no doubt be seducing the girl into the barn at the rear of the house by now.

"Mister MacDairmid," she said coolly. "Please excuse us. We are on our way to market."

Damn, Fall thought. He had hoped to run into Claire on just some occasion as this. How unfortunate it should be right at this moment.

"And Mistress Alyce. How are you this fine day? Are you enjoying your stay in New York?"

Alyce smiled timidly at Fall and ducked her face away, keeping her unblemished profile toward him.

"Very much, thank you, sir," she murmured and Fall thought again how lovely that profile was. He turned back to Claire, who was intently studying the traffic on the street.

"Where are you staying, Miss Montcrieff? Did your

221

father find you a house?"

"Yes. No. That is, we are staying at the Hawk and Crown for the time being."

Beside her Alyce looked up in surprise but Claire went on easily. "Papa likes it very much and it has given him the opportunity to get acquainted with several other men in the town. They have been most kind about showing him the sights."

Fall knew she was up to something but could not imagine why she would be lying to him. "I've heard about the Hawk and Crown. It's one of the most pleasant inns in the town. I'm sure you must enjoy it."

"Very much, thank you. And now, if you'll excuse us, we must get to the market."

"Perhaps I could walk part of the way with you."

"Oh, please don't go to that trouble. I can see you were traveling the other direction, and I wouldn't inconvenience you for the world. It was pleasant meeting you again. Good day."

Grabbing Alyce's arm, Claire pushed past Fall and darted across the dirt road, dodging a cart piled high with wood and a small carriage with a faded crest painted on its doors. The dust settled behind them as Fall watched, annoyed and perplexed. He glanced back at the house long enough to see that the serving wench had disappeared inside, then continued on down Whitehall Street. Once he got this trip behind him, he would make his way to the Hawk and Crown and force Claire to talk with him.

Claire hurried the other way, almost propelling Alyce along beside her.

"Why did you tell him we were still at that expensive inn?" the girl asked breathlessly as she hurried to keep up.

"Because—because I don't want him to know where we are living."

"Claire, slow down. I'm out of breath. Why are we in such a hurry all of a sudden?"

Claire stopped, looking guiltily at her sister. Alyce, breathing heavily, set her basket on the ground and leaned on a nearby gate.

"I'm sorry, love," Claire said, shifting her own basket to her other arm. "The Hawk and Crown just sounds like a much nicer place to be staying than Madame Hoppen's boardinghouse. And the Mac-Dairmids are such fine folk, you know. I just—I just didn't want to admit we had been forced to move."

"Don't you like Mister MacDairmid, Claire? I do. He was kind to me on the ship. And he seems to like you quite a lot."

"Humph! He only likes me the way he likes all women. Did you see the way he ogled that servant back there? Just like a man. I don't need that kind of attention from any gentleman. Are you rested? We really ought to get along, or I'll never find all the items on this list Madame Hoppen gave me."

Alyce picked up her basket. "I'm quite all right now." She followed after her sister smiling to herself. Claire's flushed cheeks and bright, glinting eyes betrayed the feeling she denied having for Fall MacDairmid. She might say that he did not matter to her, but Alyce knew her sister well enough to know better.

Adolph Philipse turned out to be a pleasant surprise for Fall. In his late twenties, he was tall and broad-shouldered, with full jowls on a heavy face, a long nose, and slightly lidded eyes. It did not take long for Fall to conclude that he was an even shrewder merchant and trader than his father. He took Fall on a tour of the Philipse shop, a large warehouse, and two ships that happened to be in port and gave him innumerable tips on the best stables, the finest inns, the town's most artistic tailor, and the most satisfactory places of entertainment.

For his part, Adolph had heard such glowing praise of Fall from his father than he half-expected to loathe the young man. To his surprise he found that he was as taken with him as his father had been.

"I can show you around," he said as they moved up the wharf back toward Pearl Street. "New York society is no doubt tame compared to London or Paris, but we do manage to entertain ourselves tolerably well. I shall see that you are invited to the best soirees, balls, supper parties—"

"Hold on a moment," Fall said laughingly. "Though I have certainly seen my share of London and Paris, you must remember I came here from Edinburgh—not exactly one of the more glittering cities of Europe. And besides, I'm here to earn my fortune. I must save a little time for work."

"Oh, never fear for that. We all of us put in our time, you may be sure. There are fortunes to be made here, but they usually require effort. They are not likely to fall into your lap!"

"I had not supposed so."

Adolph studied Fall through hooded eyes. "Forgive me, but I understood you to come from a titled family of some sort."

"Titled but impoverished," Fall said laughingly. "What wealth there is, my greedy older brother has appropriated for himself. I am most anxious to return with more than Edgar has accumulated and throw it in his venal face."

Adolph chuckled, not unlike his father. "I can understand that though I have not been blessed with brothers. They all died in infancy. Of course, there is one road to quick wealth, which a man like you might

224

be well advised to try."

"Let me guess," Fall said. "A well-to-do widow."

"Exactly. There are several here in town, none of whom will remain unmarried for long. There is one — Immetje Strycker — a divine woman of many — and I do mean many — accomplishments. Now there is a woman who would grace both your purse and your bed equally well."

"I think I must meet the lady," Fall said without enthusiasm. "But I wonder that you haven't grabbed her for yourself."

Adolph shrugged. "I'm already one of the richest men in the province. I don't need her money. Before I am finished, I intend to be *the* richest man." He looked out over the harbor and his hawk's eyes took on a visionary hue. "Land. That's the secret. You must get away from this town, Fall, and see what wealth is lying out there, just waiting for an enterprising fellow to come along. My father has become a rich man in trade and that's fine for him. But it's land that will make him — and me — truly wealthy."

Fall hesitated under the intensity of Adolph Philipse's words. He did not doubt for a moment that this young man would do exactly as he said and accomplish exactly what he intended.

"I look forward to seeing that land," he muttered. Adolph shook off his fascination with the future and clapped a hand on Fall's shoulder. "We'll leave tomorrow morning to sail up the North River. Can you be ready at dawn? We'll need to catch the tide."

"I'll be ready."

For Claire, it seemed that, if there was one single experience which most pointed up the difference between the old world and the new, it was going to the market in New York. Recalling the sparse stalls of Crief, she wandered with an amazement that grew greater each time she entered the square at the end of Pearl near the shell-strewn beach. The bounty of the farmlands beyond the palisade wall separating the town from the rest of the island was beyond her most extravagant imaginings. She had heard that the New World was a rich land but this was almost beyond belief. The long tables that made up the rows of the market were piled high. Baskets overflowed with pungent onions, larger than any she had ever seen. There were turnips, carrots, cabbages, and all kinds of fresh vegetables, dried fruits, and tart apples. There were kegs of salted beef and pork, barrels of oysters and clams—some of them nearly a foot across—and all varieties of fish from the harbor. Pastries and freshly baked bread gave off such mouth-watering aromas as to force one to reach for the purse. Elaborate cookies baked into fantastic shapes, Dutch style, drew the adults as well as the children. Squat stoneware jars of honey and molasses and round buttery cheese wheels were stacked invitingly. Kegs of homemade beer, cider, and ale, were noisily hawked. Some tables even held leaves of precious tobacco to be sold in small quantities for those who could afford it.

She knew by now that the shops of the town held every luxury that the world could send to their door—fabrics from France, wines from Spain and Portugal, porcelain from Germany, and many, many more. That did not surprise her, but that a country could grow such healthy vegetables, fruits, and grains and in such quantities was a source of never-ending wonder.

Market day was also a pleasure for the opportunity it gave her to see the only people she knew in New

226

York. Many of the newly arrived immigrants, most of them not yet situated in any permanent way, used the time to greet one another and see how each was faring. The bustle of the square was itself a source of comfort. Children darting and calling to each other underfoot, the cries of the people manning the stalls as they urged their wares, the sound of horses' hooves on the cobbled streets and the shooing of pigs and dogs, many of them grubbing in the rotting peelings thrown underfoot. Even the cries of the sea gulls overhead and the distant towering of the masts in the harbor at the end of the square somehow gave her a sense of belonging.

There were many people in the crowd she did not know — some of them obviously the well-to-do who looked disparagingly at the crowds that grew larger with each arrival. A Wappinger Indian wandered through the crowd, followed by a squaw hugging a blanket around her; farmers from the countryside in shirt sleeves and round hats meandered among the stalls, their wives in kerchiefs and aprons, their several skirts pinned up around their linen petticoats.

The crowd was so thick today that Claire was relieved to see Caleb's familiar face. He was waving at her from the next row. He hurried over to claim Alyce, telling them he wanted to show her a booth where shells from the river had been laid out. Claire sent them on ahead and paused as she spotted Lace and Esther Varn standing at a table not ten feet away. Lace was angrily gesturing at the table and berating his wife for spending too much money on what she had purchased while Esther stood silently, her lips in a thin, tight line. Claire was relieved to see that Daniel was not with them, and she wondered if perhaps this might not be the appropriate time to ask Esther about Alan. She had not been able to find anyone in the

227

town who knew of Alan or who had any idea where he was, and it had become clear to her that if she ever hoped to find him it would only be through his relatives. Yet something within her made her hesitate. There had been so much unpleasantness between the Varns and her family, and in her secret heart she held so much resentment toward them that it seemed almost hypocritical to ask anything of them.

"Why, bless my soul. Isn't that you, Claire Montcrieff?" said a familiar voice behind her. Turning to the table at her left hand Claire was surprised to see Nell Nelligan standing behind it, her hands on her ample hips and a startled expression of delight on her wide face.

"Nell! Why, Nell, how wonderful to see you again!"

"Why, look at you, how lovely you look," Nell cried, hurrying around the table to sweep Claire up in her arms. She gave her a wet kiss on the cheek, then held her at arm's length. "New York must be treating you well, my dear. Your color's so much better and you're plumper too."

"Is it treating you well, Nell? Have you found a husband?" Claire asked, glancing at the table with its pile of cabbages and dried peas. "What did you do? Catch a prosperous farmer the first day ashore?"

"Oh, that," Nell said, grimacing slightly. "No, as a matter of fact, this is just a little job I took on so as not to waste my time. Keeps one busy, you know, and adds a little silver to the purse." She leaned closer to Claire's ear. "Met a gentleman, though, who's very serious. Yes, indeed, very serious. Meantime, my landlady and her husband, who have a fair-sized garden beyond the wall, asked me to help them out."

"Well, I'm glad to hear it, Nell. I've wondered so many times what became of you."

228

"And I wondered about you as well. How is your father getting on? And your little sister?"

"Alyce is up ahead with Caleb Browne. You remember Caleb?"

Nell gave a disgusted frown. "I prefer to forget that unpleasant fellow."

"Papa is very happy here. He's made many new friends and he—"

Her words were cut short as she heard a sharp cry in the crowd up ahead. "That sounds like Alyce!" Claire said as the cry became a scream. "Something's wrong—"

With Nell following closely behind her, she pushed through the people who had clustered around the small group in the center. The Indian she had seen earlier was standing in the center, his dirty blanket draped over one arm. Before him Alyce stood, cringing against Caleb, trying to avoid the Indian's outstretched hand. A powerful aroma, part bear grease, part urine, kept the spectators from getting too close. All but Lace Varn, who stood just behind the savage, his narrow eyes focused intently on the scene.

Expecting the worst, Claire rushed to her sister's aid but was stopped by Caleb, who laid a hand on her shoulder.

"It's all right, Alyce," Caleb said gently to the frightened girl. "He only wants to touch your face."

Alyce cringed closer to Caleb, horrified to have her unsightly birthmark made so blatantly obvious to the watching crowd. Pulling her shawl over the left side of their face, she turned the blemish against his coat.

"He won't hurt you," Caleb went on. "He thinks the Great Spirit gave you that mark as a sign of his favor."

Alyce looked up at Caleb, her eyes dark with mistrust and disbelief. "Favor? He does?"

229

The Indian, looking from Caleb to the girl, muttered a few guttural phrases, nodded his head up and down and gestured with his hand toward Alyce's cheek.

"Caleb, are you certain that is what he means?" Claire whispered.

"He wants to scalp me," Alyce cried, cringing. "That's what they do—"

Caleb chuckled. "Now why would he try to scalp you right here in front of all these people and with soldiers about to protect you? Be sensible, Alyce. Can't you see he doesn't mean you any harm? Just stand quietly and let him touch your face."

Alyce gave Caleb a questioning glance, then turned and faced the Indian. Reaching out his hand, his rough fingers traced the outline of her birthmark as she closed her eyes and cringed from his touch. Laying his hand against the dark skin, he closed his eyes and half-sang, half-chanted a few incomprehensible words. Then he bowed formally to Alyce and moved off, his wife following at a distance.

Claire stared after them. "How did you know that, Caleb? How did you know that was what he wanted?"

"Oh, I keep my eyes and ears open. I've picked up a lot of little pieces of information about these Algonquin natives since we arrived in New York. They fascinate me. I thought I had met every kind of life there is in London's streets, but I never saw anything like these Indians before."

Lace Varn, standing behind Caleb, made a scoffing noise with his tongue. "Humph," he uttered. "Just like one of them savages to take to something every civilized man knows is a sign of the devil. Thieves and murderers, that's all those red men are. They're not even human, you know." He leaned close into Caleb's face. "They don't have souls."

"Who says so?" Caleb snapped, glaring down at Lace's twisted face. "They're men just like the rest of us. They just have a different way of thinking, that's all."

"That shows all you know. Have you talked to any of the farmers who work outside the town? Well, I have and they'll tell you all about these savages. Come on your land anytime they please and just take what they want, no mention of who owns it or what's to pay. And when they get riled, they come in a party at night and burn and loot and murder—not just the men but women and children too. Savages! That's all they are."

Nell leaned around Claire's shoulder to shake a finger at Lace. "Well, they were here first, you know. It was their country. Besides, you never liked anybody, Lace Varn. Anybody who was different from you."

Not wanting to get involved, Claire stepped back from the three people who took up the argument with a vengeance. She wanted nothing so much as to get well away from the Varns and their superior attitude, but she hesitated to leave before speaking to them about Alan. They were her only link with him. Taking her courage in hand she stepped up beside Esther and spoke softly.

"I thought perhaps you might have left to join your nephew by now," she casually remarked.

Esther turned to look at her, her face a cautious mask. After a long pause she spoke: "No. We don't know yet where he is living."

"Oh. I don't suppose when you discover his whereabouts, you'd send me word? I would like him to know I'm here."

"He's not been easy to find. But if I hear anything,

231

I'll send his address around. Where are you living?"

"At the Widow Hoppen's on Marketfield Street. I'd be grateful to you, Esther, if you would."

The woman shrugged and moved to join her husband, who had decided he was getting the worst of having both Caleb and Nell against him and had abruptly left the argument. Once out of earshot he said sharply, "I saw you talking with that Montcrieff woman. What did she want?"

"She wanted to know if we knew where Alan was living."

They stepped around one of the long tables and moved into another row, putting stacks of barrels and kegs between them and the Montcrieff sisters and their friends.

"Did you tell her?"

"Of course not. If she knew where he was and that he was expecting us, she'd be right off up there to join him. You know what that would mean. With her married to Alan, our Daniel would never have a prayer of becoming Alan's heir."

Lace bobbed his head up and down. "Good. Good. Now and then you do come up with a sensible idea. Not often, of course, but now and then."

To Claire's surprise, Caleb decided that Nell was doing everything wrong at her table and made up his mind to stay and help her. Taking Alyce's arm, she steered her sister through the maze of booths and back out into the street.

"I think Caleb was rather glad to see Nell, don't you, Claire?" Alyce commented as they started back toward Marketfield Street.

"He tried to pretend he wasn't but it was obvious that he was. He talks about her as though she was anathema to him but I rather suspect he likes her a little."

"I think so too. Oh, look, Claire. What a pretty carriage. And the bay. Isn't he the most handsome animal!"

Alyce had stopped opposite a tobacconist shop with a huge elaborate pipe hanging over the door. In the street in front of the small shop, a small carriage had just pulled up, decoratively painted and gleaming in the bright sunshine. The spirited animal that pulled it bobbed his head up and down regally as a liveried footman jumped from the seat beside the driver and hurried to let down a step and open the door. As the girls watched, he handed down a woman who was the most elegant vision Claire had ever seen. Her elaborate frontage headdress was piled high, with long side curls that dangled beside her narrow, painted face. Her dress was exquisite, made of silk whose folds shimmered in the light, with elbow-length sleeves with deep frilled cuffs. The tight-fitting bodice had a low décolletage set off with satin ribbon bows. The diamonds she wore around her throat and on her fingers caught the sun's rays like lightning, heightening the aura of shimmering light that hovered over her.

Both Claire and Alyce watched mesmerized as this elegant creature stepped onto the cobbles, lifted her shimmering skirts, and moved toward the shop door. The servant made a dash to open it for her, setting a ream of bells tinkling. With one dainty foot on the threshold she stopped to return the stare the two girls had leveled upon her.

Embarrassed, Claire tugged gently at Alyce's arm to walk on. The woman, her face a frozen expressionless mask, took in Alyce's birthmark which, in her interest in the lady, she had let lie uncovered. Leaning

233

forward she stared at Alyce's cheek, clucking her tongue.

"You poor child," she said in a voice that evidenced none of the compassion she spoke.

Blushing, Alyce yanked the shawl over one side of her face.

"Here, girl," the woman said reaching into an embroidered reticule and extending a coin toward Alyce. The girl shrank bank, looking up at Claire.

"No, thank you, ma'am," she murmured.

"Take it, take it," she said, pressing the coin into Alyce's hand. "No doubt it will make your life a little less hard."

"We are not beggars, ma'am," Claire said in clipped tones. "Though we thank you for your kindness."

The eyes turned on Claire, inquisitive, questioning, assessing but without any warmth. "Is this girl related to you?" she asked.

"She is my sister."

There was something in the woman's eyes as she looked Claire over that certainly had not been there for Alyce. Something harder, more threatening.

"Take this and buy her something. I'm sure there's not much pleasure in life for her with that severe blemish. It is our duty to help the unfortunate."

Claire had to fight to keep down the rage that swelled up within her. She wanted to throw the coin back in the woman's face, but she wisely tried to keep calm, her anger making her more pointedly polite.

"Take it, take it, take it," the woman said impatiently. "I've plenty more." Thrusting the coin hard into Alyce's hand, she moved on into the shop with an air of having given them all the time she could spare for such things. With a smirk, the servant followed behind, leaving the two outraged girls on the walk.

"Well, I never!" Claire said. "Such arrogance! What does she think we are?"

"It was a nice thing for her to do," Alyce said gently as they moved on.

"It was insulting!"

"But we *can* use it, Claire. Or if you prefer, we can give it to the poor box at church. Look. It's a souverain d'or. That's worth a lot, isn't it?"

Claire realized she was clenching her teeth. "You keep it. Spend it on something you want."

Alyce thought for a moment. "No. I don't think so. It would only remind me that she gave it to me out of pity. I'll give it to the poor box."

Early the following morning Fall left on Adolph Philipse's round-bottomed sloop for the trip up the North River. If he had thought he might be bored and disinterested, he soon learned how wrong he was. The land itself was beautiful with high cliffs on one side and sloping woodland and fields on the other, but it was the accumulated effect that left him consumed with wonder. Never before had he seen such lush forests, tall trees, thick vegetation. There was so much richness, so much potential that his mouth came close to watering at the idea of acquiring it. The river thronged with fish, huge long sturgeon, oysters and lobsters and clams, every variety of fish, large and small. The wildflowers in the fields were breathtaking while those fields that had been cleared and planted gave evidence of such a harvest as would be the envy of every landowner in Scotland. After the thin, denuded forests of Europe, the barren, rocky soil of Scotland, and the fields of home which had been farmed for centuries, the very newness and richness of this virgin soil was enough to fill him with awe. No wonder Adolph had decided that his future lay here.

They spent the first night at the Philipse manor house, a modest hunting lodge on a narrow tributary of the North River called the Nepperhaen. The next morning they sailed north again, going as far as the highlands where the fields bordering the water began to grow into small mountains, breathtaking in their beauty. The river widened and narrowed, now a sweeping bay, next a small channel tunneled through the green mysterious hills. At the end of the second day they had returned south as far as the Pocantico River, a winding channel they followed eastward to a small grain mill. Here, in the two-story narrow house of whitewashed stone where Adolph made his northern headquarters, they spent the second night. The next morning, Fall was shown around some of the farms run by tenants in the area, ending up with a tour of the mill.

He left the wooden building to return to the nearby house for breakfast, pausing on the step to brush some of the white frosting of the mill from his coat. The door, a Dutch design, the top half of which was open, allowed him to see into the foreroom where Adolph and his overseer were talking with two of the tenants. The overseer had a ledger opened on the draw table and was scribbling in it.

"Name and weight," Fall heard the man ask as he brushed at his shoulders.

"Jeremy Pate, two pound, ten."

"Morehead, Alan," came the second voice. "One pound, three and a half."

Fall's hand paused but he was careful not to look quickly around.

"Now how can you possibly break it down so carefully?" the overseer said impatiently.

236

"I can," the young man's voice replied. "I'm very precise. Weigh it yourself if you don't believe me."

There was a thump on the table as the overseer picked up a bag of grain and dumped it on the scales. Casually opening the lower half of the door, Fall stepped into the room. Adolph, seeing him, left the men at the table and led him toward the door to the kitchen. As he passed, Fall glanced at the two men standing before the table, intently watching the scales.

Which one was Alan? One was slightly older and shorter than the other who was tall, heavy-set, almost stodgy. Was that the peasant face he recalled from years past on the streets of Ben Brogain? He had never really paid any attention then but it might be. Thick, slow features. A shock of brown hair, pulled back and tied with a thong. Farmer's clothes, clean and neat enough though only made of poor stuff, probably linsey-woolsey. The taller, younger man's eyes were intent on the scales as if to be certain he was not cheated. He did not glance up as Fall walked through the room.

"Might those be two of your tenants?" he asked Adolph as they sat down at a table laden with food.

"Yes. Two of the best. We have about twenty tenants at the moment living at the Upper Mills but we expect to have more every year. This is good land both for farming and for raising cattle. And the mill is extremely prosperous. We have the only one within thirty miles."

"Very convenient for you," Fall said absently as he helped himself to more beefsteak pie. "I caught the name of one of those men. Morehead. It sounds familiar."

"It ought to. He's a countryman of yours. Been here about two years, if I recollect right. A good

237

man. A hard worker."

"And very precise about what his weights are."

"Very precise about everything. Not a bad trait in a tenant."

Fall spread butter on a slab of thick bread, freshly baked that morning to judge by the delicious odor. "No, I suppose not."

With a strong wind out of the north scuddying them down the river, Adolph's substantial sloop made New York in near record time. Though it was late in the day, Fall wasted no time tidying himself up but set out straight for the Hawk and Crown on Maiden Lane.

He had done some serious thinking on the trip back, and the more he turned the matter over in his mind, the more convinced he was that Claire Montcrieff was not meant to be the wife of a serious-minded dullard like Alan Morehead. She had too much beauty, too much intelligence, and too much spirit to waste on a tenant farm in the half-cleared woodlands of a back country, even one as rich as the Upper Mills. When one came right down to it, it was only a few years removed from the hunting grounds of Indians! There was also the thought — only allowed a brief surfacing but there nonetheless — that once she saw Alan again and recognized the security and mild prosperity he represented, she would immediately settle for those dull virtues he personified and be only too happy to marry the lout.

He must not allow that to happen — for her own good.

Yet when he accosted the landlord of the Hawk and Crown and learned that the Montcrieffs had moved out nearly a week before, all his excellent intentions of saving Claire from a life of domestic drudgery were swallowed up in his anger. She had lied to him. Looked him right in the eye and lied to him without even a blink.

"Where did they go?" he snapped, leaning threateningly across the caged bar.

"How should I know? They left in a hurry, that's all I can tell you. In one hour's time. Paid the shot and left. It was that older daughter who was responsible. Old Tom was a good fellow and he would have been happy to stay here yet if she hadn't hauled them all way."

"No doubt," Fall quipped, glancing around the cozy room with its usual quota of loungers and drinkers. "And she never said anything about where they were going?"

"I never asked. It's none of my concern, long as they pay their bill."

Slapping his hat on his head, Fall stalked to the entrance and stepped back out onto the front stoop. What was he going to do now? Certainly he was not going to go searching through every tavern and rooming house in New York town. There were too many of them to begin with, even for a place this size.

And yet . . . if he waited too long Alan Morehead might arrive to claim his bride and that would be the end of it. He leaned against the door absently watching the flow of pedestrians and carts in the street and wondering which way to set out. Several young men approached, rudely shoving him aside as they made to enter the tavern door. Fall caught back his first impulse, which was to knock one or two of them into the street and instead caught one by the sleeve.

"Do any of you fellows know a man by the name of Tom Montcrieff, newly arrived in town?"

They were the usual scruffy-looking lot of town wastrals but one of them, who had already entered the tavern, stopped and stepped back. To Fall's dismay he was one of the youngest, already bleary-eyed from too much ale.

"Aye, I do," he mumbled.

"Do you know where he moved to by any chance?"

The blurred eyes peered closer, looking over Fall's cambric collar and fine brocade coat.

"And if I did, would it be worth the price of a dram?"

Not even bothering to hide his disgust, Fall reached in his fob and pulled out a brass coin, carefully holding it up.

"This ought to be worth at least two drams."

The young man reached out quickly for the coin but Fall nimbly pulled his arm back.

"I believe it was the Widow Anna Hoppen's rooms on Marketfield Street," he cried, running his tongue over his lips and staring intently at Fall's hand. Fall tossed him the coin.

"Many thanks," he muttered and strode off. Though he had a vague idea where Marketfield Street was he had not an inkling which house belonged to the Widow Hoppen. But that should not be too difficult to find out. And when he did, he'd teach Mistress Claire something about whom to tell lies to.

The next morning, dressed in his best broadcloth coat and cambric ruff, Fall set out to find the Widow Hoppen's boarding house. By asking a few judicious questions, he came upon it nearly half an hour later. Yet, instead of barging straight up to pound on the door as he had half-intended, some inner caution made him step across the street and observe the place.

It was a shabby building on a shabby street. The noises and pungent odors of the wharf at one end pervaded the whole area and were made even more unpleasant by the winds wafting from the brewery that stood directly opposite the house. He took a seat on one of the large kegs that stood outside the open double doors of the brewery, pulled his hat brim down to shadow his face, and absently watched the people moving in and out of the widow's house and its neighbors on either side. For the most part they appeared to be boarders leaving for their day's work with only one or two entering, obviously intent on their breakfast. He pulled back into the shadows as he saw several members of the Montcrieff family step outside, followed by Caleb Browne, the London fellow from the *Selkirk*. First Tom with Jamie in tow set off down the street, a definite purpose in their step, then Caleb with the little deformed sister on his arm moved off in the opposite direction. If Claire had not left earlier, she would be in the house alone—a situation that could not be more to his liking. After the family members had disappeared down the street, he casually strolled over to knock on the door.

Close up, the house looked cleaner and neater than it had from across the way though the general air of shabbiness was still strong. He had raised his hand to knock again when it abruptly opened revealing a very plump woman standing there, obviously dressed to go out. Tight yellow curls coiled from under a ruffled white cap which was in turn crushed by a large straw bonnet. She wore an apron over a purple overskirt and had a woven basket on her arm and a soft wool shawl draped over her shoulders. Her quick, small eyes moved from an initial suspicion to amazement as she took in Fall's gentlemanly, expensive appearance.

"Why, sir," she said hastily, pulling the door completely open. "Good morning to you. What can I do for you, sir? If it's a room you're wanting, I have just

241

one left — very fine. . . ."

Fall raised a gloved hand. "No, no. I don't need lodgings, thank you. I am looking for Miss Montcrieff who I understand resides at this address. Would she be in at the moment by any chance?"

The widow's smile faded slightly. "Claire Montcrieff? I presume that's who you mean and not the sister, for why would any gentleman in his right mind come seeking one so ugly. Yes, Claire is here but she's very busy at the moment."

"Perhaps she could be interrupted," Fall said, pouring on the charm. "I've been looking for her for some time."

"Well . . . I don't know. You know how it is."

She gave him a conspiratorial smirk as though they both were familiar with the problems of keeping servants. Stepping back into the shadowy hall she motioned to Fall to enter, then poked her head into one of the rooms off the hall.

"Claire! There's a gentleman to see you."

Fall could not make out Claire's response but he recognized her startled voice well enough. From her tone it sounded as though she was not anxious to see anyone. He caught the widow's hissing rejoinders. A moment later the woman stepped back and motioned him inside.

"She's in the parlor, if you please, sir. But not too long, now, I pray you."

Fall bowed with exaggerated politeness. "Thank you, ma'am. You are most kind."

"Why, thank you, sir. And if you should ever need a room . . ."

He doffed his hat. "I'll come to you first."

With a satisfied smile the widow swept out into the hall and closed the door behind her. In the silence he heard her pause, then leave through the front door.

He stood, looking around the small room. It was dark and shadowed but he recognized the familiar signs of a comfortable though not elegant Dutch parlor—the faded painted *kas* in one corner, the fireplace with its border of blue tiles, two straight chairs, a floor covered with sand into which eleborate patterns had been worked, and, in one corner, a bed, reserved for privileged guests. Claire was standing beside the *kas*, near a shuttered window. Even in the dark he could see her hands clenched in her apron.

"You!" she cried. "How did you get here?"

He moved toward her. Judging from the large apron and cap that covered her hair, she was obviously cleaning. Her skirts were hitched up around her petticoats and she wore a peasant-style laced jerkin over a white blouse that emphasized the fullness of her breasts. She had not bothered with the usual kerchief and the low rim of the blouse only half-covered the tantalizing dark cleft in the center. He felt himself growing warm even as he moved toward her.

"Why did you lie to me?"

"I never did."

"You did indeed. You told me you were staying at the Hawk and Crown."

"Well, we had been!"

"You haven't been there for a week. I went to see you—"

Claire saw she was being boxed in and quickly darted to the other side of the room.

"You should not have. I didn't ask you to go looking for me. It ought to be obvious that I don't want to see you."

"Why not?" Fall said, leaping after her. She reached out and grabbed a long, thick piece of wood, holding it up before her.

"What is that for?" he said, almost laughing. "You

don't have to beat me off, you know. I told you I wouldn't force myself on you."

"Then stay over there," Claire cried, her cheeks reddening with embarrassment. "Besides, I'm not trying to defend myself. This is only a bed key and I have to use it for one of my chores."

As if to prove her point, she threw up the quilt on the bed and began tightening the ropes that supported the mattress.

"Why are you living in such a place? Couldn't you afford the tavern? I told you if you needed help you had only to ask."

In spite of his good intentions he moved toward her again. Claire pulled the bed out away from the wall and worked her way to the far side.

"And I told you I'll never ask a MacDairmid for help. You only want to make me beholden to you."

"That's not true. And what is all this about 'chores'? You've got no business working as that woman's servant. It's—it's demeaning!"

"Oh. And I suppose I'm above such as this. Well, hard work never hurt anyone though I don't suppose I should expect you to know about that. We don't have a farm any longer, as you know very well, and I have to do something to make myself useful."

He reached across the mattress, but she pulled away to the other end, still yanking on the ropes with the key.

"Will you be still! What did that woman do, charge you less in return for using you as a servant? I can't see Tom agreeing to any such thing as this."

"Papa doesn't know. And you had better not tell him."

"I'll wager he doesn't. Now, look here, Claire—"

"Mistress Montcrieff, if you please."

They had circled the bed by this time and Claire

had worked her way to the end where the last piece of rope was pulled and knotted. Giving it a mighty yank she forced it into a fat knot, then stood back, the wooden key still in her hand. Across the quilt Fall leaned toward her, his lean face angry.

"Why did you come here?" she cried. "What do you want?"

"I only wanted to see you again. To know where you were. To help you if you needed it."

"I don't believe you! There's some self-serving reason behind everything you MacDairmids do. Leave me alone. Go away. I don't want to see you."

"And I don't believe you. You say one thing with your lips but your eyes, your body all say the opposite."

"Oh! You're impossible."

Throwing the key on the bed, she rushed past him toward the door and threw it open. "I tell you, leave me alone!" she cried and was gone. Fall went after her and saw that she had run through a door at the rear of the hall into a small grassy plot behind the house. Furious, he followed, determined that she should not leave everything shattered like this. She would face him and talk reasonably to him if he had to hogtie her down to do it.

There were several small outbuildings behind the house scattered around a small field where a thin calf stood tied near a pen. Two goats looked over the side of the fence, mildly curious as first the woman came running across the yard to gather up a bucket and disappear inside the barn, and then the man came galloping after her.

Sending chickens scrambling, Fall crossed the yard and ducked into the barn. Claire was at the far end, yanking up a stool and clanging the wooden buckets against the planks of a stall. Inside a bored cow

245

munching at the straw turned her head to stare at him with large, liquid eyes.

Fall darted into the empty stall where Claire was fussing with the buckets and managed to grab her wrist.

"Stop it, Claire. Even I know enough to realize that cow was milked long ago."

"Take your hands off me," she cried, pulling back and twisting her arm in an effort to get free.

"No, I won't! Not until you talk to me in a civilized and sensible way. I won't ask you to be polite for that's obviously beyond your abilities, but we will have this out in a reasonable manner."

"You can't reason with a MacDairmid!"

"Oh. And I suppose the Montcrieffs are the epitome of rationality!"

"Let me go!"

Twisting her arm she struggled to work free of his grasp but his hands were like iron. Without realizing it, he had backed her against the high wall of the stall, her feet slipping on the thick straw. Her nearness was intoxicating. With the blood rising in his body, he pressed against her, bending over her, his hands sliding up her arms to her shoulders. She tipped her head back and the closeness of his lean face, his lips, his thickly fringed eyes made her breath catch in her throat. Her arm went slack, then her whole body. Fall caught her in his arms, pressing her against the wooden wall as they both slid downward onto the straw.

"Oh, Claire," he moaned, full of a tormenting ache that had only one driving goal.

Her voice was low, "No, no . . . " she murmured so softly he could barely hear her. Her arms went around his neck and she clasped his body to hers, both of them molding form to form, heat to heat.

246

His lips searched out her flesh frantically, savoring the sweetness of her cheek, the lobe of her ear, the soft curve of her throat, the delicate hollow of her neck. She arched her back in an automatic reaction to the caress of his lips, and he buried his head in the curve of her throat. His hands restlessly searched out her shoulders, sliding the sleeves of her bodice away and slipping beneath the narrow lace edge to cup her breast in one hand.

"I've wanted you so," he said hoarsely. "I never even realized until this moment the torment needing you has been."

Claire could not answer. A sharp little cry escaped her lips as he lifted her breast free and took the taut nipple between his teeth. Fire raced through her blood as she stretched and writhed beneath him.

Claire recognized the same intoxicating excitement that had possessed her in Fall's cabin on the *Selkirk*. Under his deft hands her blouse slid away, baring her breasts. He took them, one after the other, drinking, sucking, and licking until she felt as though she would die from the delicious torment.

It was a simple matter for Fall to slip his hands under her skirts. How he managed to rid himself of his clothes Claire never knew.

She felt his hands slip up her legs and her hands frantically sought under his shirt to the taut warmth of his chest. Deftly he pushed her thighs apart, freeing her of her skirts. With a longing beyond any she had known, she felt him move into her, hard, driving as though the need to be one was more than he could bear. She felt her own body draw his into its luscious depths, filling some aching void. He moved against her rhythmically, easy at first, then increasing in intensity. She moved with him, sensing his mounting excitement with something that seemed like tri-

247

umph. Faintly she heard her own moans as he carried her to the edge of a precipice that seemed the end of all being and sensation. Grasping her with all his strength, Fall's body arched, then just as suddenly went slack, and he slumped against her, groaning as he buried his head in her shoulder.

They lay, spent and exhausted. Almost of their own accord, Claire's fingers moved to touch his hair, stroking it softly away from his damp brow. She felt all at once such a tenderness and joy as she had never known before. How odd, she thought. When this happened the first time, on the *Selkirk*, she had felt only anger at him for taking advantage of her. There was none of that now. In its place was a warmth, even a gratitude. She could not pretend to understand it, but this time she did not fight it. She lay content and happy and simply let it be.

Fall seemed to recognize that something was different. At length he rolled off her, lying on his side with his head propped on one arm, the other protectively across her breast.

"You seem to always have this strange effect on me," he quipped. Claire glanced over sharply and saw the smile that played about his lips. She gave a deep, throaty laugh.

"You have a rather striking effect on me as well."

"We're very good together," he said more seriously. "I thought, when I came here looking for you, that it was only to be certain you were getting along all right. Now I know that this is what I really wanted all along."

Claire cocked one eyebrow at him. "You mean that I am another one of those wenches you lust after. It doesn't say much for me that you always seem to have your way with me. I never mean for it to happen but somehow . . . "

Gently he stroked the smooth skin of her long, graceful neck. "No. Not simply lust. I *am* concerned for your welfare. And a wench to tumble with is usually one you never care whether or not you see again. You draw me back somewhat against my will."

"Oh. Thank you for the compliment."

He turned her face toward him and brushed her lips with his, lightly, as though the tip of a feather had crossed them.

"It is a compliment."

Claire gave a soft sigh. "All the same, it is not the best thing for either of us. I think that is why I try so hard to stay away from you."

"I told you we have something special between us. Why fight against the inevitable? It's too precious and delightful."

"But, Fall, don't you see? There's nothing for us. You are well-born and will eventually marry someone who is well-born. And I am promised to Alan Moreland. If we were wise, we would both accept our destiny and not confuse and complicate matters by— she waved her hand to take in the small stall with its scattered matting of straw—"by acting in such a way."

He caught her to him and rolled over on his back, pulling her on top. "But this is so much fun!"

"Spoken like the hedonist you are," she answered, kissing him lightly. "Sometimes people must be practical."

"Claire, Claire! You have the most annoying way of saying 'no, no' when everything you do cries, 'yes, yes'! Your mind and your body are not working together."

"All the better for you."

"Besides, I intend to be practical." As if to emphasize his words, he sat up suddenly and leaned against the wall, drawing up his knees and resting his elbows on them. Claire slid her blouse up over her white breasts and casually picked the straw from his hair. "I have decided to rent a house," he went on, "where you and your family can live. There will be a room for me when I'm in the city, but, in the meantime, you will be more comfortable and safe and will want for nothing."

Claire's hand stilled in midair. "I don't understand," she said softly.

Fall's enthusiasm began to grow as he considered the idea. "Don't you see? I can take some of the commission I received for the sale of Sir Francis's cargo and use it to rent a house. It will be bigger and more comfortable than this hovel of the Widow Hoppen's, and there will be plenty of room for your family. You can take care of it. In fact, you must think of it as your home. I shall be on trips with Mister Philipse in all likelihood much of the time, but, when I'm in the city, I shall stay there. With all your relatives along it will appear most proper."

"But in actuality I can slip into your bed as often as you like. Is that what you're thinking?"

"It had crossed my mind."

"It's absurd. We could never accept such charity. And what about your return to Scotland? And my marriage to Alan?"

Fall frowned at her. "We can face those things when the time for them comes. In the meantime, you can pay me a nominal rent if that makes you feel better. But I want you, Claire. I want you near me. I want you in my bed. No more of this rolling around on the floor of a barn or a ship's cabin. I want your naked body next to my naked body, closed away from the world, only we two."

Reaching out he drew her close to him, stroking her hair back from her white forehead and crooking his

250

arm around her neck. She nuzzled the strong flesh in the hollow of his throat while her hand slid up his chest, savoring the feel of the soft tufts of blond hair. It was what she wanted too, much as she hated to admit it. It was all she wanted.

"Oh, Fall. It sounds so tempting, yet I cannot help but feel it would be a foolish mistake. We would only be letting ourselves grow to love all this more and more when there is no future for us."

He thought for a moment. There was truth in what she said, but somehow all that mattered was to have her near.

"We'll let the future worry about itself. For now, there is only the joy to be taken."

Twelve

Fall was as good as his word. Within a week he had rented a substantial house in the growing area of the town beyond the original old wall but still within the palisaded breastwork that now separated New York from the woods and fields beyond. After bribing Tom with an offer to find an apprenticeship for Jamie, he moved the family into his new house just a few days before he himself had to leave for a trip to Fort Orange with the group of soldiers from the garrison.

Though Claire was still ambivalent about living in Fall's house, the fact that he was not there made it seem less like charity. And she had to admit, the pleasantries and comforts of their new home almost made it worthwhile under any circumstances.

The house was large compared to the older Dutch homes that still covered most of the town. It had four rooms below, including a parlor, dining room, office, and kitchen, and four bedrooms over them. Fall decided to take the downstairs office as his own room so he could come and go without disturbing the

252

others. Tom had one bedroom—one of the main reasons he agreed to the arrangement—Jamie another and Claire and Alyce shared the third. Fall had given Claire leave to hire a servant and a cook, and, after taking on a young, slightly dull Dutch girl named Katrina Mallard, she lost no time in seeking out Nell who willingly agreed to join them. She was given the fourth room, which doubled as a small office for household matters—an arrangement that seemed to her as a gift from heaven. Though she did not tell Claire many of the particulars, it was obvious that Nell had not stumbled onto a rich wife-seeking burgher quite as quickly as she had hoped. In fact, she had been in desperate straits since leaving the *Selkirk*, taking odd jobs where she could find them in exchange for a roof over her head. The pleasant house and congenial companionship of the Montcrieffs were such a blessing as she had given up hoping for, and her estimation of Fall MacDairmid had grown accordingly.

"Though it's little enough I've seen of the gentleman," she said to Claire one fine morning after they had been settled for almost a month in the house on Fair Street. "He's almost like a rich benefactor who has died and left a legacy. Is he never coming back?"

"Oh, I'm sure he'll come striding in one of these days," Claire answered absently, rearranging a table for the third time. It was almost like playing house to set the furniture in these grand rooms, and she never tired of trying them in a new way. "That's why he wanted this place—so he would be free to come and go and not have to worry about where he was going to sleep."

Nell, who was busily arranging a large bowl of dried flowers, glanced up, her brows furrowing. "You don't think he'll mind me being here when he comes back, do you? It's bound to be a surprise, and maybe he would prefer not to have someone who was on the ship with him."

"Nonsense, Nell. He told me to hire as many people as I need to run the house, and you are so efficient it's saved looking for anyone else. Besides, aren't we all good Scots? I'm certain he won't mind."

"Well, I do hope not since I've become quite accustomed now to this grand style of living." She looked around the room nodding in approval. "This was a nice house to begin with but you've made it a real home, my girl. I hope he appreciates you."

"I don't think he cares. He did us a favor by allowing us to take care of this place for him. The least we can do is make it as livable as possible. Besides, I must admit, it's far more pleasant than any home we've had before. I could almost get used to living like this."

"I do hope he returns soon. It will be nice to see the gentleman again."

Claire stopped and glanced out of the window, her eyes taking on a faraway stare. "Yes, it will be, won't it?"

Actually she was not certain whether or not she was anxious to see Fall again. Since he had left the city before they had had a chance to share the same roof, she was still unconvinced that it was going to work out once he returned. Her body longed for him, sometimes with an almost unbearable ache, yet her mind told her it was foolish to want him too much.

And then he came home.

Claire was sitting in the upper kitchen with Nell, counting and packing an assortment of tallow candles they had just finished making when she heard the front door open. Heavy boots stamped on the floor and Katrina's childish high-pitched voice was heard in a rather flustered response to a deeply modulated male voice. Claire looked up sharply, her heart missing a beat as she stared at the closed door separating the two rooms.

"Why, I do believe that's the master," Nell cried, jumping up from the table. "Doesn't that sound like his voice?"

Claire didn't move. Very deliberately she went back to sorting the candles.

"It does rather sound like him."

Nell fussed with smoothing her cap and straightening her ample apron. "Well, get up, then, my girl. We ought to make him a welcome—"

The door was thrown open and Fall stood on the threshold. His clothes were dusty and disheveled and he still wore the metal breastguard of the garrison soldiers. His boots looked as though he had been traipsing through a slough of mud. Claire rose from the table, staring across it at his lean face. His eyes were full of smiles as he stared back at her.

Bobbing him a curtsy, Nell began to babble about how unfit it was for him to arrive like this without a proper welcome. He turned to her, taking a moment to recognize her and then to wonder why she was in his kitchen.

It seemed to Claire as she moved around the table toward him that her legs were stiff. She felt her cheeks grow warm and realized she was embarrassed, berating herself for being so silly.

"Welcome home, Mister MacDairmid," she said formally.

Fall strode into the room, throwing his cloak over the back of a chair and looking around.

"Thank you, Mistress Montcrieff. You've done a lot to make the place habitable while I was away. I'm very pleased with it."

With a start Claire realized that he was as stiff as she over seeing her there in his house.

"Now you must let us do for you, Mister MacDairmid," Nell went on breezily. "Would you like a nice hot bath? We can have Katrina draw some water for you. Or perhaps a simple meal. Are you hungry, sir?"

Fall looked at Nell again and turned to Claire, his face full of curiosity.

Jumping in Claire said hurriedly, "You remember Mistress Nelligan from the *Selkirk*, don't you? I asked her on to help with the housework. You did say to hire as much help as I thought proper."

"Of course. I did indeed say that. You are welcome in my house, Mistress Nelligan."

Nell fairly beamed. "Why, thank you, sir," she said, bobbing again. "It's very pleased I am to be here, Claire being such a dear friend and all."

Fall turned back to Claire as though dismissing Nell's presence. "I think I would like that bath if you don't mind," he said casually, wondering at the same time at how different it was for him not to demand service.

Claire moved toward the door. "I'll get Katrina right to it. Nell, perhaps you would show Mister MacDairmid his room?"

"Oh, I'd be delighted. Right through here, sir, if you please. We've done our best to make it as comfortable for you as can be."

Fall watched Claire disappear into the foreroom, wondering to himself at her stiff formality, then reluctantly followed Nell through the other door leading off the kitchen to his bedroom. He was a little

256

disappointed that Claire had not shown him to it so that they might have a moment alone, but that would come in due time.

It wasn't until after he had washed and had had lunch that he sent for her. He was sitting at the desk in his room when she knocked and entered, closing the door behind her. He offered her a chair opposite his and she sat down stiffly, folding her hands in her lap.

"Are you pleased with the house, sir?" she said in as formal a manner as possible.

"Now, none of this 'sir' between us, Claire. I am not your master and you are not my servant. We must make that clear right away."

Some of the stiffness went out of Claire's shoulders. "I confess I don't quite know where I stand. While you were away, it was not so difficult pretending this was your house, and I was simply taking care of it for you. But with you here, especially with Nell . . ."

"Yes. Perhaps it might have been better if you had hired two Katrinas instead of someone who knows us both."

"But she was in such need of a place to stay. And I do enjoy her company."

Fall waved his hand. "Oh, it's all right. It just seems a little odd at first. She'll have to become accustomed to our peculiar arrangement."

Suddenly Claire rose and moved to the curtained window. "I am not so certain I understand our arrangement, Fall. It's been so pleasant living here, so good for my family and for me as well. But now . . ."

In a hurried motion he was across the room and stood close before her. Laying his hands on her shoulders, he bent close to her face.

"God, Claire, but I've missed you. All that wandering and marching, sailing up the North River, camping in woods so thick I never knew they could exist, so much to see and do, so many new experiences — and, through them all, all I could see in my mind was your face. All I longed for was the touch of your skin, the warmth of your body." He laid the palm of his hand on her cheek and bent to kiss her lips. She wavered a moment, reluctant to let go of the barrier between them that different circumstances and unfamiliarity had thrown up. Then his lips touched hers, soft as down, gentle as a spring wind, warm and sensuous. Her arms went around his neck and she pressed against him. The old fire engulfed them both and he kissed her harder, pressing against her lips, his tongue burying into her mouth.

"Come to me tonight."

"But how? Alyce . . ."

"To hell with Alyce. She sleeps, doesn't she? I want you beside me, in my arms, for as many hours as I can have you. Come to me." His hands slipped along her arms, sliding to her waist and up to lightly graze her white shoulders and down, down beneath the bodice of her waist to cup her breast. "I could take you now, right here! I don't think I can wait until tonight."

Claire tried to pull away, reluctant as she was to do so. "We mustn't. Papa will be back any minute, and then Jamie. I can't be so brazen, no matter how much I want to lie with you."

"Then promise you'll come."

She took his face between her hands, her lips grazing the sculptured line of his own. "I promise. The moment I see Alyce is asleep."

Fall held her close in his arms, stilling the desire

that swept over him, willing it to wait a few more hours. Filled with happiness, Claire savored the good feel of his strong body against hers, the strength of his arms engulfing her. How could anything that seemed so right, that felt so natural, be wrong, she wondered. Why must she hide from the world something so full of health and joy?

"Do you like what I've done with the house?" she finally whispered.

He stood back, laughing. "Yes, I do, though I'm a poor judge. You can do anything you want with it as long as you come to me when I need you. Keep pigs in the parlor, hire out the upper rooms — I care nothing about where I live. I only want a convenient place to sleep with you."

"And after all my work!" Claire protested.

He kissed her again. "If you enjoyed it, that's all that matters. I want that for you. Now, sit here and tell me how much you missed me."

"Don't you even want to hear about the household finances and arrangement?"

"As long as you stay within my expense account, you can do what you please. You have stayed within my expense account, haven't you?"

Claire chuckled. "Yes. I was very careful to do so and certainly what you allowed me was generous enough!"

"Good. Had you been a spendthrift I might reconsider. What of your family? Have they accepted all this?"

"Oh, yes. And it is such a relief to me to know they are so well situated."

"And your father?"

"Well, he still frequents the taverns too often. And he sees more of Lace Varn than I could wish. The

Varns moved away, somewhere to the north, but Lace still comes into town frequently. Somehow, when he does, he and Papa nearly always end up in the same grog shop and nearly always have a row of some sort."

Lace Varn reminded Fall suddenly of Alan Morehead at the Upper Mills. He took the chair opposite Claire and swiveled to the side so as not to face her directly.

"Lace is harmless enough."

It was an hour later that a young lad came running up to the door to lean over the lower half and ask if Fall MacDairmid lived within. He had been sent by the captain of the ship *Glasgow Flyer* to tell Fall there were letters aboard for him. Thinking they might be from Sir Francis Murray, Fall hurriedly donned his coat and hat and went striding off toward the other end of the town.

Claire, filled with anticipation over the night ahead, tempered by apprehension over how she was going to manage to sneak away from her family, watched him leave and told herself he would return in an hour or less. By the time the shadows had lengthened to twilight and Fall had still not returned, she began to wonder if their assignation would even take place.

With Nell's help she laid the table for Fall in the formal dining room rather than the informal upper kitchen where they usually ate. Fall did not own the more elegant Delftware or porcelain, yet the common stoneware cups and bowls and wooden trenchers gave the table a cozy, familial touch. She had carefully arranged a bowl of fruit in the center, all of it laid over a fine linen cloth found for a song at the last market day.

Claire entered the room to find Alyce and Jamie already seated. She could hear her father's heavy boots stomping through the kitchen. Tom's face, as he ducked to come through the low doorway, wore a magenta hue customary these days, but his scowl was even harsher than usual.

"What's wrong, Papa?" Claire asked as she took her place at the table.

Tom yanked a ladder-back chair away from the table. "And where is the laird?" he asked sulkily.

"He went down to the wharf to fetch some letters that arrived for him last night. He should be back soon."

"It's his first night home. Are we going to eat without him? It isn't right or proper."

"I don't think he would want us to wait. He told me before he left to go on with our usual routine. Nell will see that something is saved for him."

Tom gave an incomprehensible grunt and threw his body into the chair. "Humph! The old laird would never stand for such as this."

"Papa, your sleeve is torn and you've got a bruise on your cheek. What happened to you today?"

Tom picked up the bowl of peas and began dishing them into his plate. "It's naught. A simple misunderstanding."

"With whom? Not Lace Varn again?"

"Yes, if you must know, with Lace. The most despicable, bull-headed, black-hearted rogue who ever walked on two feet."

Alyce looked up from her trencher and spoke in her gentle voice, "but I thought the Varns moved away from New York?"

261

"They did that. Moved somewhere to the north of the town on the river. But Lace, he comes down here all the time, usually carrying something from his new farm to show off. Today it was a basket of pears. Not such bad ones, either, though I didn't tell him so. Wouldn't give him the satisfaction of thinking I approved of anything that belonged to him."

"Surely you did not get into an argument over a few pears," Claire said, setting her spoon briskly on the table.

"Well, we did, if you must know." In exasperation Tom threw down his knife, his voice rising. "One of those savages, a dirty squaw, took a fancy to them pears and stole two for herself without so much as a by-your-leave. You know Lace. He feels about Algonkian like we used to feel about wild boars. Called her a dirty thief and picked up a rush and started to wale the tar out of her. It made me sick!"

Claire could feel a sickening sense of distress growing deep within. She pushed her plate away. "What did you do, Papa?"

"What any decent man would do in such a situation. I grabbed the switch out of his hand and gave him a few licks of his own with it. Told him too, he has no right to call others thieves after the way he stole my whisky. Nay, I haven't forgotten about that."

"Oh, Papa," Claire cried, laying her elbows on the table and sinking her head in her hands. "I'm proud that you tried to help that poor savage woman but I'd be willing to guess that Lace turned on you when you stepped in."

"Did he fight you, Papa?" Jamie cried, his eyes round with images of what he had missed. "Is that how you got that bruise on your cheek?"

Tom shrugged nonchalantly. "He tried to use the

262

switch on me but it didn't do much good. He's brave enough with a cowering squaw but helpless as a babe around another man. This bruise was just a lucky swipe. The squaw got away though while we were going at each other, and I think that made him madder than anything."

Claire shook her head. "How many times have I asked you to leave those people alone! It only makes for trouble for all of us to antagonize them."

"Don't lecture me, daughter!" Tom yelled. "It will be a warm day in hell when Tom Montcrieff stands by and watches a cur like Lace Varn whip a woman, even if she is a savage. Now stop all these questions and let me eat my dinner in peace. By God, I wish the laird *was* here so I wouldn't have to put up with a parcel of women and boys."

His three children exchanged glances and Claire bit back her own anger. No purpose was served by antagonizing Tom further. The damage, if it was such, was already done and there was nothing she could do about it. She picked up her spoon and bent to her plate in grim silence.

The meal had been cleared away and night had fallen thoroughly by the time Claire heard Fall's steps on the road outside the door. He came straight to the cozy kitchen and sat near the fire opposite Tom to eat his supper, giving her a brief smile. The two men went on talking long afterward and, though Claire strained to hear their conversation, she could make out little of their words from her corner of the room where she plied listlessly at some hackling. Once she thought she caught Alan's name but she could not even be certain of that. She had no chance to speak to Fall before taking up her candleholder and going quietly up the stairs behind Alyce to the room they shared above. She could only wonder whether or not she should attempt to go to his room later and, as she slipped off her outer garments to stand in her chemise, she toyed with the thought of going straight to sleep and letting him wonder why she didn't come.

"It'll serve him right if he lies there wishing I were with him," she thought, pursing her lips grimly. And yet, once under the covers, she found herself wide awake, staring at the curtain over the bedframe, every nerve alive.

It seemed to Claire that the house was never going to become quiet. Long after everyone had gone to bed, she lay next to Alyce, listening for the sounds of her quiet breathing or a step on the creaking floor. She herself was wide awake, filled with dread and anticipation, wondering if she should go to Fall and yet unable not to.

When the soft, raspy breathing of her sister told her she was sound asleep, Claire slipped from the bed and, without bothering with a candle, felt her way to the stairs. Carefully she made her way to the upper kitchen, pausing after each groaning complaint of the floorboards and terrified that her father or Nell would come down and poke a head round the door asking what on earth she was doing wandering about so late at night.

But no one came. The house remained still and drowsing until she found herself standing in front of Fall's door, her hand reaching for the latch.

It was opened softly from the other side before her hand touched the ring. His room was diffused with a soft light and his tall form was silhouetted against it in the doorway.

"I thought I heard your step," he whispered. He pulled the door open and she slipped inside. From the hearth a pile of banked embers glowed hotly. The only other light came from a rush lamp across the room, throwing shadows everywhere.

"Thank God, you came," Fall breathed and his arms went around her. He was wearing his shirt, open at the neck, breeches, and slippers. It was the first time Claire had had the leisure to appreciate his body unswathed in the layers of clothes which were the common form of dress, and something inside her grew warm and delicious at the feel of his body against her thin nightdress.

"I wasn't sure you wanted me to come," she whispered back, her lips on his neck. "You returned so late . . ."

"I know. And there was no time to speak to you alone afterward. If you hadn't come, I think I would have gone upstairs and got into *your* bed."

Claire giggled softly. "That would have been quite a shock for Alyce."

Fall's hands roamed over her back. "I want you so I don't think I'd even care. God, but you feel so good, smell so good, taste so good . . ."

She clasped her arms around his lithe, firm body, reveling in the feel of his hands on her back, her arms, her shoulders. He slid his lips over her face, lightly, invitingly, searching out the soft crevices and swells. It was the first time that he had gone so slowly. Twice before they had both been in such a fever of longing that nothing else mattered. Now it was a luxury to take time to simply enjoy the sensation of touching, kissing, fondling.

Easily he reached up and slipped off her nightcap, allowing her long golden hair to spill around her shoulders and down her back. Grasping handfuls of its strands, he found her lips, tasting them gently.

265

Gradually Claire allowed her own fingers to wander over his body, his broad shoulders, the swell of his chest showing tantalizing tufts of dark hair that disappeared beneath the open collar of his shirt.

Fall worked the neck of her nightrobe over her shoulders and let it fall around her ankles. He stood back, drinking in the lines of her body bathed in the mellow light of the hearth.

"You're more beautiful than I remembered," he cried, and, lifting her up in his arms, he laid her across the high feather mattress. She lay there watching as he pulled off his shirt, yanked at his wide leather belt, and slid out of his breeches. She could not take her eyes off him as he knelt on the bed and bent over her. She was fascinated by his body, the long thin spread of dark hair that covered his chest, thinning to a line down his stomach and below it fanned out again above his stiff, protruding maleness. She felt that he too was beautiful. His broad shoulders, tapering waist, narrow hips, muscular thighs, and that glorious, protrudence that she longed to take deep inside, filling her with its length.

She sighed as he slipped an arm beneath her and bent to clasp her hard, erect nipple between his lips, sucking at its sweetness, lapping it with his tongue. She closed her eyes and forgot everything except this swelling sensation, a body that was all feeling and wonder. He fondled her as a musician plays a choice instrument, bringing her to a wildness with his hands and his tongue, sliding his fingers up the silken inner flesh of her thighs to fondle her most secret places, driving her to ecstasy with his skilled fingertips.

Claire groaned and writhed under him. Rolling her over on her back, Fall forced his way into the moist, throbbing essence of her, driving and thrusting again

266

and again until they were both unconscious of anything else on earth beyond their mutual desire and fullfilment.

When it was over, he fell against her, both of them breathing heavily. Claire clasped her arms around him and moved so as to take his head against her breast, stroking his hair away from his damp forehead. She had never been so happy.

For a long time they lay quietly against each other, resting and content. Later, when desire awoke again, he taught her new delights. Very slowly and deliciously, she learned to stride over him, taking him deep within her as she leaned over him, the nipple of one dangling full breast caught between his lips. She found that there were special little things he enjoyed, like the feel of his erect manhood lightly rubbing her nipples or caught between the fullness of her breasts. They never tired of exploring each other's contours, the hills and valleys of two healthy bodies, each so different and each so satisfying. It was almost instinctive for her to let her lips wander casually down his chest and stomach, tasting his thighs until she took the pulsating end of his maleness into her mouth, sending him into his own realms of ecstasy. By the time she slipped away to her room she had lost count of the times they had scaled that heavenly barrier together. She felt completely a part of him, very tired and very, very happy.

She slept later the next morning than usual and came down hoping that her delight and satiation were not too obvious to Nell and Alyce. Neither woman made any comment and soon Claire was absorbed in the tasks of the day, dreaming to herself about the previous night when she had a moment alone.

She was in the barn behind the house when she saw

Fall leave. He spotted her from a distance and waved in what others might see as no more than a friendly manner. She tried to return the wave in the same offhand way, but she was grateful that there was no one around to see the glow that she felt was written on her face.

It was later that afternoon that she finally had an opportunity to slip into Fall's room on the pretext of straightening it. Katrina had been there before her and the bed was neatly made, the clothes hanging from the pegs or put away in the press. Claire lingered, stroking her hand across the quilted covers of the places where she had known such delight, picking up a clay pipe with a broken end that still smelled of tobacco and of Fall, holding his cloak to her face to try to evoke his presence. After fifteen minutes of this she found she was only dissatisfied wanting him so much and turned to leave.

The box on the table near the window was open. In it a letter was spread, thrown casually there without folding. Claire had no intention of looking at it, much less of reading it, but the signature caught her eye and she was riveted to the spot. Her common sense told her not to look closer but it was impossible to walk away. She reached out, took up the letter, and spread it on the table.

"Father is dead . . ."

The laird? Morgan MacDairmid? But they had heard nothing.

"Father is dead. But before he died he told me everything. It is as much your doing as mine that old Tom left Scotland but, since you are there too, I suppose in your usual venal way, you are doing everything you can to take advantage of the situation. Well, dear brother, don't imagine for a moment that I am going to allow you to get away with it."

It was signed, "Edgar." Claire's hand began to tremble and the thick paper fell to the floor. That signature alone evoked all the dread memories, the fear, the powerlessness, poverty, and rage. She wanted to rush from the room and pretend she had never seen the letter. Instead she forced herself to pick it up again and read it carefully.

What did it mean? Her beautiful dream, sustained for nearly a whole day, came crashing down around her. She should have known Fall MacDairmid would do nothing out of a generous nature, nothing without wanting something from it for himself. "It was as much your doing as mine" — There it was, proof that he had been involved with Edgar in driving them from Scotland and cheating them of their home. "Father told me everything" — what did that mean? She had no idea but it wasn't necessary that she should. It was enough to know that whatever Fall did or said, he always had some ulterior motive behind it. All the soft, gentle love-making and kind words were false. He had pursued her for a reason — brought them here for some self-serving purpose. She did not need to know what it was — that would no doubt come in time. For now it was enough to be aware of what he was really doing.

Throwing the letter into the box, she slammed down the lid and fled from the room.

It was an hour later that she heard the soldiers. The sound of their deep voices, full of authority, contrasted with Katrina's high-pitched frightened responses, and it drew Claire to the foreroom as much from curiosity as anxiety. She had seen men such as

269

these wandering the streets of the town many times but here in the low-ceilinged room they seemed immense, filling it with their high helmets and thrusting metal breastplates. Claire paused in the doorway.

"What is it, Katrina?"

"Oh, mistress," the girl cried, cringing close to Claire. "These soldiers would be wanting Mister Montcrieff and they don't believe me that I don't have an idea of where he is."

"What do you want with my father, gentlemen?" Claire said, stepping up to the draw table with an assurance she was far from feeling.

"Would you be the mistress of this house?" The tallest one was obviously the officer in charge. His gaze as he looked Claire over remained stern yet revealed his interest.

"This house belongs to the MacDairmid of Ben Brogain. But we are his — his guests. Tom Montcrieff is my father."

"Fall MacDairmid?" the captain answered.

"That is correct."

The captain glanced at his two comrades. It was obvious to Claire that he had not known this was Fall's house.

"Well, we have no business with Master MacDairmid. It's Tom Montcrieff we're seeking and, if you know where he is, you had best fetch him round."

"Why?" Claire asked as Katrina threw up her hands and began to whimper.

"Oh, miss, miss. Something terrible . . ."

Claire fought to keep her mounting anxiety under control. "Why do you want my father?"

The captain had the grace to look embarrassed. "It's something he's done. Something very serious."

"You must be mistaken —"

"We can't mistake murder, mistress. And that's what your father is wanted to answer for. Now fetch him at once if you please."

Claire braced herself on the edge of the table. "Murder! I don't believe it."

"You had better, mistress. We've a dead body lying now on the beach near the market as cold as the grave, and Tom Montcrieff was the last person to be seen near him. And threatening him, at that."

"What dead body? Who?"

She knew the answer before the captain spoke the dreaded words. Lace Varn! A knife straight through the heart just as clean as you please. Slowly Claire groped for the chair near her and lowered herself into it.

"I see that you bear no surprise that your father would be accused," the captain said with some satisfaction. "Now if you would please—"

"My father is not here. I don't know where he is. He often frequents ale houses and taverns during the day. But he would never murder anyone. Not even Lace Varn. You must be mistaken."

The captain hitched up his sword belt and turned to go, his boots clattering on the wooden plank floor. "That's for the magistrate to say, mistress. We only bring him in. Jacob, you stay here to watch the house in case Tom Montcrieff returns. Vandenburg, you come with me. We'll start making the rounds of the taverns."

They were halfway out the door before Claire realized they were leaving. "Wait!" she cried, rushing after the captain. "You must have made a wrong identification. The Varns don't even live in this town any more. They moved away, somewhere to the north."

271

"That may be but Mister Varn was certainly here last night. He was seen drinking with your father, after which the two of them got into some kind of argument and Tom made threats against him. Furthermore, he went so far as to thrash the deceased with a rush switch. We have witnesses who saw and heard it all."

"But my father told me about that. Varn was abusing an Indian squaw. My father was only trying to protect her."

"Protect an Indian! Come, miss. You'd better work up a better story than that. Anyway, it's not my concern. I've only to bring him in. Now, if you'll excuse me, I'll be about my work."

With that he stamped off, one of the soldiers in his wake, the other taking a desultory stance beside the door. Claire glared at him, then rushed inside to where her shawl was hung on a peg near the kitchen. She ran straight into Nell. For once the widow had few words.

"I heard everything, Claire. Oh, my dear girl. It can't be true—"

"Of course it's not true! I don't even believe Lace Varn is really dead."

"Where are you going? You can't go out now. Suppose your pa comes home."

Claire swirled the shawl around her shoulders. "Then he'll be taken off by that soldier at the door. I want to see this corpse for myself."

"But Claire . . ." Nell ran after her as she darted to the door. Claire paused on the threshold. "Try to keep this from Alyce as long as you can, Nell. I'll explain to her when I get back."

"Claire, you're crazy to go down there . . ."

Claire soon lost the sound of Nell's voice as she ran

down the road to Broad Way and turned up it toward the harbor. Her breath began to tear at her throat and to save her energy she slowed enough to breathe a little easier. There were many people on the streets, and several of them looked up with curiosity at the girl hurrying past. Claire thought she could already see accusations in their eyes, as though they all knew who she was and where she was headed.

A small crowd was clustered on the beach. Working her way to the center she saw the object of their attention lying on the shell-littered sand. Someone had put together a hastily nailed raw pine coffin and Lace Varn lay enclosed, stiff and crowded, his arms pressed by the boards against his narrow torso. His face wore, even in death, the bad-tempered scowl so common in life, now made even more grotesque by the large copper coins over the eyes and the cloth handkerchief under the chin, pulled up and tied neatly in a knot at the top of his head.

Claire stood transfixed, horrified yet unable to turn away. She could not be sorry this man who had done her family so much harm was dead, and yet she felt that even in death his long, malevolent arm reached out to bring ruin on those she loved. She shuddered and turned aside. Dead he may be, but she knew with an unfailing certainty that her father had not done this deed. But who then? And how was she ever going to prove her father's innocence?

"They really ought to remove this body from the hot sun," a woman's voice behind her spoke petulantly. Moving through the crowd Claire noticed several members of the gentry standing at the edge, resplendent in their fashionable clothes and feathered hats. As Claire passed them, she recognized the woman who had given Alyce money — a striking figure, tall and proud and wearing a beautiful fur-trimmed samare. She remembered that haughty demeanor as the woman had forced a charitable dole on Alyce that morning in the marketplace. The two men hovering around her echoed her comment, noting how the flies had already evidenced an interest in the corpse, while a third man disengaged himself from the group and came hurrying toward Claire. With some surprise she saw that it was Fall MacDairmid and her relief to see him here for a moment almost made her forget the letter she had seen earlier.

"What are you doing down here?" he asked, laying a hand on her elbow and smiling down at her.

She carefully moved her arm away. "Lace Varn has been killed and they think my father is responsible." She felt tears smarting in her eyes in spite of all she could do to hold them back.

Fall glanced over at the obscene coffin on the beach. "Is that who lies there? 'Sblood. Though I cannot be too surprised. He was a cantankerous fellow who was always asking for someone to turn on him."

"But Papa wouldn't do a thing like this. I just know he wouldn't. It was terrible, Fall. Soldiers came to the house to carry him off to gaol. He wasn't there at the time but they'll find him and when they do—"

"Fall!" the woman's imperious voice came wafting over to them. Claire was facing her and could see how she kept an eye on the two of them as though she was waiting impatiently for Fall to return to her side. "We'll be late for the governor's reception if we don't hurry," she went on in a voice that everyone around them could plainly hear.

Fall barely nodded an answer. He was still studying Claire's face.

"Come along, MacDairmid," one of the men joined in and, to Claire's dismay, began ushering the entire group toward where they stood.

"Who is that woman?" she heard herself say in a voice that betrayed her annoyance. It would be better not to care.

"That is Immetje Strycker, the wealthiest widow in the province," Fall whispered back in a preoccupied way. His preoccupation suggested his mind was more on Claire's problems than the widow's demands.

"She appears to be a lady who likes to keep her attendants dangling. Perhaps you had better hurry back to her."

A faint smile touched Fall's lips. "You've taken her measure very quickly. It's true, she does not like to be kept waiting."

The sudden surge of anger Claire felt almost brought her tears spilling over. "Then you must certainly go at once," she snapped as the woman drew abreast. Immetje eyed her, she thought, with more interest than the occasion warranted.

Carefully arranging the delicate sleeve of her samare, Immetje spoke to Fall as though she already owned him. "My dear, we mustn't keep the governor waiting." She laid her gloved hand on his arm. "He's a very particular man as you know. And I have a reputation for punctuality to uphold as well. I've spent years cultivating it and would hate to see it tarnished at this late date."

"A moment, madame," Fall muttered, obviously annoyed by the widow's pointed attention. "This is a family matter requiring my immediate attention."

"Oh," Immetje said with feigned delight. "And is this sweet creature one of your family?" she asked as she extended a gracious finger to tip Claire's chin

275

upward. "A sister perhaps? Or a cousin?"

"No," Fall said grimly. "Madame Strycker, may I present Claire Montcrieff. Claire's family are from Ben Brogain, my ancestral home in Scotland. They are currently living with me here in the city."

Claire noted how one sleek eyebrow inched upward on Immetje's smooth brow. "Living in your house? How very kind of you. I do hope the young lady is properly chaperoned however. One must consider those things, you know."

"Both her father and her sister live there, too," Fall answered, in a voice that suggested it was none of her business.

"Oh, well. Were it not for that I might almost envy the sweet creature." Her voice was full of meaning that was not lost on any of the company present.

Though she knew she should make some kind of polite response to Fall's introduction, the latent hostility and patronizing tone of Immetje's remarks were too much for Claire to bear—especially now when her mind was burdened with fears for her father. The widow Strycker was a woman who was so sure of herself and her power that Claire might as well have been a worm under her delicately fashioned kid shoes. And her possessive attitude toward Fall infuriated Claire even when she told herself that he was not worth bothering with. And besides, she hated him.

"Why don't you go on ahead?" Fall said pleasantly. "This is a matter of some importance I need to discuss with Mistress Montcrieff. I'll catch up with you shortly."

"Oh. Well, of course, we mustn't intrude on family business," Immetje quipped, smiling at the other gentlemen who waited at her elbow. "On the other hand, I should so like to have you arrive with us.

276

There are so many people I long to have you meet. Important people. Why don't we just wander a bit ahead and wait for you there? Come along, gentlemen, let us give them their privacy. So nice to meet you, my dear."

With her entourage in tow Immetje went smoothly off, her laughter at some quip from the fellow on her arm floating back to where Claire stood glaring after her.

"Where did you make her acquaintance?" she asked, unable to keep her irritation from her voice.

"Adolph Philipse introduced us. He has some idea that she might be so taken with my charms as to make my fortune by marrying me."

"He may be right. She seems to have already added you to her servile retinue."

Her snappish comment brought his own irritation to the surface. "If you knew me better, my girl, you'd know that that is probably the least successful way to win my interest. Besides, I am already captivated with someone's charms." Reaching out, he touched her cheek lightly. "A lass with golden hair and eyes blue as cornflowers and—"

Claire turned her face away. "Stop! This is not the time for blandishments. What am I going to do to help my father?"

The widow and her courtiers had paused a few feet ahead and were busily engaged in studying the contents of a silversmith's shop window. Observing them, Fall took Claire's arm and led her in the opposite direction.

"Don't worry," he said quietly. "I'll see what I can do about it. If he's innocent—"

"Of course he is innocent!"

"Then we will find a way to prove it. Don't make

the mistake of trying to hide him away or warn him off. This town is too small and it will only make him appear guilty. Let them take him to gaol. I'll find a way to get him free."

"But suppose they don't wait for a trial? Suppose they —"

"Don't start wearing the mourning broach yet, Claire. Let me look into the situation."

Claire's hands were knotted in her nervousness. "Caleb told me once that when New York was a Dutch town there was a gibbet right here on the beach that was never used. Not even once. Its purpose was to frighten and warn people not to commit crimes."

Fall gave a bitter laugh. "Don't expect such generosity from the English. Two years ago they executed their own governor for treason. They called it a rebellion of course, but two men lost their heads nonetheless."

At the horror in her eyes he realized his mistake and put a comforting arm around her shoulder. "Now don't take on so. I only say this so that you don't raise false hopes. Our best procedure is to discover who actually did murder Lace Varn and prove that Tom is innocent. Go home now, Claire, and wait for me. Can you get there all right?"

"I don't want to go home. I'm going to look for Papa. I want to be with him when he hears this."

"And what about Alyce and Jamie? They need you now. Tom can take care of himself. Go home and trust me to handle everything."

She glared up at him. "Why should I trust you!"

The genuine confusion in his face threw her off guard. "What is wrong with you? After last night . . ."

"Last night does not matter now!" Claire said,

278

pulling away from him and yanking her shawl across her breast. "Go back to your wealthy friends. I'm going to find Papa."

She darted away and was quickly lost in the traffic on the streets. Fall stood looking after her. "Headstrong. Stubborn. Butt-headed idiot!" he said under his breath.

Behind him Immetje had missed nothing—not his arm around Claire's shoulder, the concentration of their two heads so close together, nor Claire's abrupt pulling away. She was conscious of the fact that her customary mask of detached civility had been allowed to slip, revealing her extreme displeasure at what she had witnessed. But, as Fall turned to join them, she hastily put it back in place. By the time he had arrived at her side she was smiling and gracious, seemingly grateful for the pleasure of his company.

Thirteen

In spite of Claire's intention to find her father, a cursory look at two of the local grog shops convinced her that it would be wiser to follow Fall's advice and go home. When she finally reached the house on Fair Street, she found Caleb in the kitchen trying to console a hysterical Alyce. By this time Claire was almost too worried about Tom and too full of tumultuous emotions over the scene with Fall and the Widow Strycker to be overly solicitous of her frightened sister. Besides, Caleb and Nell between them were doing a good job of handling things. Alyce was receiving the kind of warm support from these two good friends that she herself had hoped for from Fall.

But Caleb turned out to be helpful to her as well. He had just arrived at the house behind Tom, followed almost on his heels by a small contingent of troopers that the watching guard had hastily summoned. After Tom had been hustled off, Caleb had slipped along behind them and seen that he was safely in gaol. He had even spoken to Tom long enough to learn the charges. He was as convinced as Claire that Tom Montcrieff could never have put a knife through

Lace Varn's heart.

"But proving it will be something else," he said without a trace of his usual good humor. "The captain of the guard seemed to feel that your father had both a good reason and the opportunity to kill Varn, and from what he says there are a number of witnesses who agree. It's going to take more than our belief in your father's innocence and in his good name to change their minds."

Claire was already reaching again for her cloak. "I'm going to him," she declared. "I'm sure he is feeling frightened and alone and God knows what the conditions are at that prison."

"Then I'm coming with you."

Alyce had been watching them both as they spoke and now she jumped up, reaching for Claire's arm. "Oh, please, Claire, let me come too. I want so much to comfort Papa and let him know how much we love him and believe in him."

Claire shook her head as she pulled the ties on her cloak together. "I fear you would be small comfort to him with that tear-swollen face. No, Alyce. Stay here and help Jamie when he comes in. I'll see where Papa is and tomorrow, first thing, I promise I'll take you there."

Though Alyce wanted to beg further, Claire cut her short by darting out the kitchen door. A few moments later she and Caleb were hurrying down Broad Way toward the tiny stone building that served as the town gaol. Claire had barely noticed it before, but now, at the thought of her father inside alone and forlorn, in her mind it took on a forbidding aspect that implied condemnation, punishment, and even death. Back in Scotland a man could be hanged for stealing a loaf of bread. How much more severe would the punishment be for murder? And even though New York was in every way more prosperous and more relaxed than home, still what kind of government could afford to allow murder to go unpunished? Her anxiety grew with every step, and she pushed ahead leaving Caleb struggling to catch up.

The busy road was a melange of wagons and carts, some pulled by dispirited mules or broad farm hacks, others pushed by men from nearby farms. Gentlemen on elegant horses weaved among them and an occasional carriage with fancy gilded sides scattered the less significant vehicles. As Claire started across the street, she had to dodge her way among them, losing Caleb in the process. As she neared the opposite side, her way was blocked by a large farm wagon, which had pulled up to wait for the passage of a group of children. She intended to go around it, but, just as she started toward the rear, one of the children carelessly threw a stone at the horse standing in its traces. The animal shied nervously, neighing and backing, and forced the wagon into Claire. Rushing out of its way toward the walkway, she careened into an old woman carrying a basket of cabbages. Both Claire and the woman fell sprawling in the dust while the cabbages rolled in every direction.

"Oh, I'm so sorry," Claire cried, scrambling to her knees and trying to retrieve the vegetables which rolled like ninepins in the dirt.

"Why don't you watch where you're going!" the old woman cried. "My poor cabbages. And they was all washed. Now look at them! Who's going to want to buy damaged goods like these?"

"I'll help you," Claire tried to say but the woman went on carping at her while they both scrambled around picking up the cabbages. She was only dimly aware that the driver of the wagon had steadied the horse and climbed down, offering to help.

"It'll all be made right in a moment," he said soothingly. " 'Twas just an accident after all."

Something in his voice stilled Claire's hand and stirred a deep almost-forgotten memory within her. She look up quickly. He was kneeling not a foot away and he looked up at her at the same moment, their eyes widening in mutual surprise.

Alan Morehead!

For a stunned moment neither of them spoke. "It was Alan who found his voice first. "My God," he breathed. "Claire, is it really you?"

"Alan? Oh, dear. Alan!"

Gripping her hands, he pulled her to her feet, forgetting the complaining old woman and her cabbages. In her numbed mind Claire took in that he was heavier than she had remembered, the square jaw more finely hewn, the face fuller. His shirt was open at the throat, his homespun jerkin close fitting and neat. He wore his hair longer than he used to and it was pulled severely back and tied at the neck with some kind of thong.

"Claire! I can't believe it. How did you get here in New York? When?"

Over his shoulder Claire glimpsed the outraged countenance of the old woman, who was angry that they had deserted her.

"I'll explain everything," she said, pulling her hands away. Kneeling quickly she picked up the last of the cabbages.

"Here, let me do that," Alan said. In only a few moments he had refilled the basket and handed it to the irritated owner, apologizing politely for the inconvenience they had caused her. Then he hustled Claire to his wagon.

"Where are you going? I'll take you there, wherever it is."

Claire fought to keep her thundering heart under control. "To the gaol. Papa is here, temporarily."

"Your father is in New York too?" Deftly Alan handed her up next to the driver's perch. He moved around to the other side while Claire called Caleb over and told him to go ahead, that she would meet him at the gaol. By the time the wagon rolled off, she was turning over in her mind frantically what she should say and how much she should tell this near stranger beside her of the events of the past few months.

But Alan did not give her much opportunity to say anything. His amazement and surprise was slowly becoming replaced with delight and satisfaction, and he expressed both with a loquaciousness Claire had forgotten he possessed.

"What a fortunate surprise to run into you like this," he said as he guided his skittish horse deftly down the crowded thoroughfare. "It must be providential. I want to hear everything. How did you manage to come this far from Ben Brogain? I didn't have an idea you had left Scotland, much less that you were in New York."

"How could I write to tell you?" Claire said testily. "I didn't know where you were."

"But I told you I was moving to the Upper Mills in my last letter."

"I haven't received a letter from you in nearly a year."

"That cannot be. I must have written at least four since last twelvemonth. They couldn't have all been lost. Well, no matter. You are here with me now and that is all that counts. I had thought to wait another year or two until I got my farm making a good profit before sending for you. But since you've already come, we might as well go ahead and get married now. If truth were told, I've been feeling the need of a wife for a long time now."

He gave her a long, suggestive sideways glance, and Claire felt her cheeks grow warm. She looked quickly away, hoping her embarrassment masqueraded as shyness.

"I thought perhaps you had married someone else," she said softly.

"When I was promised to you? I would never do that. No, I've worked hard to get a place ready for you, Claire. It's only a tenant farm of forty acres and it's not my own. But the soil is rich and already I've put a little away. I have a sturdy house and good crops of rye and barley and buckwheat. And in a few years I ought to have enough to buy my own place."

He swung the wagon off Broad Way into Bridge Street where the pedestrians and carriages were much less thick. Claire could feel a sudden, choking panic swelling in her breast.

"Alan," she cried, "listen to me. You don't understand what has happened. Your Uncle Varn came over on the same ship with us and—"

"Why, Aunt Esther never mentioned you were aboard the *Selkirk*."

It was Claire's turn to stop and stare. "You've seen your Aunt Esther?"

"Of course. They are living with me up on the North River. They came over to join me, in fact. But they never spoke of you or old Tom being along."

Claire was all at once aware that her hands were gripping the seat, her knuckles white. "No, they wouldn't," she said bitterly. "But now your uncle has had—a terrible thing—"

"I know." He snapped the reins against the broad rump of his horse. "That's why I came to the city. I'm here to bury him. My aunt and Cousin Daniel are

285

staying at the White Hart near the wall. I came in to identify the body and carry it back. I never expected to see you."

Claire twisted her hands in her lap. "Listen to me, Alan. You're going to have to know sometime. Your uncle was killed by someone, and they are saying it was my father who did it."

"Old Tom! That's ridiculous!"

"They quarreled on the ship and again yesterday, just before Lace was murdered. People heard them and will swear that Papa made threats against your uncle. He could even hang!"

Her voice broke on a sob. For a moment she thought Alan was going to lose his hold on the reins and reach for her, but he caught himself and merely squeezed her hand.

"Tom Montcrieff could never stab anyone to death. I don't know who is responsible for Uncle Varn's death but I do know it could not have been your father. Don't worry, Claire. Everything will work out."

"That's what everyone tells me," she cried. "I only wish I could be so optimistic. Anyway, I must see Papa and talk to him. I must find out what really happened last night."

"Look. I have to go the end of Pearl Street to claim Uncle Varn's body and carry it to the cemetery. Where are you staying? I'll come by later."

"No! That is, I wish you wouldn't. It's all so awkward until we get this straightened out."

"But, Claire, I must see you again. Now that you're here, I don't want to let you slip away."

"Your Aunt Esther will object. She didn't even tell you about us being here and she has never liked me. Now—"

"I intend to speak to her about that," Alan said

grimly. Pulling on the reins he guided the horse to the side of the road opposite the yellow stone gaol house. Claire gathered up her cloak to climb down but he gripped her arm. "I won't let you go until you tell me where to find you again. It has been too long already."

"Very well. We're staying at a house on Fair Street. We're watching it for the owner who is often away."

"How can I tell which one it is? Who is the owner?"

"It's the only one made of red brick instead of yellow," she cried, pulling her arm out of his grasp and swinging down off the seat. "Thank you, Alan, for bringing me here."

He stretched across the seat to reach for her hand. Reluctantly she laid her fingers in his large paw of a hand. Gazing down into her face, he squeezed her fingers until the pain made her wince.

"Claire, it is just so wonderful to see you again. To have you here with me."

Claire tried to smile but it was a poor, wan effort. She only hoped he would lay her lack of enthusiasm to worry over her father.

"Good-bye, Alan."

"Until we next meet."

She nodded and he released her to grasp the reins and snap them on his horse's back. With a lurch the wagon rolled on down the road, sending up a cloud of yellow dust. Claire never looked after it, but, pulling her cloak tightly around her, hurried across the street and up the low steps of the gaol house, more confused than ever.

The gaol was a shabby affair, constructed to allow as little light as possible and acquiring somehow a

287

forbidding atmosphere that reminded Claire of Dante's inscription over the doorway of Hell: "All hope abandon, ye who enter here." And yet she must not let her father think that hope was beyond them. She was determined to appear cheerful and even nonchalant, a conviction that carried her only as far as the gloomy, cramped cell where he stood near a barred window. Claire took one look at his thin, discouraged profile and burst into tears.

"My girl, don't cry," Tom said, hurrying to meet her as the gaoler opened the door for Claire to enter.

"I'm sorry, Papa," she said, wiping her eyes. "I wouldn't allow Alyce to come with me for fear she'd be weepy and here I am, worse than she could ever be."

"Our Alyce has more strength than you give her credit for."

Tom put his arms around his daughter and held her close for a moment. There was nothing to sit on in the cell other than a pile of straw and a thin blanket in one corner so they stood, clinging to each other. When Claire was able to bring her crying under control, she wiped at her eyes with her sleeve and stood back.

"And how is Jamie?" Tom asked. "Keeping brave above all this, I hope?"

"Yes," Claire answered. "I think at first he was fearful that all this trouble might prevent him from starting his apprenticeship with Mr. Johansen next week. But he's assured us it won't make any difference. He's even offered to allow Jamie to attend school with his own children."

"I'm glad of that." Tom rubbed his eyes in a gesture that spoke more of his anxiety than he wanted to show.

"Papa, you must tell me what happened last night.

Why do they think you killed Lace? Surely you were home in bed when he was killed, weren't you?"

Abruptly Tom turned away, throwing himself down on the straw, his knees drawn up and his elbows resting on them.

"I'm sorry to say, Claire, that I did leave the house last night after you had gone to bed. Oh, I tried to lie down and sleep like all the rest of you, but sleep simply wouldn't come. Finally I rose and pulled on my boots and slipped quietly out so as not to wake anyone."

Claire had a bad moment as the image of her father meeting her on the back stairs flashed across her mind.

"But where did you go?"

"Back to the Dove, of course. I had a bit more to drink—"

"Only a bit?"

"Well, a lot then. So much that I cannot for the life of me remember getting home at all. I woke in my bed this morning but I don't know how I got there."

"Oh, Papa!"

"I don't recall seeing Varn again either. I remember the thrashing I gave him earlier but, as to whether or not he was around later, well, I just don't know. There are those who say they saw me with him, so I suppose, I must have been."

Claire moved to the window as much to lean against the wall as to stare out at the weed-choked yard behind the building. At the far end some children were playing with sticks and a leather ball, laughing and shouting as they ran back and forth. Their voices sounded so normal, so ordinary in contrast to the gloom of the gaol that her tears almost started afresh.

Tom laid his head on his hands in a gesture that

bespoke his hopelessness and spoke softly. "Daughter, do you suppose I really did put a knife in Varn's scrawny chest? I've wanted to often enough, but would I have done such a thing and not even recall it?"

"No!" Claire knelt beside her father and lightly stroked his bowed head. "Don't think that way, Papa! You would never do such a despicable thing, no matter how provoked you were or now much ale you had consumed. There has to be another answer and we'll find it. Believe that we will."

He shook his head. His eyes as he looked up at her still bore the bleary grayness of his heavy drinking of the night before. And there was something more there, Claire thought. Something weary and discouraged and resigned. She gripped his shoulders.

"We are going to get you out of this, Papa. It's not just me who says that. Fall will help and Caleb and even Alan Morehead."

Tom's head shot up. "Alan? You've seen him?"

"Yes. On the way here I accidentally came across him on the street. He did not even know we were in New York."

"But Lace Varn was his uncle."

"That's true. Yet he doesn't believe for a moment that you could have killed him. He told me to tell you that."

"I'm not so sure that I want help from any of the Varns."

"Well, I'm not so proud. I'll take any help we can get, no matter what the source."

"Alan Morehead," Tom muttered, rubbing a finger along his chin. "Perhaps it's providential. He at least will take care of you and the children if . . ."

"Papa, don't say that! You are going to get out of this, I promise. Now, in the meantime, what do you need? Food? More blankets? Does the gaoler have to be bribed?"

"A little money always helps if you can lay your hand on a few coins. And a thicker quilt. These stones . . ."

"You shall have two just as quickly as I can get them here," she cried, throwing her arms around Tom and hugging him close. He patted her back gently, trying to reassure her though he himself had none of her resolution.

"The MacDairmid will come up with something. He's a good man for all his wild ways. We'll try to trust in him."

Claire fought to keep back her tears even while her common sense told her this was the worst time for weeping. She could hear the thump of the gaoler's boots approaching from outside, keeping time to the clink of his heavy keys at his belt.

"I have to go for now but I'll be back tomorrow. I'll ask Caleb to bring you the things you need for tonight. Alyce wants to visit you too. Will that be all right?"

"Yes. Let her come. She's a good lass and she worries. It will be a comfort to her just to see that I'm alive and well."

With a sharp metallic thrust, the key turned in the lock and the door opened on the gaoler, a thick Dutchman with a severe but not unkindly face.

"Come along, miss," he said brusquely. Claire kissed her father.

"I'll see you tomorrow. And don't forget. You are innocent and we are going to prove it."

Tom nodded without answering. She left the building more distracted than she had ever expected to be. Was it possible that her father had actually killed Varn and then blacked out? Lace had a way of taunting people beyond their capacity to bear. He was cowardly that way. Had he picked a second quarrel with Tom when he saw how drunk he was, hoping perhaps to have him arrested? And had the plan backfired when Tom drove a knife between his ribs?

No, she shuddered. It wasn't possible. Still, there was the damaging fact that Tom could remember nothing of what had happened and there were others who had seen them together.

And the worst thought: Was it possible that she and Fall had been lost in the passion of those entwined bodies on his bed at the same time her father was killing a man in a drunken rage?

She stood on the steps waiting for her panic to subside. Across the road she saw Caleb sitting on a barrel waiting for her. Hurrying across the road she went to meet him.

That evening Claire took special pains to avoid meeting Fall. She asked Nell to set aside his supper since he was late in arriving, then went to her room, and kept there until it was time for bed. When Alyce came up later, she pretended to be asleep, but in fact she spent a restless night hovering between restless dozing and anxious insomnia.

The next morning she was down early and kept busy with chores she ordinarily left to Katrina and Caleb. Near eleven she was in the lower kitchen when she heard Fall upstairs asking Nell about her. Throwing down the rushes she was trimming, she made a dash for the small stone cellar off the kitchen which was used as a buttery. She could plainly hear his boots on the stairs as she closed the door.

She began absently turning cheeses and calculating that with any luck he would go searching for her outside.

But Fall had heard the soft clink of the buttery latch. He threw open the door and marched into the room just as Claire made a dash for the outside door. He confronted her before she could dash outside, standing with his hands on his hips and looking her over.

"Where were you last night? I waited for you the whole night."

"I fell asleep," she commented lightly and went back to turning the cheeses.

"Without a word to me? I looked for you when I came in, expecting you would bring me my supper. Why didn't you wait up for me?"

"I was tired."

He took two sudden steps toward her, pulling her hands away. "Let those damned cheese be, Claire. I wanted you, longed for you." Tipping her chin, he kissed her, hard and bruisingly. His hand cupped her breast, gently squeezing.

"Why didn't you send for the widow?" she said and instantly regretted it. He laughed as though her jealousy amused him.

"Is that what's bothering you? I don't want the widow. She can have any young buck she crooks her finger at. I want you." He tried to pull her into his arms but she pushed him away.

"Stop it, Fall! I cannot think about such things now. I saw my father last night —"

"I saw him yesterday too. He is all right for the moment. There is nothing that can be done for him until after the hearing. I have the governor's word that he will be safe until then."

"You saw the governor? You asked him about Papa?"

"I told you I would, didn't I? Come, sit here beside

293

me, Claire, and I'll tell you everything he said."

"No! I don't want to get that close to you. It always leads to more."

His sudden anger was like a door slamming between them. Taking a step back he said with some bitterness, "I rather had the impression you enjoyed it."

"Perhaps I did. But now there are more important things to think about. Much more important."

"What's the matter with you, Claire? One moment you're hot to take me, the next you're cold as a winter herring. It's damned confusing."

Claire glared at him, longing to say that her behavior was not half so confusing as his brother's letter. Or as damning.

"I've seen Alan Morehead," she said instead. That took him by surprise.

"Where?"

"Here in town. He came in to collect Lace's body for burial. He had no idea I was here. We were both astounded, to say the least."

"But he can't mean to marry you still. He didn't send for you or prepare—"

"He mentioned it nonetheless."

"I see." Fall folded his arms across his chest, appraising her with cold eyes. "And, of course, that means I am no longer quite so desirable as before."

"*You* don't intend to marry me. Especially not now, with a rich widow just waiting for you to crook your finger."

Furious, Fall reached out and dug his fingers into her arm. "You stubborn, blind little fool. I never met a more maddening, irritating woman. I don't know why I bother with you at all. I ought to turn you and all your family out into the street. Maybe then I'd get a little peace."

"Go ahead. Do it. You owe us nothing and for certain we owe you nothing."

Fall controlled his anger with an effort. "All of you need a home and you shall have one as long as I am able to give it to you. And I'll do what I can for old Tom, even if he probably deserves to hang."

"Oh!" In a frenzy of anger Claire pummeled him with her fists. "Damn you for saying that. You know he didn't kill Lace Varn!"

He caught her hand in an iron grip. "I don't know it and neither do you. But I'll try to get him off. Then you can go into the sunset with your stodgy Alan Morehead and the whole Montcrieff clan be damned!"

Turning on his heel, Fall stalked through the door, slamming it after him. Sinking to the plank bench that stood against the stone wall, Claire twisted her hands in frustration.

"And be damned to the MacDairmids too," she muttered and burst into tears.

During the next two days Claire barely saw Fall. He was gone from the house most of that time and, when he did come in, it was to change clothes or eat a quick bite of food. He gave her a few hard glares and one monosyllabic grudging comment and nothing more. She noticed that his bed was barely slept in.

On the morning of the hearing she rose early, washed her face, braided her hair, and dressed very plainly and neatly. It was important to give the impression of quiet dignity, she felt. She found Alyce in the kitchen in her work clothes — full apron over her linsey-woolsey dress and mobcap.

"Aren't you going to dress?" Claire asked in some surprise.

"I decided it would be best if I did not go to the hearing. I was afraid that I might bring Papa bad luck."

"Nonsense. You could never bring anyone bad luck. And I am certain you want to be there."

"Oh, I do. But, well, you know, with my mark . . ."

Deliberately Claire bent and kissed Alyce's flamed cheek. She knew very well the danger that might follow if anyone, Esther in particular, took pains to make an issue of Alyce's birthmark at the hearing. In fact, it had crossed her mind earlier to ask her sister to remain at home. She was vastly relieved that Alyce had volunteered to do so.

"Perhaps it would be for the best, dear heart. Not because of your mark but because it is bound to be painful and you know how easily distressed you are. I'll tell you everything that happens. Word for word."

"And do tell Papa that I love him and am praying for him."

"I will, I promise."

Alyce reached for Claire's hand and pressed it against her cheek. "Oh, Claire, do you really think they'll allow him to go free?"

Claire hugged the girl's thin shoulders. Worry had taken its toll on Alyce. She was none too robust to begin with and now she seemed more fragile than ever. There were dark bands under her eyes and the normal side of her face was wan and sallow, whether in contrast to the livid pink of the birthmark or from staying too much indoors and brooding, Claire could not be sure.

"I'm certain they will," she said with more confidence than she really felt. "Papa is a good man. It's just not possible that he could be declared guilty of a murder he did not commit."

296

Yet, an hour later, when she entered the fort at the end of Manhattan and made her way to the governor's palace, she grew more anxious with every step. To begin with, she had never expected so many people to be there. A few, judging from their dress, were tradesmen and mechanics who had left their work for the excitement of a hearing. What surprised her more was the number of gentry present, most of them elegantly dressed and laughing and dawdling as though on their way to a party. Something in Claire blazed with anger at the sight of them. She recognized Immetje Strycker right away, surrounded by her usual bevy of suitors and looking gorgeous in a drawn silk overskirt and ermine-trimmed samare. At least today Fall was not among the servile retinue that hung about her, though it would not have mattered had he been, she told herself. A few steps behind Immetje came a heavyset young man with a long nose that she recognized as Adolph Philipse. She remembered him from a visit he had made to the house one evening to collect Fall. Stephanus Van Cortlandt was the man in the beautiful green velvet coat while the gentleman accompanying him wearing a large, beautifully coiffed full-bottomed wig that fell in cascades of curls over his shoulders was Lewis Morris, one of the wealthiest men, it was rumored, in the province.

I hope they are enjoying themselves, Claire thought with some bitterness as she climbed the stairs to the governor's house and entered the already crowded chamber room. At once she spotted Fall talking with Governor Fletcher at the other end of a massive oak table that ran down the center of the chamber. He looked up and caught her gaze, then came straight over to her side.

"I've arranged for you to sit here," he said in a businesslike manner indicating the end chair of one

of several rows arranged along the sides for spectators.

"All these people!" Claire cried. "Why are they
here? Just to gloat? To be entertained?"

"New York obviously does not have the excitement
of a murder very often. It draws them out."

"The excitement of a hanging, you mean. They
care nothing about my father. They're just—just
ghouls!"

Taking her elbow, Fall steered her toward the row of
chairs. "Please keep your voice down. There is no
need to antagonize these people. They are the ones
who hold your father's life in their hands."

Claire jerked her arm away from his fingers.
"You're one of them, aren't you? And just as bad."

Angrily he gripped her elbow, his fingers digging
into her flesh. "You little fool," he hissed. "Will you
control that miserable temper long enough to do
some good for Tom. I've talked myself blue in the
face to the governor and his council trying to convince them of his good character. If you come in here
and act like a shrew, you'll undo everything."

It was the first time Claire knew that he had done
anything on Tom's behalf and it gave her pause.
Relenting a little, she let him lead her to her chair
without another word. She was about to take her
place when a familiar face across the room brought
her to an abrupt halt. Fall followed her gaze and
leaned closer, whispering in her ear.

"Don't let your shock be so obvious. Pretend you
never saw him before."

"But that is the captain of those pirates. I'll never
forget that face."

"His name is William Kidd and he is a very
respected fellow in this town."

"Respected! Why, he's nothing but a common—"

He laid a finger on her lips, cutting her short. Claire's heart sank. What kind of people were these New York gentry? If a notorious pirate could appear openly in the governor's chamber room, what chance did her poor father have for justice?

"This is a mercantile trading center, Claire," Fall went on quietly. "Sometimes it is easier to ignore how goods are obtained than to make an issue of it. Now please, sit down and be quiet. The best thing you can do for your father is to look pretty and demure and innocent. And for God's sake, keep your mouth closed. Caleb, I'm counting on you to see that she does."

Once again Claire snatched her arm from his grasp. "Really, you are too much! I know how to conduct myself."

With a flounce of skirts she took her place, a grim Caleb in the seat behind her. At that moment her father entered between two stout soldiers, and she immediately forgot her irritation with Fall's overbearing ways to concentrate on giving her father an encouraging smile. A few moments later the governor was seated at the head of the table, his council seated along the sides and Tom standing at the far end near Claire. The crowd had begun to grow quiet when a murmur spread among them, and Claire saw Esther standing in the doorway leaning on Alan Morehead's arm. Both of them spied her at the same time, and Alan smiled wanly while Esther shot her a look of pure hatred. Then they moved to take two empty chairs on the opposite side of the room.

The emotional turmoil of sitting in the same room with Fall, Alan Morehead, and Esther Varn with her open hostility almost caused Claire to ignore the droning of the bailiff's voice until she recalled that she had promised to recount every word for Alyce.

299

She tried to concentrate on the charges and the testimony, but, as the hour wore on, her heart grew ever heavier. First there was the graphic description of finding Lace's body face down on the oyster shells on the beach at the end of Pearl Street. This was followed by a detailed description of the knife wounds that had killed him and other incidental bruises across his back and on his face. Then came the testimony of witnesses, each of them more damaging than the last, until it seemed that the collective accusations were almost beyond refuting.

Jacob Lister, a journeyman wheelwright, was present during the first argument Tom had with Lace over the stolen pears. His description of the thrashing Tom had inflicted on the victim was graphic and embellished, Claire felt sure, by his sense of importance at being called to testify before so august a body.

Then came Geertie Menson, a scraggly-looking old woman with an obvious fondness for gin who had overheard the two men arguing again at the Sign of the Dove near Pearl Street later that night. A crony of hers, one Teunis Obe, was certain he had heard Tom make threats against Mister Varn.

"Can you recall his exact words?" the governor asked in a voice bordering on boredom.

"Yes, your honor. He says somethin' like, 'I can whip you to death anyday, Lace Varn.' Somethin' along that line. It was a threat, right enough. A threat to kill him."

"Your honor," Tom interrupted. "If it please, your honor, he threatened me first, Lace did. Said he'd get even if he had to kill me to do it."

Governor Fletcher waved a ring-encrusted hand. "You shall have your time to speak, Tom Montcrieff. For now, just remain quiet and hear the evidence against you."

With some reluctance Tom grew silent, contenting himself with glaring at Teunis Obe. Fall leaned over and spoke softly to the governor, "You will recall, sir, the victim was killed with a knife, not a thrashing. Was there any threat to kill him that way?"

The governor nodded, laid his elaborate wig back against the tall back of his chair and examined Tom through his glass. "Did the defendant threaten to kill the hapless Mister Varn in any specific way? With a knife or a gun perhaps?"

Teunis Obe looked down at his thick fingers, examining the broken nails. "Not that I heard, your honor. But it was a terrible argument, you understand, and went on for a long time. I could have missed a few words."

Two more people came forward to speak. One was another of the late-night revelers at the Sign of the Dove who placed both victim and defendant inside shortly before dawn and who saw Lace leave alone with Tom following shortly afterward. The second was a farmer from the Upper Mills who testified to the character of the deceased — that he was a taciturn fellow but seemingly a family man who worked hard in the short time he had lived with his nephew north of the town.

Claire held her breath for fear that Esther might be called next. There was no telling what that vindictive woman might say if given the chance, even to implicating Alyce if she thought it would strengthen her charges against Tom. When Tom was at length allowed to speak for himself, she breathed a sigh of relief.

It was quickly dispelled. Though Tom adamantly denied killing Lace Varn, he freely admitted the earlier argument and the thrashing. Under the gover-

301

nor's skilled questions, his certainty began to waver.

Yes, there had been a long emnity between the two families, but then Lace Varn was a difficult man. Quarrelsome, mean, and venal. Yes, there was some suspicion that he was responsible for forcing Tom and his family to leave Scotland. Where had they got that information from, Claire wondered. But there were others who could testify to Varn's personality, those who had crossed with them on the *Selkirk*.

Yes, he had quarreled with Varn on the ship. He had stolen a bottle of good whisky from him. Yes, he was certain it was Varn who was the thief and, no, he had not forgotten or forgiven.

No, he could not recall what he had done after leaving the Dove though he believed that he simply went home to bed. That was what he always did. No, no one had accompanied him. He did not know if anyone saw him or not.

Yes, it was true, your honor. He could remember nothing of that night beyond entering the tavern for the second time very late. It was the grog, you see. It does that sometimes, especially when you have too much of an evening.

All at once Claire was aware that she was twisting her hands painfully. Even her father had seemed to shrink into himself as he talked, as though he could hear his own testimony getting weaker. While the governor leaned across the table to converse quietly with the men on either side of the table, her anxiety began to mushroom painfully inside her. She attempted an encouraging smile at Tom once when he glanced over at her, but the despair in his eyes was too much. Claire had to fight back her tears.

At last Governor Fletcher sat back. "Tom Montcrieff," he began in a stentorious voice heavy with authority. "We find that there is enough credible evidence to place you in the vicinity of Lace Varn's murder and to give you sufficient motive to have committed the crime. In the absence of any other suspect with as good motive or availability, we have no other choice but to charge this crime against you. The victim may have been a man of obstreperous character, but there is no record of any prior argument with another man who might have instigated this despicable crime. There was, of course, the incident with the savages, but the details here are in no way typical of Indian revenge. Therefore, we charge you, Tom Montcrieff, with the crime of murder, a capital offense for which you shall be duly tried and, if found guilty, hanged."

There was a murmur around the room, low and curious. Satisfaction? Claire was too distraught to care. Blindly she reached out behind her, and Caleb grasped her hand, holding it tightly.

"However," the governor's cool voice went on, "though we must see the king's justice done, we have no wish to impose an injustice on one of our own citizens—even one so newly arrived. Since you cannot recall—or claim that you cannot—the incidents of that fateful night, we will allow you a grace period of two weeks to attempt to discover some witness who can verify that you actually did go home to bed and did not follow the hapless victim to the vicinity of the beach where he was murdered. You shall remain in gaol during that time—"

"But, sir. Excuse me, but how am I to search for someone to help me if I am in gaol?"

"I suggest you put your family and friends to the search. You shall remain for safekeeping in gaol until the end of these two weeks, whereupon we shall proceed with a speedy trial that justice may be served."

Blindly Claire watched her father being led away. "Don't worry," she whispered, hoping he could read her lips. He was barely out of the door before Fall was at her side. She looked up at him with despair in her eyes, all her former irritation forgotten.

"Oh, Fall. Two weeks. Only two—"

"It's something, at least, and bless Governor Fletcher for giving it to us. Listen, I have an idea which I intend to pursue. It will mean I'll be away for a while."

"You wouldn't leave now!"

"I must. It may be important. Meantime, you and Caleb and anyone else you can call a friend, start searching for someone who might have seen Tom going home that night. Find out everyone who was at the Dove that evening and—"

"Hello, Claire," a man's voice broke in. Over Fall's shoulder Claire saw Alan advancing toward them. Esther, blazing her displeasure, stood near the door glaring after her nephew. Yet Alan came on, smiling at Claire. Fall, seeing him, stepped away from them both, his expression unreadable.

Claire stammered a good morning and a hasty introduction. Fall's acknowledgment was chilly while Alan evidenced some surprise at the rakish young MacDairmid being in New York, then turned his attention wholly to Claire.

"It looks bad, I know, but—"

"I must go," Fall said abruptly. "Don't forget what I told you, Claire."

Slapping his hat on his head, he hurried out the door, leaving Claire in confusion behind him. "I wonder you can be seen speaking to me under the circumstances," she said to Alan.

"Why not? We're promised, remember. And I do not believe your father killed my uncle at all."

"But your aunt? She looks as though she could murder us both right now."

"I know. But she will simply have to get accustomed to seeing you with me."

His words were brave but Claire noticed how he fingered the buttonhole of his jerkin nervously. He was uncomfortable. It was evident no matter how much he tried to hide it with bravado.

On a sudden impulse she said, "Alan, I don't think we should meet again until this matter is settled for good."

"Whyever not?"

"Out of consideration to your aunt and to my father. I shall have to work every moment to try to find someone who saw him that night and can clear him. Our relationship would only be a needless complication."

Alan frowned and studied his hands as though he was thinking this through but Claire was certain she detected a feeling of relief.

"If you really feel that way. But once this is cleared up, we must begin to concentrate on our own future. We've waited too long now."

It was on the tip of her tongue to point out that they would still be waiting had she not taken matters into her own hands and left Scotland, but worry and hopelessness were too strong to raise that point now. "Yes, our future," she muttered instead.

"If there is anything you need, you have only to send to me, you know that."

"I need nothing, but thank you."

"Alan!" Esther's impatient voice rang out. Claire looked up and caught her glare of hostility.

Quickly Alan laid his hand on her arm and squeezed it. "I'll see you in two weeks," he murmured, "at the hearing."

As he moved away, Caleb stepped up beside her. "Is that the fellow you came over here to marry?"

"Yes."

He shook his head. "Well, we can't be thinking of that now. Claire, my girl, we've a lot of work to do."

Meekly Claire allowed him to lead her from the room. All she wanted now was to be out of this place and away from these people, their curious stares, and whispered comments. Yet just as she was about to follow Caleb through the gates of the fort and out into Whitehall Street, she heard a imperious voice behind her.

"Young woman!"

Somehow Claire understood this command was meant for her. She turned to see close to her Immetje Strycker standing regally, her hands folded at her waist, waiting for Claire to respond to her summons.

"Young woman, I would like a word with you, if you please," Immetje went on politely but demandingly.

Claire studied her as though trying to decide whether to ignore her summons or answer it. She felt Caleb lay a hand on her arm.

"It's all right," she said softly. "Go on ahead. I'll catch up."

Standing her ground, she waited while the widow moved easily toward her. "I'll be just outside," Caleb whispered back.

"You are on your way home?" the widow asked, coming abreast of Claire.

"Yes, madam."

"Then walk with me a ways. I am also going that way."

"If you please."

"I do please." Turning Immetje gave a small wave of her fan to the young men clustered behind her and they fell back, allowing the two women to pass through the gates of the fort. Claire noticed Caleb waiting and saw him take his place behind, along with the widow's curious but obedient courtiers.

Deliberately Claire waited for the other woman to speak. They sauntered slowly up Broad Way, taking the west side, which was more open and less crowded than the east. Immetje tapped her fan against her wrist as though searching for the right words.

"You are a countrywoman of Fall MacDairmid, I believe."

"You know that I am. He introduced us."

"Yes, I remember now. And it is your unfortunate father who we witnessed just now before the governor's council."

"Yes." Her voice was clipped and its bitterness was not lost on the widow.

"A most distressing state of affairs. Believe me, I do feel for you in your trials."

Claire strolled in silence. How was she expected to answer such a comment from such a woman? The implied sympathy was most certainly false. Why would a rich widow care what happened to a poor immigrant? Did she expect the felon's daughter to be grateful for her pity? To beg for her help? To feel honored even to walk with her like this?

When she answered nothing, Immetje gave her a searching look and went on in her polite, objective way.

"I appreciate how much concern your master must feel for the troubles of a countryman—"

"He is not my master. His father was the laird of our village and we owe him our respect, but we are free subjects."

"My, my. How very touchy you are, my dear girl. I meant no offense. My concern is totally for Fall, you

307

see."

It was, Claire felt, her first honest statement. "Naturally it would be," she answered.

"I don't think you quite understand. Fall MacDairmid can have an exceptional career here in this new country. He has, well, talents and abilities that we sorely need. With just a little effort he can make his fortune here.

"And you mean to help him."

Immetje was growing impatient with the girl's surliness. "All I can. We may as well understand each other. An association with people who are accused of murder can be most devastating to a man just starting out. People here have long memories. The town is too small, the opportunities too great, and the competition too fierce."

"Perhaps he should marry a rich widow," Claire snapped. That brought Immetje to a halt. With flaming cheeks she stopped and faced Claire.

"Young woman, you are far too rude and impertinent for your own good. You might help Mister MacDairmid more by bridling your tongue."

Claire glared up at Immetje standing there wearing her wealth with arrogance. She studied the crimped curls that fringed her high forehead, the wide collar with its exquisite lace points, the proud thrust of the shoulders, and the haughty slits of her eyes.

"I neither care to help or hinder Mister MacDairmid. And my name is Claire. Mistress Montcrieff."

"Let us be honest with one another," Immetje went on patiently. "I am most anxious to see Mister MacDairmid get ahead. It might be to your advantage to discourage him from becoming too much associated with this sordid business. There are others who can help you, and I will see to it that they do. In the meantime it might be better if Fall were to leave town for a while. I have some estates in Westchester that are much in need of a good man to manage them. He has promised to have a look at them for me."

"Is that where—"

Immetje's thin lips drew into a narrow smile and too late Claire realized her mistake. Of course that was where he intended to go and just now, when they needed his help so badly. Off to look over the widow's estates. Well, why not, when they would probably be his soon?

The sudden thought of this arrogant, gaunt woman in Fall's arms was almost too painful to bear. Something in her look must have given her thoughts away for Immetje all at once grew wary and her eyes narrowed. She is wondering about me, Claire thought. How well do I know her dear Fall? Has he held me in his arms? Has he bedded me?

Turning away, she started down the street again. If Immetje only knew. I care nothing for Fall MacDairmid. She can have him.

"I can do nothing for you until you give me your assurance you will stay away from him," Immetje said behind her. Claire paused, then turned back to face the woman.

"I will not give you that assurance. What Fall MacDairmid does is his own concern. I have not asked him for his help, nor will I ask for yours. My family has friends here who will help us find the means to clear my father. And now, madam, if you please, I have much to do. Good day to you."

Immetje made a low clicking sound with her tongue. "You are a very proud young woman, Mistress Montcrieff. Perhaps a little too proud."

Claire drew herself up. "It has been my belief, madam, that one cannot be too proud."

"Ah, but, when one pulls oneself up too high, it means that one must fall that much farther and faster."

"Perhaps you should tell that to Mister MacDairmid. Good day to you."

"What was that all about?" Caleb said as he caught up with her. Claire had set off at such a pace that he could barely keep up.

"That arrogant, self-centered woman! How can he stand to even be around her!"

"Who? What? Slow down, Claire, and tell me what she said. After all, she's one of the most important people in this town."

"Never mind what she said. It doesn't matter. Come on, Caleb, we've got to get to work and find someone who saw Papa go home the night Lace was killed. That is all that matters now."

Fourteen

For the next several days Claire, Caleb, Nell, and Jamie scoured the town trying to find anyone who might have seen Tom on the night Lace Varn died. But no matter how many people they asked, no matter how many seedy, dark taverns they braved or how many doors they knocked upon, they were not able to find a single person who could verify Tom's story that he had made his way home to bed in the early hours of that fateful morning.

Claire was not surprised. Most of the people who frequented taverns and grog shops at that time of night were sailors from the ships in the harbor, and they either recalled little or had already sailed away. If any of the ne'er-do-wells, who spent their lives hanging around these places, actually had seen Tom, they were either too intrigued by the idea of a public hanging to speak up or had been bought off by Lace's friends. Claire would not have put it past Esther to do something like that although she refused to believe Alan had a hand in anything so dishonest.

She returned from another weary round of inquiries late on an afternoon a week after Tom's hearing more discouraged than ever. As she passed along the

311

street to the doorway, she could see Caleb and Alyce sitting in the garden at the rear of the house. Instead of going inside, she walked around to join them, thinking it would be refreshing to sit under the shade of the trees there and share her misery.

She paused at the edge of the house to observe the scene at the other end of the garden — Alyce on the ground deep in conversation with Caleb, who was sprawled beside her, and Nell sitting on a bench built beneath the tree, working at her mending. As she walked nearer, she caught Alyce's words and all thoughts of Tom flew from her mind.

"It grows very tall," she heard Alyce say, "and it has bright red berries and leaves like fine lace. And the most amazing thing is that, just where each berry is attached to the stem, a perfect star is formed."

"Why it's nothing but a locust tree," Caleb said dryly. "I've seen a few like it in my travels around the other end of the island."

"And when did you go traveling around Manhattan?" Nell commented dryly.

"Oh, I've seen more of this place than you know, woman. I find it of interest to learn about this New World. You never know when information will prove useful."

"Seems to me you're always loafing about the house here. When have you had time to go traipsing about the island?"

"Well, you don't know everything about where I go. Just because I don't talk of it all the time like some people I know don't mean I ain't been busy."

"But, Caleb, you couldn't have seen this tree. I brought it with me from Scotland. It's mine. I don't think there's anything like it in the New World at all."

"Ah, but you're mistaken, missy. There's a similar tree that grows in high places, much like this one. It

312

has a different name that's all. Mountain ash, it's called over here."

"Alyce!" Claire cried, stepping into the group, her displeasure written on her face. "You haven't planted that tree here!"

Immediately Alyce jumped up. "Oh, dear. I didn't want to tell you yet. I didn't hear you come up, Claire."

"Alyce, I told you not to plant that tree anywhere. We don't know yet where we will be living, and this place is only temporary."

"Then I'll dig it up if we have to move. It needs earth, Claire, and sunshine."

"What am I going to do with you, you difficult girl? You never should have brought that thing with you. I told you—"

Caleb looked from one to the other mystified. "Such a to-do over a little plant. Come now, Claire, it can't matter that much."

"Sit down, Claire," Nell said soothingly. "You look worn out and no wonder, wandering all over town in this heat. Let me get you a cool drink."

It was a relief to Claire that Nell laid her distress over the tree to weariness and worry. She sat down on the bench and admitted she would love something cool. Calling Alyce to help her, Nell disappeared into the kitchen, leaving Caleb sitting on the ground beside Claire, studying her face.

"What's the real reason you're so bothered about this little tree? Did you have another disappointing day? No luck finding anyone who could help your father?"

Claire leaned back against the broad trunk of the oak and sighed. "No, I didn't find anyone and I am worried and disappointed although by this time I hardly expect to have any luck with that problem. No,

Caleb, it's something far worse that bothers me about Alyce's tree. In Scotland the rowan tree is associated with witches and Alyce knows that. She has such a hard time anyway what with her mark taken as a devil's touch. To carry on as she does about a stupid tree only makes everything worse."

She half-expected Caleb to laugh but he didn't. He seemed to understand her anxiety and sympathize with it.

"The poor bairn does not have much to fuss over, you know. No friends, no girls her age, no young men calling on her. She spends a lot of time alone, Claire, and that can twist the best of spirits. It's hardly surprising that she would try to make a friend of objects like plants or trees. Why don't you let her have a pet of some kind? A puppy or a kitten?"

"I can't! Don't you know that any pet Alyce might have would be taken as her familiar? It's too great a risk."

Caleb shook his head at the perversity of people.

"Of course, maybe it's not the same here," Claire went on almost to herself. "This is a new country with new attitudes. Look how easily different churches get along together here in New York where in Scotland they'd be at each other's throats. Perhaps I worry needlessly."

She had almost talked herself into believing her fears were unfounded and she expected Caleb to agree with her. When he shook his head, his brows beetling, Claire sat up.

"No. You do right to be concerned," he said quietly.

"Why do you say that?"

He shrugged his thin shoulders. "Only that—it's always better to be prepared." Then his eyes met hers and the casual attitude dropped away. "No, I'll speak clearly even if it must cause you some anxiety. You do right to be concerned because even in this New World the scourge of fear over witches can take its toll. I heard about it just last week. Some fellow at the Sign of the Dove was talking about something that happened up north, somewhere near Boston. There was a fearful calamity over witches in the town and somewhat like eighteen people were hanged as witches."

"My God!"

Quickly Caleb laid a hand on her arm. "Now don't get alarmed. According to him it never spread to the other colonies. In fact it was pretty localized in that village. There was never any trouble of the sort here in New York."

"But eighteen people actually killed! Who were they? Were any of them—young girls?"

"No. As I recall, he said they were mostly old women and a few men. I only tell you this, Claire, so you'll keep your guard up. You do right to protect Alyce, even in this new country."

Claire spotted Alyce and Nell in the kitchen doorway, carrying a jug and two wooden mugs. "Caleb," she dropped her voice, "do you think it is possible people here in New York don't know about what happened up there in Boston?"

He nodded. "News is very slow to get from place to place in all this wilderness. And it was some time last year all this happened. Mayhap it's all been forgotten by now."

"And here you are," Nell said brightly as she walked up to the bench and handed Claire a mug. "Lemonade. Made it myself and kept it in the buttery to keep cool."

"Thank you, Nell," Claire answered and put the mug to her lips. Something inside her felt more sick than when she had first walked into the garden. She didn't want to think about it now, but it lay there, heavy and depressing, in her chest. All her hopes that in this New World the worst of the Old would be gone forever, dying at her feet. Even here the scourge lingered, threatening accusation and misery and perhaps even death. Even here in this bright new land, she must never relax her vigilance. Added to the thought of her father languishing in gaol, it was almost enough to make her wish she had never left Scotland.

The next morning on her way to the gaol to see her father, Claire decided to make one last detour to the Sign of the Dove. Perhaps if she prodded old Maude, the proprietress, one more time, she could get her to remember just one more name, one more face, one additional person they could search out. It was a lowering day overcast with gray much as her mood. Claire paused before the drab exterior of the building with its forlorn, paint-chipped blue dove clinging to the side. It was a seedy place, dank and dreary, frequented mostly by the sailors on leave from their ships tied up at the piers. Claire did not really want to go inside again among the men — rough, silent men who sank into an alcohol-induced fog and were content to lie there. She did not like the way they looked at her, she did not like the questions in their eyes or the way they mistook her interest for something other than what it was. But it had to be done. If she was going to help her father, she had to continue the effort. There was no where else to turn.

So, steeling her nerve, she stepped across the dingy threshold and into the dark room. It was early and not very crowded. Around the walls she could make out the dark outlines of several figures bent over their tankards of beer. They barely looked up as she walked across the room. She found Maude at the other end giving a cursory wipe to some wooden tankards with a dirty towel.

"You back again," the old woman said, clicking her tongue. "Haven't I told you all I can? There's no more to be said."

"I thought perhaps you might have remembered somebody else."

"Why should you think a thing like that? I told you already everythin' I know. How am I supposed to know everyone who comes in here, especially on a crowded night when there's more faces than I can recognize? Place was thick that night. Ship come in just afore sundown. Most of them seamen already gone out again."

"But it's so important. It's my father's life. Everything depends on it. Isn't there any face you can recall, anyone who might have seen him leave? Did you see him walk out?"

"All I remember was a blazin' argument. Had to yell at the both of them two, three times to break it off. Don't like that kind of thing going on in here. It's rowdy enough as just naturally." Something in Claire's face made the woman's hard visage soften. "What about old Nathan Bright. Seems like I recalled him the last time you was in. Did you speak with him?"

"I tried to but he was so gone in drink he couldn't even carry on a conversation. One night is like another to him."

"Too bad we don't have a watch in this town. They might have seen your pa."

Claire pulled her shawl up over head and around her face. "Well, I'm grateful to you, Maude, for what you've given me. If you do remember anything,

317

please, please send for me. I've only got a few more days."

Maude's hard eyes softened slightly as she studied the distressed girl standing before her. She could barely remember when she was that young. A flicker of recognition touched her—the pain and distress one could feel so keenly at that age. Long since it had all been walled in by experience and sorrow. "All right," she mumbled. "If'n I do remember anyone, I'll tell you for sure."

Claire muttered a thank you and turned to leave. As she crossed the room, she glanced quickly at two men seated in the booth nearest the door, both of whom glanced quickly away. One of them turned his head so that all she could see was the outline of his cap. The other was a bearded sailor, whose hard little eyes fastened on his tankard. She hurried through the door and back into the gray light of the street, thankful to be out of the place. Behind her the sailor in the cap turned back to stare at the door.

"I know that little girl," he said quietly.

His companion, concentrating on his beer, barely looked up. "Aye, I'll just bet you do."

"I didn't know she was still in New York though."

"Well, she's not going to have anything to do with the likes of you, Jimmy. Come on. Let's have another. We've a lot of prize money to wet our throats with."

Jimmy Cole nodded, his narrow eyes still glued to the door through which Claire had disappeared. "Aye, another," he answered, his mind clearly not on another drink.

Claire made her way down the weed-choked streets to the gaol wondering how she was going to buoy up her father's spirits when she herself was so discouraged. If only Fall were here! If only he hadn't gone north to inspect the widow's holdings. How unkind

318

of him, how mean, how venal! Of course, he thought that someday they would all be his and naturally that would take precedence over any other concern. All his comments about how "this was not the way to win him." Evidently the widow *had* found the way to win him and without waiting too long for it. Her anger put a new briskness in her step, and she reached the stone gaol house before she knew it. It was easy to get in to visit her father. They were used to her stopping by now. Tom looked up eagerly when he heard her step, hoping she had brought some good news. One good look at her eyes and he knew better.

"You haven't had any luck, I see."

"No. I tried so hard but there's no one. Papa, if only you could remember. You must have passed someone as you walked home."

Tom shook his head. "It was the grog. It fogs the mind like a blanket and you don't see anything or anyone. Did you bring some tobaccy?"

Claire nodded and reached inside her basket. Tobacco was very hard to come by but, by dint of saving on their household needs, she had managed to put by enough to bring him one pipeful. He took it gratefully, almost humbly, as though one good smoke could make up for the lack of drink which imprisonment had imposed on him.

"And no word from the MacDairmid?" he said, drawing on the long clay stem.

"Nothing. I didn't expect any. You cannot depend on those MacDairmids. When will you ever learn that?"

"Ah, that's not true, lass. Morgan MacDairmid was once as fine a man as any I ever knew. 'Twas a shame he was brought so low by forces he couldn't help."

Claire had heard all this many times before but this

319

time her patience snapped. "Papa, how can you defend them? Practically everything that has happened to us is their fault."

"Now, what do you mean by a statement like that?" Tom asked, looking up at her sharply.

Claire hesitated. She had never mentioned Edgar's letter to her father but it had rankled in her mind for days now. Since Fall had been away, she had gone back two or three times to read it over, always wondering what it meant. What was Edgar responsible for and how had he and Fall conspired together to bring them here to New York? Was her father's imprisonment and possible execution part of the plan? It was almost unthinkable that Fall would go to such lengths to have Tom accused of murder, but, if there was money or land involved, how could she be certain he would not do it?

Finally she decided to speak. It was long past time. "Papa, there is some kind of conspiracy between the MacDairmids and our family. I don't know what it is."

Tom took the pipe out of his mouth. "What are you talking about?"

"I don't know what I'm talking about. I haven't been able to figure it out. I only know there is something going on that is bigger than we know, something that involves us."

In a nervous gesture Tom ran his fingers through his lanky hair. "If you mean that business with Edgar, why he admitted as that he did it to get our land. There's no conspiracy in that."

"That was only part of it. There's more to it, I know there is."

"Ah, you're imaginin' things," Tom said. Yet he could not put her off. Even as he tried to sound casual about her accusations, she could see his agitation growing. His hand began to tremble and his eyes looked everywhere in the room but directly at Claire. Like a light breaking through a cloud, she all at once knew for certain that she had spoken the truth and Tom knew it.

"Papa, there *is* something going on and you know what it is! It's something you're not telling me. What is it?"

"Stop it, Claire! You're just imagining things. There's nothin'!"

"There is," she cried, gripping his arms. "And it has to do with everything that has happened to us — all the accusations against Alyce, the way our land was stolen, the money to send us here to New York. And there is more. I don't understand it at all but it's there. And Fall is involved in it somehow."

Tom threw down his clay pipe, breaking the stem and scattering the tobacco. "I tell you there's nothin' going on!" he yelled. "There never was and there never will be. Put such ideas out of your head. I never want to hear a word said about them again. Never!"

"Papa!" Claire cried, taken aback at the depth of his rage. He stalked the length of the tiny cell, back and forth, slashing his arm up and down in the air.

"Shut your mouth. There's nothin' going on. There never was and never will be. I won't have it. I won't hear no more about it. Not another word. Haven't I got enough to trouble me without being plagued by my own daughter this way!"

"Papa, please. I didn't mean—"

"Go on now! Get out of here! Go home and don't come back no more until you can bring me some news that's good for a change and not fairy tales."

His loud yells quickly brought the gaoler, who unlocked the door for Claire and pulled her out of Tom's cell. There were tears in her eyes as she left her

321

father raging behind her in a way she had never seen him do before. The gaoler patted her on the shoulder in a kindly way.

"Don't worry about it, mistress. It's the closeness. It often gets to a man after a length of time like this. He'll be the same as before once he gets free."

If he gets free, Claire wanted to say, but she hadn't the heart even to talk. She nodded her thanks and went home, more mystified than ever. She had never expected such a reaction from old Tom, neither in its quality nor in its depth of feeling. And yet, in spite of his loud protests, there was a gnawing recognition deep within her that her father knew more about this problem with the MacDairmids than she had ever imagined. Somehow Tom was involved in it, but how she was ever going to get him to share what he knew with her, she didn't know.

And yet as the long week wore toward its close and Tom's last hearing drew near, she became so obsessed with concern over her father's danger that thoughts of the MacDairmids and their mysteries were pushed from her mind. If she thought of them at all, it was to rage at Fall for his callous and insensitive ways and at herself for giving herself to such a man so easily.

And then he came home.

He arrived late on the afternoon before the hearing the next morning. Alyce came running down to the sheep pen where she was helping Caleb with a new calf to tell her he had just ridden up. Claire jumped to her feet before she remembered how angry she was with him.

"Aren't you coming up to the house?" Alyce said as Claire went back to helping the calf to stand on its wobbly legs.

"I'll be up when I'm finished. You and Nell can see that Master MacDairmid has everything he needs."

"He looks as though a good washing and a strong drink would be all he wants. I never saw a man so dusty and disheveled from a journey. But you should come up, Claire. There's a note arrived for you just a few minutes ago."

"What note?"

"I don't know. It was brought by a young boy who was most adamant that no one should have it but you."

"Oh, very well. I'll be right up." She handed the calf to Caleb thinking the note was probably meant for Fall from his widow lady and walked up the winding path to the house, taking off her straw bonnet to let the air blow through her hair.

She was more upset at the idea of seeing Fall again than she wished. She wanted to be all cool and contained, even nonchalant. Instead her heart raced and her breath came short just like a foolish, silly child, she chided herself. When she walked into the kitchen and saw him standing beside the table, a knife in one hand and the other pinning down a haunch of ham, her miserable emotions threatened to do her in completely.

He looked up and gave her a warm smile. It quickly faded at the coolness of her look that completely masked the turbulence she felt.

"That's not a very warm welcome," he commented drily.

Claire looked away. "How did you find the widow's holdings? Are they worth marrying the lady for?"

For a moment she mistook his surprise for puzzlement. Then he gave a sharp laugh.

"Well worth," he commented casually and went back to slicing a piece off the ham.

"You didn't think I knew where you had gone, did you? Well, I heard it from the lady herself. She stopped me on the way out of the governor's house the day of my father's hearing."

"Oh. You never mentioned it to me."

"You were too eager to be off. Of course, that's not hard to understand. What chance does an old man's danger have against the lure of an estate worth a fortune?"

"You sound very bitter. What's the matter? Weren't you able to find anyone who could verify Tom's story?"

Claire was unable to look directly at him. Feeling suddenly very weary, she sank down on a bench beside the table and stared into the fire.

"No."

Fall speared a slab of meat, set one boot firmly on the bench beside her, and leaned on his knee, nibbling at the ham.

"That's too bad. I was certain you'd come up with someone."

She turned on him furiously. "Is that why you left us to go off and satisfy your venal desires for money? You said you would help us. You told me to trust you, that I could depend on you."

Fall laid down the knife. "And so I meant —"

He was interrupted by a voice from the doorway. "Excuse me, mistress, but would you be Mistress Claire?"

They both turned to see a young urchin standing in the doorway. He was obviously one of the children from the wharfs, shabbily dressed and very dirty.

"I am," Claire said, recalling for the first time that Alyce had told her a boy had come with a message. "Are you the boy who was sent with a note?"

"No note, ma'am, but a message that I'm to give to you and to you alone."

"Who is it from?"

The boy glanced at Fall, shifting his weight from foot to foot uncomfortably.

"You can speak here, child," Claire said kindly. "Tell me who sent you."

"Beggin' your pardon, ma'am, but I was told most clear that I was only to talk to you, private like. 'Twas Mistress Maude who said it."

Again the child looked warily at Fall as though he had not meant to divulge that much.

"Come," Claire said, moving quickly to the door. "We'll walk in the garden together." Laying a hand on the child's thin shoulder, she steered him outside and far enough away from the house that they could speak without being heard. Then she knelt, looking into his young, worldy-wise eyes.

"You're a good boy, and I commend you for trying to do what you were told. Now, tell me exactly what Maude said, just as she spoke it to you."

"She says, if you want to find someone who can help your pa, you're to come to the old grain-mill warehouse on Beaver Lane just after sundown tonight."

Claire waited. "That's all?"

"Yes, ma'am. Oh, she did say too that you was most certainly to come alone and not bring anyone with you. That, if you did, it might ruin everything."

"You're certain she said that?"

"Yes, ma'am. She says that. She says that if you want to find someone who can help your pa—"

"You needn't go through it all again. I understood it the first time. But are you sure there was nothing more?"

"Nothing, ma'am. That was all of it."

He stood waiting for his expected reward, but Claire was so busy thinking over his message that she did not realize at first why he was still there. Why the old warehouse and not the Sign of the Dove itself? And why alone? At the very least she ought to take Caleb with her.

"Did Maude say she would meet me at the old warehouse?"

"She didn't say, ma'am, but I suppose that is what she intended."

"I suppose so too. Very well. Do you see that lady over there by the well? Her name is Mistress Nell. Go to her and tell her Mistress Claire said she is to give you some supper and a half-penny for your trouble."

"That gentleman —?"

"Don't worry about him. He won't bother you. Run along now."

The boy took eagerly off toward the house while Claire stood in the garden thinking. She still did not like the idea of going to the old grain mill alone and at night, yet what other choice did she have? It was too important not to follow through. It might make the difference for her father between life and death.

But why so much secrecy? Should she trust Maude at all — a cantankerous old hag even if her shrewd little eyes did now and then seem to be aware of far more than she pretended to see. Yet there was no one else and nowhere left to turn. And the hearing was tomorrow morning.

In the end she said nothing, not even to Caleb. Toward sunset she wrapped her plaid around her shoulders, murmured something to Nell about walking to the old India Company garden to watch the sun go down and slipped from the house before Alyce could volunteer to go with her. Nell assumed she wanted to be alone — after all, Claire had been under a lot of stress and worry these past two weeks — so she let her go and gave it no more thought.

Once out of sight of the house Claire hurried down

Broad Way to the docks, trying not to call attention to herself. The streets were still moderately crowded with apprentices hurrying home to their supper, soldiers from the fort casually ambling by filled with their own importance, and, now and then, a family out for a stroll in the pleasant weather.

But as she neared the harbor and twilight began to deepen, she began to see more and more of the people who, like insects, came out at night: seedy sailors from the ships in port, town tipplers shuffling along toward their favorite dram shops, and even one or two women who looked as though their reputations would not bear too close a scrutiny. By the time she reached the Sign of the Dove the gray night was deepening and Claire was beginning to grow uneasy. She wished she had at least spoken to Caleb and had had him follow behind her, just in case. In the bright afternoon this mysterious summons had seemed worth obeying, but now, as night was falling, she began to see it as pure folly.

Yet she had come this far and she would not turn back now. Ignoring the comments several of the passers-by directed at her, Claire pulled her plaid around her head and turned in at the path called Old Beaver Lane which led past the tavern. She went quickly past the yellowed building, ignoring the lights and noise inside, and slipped toward the river where the old, dilapidated warehouse stood. It had been originally built to store grain from the windmill that used to stand just north of the fort. It was isolated and alone now, with the mill gone—a decaying, abandoned structure giving last homage to the mill that had been one of the town's Dutch landmarks, a black shadowy hulk against the somber gray of Hudson's River in the distance.

The doors stood open, one of them hanging crazily

from its hinges. Claire moved cautiously to the black interior and peered inside.

"Maude?" she whispered.

A sudden clatter within made her jump nervously until she saw a gray cat come running through the doorway. She realized that her heart was racing and she forced herself to be calm. After all, what was there to fear from old Maude?

"Maude, I'm here," she whispered more loudly. "It's Claire." She stood by the door trying to see through the blackness inside the building, still reluctant to go inside. Then came a return whisper.

"Over here—"

Claire took a few steps inside the building. "Where are you? Don't you have a candle or a lantern? I can't see anything."

"Too risky," came the hoarse reply. Now she could pinpoint the direction—to the left and near the middle of the long, open room. She stepped closer. The old warehouse smelled strongly of decaying grain and mold. Long rotted residue of grasses and flour crunched under her feet.

"I won't come any farther," Claire declared. "If you want to tell me anything, you will have to come to me."

In the long silence that followed her defiant outburst, she thought she must have offended the old woman, but then she became aware of a silent figure moving near her. A hand reached out and lightly touched her arm, and Claire stifled a scream and pulled away.

A voice spoke softly near her ear, "Don't be alarmed, mistress. I've come here to help you."

"You're not Maude," Claire cried and started back for the door. She was stopped by an iron grip on her arm, the fingers digging into her flesh.

"Don't be alarmed, I say. Don't you want to hear what I want to say?"

"Let me go. I don't like any of this. I came here to talk to Maude. Where is she?"

The voice was near enough now that she could feel a warm breath on her cheek. Something cold crept down her spine as she realized she had heard this voice before.

"We don't need Maude. You wanted someone who had seen your pa, right? Well, I'm here to help you, Mistress Claire. You and your pa. That's what you want, isn't it?"

"I know who you are," Claire cried, shrinking away from the man's shadowy form. "You are the first mate from the *Selkirk*."

"Master Cole. That's correct. Here at your service."

Claire could feel her flesh crawl under Jimmy Cole's tight grip. She tried to ease toward the doorway, but he was too strong for her and, even as she attempted to move away, he pulled her farther inside the warehouse.

"Come now," he said soothingly. "We have no argument with each other. I'm here to save your father from a hanging. Seems as though you'd be welcoming me with open arms."

"I want nothing to do with you. There is no way you could help my father. Go back to your cutthroat pirates—that's all you're fit for. Not decent people."

Jimmy's voice grew mean. "You're mighty uppity for a girl who is about to see her father go to the gallows. Suppose I just happened to see him making his way home the night Varn was killed. Would I be only fit for cutthroats then? You'd be glad to give me a warmer welcome then, wouldn't you?"

"I don't believe you."

"That's no matter. Whether I really seen him or

didn't don't matter as long as I swear I did. And I'm prepared to do that. For you, mistress."

Her struggles were only getting her pulled farther inside the darkness of the building so Claire decided to try something different. She grew very still as though she was thinking over his proposition.

"You'd be prepared to swear before the governor and his council that you saw papa that night? Even if you didn't."

Cole eased the grip on her arm and moved closer. She could feel his other arm sliding up her shoulder.

"That's right. What's a lie more or less to a cut-throat pirate?"

"They won't believe you."

"I can make a very convincing liar when I want."

"But why? What do you want in return? I haven't much money."

"It's not money I'd be wanting from you, miss."

Her flesh grew colder as she felt his arms enclose her and smelled the offensive odor of sweat and beer. Turning her face aside, she strained against him, still trying to appear compliant and reasonable but with fear flaming into near panic within her.

"Please. We can't talk like this. Let's go into the tavern and sit in a booth and discuss this reasonably over a dram—"

But Jimmy had longed for this too long and the force of her soft body pressed against his was intoxicating enough to make him forget everything else.

"I've wanted you for such a long time," he breathed, nuzzling her neck. "All that time on the voyage, watching you, imagining you in that bunk with me below decks. And ever since then, when I took a woman, I pretended it was you. When I dreamed of a woman, it was your face, your body . . ."

His urgency was growing, driving her into panic. She was aware now as she had not been before that she was his victim and he was fast getting beyond reason. His hand slid up to cup her breast. She struggled against him but his arm held her tightly, forcing her to her knees as he began to kiss her wildly, his hands sliding over her flesh, fondling, gripping . . .

Claire was beyond being careful now. "No!" she yelled. "Let me go!" But his mouth clamped on hers, stopping her words. His wet tongue writhed against her lips. He pushed her down on the floor among the rotted grasses and threw himself on top of her. She tried to roll away but he grabbed at her hair and pulled her back, throwing himself on top of her. She pelted him with her fists until he hit her viciously on the cheek, knocking her senseless for a moment. Her arms fell slack and she felt him yanking up her skirts, thrusting his knee between her legs to push them apart.

"No . . . no!" Claire moaned. The rotted effluvia on the floor made her stomach turn over. She tried vainly to force her knee up against his groin, but his heavy, gyrating body prevented her. She felt utterly helpless, sick, and revolted to the core, furious at being forced like an animal to satisfy the lust of this dreadful man. Throwing back her head, she let out one agonizing scream.

There was a sharp crunch and crack that she somehow heard through her agony. The body above her was jerked backward, the heavy weight pulled away, and she felt freedom. She rolled to the side, able to make out two dark shapes, one of them gripping the other and pounding his head against the floor with a series of thumping crunches.

Claire scrambled to her feet ready to run for the

331

door, which was only a sliver of light in the distance. She was almost there when she heard Fall's voice.

"Claire!"

She stopped, careening against the old wall, leaning against it until he reached her.

"Claire," he cried, pulling her into his arms. "Are you all right?"

She couldn't speak. She nodded and slumped against him, letting him support her. The tears began to stream down her cheeks. He soothed her, stroking her hair gently away from her face, "It's all right now. He won't bother you any more."

"It—it was the—first mate from—" she stumbled.

"I know. The lecher. He always had his eye on you, but I never thought he'd stoop this low. Well, he won't bother anyone again. Ever."

Claire shuddered as she remembered that awful weight on her. "Did you kill him?" she asked softly.

"I don't know. I might have. His neck gave an awful crack when I pulled him backward."

"Oh, Fall. You'll be in terrible trouble. We ought to call the bailiff or something."

"No. I don't think the Montcrieff family can take any more scandal, especially not tonight. Come on, we'll slip out and go home. His fellows will find him."

Claire needed no urging. All she wanted was to leave this terrible place behind her, but, as they stepped outside into the now dark night, she remembered her shawl.

"My plaid. It must be back there."

"You wait here. I'll get it."

"No! I'm coming with you." She grasped his hand and followed Fall back into the building where they came upon the still prostrate form of Jimmy Cole lying in a heap. Claire felt around until she touched the bunched edges of her shawl but, when she tried to pull it away, she realized it was underneath the lifeless man.

"Let me," Fall said and, taking the end, pulled the cloth away. He tried to put it around her shoulders, but she did not want to touch it so he clumped it into a ball over his arm as they fled the building.

They passed no one in the lane and, by the time they reached Broad Way, Claire had managed to achieve some semblance of calm. She smoothed back her hair hoping no one would look too closely, and they walked as hurriedly as they could without attracting attention back toward the end of the town.

They slowed their steps as they neared the road that turned off Broad Way to the house. When they reached the cross street, Claire stopped suddenly. "I can't go in yet," she cried, shuddering. Her knees gave way and Fall clasped her around her waist to hold her up. She was trembling like a leaf in the wind. She fought to still the shudders, but her body was racked with them.

"There's no need to go home yet. Come on. We'll walk a little farther."

They continued down Broad Way, past the old remains of the wall to the common. Though it was night by now, there were still a few people out enjoying the mild evening, and they could make out the dark shapes of animals grazing the fields. Without speaking Fall led her away from the road down to a narrow path toward the river. There was a large grassy knoll there with a sloping lip of a half-buried boulder. The bank sloped downward from it to the river beyond, pewter gray and shimmering with the light of a moon just rising.

Claire sank down on the stone, twisting her hands in her lap. "I'm ashamed to have so little control," she said, still shuddering.

333

Fall sat beside her, put his arms around her and pulled her to him, cradling her head against his shoulders.

"There's no need to feel shame," he said gently. "It was a horrible experience. Any girl would be unnerved. The idea of that—that bastard laying his slimy hands on you makes my blood boil still."

"I never expected to see Master Cole. I never expected to see him again ever. I hate him! I hated him on the ship and I hate him even more now."

Fall stared out over the water, his face grim. "If he's not already dead, someday I will kill him!"

Claire's body gradually grew quiet as she lay against him, comforted by the soothing feel of his fingers lightly stroking her back. His body was firm and solid and exuded a strength she needed now more than anything. After a few moments she sat up.

"Fall, how did you know? Why were you there?"

He gave a laugh. "Did you really think I'd allow that young lad to sit in the kitchen and eat his supper without finding out what had brought him? I knew something was up or he would not have come so mysteriously."

"I told him he would not have to speak to you."

"Well he did. And after a few well-placed threats he was so cowed he was glad to tell me his message. I was undecided at first as to what to do. I almost decided to let you go alone to deal with the results of your own folly, but in the end I thought that might prove to be too dangerous."

"But I didn't think I could depend on you. If you hadn't run off. If you'd stayed and helped us, I would never have been so secretive."

"Oh, Claire. Don't you think I was helping you? Where do you think I've been these last two weeks? Was it so easy for you to believe I had gone off gallivanting to look over the widow's lands in the hope they would soon be mine? You must have a very poor idea of my character."

Claire pulled away from him, staring at his indistinct face in the soft light. "But where were you then?"

"I was trying to find the tribe that savage belonged to. It was obvious to me from the first that he must have been the one to kill Lace Varn. After all, who had more reason? His squaw had been publicly thrashed by the man just that morning, he had been accused of thievery and called a dirty savage in front of the town. It's a mistake to think that you can say anything you want to people like that, even though they are Indians, and think that they don't feel some loss of pride. That was something Varn never learned."

"But the governor said it did not look like an Indian killing? That it wasn't the Indian manner?"

"So. He was just a little smarter than most. At any rate, I felt that that was our best hope to help Tom. So with Adolph's help I tracked down the tribe he belonged to and managed to speak to the Sachem Canopus before they could kill me. And with the chief's help I brought him back."

Claire stared in disbelief. "You mean he's here in New York? He's going to admit what he did and give himself up?"

"Not willingly, of course. But, with the power of his tribe behind us, supported by the force of the soldiers at the fort, yes. I have to admit there were plenty of other braves who did not think it was such a good idea and who still feel some resentment about it. But the chief is a wiser man and he wants peace at almost any price. Adolph had told me all this before I went or perhaps I might not have felt so confident about walking into their village."

"Oh, Fall," Claire cried. "How I misjudged you! I'm so sorry and so ashamed!"

He laughed. "You should be."

"I was so worried about Papa. I thought there was nowhere left to turn and, when it seemed that Maude had found someone, I had to follow through on it. But it was not Maude at all. It was a terrible trap."

"Sometimes I don't know what I am going to do with you, Claire. You trust people you shouldn't trust and you don't trust those you should. Those who care for you and love you."

"And do you love me?" Claire said quietly.

He laid a hand on either side of her face and looked deeply into her eyes. "You know I do."

"I don't know it," she cried. "What you call love is so strange to me. I know you love to have me in your bed but as your mistress, not your wife. And what about all those other women you've had? What about the widow?"

Fall shrugged and took his hands away. "Don't you realize, Claire, that there is a wide difference between loving someone and marrying her? Marriage is a business proposition. For a man like me with no fortune of his own, it is a way of getting a hold on the future. The widow is an attractive enough woman, but do you think for a moment that I really want to marry her?"

"She assumes you're halfway to the altar by now."

"It amuses her at the moment to think so. She toys with men that way. Oh, I've no doubt that, if I wanted to marry her, I could do it."

"You're very sure of yourself."

"I had enough success in the past to know."

"So marriage is a business."

"That's right."

"And is that true for me as well. Is that why I must marry Alan, for security?"

"There are worse reasons."

Something within her began to grow more and more distressed at the tone of his words. Somehow it was not what she wanted to hear and yet the need to be in his arms, the longing to have him hold her close overcame her distaste at what he felt love to be.

"It seems to me," Fall said, "that, speaking of love, you've shown little of it to me lately. I tried to take care of you and your family, I've tried to help your father, and all I receive for it is your poor opinion of me."

"Oh, Fall," Claire cried, "I do love you. You know I do."

"You have a strange way of showing it."

"And how should I show it?"

Slipping his arms around her, he pulled her to him, lightly kissing her neck. "I know a way," he breathed. Claire's skin seemed to come alive under his touch.

"Oh, you do, do you?"

"Yes. And it's been too long since you were there."

It took her only a moment to let go of the disappointment she had been feeling. She would worry about that later. For now nothing else mattered but this.

Taking her hand he led her back to the house, moving quickly through the dark. They paused in the kitchen just long enough to see that it was empty, then they slipped into Fall's room, closing the door softly behind them and turning the key in the lock. He turned to her, put his arms around her, and kissed her hungrily. Slipping her blouse over her arms, he nuzzled her shoulder. Then all at once, he paused and looked at her. "Are you sure? Is it all right?"

By this time Claire's body was growing so alive

under his touch that all the unpleasantness earlier in the evening was forgotten. Her answer was to clasp him in her arms and kiss him.

"Yes," she moaned. "Yes, oh, yes."

He lifted her easily and carried her to the bed, laying her supple body on the coverlet. Claire reached to undo her laces but he caught her hand.

"No. Let me do it."

She lay quiet as Fall slowly and gently began to undress her. As he moved each garment away, he bent to kiss and nuzzle her responsive flesh, slowly tasting the curve of her throat, the wide swell of her breast, the sweetness of the firm, erect nipple.

She writhed and moaned under his insistent lips and gently probing fingers. Slowly, tantalizingly, Fall raised her hips and slipped her petticoats and skirt down around her ankles. She lay white and lithesome, stretched on the coverlet, her golden hair spilling around her shoulders. He stepped off the bed long enough to remove his own restrictive clothing while Claire scrambled to her knees to watch. She loved the look of him—so solid and firm, his lithe muscular legs, his flat stomach, and broad shoulders, his erect manhood jutting out from his slim hips, throbbing in expectation. She thought he would lay her back on the bed and stretch out beside her. Instead he moved to where she was kneeling, her head almost on a level with the protruding shaft that preceded him. Instinctively Claire bent to take the moistness of it into her mouth, curling a finger lightly around the sensitive tip. This was a new sensation and a very pleasant one. A faint salty taste accompanied the soft warmth that filled her mouth. Lightly she ran her tongue around its delicate softness and felt a surge of pleasure when Fall groaned in ecstasy. She might have gone on longer probing and exploring with her tongue but he was beyond waiting. He put his hands on her shoulders and gently pushed her back on the bed, cradling her head in his arms as he stretched beside her. Now his fingers probed, seeking the soft warmth between her silken thighs, opening and inserting as Claire moaned with the pleasure of it. When he shifted his body onto hers, she felt the pressure of that throbbing shaft as it pushed into her, gently at first, then forcefully, seeking the farthermost regions of the mystery that was her woman's body.

His rhythm carried them both along, pushing, pulling, all else forgotten save the wonderful sensation of pure feeling. Just when Claire thought she could stand it no longer, Fall suddenly withdrew, cradled her in one arm and with the other hand began to stroke that secret nodule that he knew. She was beyond thought now, crying out to be filled with that delightful fullness that only he could give her. Just as she came crashing to the ultimate reaches of ecstasy he finally gave in to her pleading, thrusting into her, and together they soared across that far shore where two people for a few brief moments are melded into one.

Afterward they both lay spent and silent. For Claire, to be in Fall's arms, after having given him as much of herself as was possible to give and having received a like gift of himself, was a comfort and joy only a little less than that ecstatic moment of completion. It washed away the evil, the cold, and the disgust she had felt earlier when Jimmy Cole tried to violate and take by force what she had now joyfully given. She nestled against Fall's chest, burying her head in the soft curve of his neck, safe in the circle of his arms, the beloved body pressed hard and strong against her own.

Whatever happens, she thought, for a little while we have shared something that will be forever ours. A precious memory to carry her through the barren and worrisome future that lay ahead.

The hearing the following morning was almost a disappointment after the dramatic one of two weeks before. Fall immediately produced his Indian, got him to admit that he had been the one to kill Lace Varn whereupon Tom was dismissed. The crowd, only slightly smaller than the one before, seemed let down by such a simple solution and yet felt some admiration toward Fall for having been clever enough to find the real culprit.

As the governor announced Tom's dismissal, Claire rushed to her father, who looked as though his knees were about to give way beneath him. Throwing her arms around him, she led him from the room as quickly as possible. All the way down the stairs and out of the governor's palace, she had to push away those friends of his who were anxious to shower him with their congratulations. She pushed through the crowd, with Caleb on one side of her father and her on the other tightly gripping Tom, as they made their way to the street and down Broad Way. She was worried about her father. He looked very pale and acted somewhat disoriented as though the two weeks in gaol had taken more of a toll than only the physical confinement could account for. She had expected to have to pull him away from the several taverns they passed, so certain was she that he would want to go immediately back to his old haunts. Instead he barely looked up as they walked by and showed no interest in anything or anyone at all. By the time they reached home, she was more certain than ever that something more drastic than a simple depression had possessed her father. She tried to talk with him, but, aside from repeating over and over, "it was a miracle," he had nothing to say. At length she insisted that he go up and lie down for a while, and he agreed without argument as though glad to be led. Taking his arm, she led him up the narrow stairs to his room. Tom shuffled along the hall, still disoriented as though he did not know where he was. Claire helped him stretch out on the bed and was laying a quilt over him when Nell appeared at the door.

"Master Morehead is downstairs to see you, Claire," she said. "You go ahead. I'll take care of getting your father settled."

She had not expected to see Alan so soon. Laying a hand gently on her father's cheek, she saw he was already asleep and left to go to the formal foreroom below. In the tiny room Alan's large body seemed larger than ever. He was standing near the table, and, when she stepped into the room, he moved quickly to her, grasping both her hands tightly.

"I'm so happy for you, Claire, that your father came out of this safely."

"That's kind of you, Alan. I still can barely believe it. It's been a nightmare and it doesn't seem possible that it's really over."

"I can understand that," he said as he helped her to sit on one of the high-backed oak chairs near the table. Pulling up a footstool he sat at her feet, still clasping her hand.

"I wanted to say that, now that all this is finished, it is time for us to begin to think about our future."

Firmly Claire pulled her hand away. "Are you sure, Alan? Considering all that has happened, do you still want me?"

"Oh, yes. I need a wife, and I believe you'll make

me a good one. Ever since I knew you were here in New York I could hardly think of naught else but you, even with all this trouble. That's behind us now and it's time to look ahead."

"But there are some facts that must be faced, Alan. I don't have a dowry—"

"Did I ever ask you for a dowry in Scotland? I've never expected one. We'll live fairly simply and I've enough for the both of us."

"But my father does not seem to be well. His confinement has left him sickly and we cannot stay here. This is not our home."

A frown creased Alan's stolid features. "Well, it's not what I would have wanted. I would have sent for only you, had you waited. But, since they're here and they're your family, we'll have to take them with us to the Upper Mills. It'll be a mite crowded but I suppose you're used to that."

"Alyce too?"

"I'll speak frankly, Claire. It seems to me that, where Alyce goes, trouble is never far behind. But I know you're fond of the girl so I'll just have to accept having her around."

Claire twisted her hands in her lap. "But your Aunt Esther? She'll never accept me. She hates me and she hates the idea of my being your wife."

Alan's wide face grew hard. "I told you before, Claire, she will just have to accept it. Now that my uncle is dead I'll have her to care for as well. It's almost too much family all at once, but that can't be helped."

"In the same house! Alan, it will never work."

He turned to her quietly. "It will work," he said, with such utter finality that she knew it was useless to argue. "I have a pretty solid little farm. We'll manage."

342

Claire jumped up quickly from her chair and strode across the room to the wide window ledge where she began fussing with some flowers Nell had put there that morning.

"I don't know what to say, Alan. It's too soon."

That hard edge on his features grew even more severe. "But you said before that you only needed to know your father was safe."

"I did. At least, I did then. But it's so soon after. Give me a little time to think. I know I must make this decision but I need to think for a while first. I haven't been able to give a thought to the future these last two weeks."

Alan stood up, his huge form towering over her. His hands at his sides were balled into fists. "How much time do you think you'll need now?"

"A few days. A week?"

The hands slowly relaxed. "Very well. If that's the way it must be. I'm a patient man, Claire, but my patience does wear thin with too much usage."

He took a few steps toward her. "It seems I want you more and more now that I know you're here."

To Claire's horror he reached out and drew her to him, enveloping her with his arms. Crossing her hands across her breast, Claire tried to block out all memories of the previous night as she felt Alan crush her body against his. His energetic embrace was suffocating. She pursed her lips as he leaned back, tipped up her chin, and kissed her, his lips wet and thick. She felt like stone beneath his flesh.

"We've a lot of time to make up for," Alan said hoarsely.

Claire closed her eyes to block out the nearness of his face.

"I suppose we do."

Alan seemed completely unaware of her lack of

enthusiasm. He kissed her again, then stepped away, and reached for his battered round hat on the table.

"Very well then. I'll go now but I'll be back in a week. Try to have your things ready so we don't lose much time. It's seeding time for the barley."

"I'll try," she murmured.

She watched him leave through the door, then stepped back to the window to see him throw himself up on the wagon that stood in the road outside. Without a backward look at the house, he snapped the reins and lumbered off. Claire leaned against the checkered curtain and closed her eyes.

A week. One short week.

Fifteen

The noise from the Sign of the Dove was evident all the way up the lane as far as Broad Way. The *Flying Dolphin* had dropped anchor in the harbor that afternoon. Ostensibly a merchant brig carrying timber and tar to Bristol and returning loaded with fine cloth and French wines, it was common knowledge among the riffraff of New York that she was actually a pirate ship. Her captain, Raef Duvall, was known as one of the most ruthless men to walk the boards since he preyed on English, French, Spanish, and Dutch vessels alike, all with the quiet blessings of the merchants of New York. He led a boisterous, villainous crew, and most of them had come straight to the Dove to work off several weeks of boredom at sea.

Old Maude stood behind the caged bar fiddling with some dishes on a tray. At the sudden eruption of a racket at the far end of the room, she glanced up to see that one of the sailors from the *Dolphin*—the one with the ravaged face and a handkerchief wrapped around his head to cover one eye—was poised on the table and reaching for the throat of a mate from the *Coral Island* who was sitting across from him. Without a word Maude grabbed up a wooden tankard

345

from below the bar and heaved it across the room, where it caught the seaman on the side of his head. The man staggered and cursed, looking quickly around.

"Take it outside," Maude yelled and was satisfied to see him back off the table, glaring at his adversary. Maude went back to fussing with the dishes on her tray. When she had arranged them to her satisfaction, she nodded to a burly man sitting to one side. Without a word he rose from his place and stepped behind the bar.

"Keep one eye on these cutthroats and the other on the liquor," she said humorlessly. "I'm going above."

The man nodded again as Maude picked up the tray and hobbled over to a narrow stairway along one wall. Taking them one step at a time, her greasy skirt clutched in one hand, she eased her bent body up the steep stairs. The short dark hall above was only slightly less noisy than below but Maude was relieved to be there. She moved to the closed door at the far end, opened it with one hand, stepped inside, and pushed it closed behind her. It was a tiny room, airless and with one tiny window that gave little light in the gray afternoon. That was enough, however, to satisfy her that the figure on the bed had not moved since her last visit. She set the tray on a small square table next to the bed—the only furniture in the room—pulled back one corner of the sheet, and poked one finger at the bloody bandage around the head of the man lying there. To her surprise he moved imperceptibly.

"Oh, so you are alive," she mumbled.

Jimmy Cole stirred under the covers and gingerly moved his head to where he could focus one eye on the old crone bending over him.

"Oh. It's you," he croaked hoarsely.

346

"Yes, it's me. And you'd better be thankful for it's due to me that you're here at all."

"Thought maybe I'd died and gone to hell."

Old Maude chuckled softly to herself. "Hell it is, but it's still on earth." She eased her ancient bones down on the bed. "I thought you were done for, for certain. Never saw such an apparition since I've been here. Went out to the necess'ry house, I had, and in the dark, when this figure rises up before me like a demon from the nether regions — blood runnin' down your face, bent over, clutchin' at the air — gave me such a start as to add ten years to my life."

"Ten years to your life, old woman, and you wouldn't be here."

Maude chuckled again, appreciating the joke. "Still got some life left in you, I see, in spite of your broke head."

Groaning, Jimmy reached tenderly up and touched the bandage. "Feels like I was kicked by a horse. I'll get 'em for this!"

"Your plan didn't quite work, did it? What went wrong? She didn't want you to lie for her?"

He muttered something but Maude only caught the blasphemies.

"I'm not surprised. With such as you a lie would never of held up in the governor's council. Don't know why you wanted to do it anyway. Never knew you to do a favor for anybody."

Jimmy only glared at her in response and eased his body away from the edge of the bed. A sudden noise from below brought Maude to her feet, shaking out her skirts.

"Got to get back afore they break every piece of furniture in the place. I brought you some gruel."

"I'd rather have ale."

"Brought you some of that too. Take what you can.

347

No matter to me. I'll add it to the shot."

She hobbled to the door, still chuckling to herself, and closed the door behind her. Jimmy lay looking up at the cracked ceiling, turning over the crowding memories. How long had he lain here knowing nothing? How many days had passed since that old crone had dragged him more dead than alive to this stuffy room? He ought to have asked her. He had to get out of this place. He must pull himself together and get up from this bed. Had his ship sailed without him? He did not want to miss it and yet he knew he was not leaving New York until he had had his revenge. A silly wench and an arrogant dandy were not going to get away with pushing Jimmy Cole around. He would get even with them if it was the last thing he ever did.

But how? He must think of a way.

A slow smile spread over his broken lips. Of course. There was a way; he had known it all along and not seen it. But he had to be on his feet to make it work.

He tried to raise himself up in the bed, but the room whirled around him so dizzily he was forced to sink back on the pillow. All right. So he couldn't do it yet. But he would. He would keep trying and forcing himself until he was on his feet again. He would see them suffer for this if it was the last thing he ever did!

"I'm worried about Papa, Fall."

Reluctantly Claire pulled her eyes away from the far end of the garden where her father sat under the tulip tree.

"I don't know why. He's safe now. What is there to worry about?"

"He's been acting so strangely. Haven't you noticed? All day he does nothing but sit and stare into the distance. I almost wish he would go back to carousing with his friends. This is so unlike him."

"There's bound to be some lingering effect from his weeks in gaol. Being caged up does something to a man—especially a man like your father."

Claire felt some annoyance that he would not take her concern seriously. She stared back at Tom sitting so morosely. Alyce had joined him and was kneeling on the ground with her head in his lap as he gently stroked her hair away from her forehead. Alyce seemed to be the only person now who could break through the fog surrounding him and reach the man inside. Tom showed no interest in the rest of them, only an indifference bordering on hostility toward herself or Jamie or Nell or Caleb. Only for Alyce had he still a gentleness, a sympathy.

Tipping her head back, Claire rested against the stones on the outside of the house and lifted her face to the warmth of the sun. It was so warm, so strong. Much stronger than any sun she remembered in Scotland. And yet she loved it. Nell admonished her constantly that no self-respecting woman would dare risk the blemish of a freckle or, even worse, a dark tan you got from being in the sun too much. Yet in spite of such horrors, she reveled in it.

When had Tom changed so? It wasn't difficult for her to remember. It had been like going from night to day, and it had come after she had faced her father with the mystery that hung over their family, the same mystery that seemed to be related to the MacDairmids. Even though he had protested vehemently that she was fantasizing, that there was nothing wrong between the two families, she could not deny that he had not been the same man since that day. He had retreated into some far place where she could not reach him. Even at the hearing he had been withdrawn, almost as though he did not care what happened to him.

She felt Fall stir on the bench beside her. There was such a comfort in sitting here in the sunshine with his firm body next to hers that it almost made her forget her concern for Tom. It gave her so much pleasure to have him near, and yet . . . the days were going by so quickly and still she had not been able to bring herself to speak to Fall of Alan's ultimatum. Neither had she been able to make up her own mind about what to do. At times the two of them seemed so close even though there was this great chasm between them—one she did not know how to cross.

"You're frowning," Fall murmured. Protectively he squeezed her hand. "Don't worry about your father. He's a sound man. He'll come out of this."

"I hope you're right," Claire said, smiling up at him.

He almost leaned down to kiss her until he remembered that there might be other eyes watching.

"Excuse me, Mister Fall." It was Nell standing in the doorway, wiping her hands on her long apron. "There's a soldier here to see you."

"Soldier? What soldier?" Before Fall could get to his feet, the man came striding out the kitchen door at the back of the house.

"Master MacDairmid?"

Fall stood up with his hands on his hips. "Yes. I know you. It's Captain Rafael, isn't it? Of the governor's guard?"

"Aye, that's right, sir."

"You were on the expedition I accompanied to Fort Orange a few weeks ago?"

"That's correct, sir. I was."

"Well, what's wrong? What is it you want with me?"

The captain stirred restlessly in his heavy armor. "Sir, the governor has sent me to fetch you at once."

"What's the matter? Is there trouble with that Indian I returned to justice?"

"Don't know, sir, and, if I did, 'twouldn't be my place to say. All I know is that the governor says to fetch you at once. That it's a matter of some urgency."

Fall and Claire exchanged glances. There was something in the captain's manner that suggested this was no trivial matter. Since he had been sitting in his shirt sleeves and jerkin, Fall begged enough time to get his hat and coat and make himself presentable. The captain, grateful not to receive an argument, gladly agreed.

"Would you like me to come along?" Claire whispered as she followed him inside.

"No. Whatever it is, I'm obviously not under arrest. He may simply want my advice on that Indian matter. I know he's concerned lest it mushroom into real trouble with the tribe."

She reached up and kissed him on the lips. "Come back soon. I don't want to have to worry about you too."

He reached around and squeezed her ample skirts. "As soon as I can."

The two men spoke little on the walk back to the fort at the end of Manhattan. The captain did not seem to relish his duty, and Fall was more concerned than he had pretended to Claire. He was glad when they finally walked through the old walls of the fort, dusty as it was inside from the marching of a listless troop practicing drills. The small courtyard was nearly filled with soldiers and civilians alike. Most of the townspeople milled around the governor's door hoping to get inside to see him. The noise from the

351

wharves on the south side added to the confusion within the fort, as did the overpowering aroma of fish from the market just beyond.

Fall made his way straight past the knots of people waiting by the door, most of whom eyed him with varying degrees of jealousy and irritation, and stepped inside the cool dark interior. The governor's parlor had two small windows with tiny panes of leaded glass that allowed little light so the room seemed cooler than it actually was. From the doorway Fall saw Governor Fletcher standing behind a table near the hearth facing him and, as he entered the room, a figure rose from one of the high-backed tapestry chairs on either side of the table. The man was very tall and thin, and he wore a wig that curled to his shoulders and fell gracefully over a lace-pointed collar.

"Come in, Fall," Governor Fletcher said in a un-smiling manner. More accustomed to the man's friendly, casual attitude, Fall felt a stir of concern.

"I was sorry to have to summon you so abruptly but a matter of some importance has come up. You've met Mister Wisham?" he indicated the tall gentleman who bowed pompously.

"I don't believe I have had the pleasure," Fall said, searching his mind. He had seen that long face before, but where?

"Richard Wisham, Commissioner of Tariffs and Custom for Their Most Sublime Majesties, William and Mary, of England," the man answered, intoning his title as though it was about to be bestowed on him.

"McFall MacDairmid," Fall answered, keeping his expression as nonchalant as possible. He turned back to Fletcher. "What has happened? Has my savage been giving you trouble?"

"Oh, no. He's very docile for the moment though we are keeping a watchful eye on him just in case his fellow savages attempt a rescue. No, this is a quite different matter." Fall noticed that Fletcher looked decidedly uncomfortable and his own sense of unease began to grow. "Perhaps Mister Wisham might like—"

Fletcher eased himself into one of the tall chairs and in effect retired from the field, leaving it to Wisham and a more and more bewildered Fall. Fall refused to sit where he could be towered over by Commissioner Wisham and so perched on one end of the table, resting his gloved hand on his knee. He hoped he presented the picture of an interested observer even though he had a strong suspicion of what was coming.

"It has been brought to our attention," Wisham intoned in his most officious voice, "that certain 'discrepancies' exist in the cargo manifest of the *Selkirk*. You arrived on that vessel, I believe, some weeks ago."

"That's correct. We sailed from Leith in Scotland, with one stop at Plymouth to take on both cargo and passengers. But if there was a problem with either, you should talk to Captain Mendel, not to me."

"We intend to do that as soon as the ship returns to port. Unfortunately, she is now in the West Indies and not expected back for another month."

"Well, I hardly see—"

Commissioner Wisham set one hand on his hip beneath his elegant flowered coat and dismissed Fall's objections with a deft wave of his large, lace-edged handkerchief. "Let us not waste time, Mister Mac-Dairmid. We have strong evidence that certain shipments were taken aboard the *Selkirk* at Leith bound for the merchants of New York and sent by one Sir

353

Francis Murray of Edinburgh. I don't need to elaborate on the fact that such an act consists of illegal importations for the purpose of profit and is strictly against the laws of custom."

Fall tapped his glove against his knee, smiling without humor. "How interesting. I should have thought Sir Francis would know better."

"And we have your name on a list as agent. So please do not pretend this is the first you've heard of the matter."

Fall gave the governor a surreptitious glance. He was looking everywhere but at the victim, obviously unhappy to be dragged into this but too friendly toward Fall to abandon him to the lions. "I know nothing of any illegal cargo," he said with some belligerence.

"Come now, Fall," the governor spoke up impatiently. "It will do you no good to protest your innocence. Commissioner Wisham came to me with the lists that prove you were involved, and it was only because of our friendship that he allowed me to have this private meeting with you first!"

"I suppose I should be grateful."

Wisham dabbed at his long nose with his linen square. "This is a very serious matter, Mister MacDairmid. His Majesty cannot tolerate flagrant abuse of the Navigation and Staple Act. Foreigners are strictly prohibited from taking part in trade with the colonies as, I suspect, both you and Sir Francis well know."

"That act was aimed more at the Dutch than the Scots."

"Be that as it may, it included all foreigners. And there are very severe penalties."

Fall made a quick decision to try bravado. "Gentlemen," he said, smiling at them both. "We are a long way from England. Surely a matter of a few small bits of furniture and cloth—"

Wisham drew himself up, towering over both men. "I must ask you to remember, sir, that I have been entrusted to carry out the king's mandate. These 'few bits of furniture and cloth' were brought illegally into this port without authority and without paying custom. I cannot simply overlook this. It is a matter of thievery."

Fall's temper got the best of him. "Then why come to me? What about the merchant of New York who accepted the goods and sold them privately. Doesn't he deserve to be here as well?"

He saw Governor Fletcher turn a shade lighter. They both knew whom he was talking about but something in the governor's manner told him that was the last name he wished to hear spoken.

"We are accusing no one in the city at the moment since we have no proof that points to anyone receiving the goods. That is, unless you would like to tell us."

Fall caught the governor glaring him a warning. He gave a short laugh. He was not the man to try to shift the blame on someone else's shoulders in the hope of escaping his own guilt.

"I neither confess that I brought in such goods nor admit that I sold them to anyone else."

Governor Fletcher stifled a sigh of relief while Wisham walked around to stand facing Fall directly.

"You may claim innocence all you wish, but the facts are that we have proof you were involved."

"What proof? And from whom?"

"A manifest of the entire cargo from Leith and two pieces with Sir Francis Murray's name, which were reclaimed from the *Osprey*, the pirate ship. One of their seamen will testify that they were taken from the

Selkirk when it was pirated at sea."

It was beginning to make sense. "And that sea-man's name?"

"That is not important now. What is more to the point is what to do about you."

"Am I to be thrown in jail? Hanged on the gallows? Sent packing back to Scotland? Come, gentlemen, let's get to the point. I suspect you would have not called me here today if you had not already decided on some proper punishment. You would have simply sent the guard to arrest me."

"Now, Fall," Fletcher said, rising from his chair. "You do me an injustice. It took some convincing to allow Wisham here to agree to this meeting. He was all for hauling you off to gaol and making an issue of the whole thing. He had you brought here as a favor to me."

And to keep Philipse's name out of it, Fall thought bitterly. "I'm grateful," he said with heavy sarcasm. Fletcher ignored his tone and went on.

"This Navigation and Staple law is most injurious to free trade in the town, and I, for one, wish with all my heart that Parliament would repeal it. But since it is the law, we must live with it for the time being."

"Which leaves me where?"

Wisham took the seat the governor had vacated, crossed his knees, and tapped his long fingers together. He had the elegant hands of a woman, Fall thought — soft, manicured, heavy with embossed rings. A man who obviously lived well.

"Because of your excellent services to the governor since your arrival in New York," he intoned, "I have agreed to reduce your punishment to a simple fine. You pay the crown two thousand florins and the matter will be dropped."

"What!" Fall jumped up from the table as his

gloves fell to the floor.

"That is, of course, as long as the crime is not repeated. Should you be tempted to flaunt the law a second time, you will not receive such easy terms."

"Two thousand florins! Why, that is a fortune! I've never seen that amount of money in my entire life. I can't pay a fine of such exorbitant proportions."

"You have friends, Fall," the governor said almost apologetically. "We'll help you find a way."

Fall gave him a long look. Was this a reference to Frederick Philipse? Was that gentleman going to bear some of the blame by paying part of the fine? Even so, where on earth was he going to find the rest?

"It's too high. Far too high."

Wisham continued to tap his fingers together. "Perhaps you would rather take up residence in the gaol house until we can have a trial? It's not the most accommodating place I've heard."

Fall glared at the man, wishing he could grab him by his lace-collared throat and drag him out of his chair. "I won't do it," he snapped. "It's robbery, pure and simple, and I won't accept it. You think I don't know where most of that money would end up? Certainly not in the crown treasury. How much would go to you, Governor? And how much to keep this dandy in his gold rings and brocade silks?"

The governor gasped while Fall had the satisfaction of seeing Wisham's aplomb finally give way. Two bright spots appeared on his pale cheeks and his eyes narrowed like a snake's.

"Really, Fall. You do us both an injustice," Fletcher spluttered.

"I've heard enough," Wisham snapped, rising to his feet. "I have offered you a perfectly appropriate solution but, if you would rather suffer for your crimes, it is of no concern to me. I shall call the

357

guard."

"No!" Fletcher cried and grabbed at the man's arm. "Mister MacDairmid is reacting hastily, out of pride and poor judgment. I feel certain that, if we allow him a little time to think it over, he will come to see the wisdom of our plan. Take a few moments, Fall. Come, Commissioner. You and I will leave him here for a while to ponder the matter."

"I don't like it," Wisham glared. "What's to keep the man from bolting out the nearest window?"

"To go where? We are not in England, after all. New York is surrounded by wilderness. Besides, Fall is an honorable man. Give me your word you will stay here, and we will leave you alone to think the matter over."

"You can both go to the devil," Fall mumbled.

"You see?"

Fletcher patted Fall's shoulder good-naturedly. "It's only his high spirits talking. Come, Wisham. Let's go have a glass of my fine French brandy. I guarantee Fall will be here when we return."

Reluctantly Wisham let the governor lead him to the door while Fall watched them go. He felt certain the governor had something up his sleeve, but what it was he could not tell. He had only to wait a few moments after the door had closed to learn that he was partially right, at least. He had only been alone long enough to pace the room twice when there was a soft tap at the door. It opened and a serving girl poked her head around and laid a finger to her lips.

"You're to come with me, sir," she whispered.

"Who are you?"

"Shh," she cautioned, looking back into the hall. "Be quiet, please, sir, and just come with me."

What now, Fall wondered, but he followed the girl out of the door and into the hall, half-amused at the way she looked in each direction, then scurried down to the end where a short stairway was recessed in a wall. Hurrying up the short flight, she tapped softly on a door, waited for a muffled "enter" from inside, then opened it just far enough for Fall to step through, and closed it behind him.

He was standing in a small office furnished very practically and simply with a tall desk against one wall, a square plank table in the center, and two chairs at the far end flanking a narrow fireplace. And standing in front of the hearth, brilliantly attired in a scarlet overskirt and long, pointed stomacher, was Immetje Strycker. Her hands were folded primly across her waist and her aristocratic head was thrown back, which made her look taller than ever. The ruby necklace around her narrow throat caught the sunlight from the long windows and glimmered ominously.

"You'll forgive my surprise," Fall said with a startled smile. "But you are just about the last person I expected to see here."

Immetje's chin came down a notch and she smiled graciously. "Oh, Governor Fletcher and I are old friends. It is really not so unusual for me to visit his home. Please come in, Fall."

Remembering his manners, Fall crossed the room to her and kissed her hand with aplomb. "It is always a pleasure to see you, madam."

Immetje suppressed a sudden overwhelming desire to stroke the sleek head that bent over her hand. She gave a short, mincing laugh. "I wish I could believe that. Please, sit down. I wish to talk with you."

Filled with curiosity, Fall took one of the two chairs after she had settled in the other. They were only a few feet apart but Immetje spoke so softly that he had to strain toward her to hear her words.

"If this is about the trip north I promised you—" he began, but she waved a hand to interrupt him.

"No, no. I understand why that had to be postponed in the interest of your 'family retainer's' problems. You handled that matter quite well, my dear. I hope now you can put such mundane matters from your mind and think about your own future. My lands will still be there when you find it convenient to have a look at them."

"You are very understanding, madam."

"How long will it be, do you suppose, until I can prevail on you to stop calling me 'madam' and begin to use my rightful name? It is Immetje, you know."

Fall smiled knowingly at her. "Then you are very understanding Immetje."

"That's much better. Now, to the business at hand. I have learned from my friend the governor that you have come into some difficulty with Commissioner Wisham."

"News travels fast."

"Only to those of us who make it our business to know."

"I had no idea my problems were of so much concern to you."

Immetje sat back in her chair, laying her sleek arms along the polished arms, looking at him sideways through slanted eyes.

"Then you are very obtuse. I have tried in every way I know to tell you how important. Not in so many words, of course—that would not do at all. But surely you must have guessed."

Fall studied his hands. "I would not have presumed on your favors, my lady. After all, you could have any man in New York. You have only to lift your finger."

"But not you?"

"I didn't mean that."

"Good. Let us not mince words, Fall. I am a direct person and I dislike all these roundabout games men and women are forced to play. The truth is I am a widow and I must marry again. My late husband was a good man but extremely stolid and completely obsessed with building his fortune. My father was not a poor man, and, when I was quite young, Mister Stryker acquired me as one more important asset of his business. Once he made his fortune, the Lord saw fit to rob him of the chance to enjoy it and that delicious opportunity fell to me. I must marry again, but I am determined that this time I will pluck some of the fruits of pleasure in that marriage that were denied me the first time."

Fall rubbed a finger along his square chin. "You are very frank, Immetje. It is a refreshing trait in a woman."

"I know your reputation, and I know you have had your share of coquettes and married ladies. Your string is a long one. I confess I have been a little surprised and perturbed that you have not made an attempt to win my favors. On the other hand, it has convinced me that your main concern is not my fortune and that is something I feel very strongly about. There are any number of attractive but grasping young fellows who would wed me, but I would have to be very stupid indeed not to know what they are really after."

"How can you be so certain that I am not as much a fortunehunter as they? Perhaps my reluctance was contrived, just to make you think that."

She laughed. "That's possible but I don't think so. I have a certain talent for judging character."

Abruptly Fall got to his feet and leaned one arm along the mantel, rubbing his hand along the highly polished wood.

"I brought you here today," Immetje went on, "because I know you were levied with a ruinous fine for smuggling."

"Ruinous to say the least. It's absurd. Impossible."

Immetje folded her hands primly in her lap. "That is true but Wisham is a covetous man who is determined to return to England a rich one. Most of what he has accumulated in his post as commissioner has come directly from just such matters. It is more profitable for him to collect fines than to jail or hang those who flout the navigation law. This one, I admit, was worse than any before."

"He certainly has no chance of collecting it. I have never seen that much money in my entire life. And I don't have enough wealthy friends to put it together." He stopped and looked at her sharply. "You wouldn't be offering to pay it, would you?"

Immetje gave a quick laugh. "Dear Fall, you are indeed obtuse. Why don't you propose to me on the spot? It would solve all your problems."

He was completely taken aback. "Why, madam, I had not thought of marriage quite in such mercenary terms."

"I know you haven't," she said, chuckling to herself. "That is what endears you to me. That, and other things." She gave him a look so sensual that Fall could not suppress his surprise. This whole conversation made him decidedly wary. But Immetje was enjoying herself and had no intention of dismissing him yet.

"It seems I am going to have to speak for you, Fall, dear, even though I half hoped you might spare me the need. Very well, then. You need two thousand florins and I need a husband. It pleases me to think of you in that capacity. So, marry me, my dear, the fine will be paid, and you shall be a rich man."

To his dismay Fall found himself for once at a loss. "Madam . . . you do me a great honor . . . I don't know what to say . . ."

"A simple 'yes' will do nicely."

"I hadn't planned to marry at all, that is, certainly not for a long time—"

For the first time Immetje's good humor began to grow cool about the edges as she saw the possibility looming that she might be refused. He picked it up at once.

"I am completely taken aback," Fall went on, resuming his seat. He reached for her hands and tried to summon as much sincerity as possible. "You do me a great honor, ma—Immetje. Forgive me if my surprise prevents me from answering at once. It has all come so fast—the accusation, the huge fine, and now . . ."

His sincerity seemed to work. Some of the coolness faded.

"Perhaps you would like a little time to think it over. I will grant you that. I'm sure my offer was—unexpected."

"Indeed it was. You are the most gracious of women," Fall said, lightly kissing her fingers.

"A day? Two days? That is the most I will grant you. You see, my dear, I, too, would like to have this matter settled."

"Two days would be more than sufficient."

"Very well. I had hoped we could settle the matter this afternoon but, since it appears to be more of a business proposition than a love match, well, any good businessman will tell you that a decision of such long-range importance should never be made without time to think. You see, Jacob Strycker taught me well."

He was aware of the slight hurt in her tone even

though she masked it bravely. If she could not have what she wanted on the personal level, then she would have it on the business level. Just as long as she had it. Abruptly she rose.

"Now. Go and collect your things and leave this house. I shall expect you with an answer the day after tomorrow. At *my* house, this time. Never mind the governor. He will know where you are."

Fall took her hands and gave them a gentle squeeze before leaving the room. He felt he should give her a kiss, no matter how perfunctorily, but he could not bring himself to do it. It seemed too much as though it was expected of him and, besides, might give her the idea that he had already accepted her offer. Instead he collected his hat and departed quickly.

"Good lord!" he raged to Claire after he had roamed the streets of the town long enough to work up a fine wrath.

"Marriage on demand! Dance to her tune like a puppet. Pull the string and the Scotsman dangles, this way, then that! God in heaven!"

"Perhaps she really thought she was doing you a favor."

"A favor! She cooked this up with the two of them—that venal governor and that greedy commissioner. They don't care about my breaking the law—half the merchants of New York do it every day. They're not going after Philipse, you notice. 'We have no proof against anyone in the city,' " he said, mincing the commissioner's pompous tones. "It would not surprise me if the widow set that fine so high on purpose, just so she could buy me off with it."

"She must want you very badly. I had no idea your charms were so potent."

Fall glared at her. "I refuse to play lackey to a woman just because she has a fortune."

"Then that makes you different from every other man in New York. Come, Fall. It's a tempting proposition, admit it. You'd never want for money again. And she's not unattractive."

"I can't believe you said that. I thought you loved me, and here you are palming me off on this woman I feel no affection for in the least."

"You said you loved me too," Claire said quietly, "but you have not offered to marry me. And who was it said that marriage was a business. That you needed a wife with a fortune."

He stopped pacing the room. "I did say that, didn't I? But I wanted it to be *my* decision. I certainly did not expect to be bought off."

"What is the difference? Instead of your venal proposition it is hers."

"I knew you would never understand."

"So what are you going to do? Refuse her?"

He sat down on the bed, leaning forward with his elbows on his knees. "I don't know. If I refuse her offer, where will I find one hundred florins, much less two thousand? I'll have to go to gaol or slip out some dark night aboard the first ship bound for Scotland. Not a promising future either way."

"It seems you have little choice."

Her words were so sensible, so practical. Yet all the time she was dying inside. How she longed for him to clasp her in his arms and tell her he loved only her. They might go far away from New York, away from Alan and Immetje and begin life somewhere together. Yet that did not seem to occur to Fall. As near as she could tell, he did not see her in his future at all. And for this she had sent Alan away!

Suddenly consumed with a burning resentment,

Claire jumped off the bed and began pulling on her petticoats.

Fall looked up quizzically, "Where are you going?"

"I have chores to do."

"I have the most momentous decision of my life to make, and you have to go off to complete your chores! How can you be so callous? I need you."

Furiously Claire pulled her skirts over her petticoats and twisted the tabs at her waist. "You don't need me for anything except to warm your bed. Make up your own mind."

"What's got into you? You don't have anything to be angry about. I'm the one who has to yoke myself to a Dutch *huysvrouw*!"

Claire yanked at the laces of her bodice. "Go ahead and marry your rich widow. I don't care what you do!" Fighting back her tears, she stalked from the room, slamming the door behind her.

Sixteen

The night was endless. The hours inched their way toward morning while Claire turned, first one way then the next, trying to calm the teeming cauldron in her mind. It made her sick to think of Fall marrying Immetje Strycker, and then it made her furious that she even cared. She must accept the inevitable and marry Alan Morehead. That was the only security for her and for her family. Yet when she thought of Alan, all she could recall was the feel of his wet lips on her own while she stood stonelike and numb. That thought led to the treacherous image of lying in Fall's arms, his hands roaming her body, his lips against hers.

Resolutely she fought down the memory. It was hopeless to think of Fall. They had no future and never would have. Yet how could she settle for Alan after . . .

Claire had lost track of how long this interminable inner argument had gone on when all at once she was conscious of Alyce lying at her side. The girl was unusually still. She had barely changed positions while Claire had been thrashing about. Instinctively Claire laid a hand on her sister's forehead and found it abnormally warm to the touch. Not alarmingly hot but warm enough to indicate that something was wrong. Alyce had always been susceptible to fever, and for a moment Claire forgot her own pressing concerns and concentrated on her sister.

At length she slipped into a half-sleep that mercifully, when she again opened her eyes, had lasted until dawn. A gray light softly illuminated the corners of the room and outside the crowing of a rooster and the bleat of a sheep from the barn gave credence to a new day.

Alyce's forehead was even warmer than before and now she stirred as restlessly as Claire had during the night. Claire slipped from the bed, drew on her clothes, and made her way quietly to the kitchen where she found Nell already stirring up the embers in the hearth.

"Alyce has a fever," she said, reaching for a cup of the tea Nell had brewing on the trivet. It was strong and hot and provided her with a small surge of energy. Her heavy-lidded eyes, still aching from the sleepless night, began to ease. "She's an easy prey to this type of illness. I'll fix her a flaxseed posset — there's nothing like it for drawing out infection — and I think she should stay in bed today and keep warm. I'll have to go to the market alone."

"No, you won't," Nell answered as she broke some eggs into a large, brown pottery bowl. "I was going to go along with you anyway. Caleb told me that a ship I've been waiting for, the *Bonnie Brae* out of Glasgow, came into port late yesterday. I may have a letter on it from my nephew and a length of good serge I asked him to send me from home. I intended to go down there this morning anyway."

Claire was relieved not to have to venture out into

the market crowds alone. Since her terrible experience in the old warehouse she dreaded going into the lower reaches of town out of fear that she might spot Jimmy Cole's horrible face lurking somewhere in the knots of people who were always around. That was foolish, she knew—the man was probably dead. Yet there had been no mention of a sailor found killed in the old warehouse building, not in the occasional broadsheets passed around town, not in the gossip that circulated among the populace. Her anxiety, no matter how unreasoned, was very real.

So it was that later in the morning the two women set off, having left Alyce surrounded by various remedies and under strict orders not to stir from her bed.

The day was overcast with a thick gray haze hanging over the river in the distance, obscuring the hills on the other side. It was humid and warm, and Claire was glad when Nell suggested they go to Coentis Slip where the *Bonnie Brae* was moored before negotiating the crowds at the market.

As they approached the slip it seemed to be as teeming with people and activity the market itself, if not more so. The first mate was ensconced behind a table on the pier surrounded by kegs and barrels and bales stacked haphazardly all around him and along the slip almost as far as the street. Workers moved among the cargo calling orders and ribald comments while departing passengers mingled with townspeople who, like Nell, had come to inquire about messages and parcels from home.

Claire hung back as Nell elbowed her way into the crowd grouped around the first mate, leaning against a stack of bales which were being ignored for the moment by the men unloading the ship.

She was standing opposite the stern of the *Bonnie Brae* where she could look up at the decks and intricate rigging. A sea gull perched on one end of the cross spar was quarreling furiously with a spotted tern who eyed the same location. As Claire watched them with amusement, she saw the door to the captain's cabin just below open and two men emerge. She recognized the ship's master by his coat and plumed hat, and she only half-noticed the gentleman who followed him, a tall figure in a black velvet coat whose luminous folds glimmered in the bright sunlight. Claire had looked back to the gulls when suddenly her eyes riveted on the two men. She could not see their faces but there was something threateningly familiar about the black coat. His height and stance, the set of his shoulders—it was more subconscious than obvious but instinctively she felt her body press back against the bales. There was a narrow slit between the stacked boxes, and Claire moved to where she could watch without being seen. The two men started down the steps to the main deck, the captain talking energetically. As they neared the ship's railing, she got a good look at their faces and her breath froze in her throat.

Edgar MacDairmid! It couldn't be but it was. She would know that face anywhere—the dark, pointed beard and narrow mustache, the slitted eyes that always looked as though they were appraising everything in sight, the black hair falling to his shoulders . . .

Claire shrank farther back within the narrow recess, drawing in her breath. The two men stepped lightly down the ramp to pass not three feet from her. As they neared, she heard Edgar speaking.

". . . a seedy little town. Too new, too rustic, and

370

too uncivilized."

"I wonder that you came so far to visit it since you find it so little to your liking," the master answered.

Edgar gave one of the humorless chuckles Claire remembered with such trepidation.

"I told you, I have business here. Once that is accomplished, I shall be on the first ship bound for Scotland."

They passed on into the busy wharf area, and in the general confusion Claire could not make out the master's answer. She waited several long minutes before she dared to peer around her screen to see if they had disappeared. Edgar must not see her! The sight of him, much less the questions his comment about "business" in New York raised in her anxious mind, were enough to make her concern of the previous night pale in comparison. When she was satisfied they had left the area, she slipped out far enough to see across the street facing the wharf and glimpsed Edgar's black coat just entering the door to a tavern that bordered the street. Darting across the pier, Claire careened into Nell, who was standing talking with the first mate of the *Bonnie Brae*. Her fingers dug into Nell's arm.

"I have to go home, Nell. At once!"

Nell looked up at her in confusion. "But I've only just got my turn. What's the matter, Claire? You look as though you just saw a ghost."

"It's worse than a ghost. Oh, Nell, I have to leave right now. If you won't come with me, I'll go alone, but I must get home."

"But the market—"

"Forget the market. It doesn't matter any more."

At the tone of near hysteria in Claire's voice, Nell began to grow concerned. For a girl who was usually so level-headed, Claire was acting very strangely. She had already turned her back and was threading her way through the crowd.

"I'll come back later," Nell spoke to the mate and darted after Claire, managing to catch up with her a block from the slip. The girl was walking so fast that Nell was hard put to keep up with her and hadn't the breath to ask questions though her curiosity was raging. When Claire finally turned into Fair Street, she broke into a run that did not slacken until she was inside the kitchen of Fall's house. Nell was minutes behind her and leaned against the wall, gasping for breath.

"Are you going to tell me what this is all about?" she gasped. "I've never seen you in such a state."

"I can't! Trust me, Nell. Don't ask me any questions. Just be quiet and let me think. I've got to figure out what to do."

With her ample chest still heaving, Nell watched as Claire paced back and forth in the narrow room. Slowly her irritation began to be replaced with real concern.

"Very well. But you'll think better with something comforting in your stomach. Sit down and let me fix you a cup of tea."

"I can't sit down," Claire cried, twisting her hands against her waist. Suddenly she stopped and looked around.

"Where is Caleb?"

"Caleb? Why, I suppose he's back of the barn. He said something about repairing the sheep pen today."

Claire was already through the door and racing around the side of the house before Nell's words were out. She found Caleb in his shirt sleeves working a long saw on one of the planks of the fence. He looked

372

up at her call, startled at the sight of her anxious face.

"Caleb, you've got to take me to the Upper Mills right away," Claire cried without any preliminary explanations.

"Just like that? Pick up and leave?" Caleb barely managed to stifle his amazement at this preposterous demand.

"Yes. The sooner the better. Please, Caleb. I can't go alone, and I've got to get out of this town right away. Immediately!"

Very deliberately Caleb laid down the saw and leaned against the fence of the sheep pen. "You don't know what you're asking, Miss Claire. Do you have any idea how far away the Upper Mills is?"

"It's only just up the river, isn't it?"

"At least twenty or thirty miles. That's a long trip, especially when you're starting out without any preparations. It would make more sense to think about this, get together what you need and then—"

"I can't wait for all that," Claire cried with a sob in her voice. "Can't you understand? I've got to go now. If you won't take me, I'll go by myself, this very afternoon."

"Now, wait a minute, Claire. Calm down and let's talk this over sensibly and rationally. Now—what is this all about? Why do you have to go north this very afternoon?"

Claire turned her head away from his searching eyes. "I can't tell you that. You'll just have to trust me that it's absolutely imperative that I get out of this town at once!"

Caleb rubbed a hand over his thinning hair. "Seems to me that you're asking for a lot of trust considering you want me to venture into the woods on a moment's notice. What about Master Fall? What's he going to say about your leaving so hastily like this?"

"It doesn't matter what he thinks. He's not involved in this," she lied. "And I can explain to him later. Will you take me?"

"But your Pa, and Alyce?"

"They'll be taken care of later too." She laid a hand on his arm, looking earnestly into his face. "Believe me, I wouldn't ask this of you, Caleb, if I did not see it as my only choice. Please, take me to Upper Mills."

"But Miss Claire, do you know what you're asking? It's bad enough by boat though that's sheer pleasure compared to walking. There are hardly any roads, I'm told. Just Indian trails through the woods. No taverns, no inns—"

"That doesn't matter. I can manage if you can. Besides, there must be settlers along the way where we might find shelter if we need to. People go back and forth all the time."

"That's true but I don't think you have a fair idea of how they make the trip. However," he said, beginning to be both intrigued at the adventure of the thing and curious as to what could force Claire to be so desperate. "If you're really determined to go, I'm not the man to see you set off alone."

Claire took a deep breath, more relieved than she had been since she had recognized Edgar MacDairmid walking off the *Bonnie Brae*.

"Thank you, Caleb. I'll never forget you for this."

Caleb began pulling down his rolled-up sleeves. "I'd better leave this chore for when I get back. Now you run up to the kitchen and tell Nell to pack us as much larder as she can manage that won't weigh us down. I don't suppose the master would mind if we take old Charlie, though he's only fit for the plow."

374

"No. I won't take anything of Fall MacDairmid's. We'll walk. I don't mind. I'm accustomed to it."

"It'll be hard going in places, Claire. I hope you know that."

"I don't mind."

"Well, as long as you're that determined. However, I insist that we borrow one of the master's pistols or a blunderbuss. I refuse to go into these woods without some protection."

Claire thought this over and decided it sounded wise even if distasteful. "Very well. In a half-hour. We'll leave in a half-hour then."

"Please, Miss Claire. An hour?"

"All right. But only an hour!"

It seemed impossible to Claire that she was actually on her way to Alan at the Upper Mills. With every step that carried her farther from New York some of her anxiety lessened. It had taken them less than an hour to pull together the gear Caleb thought necessary for their trip and to strike out from Fair Street, through the palisade walls and down the path to Greenwich Village. She felt some remorse at leaving her family, but she had tried to explain to her father where she was going without eliciting any response whatsoever beyond a mild nodding of his head. She left Nell with strict orders to keep Alyce in bed and indoors until someone came to escort both father and daughter north, which, Claire hoped, would be in only a matter of days.

Fall she had left with no word at all. He would know soon enough that his brother was in New York and, whatever scheme they concocted between them to harm her family would at least be somewhat more difficult with the family having disappeared.

Besides, he had the widow to comfort him!

375

Once past the tiny village of Greenwich, they entered into such deep woods as Claire had never imagined existed. Trees, so thick she could not put her arms around them, crowded close together and towered over her head, shutting out the sunlight. The forest floor was dappled in places, buried deep in leaves in others. Vast pines, huge oaks, tulips and birches, elms and copper-tinged beeches fought for space on the undulating hills they traversed. There were huge gray boulders, tiny streams that whispered over rocky beds, thick bushes of bilberry and blackberry they had to cut through or work around in places where the trail had become overgrown. No more than an old Indian path, it was difficult going for Claire in her hobnailed boots, but she pushed bravely on, stopping only to catch her breath now and then. The more distance she could put between herself and Edgar before night fell, the easier she would rest.

They followed the river closely, often catching sight of the colorful sails of sloops skimming by on its silver surface. Caleb was all for waving one of them down and perhaps hitching a ride north, but Claire would have no part of it. She wanted speed and she wanted to be anonymous. The path offered both.

They made the first night's camp near the first of two rivers that had to be crossed. The terrain had grown steadily higher as they moved north until their camp had been made on a cliff overlooking a bend in the river far below. Caleb knew from what other travelers had told him that there were still Indian camps at this end of Manhattan, and he was decidedly uncomfortable. He had sensed more than once during the day that there were eyes observing their progress, and he would have been willing to wager a month's salary that Stone Eagle knew they were there and where they were going. That no one had bothered them had to be due to the chief's unwillingness to force a confrontation.

It was an oddly unsettling night. Claire barely slept though her lack of sleep the night before coupled with the long walk made her weary enough. She was intensely conscious of animals in the woods, the far-off bay of a fox or a wolf, the chatter of the night creatures, the occasional scream of a small animal falling victim to some larger creature. And the dark! She had not realized how dark woods could be. Caleb managed to keep the embers of their campfire going until dawn, which helped alleviate her fears, but never had she been so thankful to see the first threads of light at dawn or to hear the awakening chatter of birds in the trees over their heads.

The second day was better if only because Claire knew more what to expect. They managed to cross both Spuyten Duyvil and later the Nepperhaen by waiting until an obliging oarsman appeared to ferry them across. It cost them a little time but they made up for it by pushing ahead after their rest. Soon they began to pass farmhouses, particularly around the Nepperhaen. For the most part the inhabitants, mostly Dutch, were friendly and helpful and plied them with buttermilk, sometimes even a meal. It was beautiful country, hilly and rolling, green as emerald, spotted with splashes of brilliant colors in the fall foliage and wildflowers. Claire began to realize that she had really seen nothing of this New World by staying so close to New York all this time.

They reached the vicinity of the Upper Mills just as nightfall was darkening the hills across the river, the sun above a brilliant red globe spreading its scarlet haze to the surrounding clouds. In fact, they were upon it almost before they realized. They came out of a hollow dotted with two or three roughly fashioned houses to see another river in the distance with a tall wooden millhouse standing beside a makeshift dam.

"I think this is the place," Caleb said, relieved that they would not have to spend a second night alone in the deep woods.

"Do you suppose so? It looks very small."

"Aye, but there's no other mill after the Nepperhaen so it must be this one. It's near enough to the river, too. Yes, this has to be the place." He sat down on a convenient boulder, pulled off his hat, and wiped his sleeve across his brow. "And now, mistress, that we've come this far, will you at least confide in me where we're going?"

Claire took a seat opposite. Now that she was here her judgment did not seem so certain as it had been back in New York.

"We have to find a farm belonging to Alan Morehead. I don't know where it is but someone should be able to tell us."

"Your intended?"

"Yes." She could not meet his eyes.

"Well, if you've come up here to marry that fellow, it seems that you might have told me so. What's the secrecy in that?"

"He doesn't expect me, Caleb. At least, he doesn't know I'm here."

"Seems as though he's in for a surprise."

"Yes. And now that I'm here, I'm not so certain as to how he's going to take it. But there's nothing to do but press on. We've come this far, we certainly can't go back. I never want to go back to New York again."

Caleb got wearily to his feet and stretched out a

378

hand to help Claire up. "Night's coming on. Let's get over to that mill and see if the miller can direct us to your Alan's farm. I'm not anxious to sleep another night on the ground."

Alan's house was not so far from the mill itself that Claire and Caleb could not have easily walked there before night arrived. However, the miller, Jonas Fletcher, who was a very obliging gentleman, took them there himself in his cart. The shadows were long by the time they rolled up to the rough stone house, and Claire fought down her fears by thinking how welcoming the smoke curling up from the stone fireplace and the tiny candles twinkling through the windows looked.

Caleb jumped down from the cart and reached up to help her down as the door was pushed open and a curious Alan emerged. He stood there looking at the unfamiliar sight of the miller's cart in his front yard, then stared at the gray outline of a girl who was at once familiar and unbelievable.

"Claire?" he asked. "Is that you?"

Claire stepped resolutely up to him.

"Yes, Alan. It's me. I've come to you."

Alan looked from her to Caleb and then to the miller's curious face, who was watching them intently. He took her arm and led her toward the door. "Come in, then. Come in."

"This is Caleb Browne, Alan. He escorted me here."

"Then he must come in as well and warm himself by the fire. My thanks to you, Miller Fletcher, for bringing my guests to my house."

The miller nodded, disappointed that he had been

given no explanation. How like Alan, Claire thought, following him meekly into the house. No exclamations of surprise, no dismay, no delight, indeed, barely any reaction at all. Any other man would have been dumbfounded to see her turn up like this on his doorstep. Fall would have . . .

She forced that thought from her weary mind. Now that she was actually here and Alan had not turned them away, all her resolution left her and the dogged tiredness she had fought off for two days and nights threatened to overwhelm her.

As Caleb moved forward to the fireplace to inspect a pot simmering over the flames, Claire stood in the middle of the room looking around with some dismay. The house, she could see at a glance, consisted of one large room with a loft overhead that covered half the kitchen. The remaining half lay under the steep sloping roof. Though the room was sparsely furnished, it was clean and substantial. The walls were stone interspersed with huge hand-hewn logs, the floor raw wood that had been scrubbed to a shining patina. There was sand strewn across the boards and the stone walls had been carefully whitewashed.

A settle stood against one wall, a plain table opposite, several rough benches were interspersed with low stools around the room, and a large chest was placed majestically near the entrance. Otherwise the only imposing item in the room was the huge stone fireplace, large enough that Claire could have stood upright inside it, and crisscrossed with hooks and chains, guarded by a musket over the mantel and a long brass warming pan standing to one side, dark with stain. Somewhere in the recess of her mind she was aware of an intention to polish that thing as her first chore.

All at once she was aware of Alan at her side. For the first time he seemed uncomfortable, rubbing his thick hand along his chin and glancing around his kitchen with a nervous intensity.

"I had hoped to get it cleaned up before you came," he said apologetically. "It's a bit rough, I know, but—"

Claire turned to him quickly. "It's lovely, Alan. I know it must be a terrible shock to you to have us arrive like this. So unexpected. I can explain."

"That's all right," Alan replied, smiling tentatively for the first time. "Actually I was going to go down day after tomorrow to fetch you back, it being a week since we last talked and all. Saves me a trip."

Claire looked around the room for a place to sit. Her knees threatened to give way now that her trip was over and she was actually safe. "May I sit down?" she said weakly.

"Oh, forgive me. I'm forgetting my manners," Alan cried, pulling up one of the benches. "Here, sit before the fire and warm yourself. I've got a supper going. It's only venison stew but it's strong and hot. You'll be needing it, I'm sure. What about you, Caleb? Would you like some beer?"

"Oh, I would indeed," Caleb breathed, taking the opposite end of the bench from Claire. "That sounds even better than stew. It was some trip up here, let me tell you."

Claire looked up to see Alan studying her face. "Poor Caleb," she said. "I hauled him away from his chores to escort me through the woods at the very last moment. He's been a good friend."

"Why didn't you wait? You knew I'd have come to fetch you."

381

"I couldn't, Alan. There was some—some trouble. I had to leave at once." Her words caused his broad face to darken. "Oh, I'm in no trouble with the sheriff or anything like that. I just had to get out of New York, that's all."

"I'm relieved to hear it. I've lived here peaceably and that's how I want to stay. A man in trouble has difficulty buying his freehold." He busied himself pulling up the table and placing a second bench alongside. From a shelf on the wall he produced wooden trenchers and tankards, spoons and a platter with a large hunk of stiff bread. "Now, come and eat," he said, pulling Claire's bench up to the table. "I'm correct in supposing you haven't had supper?"

Gratefully Claire took up her spoon. "No, we haven't and it smells delicious. I didn't realize I was so hungry, or so tired." The stew was strong, so strong that had she been less hungry she could not have eaten it. The beer too was of a heady, unadorned homemade variety, but even that was delicious though it fogged her weary mind more than she wished.

"Do you have room for us, Alan?" she asked between mouthfuls for there was little suggestion of bedding in the room.

Alan bent over his plate shoving the stew into his mouth. "Oh, Aye. The sleeping's in the loft. I'll have to make a little rearranging but we'll manage."

Claire was about to ask him why there was a need to rearrange anything when the answer presented itself. The front door was thrown open and a disshelved Esther Varn entered the room, stopping on the threshold and staring at the three of them. Claire suppressed a groan. She had forgotten all about Esther and her odious son. If they lived here with

Alan, that was going to present a few problems beyond those she had already envisioned.

"I didn't believe it was true, but I see it is." Esther spoke more to herself than to the occupants of the room. "Madam van Orliff said there was a yellow-haired woman in the miller's cart but I didn't think—"

"Come and sit, Aunt Esther," Alan said forcefully. "Where's your Daniel got to? We're having supper without him. Mistress Claire is weary from her journey."

Esther took a few halting steps toward the table, glaring at Claire. "You weren't supposed to come for two more days."

Claire glared back at the woman without saying anything. She owed Alan an explanation, which she intended to give him once they were alone, but Esther Varn she owed nothing.

Alan made room for his aunt on the bench and she sat gingerly on one end. "I'm not hungry," she breathed when he pushed a wooden plate in her direction. "Where do you intend for all of us to bed? It's going to be crowded. I won't sleep in the same room with her, if that's what you've got in mind."

Alan threw his spoon on the table. "You'll sleep where I say, Aunt Esther. This is my house."

Esther's answer was to send a murderous glance at Claire as though her nephew's rudeness was the girl's fault.

In a somewhat milder tone Alan went on. "Besides, there's plenty of room. You and Daniel can take one end of the loft and Claire the other. Caleb and I will bed down here in the kitchen."

"Oh, Alan. I never meant to put you out of your bed," Claire cried. This whole situation was beginning to be too complicated for her taste. And the idea of spending a night in the near vicinity of Daniel Varn was almost too much to contemplate. Fortunately Esther's thoughts seemed to be along the same line.

"Daniel can stay with the van Orliff boy for the time being." she said ungraciously. Claire breathed a silent sigh of relief.

"I have to be up early anyway," Alan went on, ignoring her. "This way I can stir about without waking you." He reached out and patted Claire's hand lying on the table as though he was her protector. Esther looked quickly away

"You know I'm always up in time to get your breakfast."

Alan glared at his aunt. "Yes, but Claire's had a tiring journey and she needs her rest. For tomorrow at least, she ought to sleep as long as she needs."

"You're very kind, Alan," Claire said softly and with sincerity.

He squeezed her hand tightly, so tightly that she winced. "Soon enough we won't have these sleeping problems. We can share the same bed."

There was a tone of delight in his voice that made Claire wince even more, but she ducked her head to hide it. Now that she was here, she suddenly realized she had not faced what the next step would be. Alan obviously assumed, and not without reason, that she had come so hastily to the Upper Mills to marry him. And, when she looked at it objectively, that thought had been in the back of her mind too. But now that she was actually here . . .

Claire had occasion during the night to think more about this vexing question. Though she had fallen asleep almost immediately, once her body was stretched out on the bed Alan had fixed for her in the loft, she woke much later in the evening, staring at the dark corners of the loft and wondering where on earth she was. Downstairs she could hear the low murmur of voices — Alan's and Esther's. Where Caleb had gone she could not imagine but the two of them, aunt and nephew, were talking intensely as though no one else was there.

That is, Esther was talking. Her voice, intense and strident for all its low pitch, carried clearly to where Claire's bed lay.

"I won't be forced to live here with that woman," Claire heard her say. There was a long pause followed by Alan's low rumble.

"Then you must move."

Esther spoke again, aggrieved and petulant. "How can you speak so to your own flesh and blood! And so recently a widow, too. You have no heart."

"A man needs a wife. Claire Montcrieff has been my intended for several years. You knew that when you came."

"I thought surely you must have got over that old infatuation long ago. She worked her wiles on you well enough when you were both in Ben Brogain but here in this new country I was certain you'd see her for what she is and forget her."

"Well, I didn't."

"I wish I knew what kind of a spell she's cast on you. It's probably something that wicked sister of hers concocted. She's a witch, that girl, with the devil's mark on her. If you think I'm going to stay in the same house with that evil child, you're—"

"Go to bed, Aunt Esther."

"And what about Daniel? I can't expose him to such—"

"Aunt Esther," Alan said with stubborn resignation. "I'm tired and I have to be up early. If you don't want to live here with Claire and me, you can find some other house that will take you in. It's nothing to me where you live except that I insist you stay here until we're wed since it's only proper that we have another woman in the house."

"Such a way to talk to your own widowed aunt!"

"Good night, Aunt Esther!"

Though Claire did not hear any movement that would indicate Esther Varn had obeyed her nephew's order, the voices stopped. Evidently Esther had managed a way to sleep downstairs or was biding her time until her next attack. Claire turned on her side and pulled the rough coarse woolen blanket over her shoulders against the chilly night air. She had expected that relief over leaving New York would put to rest any other vexing concerns. Instead she had a whole new set of problems.

But she was too tired to face them tonight. She would think about them in the morning.

Hours later Claire woke to a quiet, empty house. Both Esther and Alan were gone and even Caleb was nowhere in sight. There was some home-brewed ale on the table in a wooden jug and several thick corncakes on a plate, evidently set out for her. She took her tankard and one of the cakes outside to enjoy them while she had a look around.

Her stay in New York had pushed aside memories of what a rural morning was like, but they came thronging back as she took a seat on a bench alongside the house. The trees were thick and tall except where they had been laboriously cleared in fields surrounding the house and barn. The fields showed signs of new plowing around the blackened stumps of what had been a forest. In the distance she could hear the low bellow of a cow, the soft tinkle of a bell, and the indistinct thud of an axe on wood.

The air was fresh and moist after a shower during the night. Never had she seen such thick, lush vegetation as that which surrounded Alan's little house. A garden off to the side showed promise of vegetables and herbs, richer and taller than any she had ever seen. From where she sat on a rising hillock she could glimpse the blue river far off in the distance. She might really get to like it here, she thought. Even the isolation was pleasant, though she had to admit that, right now, the fewer people who knew she was here, the safer she felt.

Esther did not appear until the day was nearly spent and Alan was too busy to attend to Claire so she had the whole day to putter around the house making herself useful. She found plenty to do for it was obvious that a tenant farm like Alan's was almost completely self-sustaining. Besides, she wanted to show him her appreciation, if not prove that she would make a useful wife.

That evening she convinced Alan to go back to New York, since he had planned to make the trip anyway, and bring back Nell and her family. She was worried about Alyce's health and her father's mental condition, and she felt that the sooner they were all out of New York the better. She would bring Jamie too, if there was some way to alter his apprenticeship. At least he would be safe even if he had to stay in the town. The cobbler, Johansen, had a large family and, anyway, why would Edgar be interested in a twelve-year-old boy. It was Alyce and herself that he wanted,

387

though why she still could not fathom.

Alan agreed to bring her family to his farm as long as she would set the date for their wedding. "There's a rent day coming up in a week or two. 'Twould be nice to have the bans spoke before, so we could have the ceremony at the end. That way everyone who was coming to the wedding would already be here."

"What's rent day?" Claire asked, hoping to turn his mind from the subject of weddings.

"Twice a year we pay our due rent to Lord Philipse who owns our farms. It's a grand occasion with lots of free beer and good food, dancing and visiting. You'll like it."

"Are all these farmers tenants of Mister Philipse's?"

"No, but most are. A few lucky ones have freeholds, as I intend to someday, soon as I'm able. He owns so much land up and down the river, he doesn't seem to mind selling off a few acres to those who can run them well and can get together the price."

Alan shoved back in his chair and laid one arm along the table. His sleeve was grimy from working in the fields all day, and there was an earthy, sweaty aroma ground so deeply into his shirt that Claire guessed a month of washing would not get it all out. He had washed his hands and face before coming in, and she stared at the line on his neck dividing that which was washed from that which was not. He was smiling at her, a look of pride and satisfaction on his broad face.

"I've done well since coming here, Claire. I've two oxen, four cows, one a prime breeder, eleven sheep, chickens, and geese. I've cleared twenty acres, planted rye, barley, and wheat, bought a loom, and raised a sheep pen all on my own. It's a substantial man you'll

388

be marrying."

Claire looked down at her hands in her lap. "You've done wonderfully well, Alan. Any girl would be proud to have a husband like you."

Could he tell the forced quality in her voice, she wondered. The insincerity?

"I'm glad you see it that way. Very well then. I'll fetch your family tomorrow, and you can start fixing up this house the way you want. It's not large but I always intended to add onto it anyway when the bairns started coming. I'll just have to move the work up sooner, that's all."

Claire felt a flush on her cheeks at the thought of children with this man. Like a silly schoolgirl, she winced and hoped Alan would take it for bashful maiden shyness. She fought the pain in her throat as Fall's image rose treacherously before her.

"Thank you, Alan. You've been very good to me."

"No more than what any man ought to do for his own wife."

Caleb resurfaced late that afternoon. As Claire had suspected, he had spent the day getting to know the surrounding area, talking with the neighboring farmers, conversing with the miller who was only too happy to demonstrate the fine qualities of his operation.

"And did you know our friend, Adolph Philipse's father, owns all this land?" he asked as Claire busied herself around the kitchen readying the evening meal.

"He's not our friend. He's Fall's."

"Well, he's rich. They call his father 'the Lord of the Manor' around here, though by rights his title hasn't been officially bestowed as a 'manor' as yet. But it will come. He's a regular squire, Frederick Philipse."

389

Alan stomped inside the door just in time to catch the last of Caleb's sentence. "Where do you know Frederick Philipse?" he said as he scraped his muddy boots on an iron rod near the door.

"I don't except by reputation. I just learned today that he's your landlord."

"That's right."

"Happens I met Adolph Philipse, his son. He's a friend of young Fall MacDairmid's and was at his house once or twice."

"He comes up here pretty often too. Stays at the mill house. In fact, either he or his father should be arriving soon for rent day."

Alan pulled off his boots, left them standing by the door, and crossed the room to pull up a bench to the table. "You'd enjoy rent day, Caleb. It's our most important festival, the one we look forward to all year. Master Philipse does well by us, and he's fairly generous in making merry for his tenants."

"So he's a good landlord, then?"

Alan shrugged and reached for a trencher of ham. "Not so bad. Better for sure than Morgan MacDairmid ever was."

Since Caleb knew nothing of the kind of landlord the Laird MacDairmid had made, he only gave Claire a sly wink and went back to asking questions of Alan. His curiosity about this new country reached out to encompass everything.

The evening passed pleasantly until Esther came slinking in as night was falling, turning her sour expression on all three of them. Claire went to bed soon after, ignoring the older woman completely in spite of the fact they were expected to share the loft that night.

The next morning she was up early to help see Alan

390

and Caleb off to New York. As she handed a basket lunch she had put together up to Alan where he sat on the wagon's driver's seat, he beamed down at her.

"What do you think, Caleb!" he said with pride. "Won't she make me a good wife!"

Claire watched them rumble out of the yard and down the narrow road with a deep sense of satisfaction. Once Alan returned with Alyce and her father she would be settled here in the Upper Mills for good. Then let Edgar MacDairmid do what he could to try to find her!

It only took Edgar one day to learn that his brother had a house in the northern reaches of New York near the old sheep walk. With deliberate calculation he waited another day before seeking Fall out, using the time to ask discreet questions about Claire and her family and to try to piece together a mosaic of Fall's standing in the community.

It did not surprise him to learn that the Montcrieffs were living in Fall's house—that would be part of his brother's plan to control them. The murder charge against old Tom might have been providential had not Fall managed to do away with it. He could not quite understand his brother's motives in seeking out the guilty savage but, knowing Fall, there had to be some self-serving idea behind it.

After three days he decided he had enough information to face his brother, and he sent word asking Fall to come to the City Tavern that afternoon. With sly amusement he pictured his brother's look of amazement when he received this invitation and long before the appointed hour he took a private room upstairs, left word with the landlord, and waited for the expected knock on the door.

It came right on time. At his brusque "Enter," the door was thrown open and Fall stood there looking as amazed and appalled as Edgar had expected.

"Good Lord!" Fall said, taking a few steps into the room and peering into Edgar's face where he sat languidly behind a wide oak table. "I see it and I still don't believe it."

"Your manners have not improved by association with this New World, brother. Please close the door behind you. I wish this interview to be private."

Fall swung his booted foot and kicked the door shut. "What are you doing here? God's blood, didn't you bedevil me enough in Scotland? Must you follow me here as well? I thought I was finally rid of you."

"You know very well why I'm here. How could you have expected anything less? If you allowed yourself to think I would retire and leave the field to you, then you don't know me very well."

"I know you only too well—and what field? I don't have any idea what you're talking about."

Edgar gave a short, brittle laugh and picked up an earthenware jug from the table, pouring a goblet of wine. "Sit down. Fall. The amenities in this uncivilized outpost leave much to be desired, but, foreseeing as much, I brought some good madeira with me. Have a glass." He pushed the pewter vessel across the table toward Fall.

"This must be a first," his brother said sarcastically, ignoring the goblet. "Let us be honest, Edgar. Yours is the last face I care to see in this or any other outpost. I don't know why you're here but I tell you now, I am making my own way. I want nothing from you or from Ben Brogain ever again and there is nothing here you can use to hurt me. So, why don't you just go back to whatever ship you came over on and make for home?"

Edgar's eyes never left his brother's face during this impassioned speech. He laughed again, humorlessly and sharply. "I have no intention of returning to Scotland until I've satisfied my reason for coming here in the first place. And for someone who has just received an astounding fine of two thousand florins, you speak very bravely. Or recklessly, I should say, since that fits your old pattern of behavior far better."

Fall studied his brother's sly face. "And how, my dear brother, would you know about that?"

"I make it my business to know what might prove useful."

"I see. Yet you don't seem aware that the matter has all been settled."

This knowledge seemed to surprise Edgar if Fall could judge by the slight narrowing of his brother's suspicious eyes. Still, the patronizing smile never wavered.

"Come now," Edgar said smoothly. "For once I am not interested in arguing with you. We have a common concern, after all. Why not agree to work together so that it might be settled to our mutual benefit?"

"I wouldn't trust you with any concern, mutual or otherwise."

Edgar lounged back in his chair, drumming his fingers on the table and making a derisive clucking noise with his tongue. "I can see I should never have bothered to try to be accommodating with you. Very well." Leaning forward abruptly, he stretched his folded hands across the table. "Where are the Montcrieffs?"

Fall's genuine astonishment at this abrupt change

of subject caused the first waver of doubt in Edgar's certain assumption that his brother shared the information Morgan had revealed on his deathbed.

"Why on earth should you care about them?"

"Father—"

He stopped just in time, thinking, waiting. Better to be cautious rather than talkative. Suppose his brother really didn't know anything.

Turning from his brother, Fall walked to the window. "Tell me about Father. Was the end—difficult?"

"No more than one would expect of a man who had seldom known a sober moment in sixteen years." His wary eyes never left Fall's form, but his fingers traced a pattern along the wooden table top. "You did receive my letter, then?"

"Yes. But I could make no sense of it except that Father was dead. I was sorry. I always disappointed him and yet somehow I thought one day—"

"He had little use for either of us. Or for anyone else, for that matter. There was a bequest—a small one—for old Tom. If you can just tell me where to deliver it . . . "

Fall turned to study Edgar's face suspiciously. "Surely you're not going to pretend you came all this way to deliver a small inheritance."

"Of course not." Too late Edgar saw he had raised the specter of doubt—something he wanted at all costs to avoid. "I came on business pertinent to Ben Brogain but as long as I was going to be here I thought I might as well expedite this matter. That will settle the estate once and for all."

"I assume there is nothing for me in that settlement."

"You know Father gave you what was yours long ago," Edgar said with obvious satisfaction. "He never

394

saw any reason to change his mind."

A cynical smile touched Fall's lips. "Oh yes, the prodigal wasting his substance on harlots and wild living while the elder brother stays home fattening up the calf. Well, sorry to disappoint you, brother, but I am not foraging among the swine looking for husks. And I don't have the slightest idea where Tom is or any member of his family."

Edgar cocked a quizzical eyebrow. Fall was lying of course, and how blandly he did it. "But I was told they were living with you?"

"They were for a time but they left. Abruptly and without a word. Such was the extent of their gratitude. I don't know where they went nor do I care. This is a large province. They could be anywhere."

Pulling back the blue-checked curtains that hung limply along the sides of the window, Fall looked down into the street below. A wagon was lumbering by with the driver's seat occupied by a stocky farmer whose round battered hat was pushed back to reveal a shock of bright yellow hair.

It was some instinctive hesitation that made him hold his tongue and not mention Alan Morehead to Edgar. He was not sure why, except that he had never willingly shared anything with his brother. Besides, he wanted Edgar nowhere near Claire. She detested his brother even more than she did Fall himself.

It was infuriating that he should even feel pain at the thought of Claire. She was an ungrateful, selfish wench who professed to love him in one breath and then ran off to a more secure man the moment she didn't get everything she wanted. And without even so much as a good-bye or a "wish you well." She might have at least stayed long enough for that. Perhaps he could have talked her out of going.

Edgar's long fingers drummed a loud staccato on the table as he watched his brother's musings by the window. He was more annoyed than concerned. The Montcrieffs could not have gone far. Someone would know where to find them. He was bound to pick up their trail sooner or later. Meanwhile, the less he saw of this foolish brother, the better.

In a flat, inhospitable voice, he said, "Perhaps you'd like to stay and take supper with me?"

"I'd prefer not to," Fall answered, turning to pick up his hat. "Let's not be so hypocritical as to pretend that we can tolerate each other's presence. I only wish I knew what the 'business' is that brought you here."

Edgar waved a casual hand. "Nothing that need concern you or Sir Francis Murray. I won't attempt to rival your efforts at smuggling, if that's what worries you. How did you manage to pay that fine, by the way?"

Fall set his hat jauntily on his head, for the first time giving his brother his old, teasing smile.

"Your spies must not be as good as they were at home if you haven't heard that news. I'm marrying a rich widow next week!"

Seventeen

Claire wanted desperately to enjoy rent day. It should be, she felt, the happiest day of her life. She was beginning a whole new existence, almost like being reborn into a newer and better world. Her family was with her, Alyce had recovered from her fever, and they were all safe from harm. Alan, decent, kind, patient Alan, had done everything possible to make her feel welcome and at home. His neighbors, with the obvious exception of the Varns, had been generous and accepting and already accorded her the respect due "Farmer Morehead's wife" though she was not yet that.

Indeed, she had been hard pressed to keep Alan from having the bans cried at this rent day service. He hadn't liked it at all and had finally given into her "need for more time" reluctantly and out of the conviction than a few more days she would be over her misgivings.

Why couldn't she revel in all the good things that had happened since the day she left New York so abruptly? What nagging doubt and old longings kept turning her mind back to the house on Fair Street, to a long face with curving, shapely lips and eyes darkened by thick lashes, to strong, firm arms and a muscled chest, to narrow hips and . . .

Claire mentally shook herself. This would never do. And yet her treacherous body ached for those arms around her and those lips on her throat and breast. The empty spaces inside her cried out to be filled by that familiar, beloved body.

Even as she wandered the crowds on the long fields near the Upper Mills with her arm through Alan's, her thoughts kept slipping away to Fall. Where was he right now? What was he doing? Had he forgiven her for leaving without a word of good-bye? Did his mind slip away to wonder about her?

Nonsense. He was probably married to the widow by now and too busy inspecting his new properties to give a thought to her at all.

"Look," Alan cried, breaking into her reveries. "There's a dance just beginning on the green. Let's join it."

"But I don't know how," Claire answered, hanging back. It still surprised her how the fun-loving Dutch took public dancing for granted. Even in the more northern provinces of the New World where the Puritans ruled the roost, such a thing would have been frowned on. But here in New York it was commonplace. Nobody knew how to enjoy themselves like the Dutch, Alan often said, and she was inclined to agree with him.

"I'll show you how," he said, dragging her toward the group that was lining up near a single fiddler. Claire allowed herself to be led, watched and followed, and quickly caught on. Soon she was tripping and twirling with the best of them and it was only when it was over and she was breathlessly gasping for air that she realized she had not thought of Fall once the whole time.

Rent day was all that Alan had claimed it to be. After a service at the new Dutch stone church, built only five years before, one by one the tenants of the area had lined up before a long table behind which was ensconced Frederick Philipse himself, with a secretary on one side and his son, Adolph, on the other, to plunk down the mid-year's rent. Mostly these took the form of an assortment of bags of grain, haunches of meat, or kegs of small beer. Occasionally a yeoman who had had an exceptionally good year had a small bag of coins. Master Philipse received it all with good humor and a friendly word to each tenant. He was rumored to be the richest man in New York, yet Claire was impressed with the seriousness with which he took this business. Once the rents due had been paid, the fun began. Long tables were laid with trenchers and trays of meats, breads, preserves, cakes, and sweets. Beer flowed like the waters of the Pocantico river nearby, in a never-ending stream. Children played at games and the grown-ups danced, gossiped, and told ribald stories over their tankards. Tenpins and bowling greens echoed with the clatter of balls and pins and the laughter and taunts of losers and winners, and over it all the merry squawking of the fiddles provided an endless accompaniment.

Alan had even managed to get Alyce and Tom to put in an appearance. Tom was thin and still preoccupied with some far country of the mind, but he came and wandered, looking about him with wonder as though he could not remember how he got in the midst of all this merriment. Alyce stayed close by him, both to help her father should he need it and out of fear that she would not be accepted. Claire had been relieved that so far no one had made much of her deformity. Though she could not say her sister had been accepted with open arms, yet there seemed to be none of the hostility so common in Ben Brogain or even in New York.

After the dance Claire, once she had caught her breath, talked Alan into going to look for Tom and Alyce since she had not seen either of them for nearly an hour. As they passed a group of housewives sitting on a grassy knoll under a tulip tree, Claire was blissfully unaware of Esther Varn's stony glare. The sight of Claire's flushed cheeks, the lovely glow that her exertion gave to her face and skin, her arm linked with Alan's as they both, smilingly, searched the crowd raised such bitterness in Esther's soul as she had never known. The thought of that girl getting everything while she was left a widow with nothing, not even a patrimony for her son, was gall in her throat. She muttered something under her breath and was surprised when the woman next to her laid a hand on her arm and leaned closer.

"What was that you said, Madame Esther?" Edith van Tanner asked.

"Nothing. Nothing." Esther mumbled. Edith was one of the women Esther had the least use for among the *huysvrouw* of the Upper Mills. She had a round, sweet face and a smile that never slipped. Her benevolence was as all-consuming as her good humor.

"Your nephew has lost his heart, for sure, hasn't he? You can see it in his face when he looks at that girl. Ah, well, it must make you happy. She's a lovely lass, Claire Montcrieff."

"Naturally, I want what he wants," Esther managed to get out.

The woman on Esther's other side, a roundly obese

400

Dutchwoman, whose voluminous skirts emphasized her huge size, leaned back against the trunk of a tree and fanned herself with a large handkerchief.

"Be happy he's not after the other Montcrieff girl. Not that he ever would be, nor any other man. What a frightful mark she has on her, that girl."

Edith turned her kindly gaze on her neighbor. "That's an unkind thing to say, Meip. A Christian ought to be more understanding. Think of the trials that poor child must have had to suffer with such a blemish. One wonders sometimes why God would inflict such suffering on an innocent young girl."

"It's not always God's doing," Esther said in a voice thick with suggestion.

"Why, whatever do you mean?"

"Only that in the old country that girl was considered a witch. She bears the devil's mark on her and it was proved time and again."

Meip sat up suddenly alert. "What do you mean? How proven?"

"Oh, it's not for me to point that out but there was proof. Things happened, and always when she was around."

Edith's smile lost some of its exuberance. "What nonsense. We don't hold with such superstition in this country and a good thing it is too."

"Speak for yourself, Edith van Tanner," Meip said vehemently. "Why, I happen to know that up in Massachusetts colony last year, no less than eighteen people were burned and hanged for witchcraft. Who's to say that the devil can only do his crafty business in Massachusetts?"

"That's dangerous talk, Meip, and I'll thank you to stop it. Where did you ever hear such a wild tale? I know nothing of it."

"That's because your husband never goes down to the town. My Wilhelm does often and he brought it back to me. For a while that's all they were talking of. Several young girls and an old darkie servant were involved. They was set upon by spells and possessions and they made accusations toward the women in the village and even some of the men. Trials were held and those found guilty were hanged. Eighteen in all!"

"I never heard any mention of witchcraft in Upper Mills since I came here," Esther said quietly. Her eyes had never left Meip's face during her long tirade. Now she strained toward the plump woman, a look on her face that Edith found most distasteful.

"No, not here, of course. But there are places —"

"That's enough," Edith said with finality. "No one around here would believe such nonsense for a moment. We've better sense." Slowly she got to her feet. "I think I'm going to go look for Samuel. He promised to bring me a plate of food but he probably got sidetracked at the bowling green. Good day to you, ladies."

Edith moved away and was soon swallowed by the crowd. When she was out of hearing Meip muttered, "Just like her to go off when there's something unpleasant that she doesn't want to know about. She's a good woman, Edith is, but always looking for the bright side of everything. Sometimes it just pure makes me sick."

Esther sidled closer to Meip's thick body. "Tell me about the witchcraft trials," she said in a conspiratorial whisper. "I want to know more. I find the subject most fascinating."

Meip brightened up at once and leaned toward Esther. "Well, as near as I know it was like this . . ."

402

The rain that had been threatening all day finally fell just after the wan sun had disappeared behind the Jersey hills — a slow, endless heavy drizzle weeping sorrowful tears for the lost day.

Edgar stood in the doorway of the City Tavern and watched the wet streets with distaste. He was going to have to wade through those mud holes and wet weeds back to his lodgings. Though it was not far he was sure to arrive wet and miserable. He had almost come to not expect such Scotland-like weather in this usually sunny province of New York and now, when it did appear, it was almost an affront. On the other hand at least the rain might keep off the riff-raff from the docks who usually roamed New York after dark.

Pulling his feathered cap close down on his head, he threw one corner of his cloak over his shoulder and started off, hunched against the rain and looking, dressed all in black, like a malevolent specter haunting the streets. At the corner he turned to make his way up Stone Street, relieved at least to be out of the worst of the mud on this one paved street in town. The wind that drove against him made the loss of the mud little consolation. Yanking his hat closer, he hurried ahead.

He was halfway down the block when an apparition stepped out from one of the stoops and blocked his way. Edgar reeled back, thrusting his head forward to peer at the man who confronted him. He was standing beside one of the houses that was required to keep a lantern lit against the evening so Edgar had a good look even though the scarred face was cast in deep shadows.

A sailor, yes, and one who had endured some

horrible punishment. His neck was permanently twisted and his head cocked at an angle as though he had been pulled down from the gibbet before the final death throes. He was short, much shorter than Edgar, but the stocky figure and horrible face gave him a menacing demeanor that more than made up for his lack of size.

"If it's money you're wanting, you'll get nothing from me," Edgar said threateningly. To his surprise the man only laughed.

"I've no doubt of that," he answered in a voice like rough gravel. "You'd be Edgar MacDairmid?"

"You're blocking my way. Stand aside if you please."

"You're a MacDairmid, all right. Arrogant as peacocks, the lot of you."

"I've no liking for standing in the rain listening to insults from the likes of you. Stand aside or I shall be forced to use my sword."

"That would be too bad," the man answered, not in the least intimidated. "I've some information that I fancy you'd dearly like to have. You kill me and you'll never know what that is."

Edgar stayed the hand that was already on his sword. "What information?"

"As to the whereabouts of a family you've been asking of all over town."

The rain dribbled down Edgar's cheeks but he was caught fast. Maddeningly the man said no more. "What name?" he finally asked.

The sailor took his time answering, unfazed by the ever-heavier rain. " 'Twould it be Montcrieff, now, by any chance?"

Edgar's hand moved away from his sword. With a quick look around, he stepped under the gable of the house, out of the light of the lantern and the rain. The sailor followed though not too closely.

"What do you want? How much for this information?"

"Well now, it's not really money I'm after, but then a little profit is never unwelcome. As a man of business you'd understand that."

"Get to the point, man," Edgar snapped impatiently. "I want to get home and out of this. If you know where the Montcrieffs are living, I'll pay you—within reason."

"I know all right. Ten guineas it will cost you. Five now and five when you find them—just to prove to you that I know what I'm talking about."

"I would never have agreed to any other terms. Who are you? And what do you have to do with the Montcrieffs?"

"That's my business. You just give me the money and I'll tell you where they are. If you want my help getting to them, well, that's all right too. I plan to go there anyhow."

Edgar turned this over in his mind silently. This whole thing sounded suspicious and certainly this sailor was as unsavory a character as he had ever seen. On the other hand, after all the inquiries he had made, this was the first time he'had come across anyone who thought he knew where Tom had taken his family. Five guineas was a lot to lose if this proved to be a ruse. Yet there was nothing else.

"Very well. Naturally I don't have that kind of money with me. Come round to my rooms tomorrow morning."

"I don't think so. It's now, tonight, or forget the whole thing. It's nothing to me if you don't want to go along. I'm going anyway."

There was a long silence. How it galled Edgar to be at the mercy of scum such as this. Finally he pulled his cloak closer around his shoulders and stepped back out into the rain.

"Very well. Come along then."

When had things started to change, Claire wondered. It had been so subtle, so quiet. Almost from one moment to the next, without any warning, all that had seemed so normal before suddenly took on the apparition of an old, forgotten terror.

When Alan's best milk cow came down with a tick fever, it seemed an awful but normal catastrophe—one of the risks that farmers run. When two of the van Tanner children came down with malaria, she was assured that every year some of the area's inhabitants caught this dreaded disease. Nothing unusual in that, everyone said. After that it seemed as though one mishap followed another. Alan's loss of a prize heifer was quickly followed by two of his neighbors losing first a fine plow horse to moon blindness and then a second expensive riding horse to an accidental fall when he stepped in a hole and had to be destroyed. A disastrous fire burned the newly sprouting wheat in one of Alan's best fields and the rye was all but ruined by the prolonged rainfall that continued with each new day. Looking back it seemed to Claire that the last pleasant day she had known was rent day. Nothing good had happened since.

And now the old rumors were beginning to surface. Claire had little doubt about where they had started. Esther's venom was as strong as ever for all that she seldom spent much time at Alan's house anymore. She was very friendly with the people of the Upper

Mills and spent most of her days visiting and talking. How easy it was for her to drop the suggestion that all this bad luck had only come upon them after Alyce had come to live in the village.

Claire had her own ideas about how Alan's fields had been burned—she would have sworn that had been Daniel's doing. The other illnesses and accidents, even the rain, were just Esther's good luck, accidents of fortune that she could put to good use against Alyce.

Even Alan had begun to change. When, at length, Claire had finally approached him to set a date for their wedding, not because she wanted to especially but because it was the best way to ensure Alyce's safety, she found him strangely reluctant.

"Perhaps we'd best wait a while," he said after a long thoughtful pause. "Just until this spell of bad weather has run its course."

"You mean 'bad luck,' don't you?"

"That too." His stocky face set in stubborn lines that turned the pleasant expression he usually wore into something unattractive, almost forbidding.

"Alan, have you been listening to your aunt's gossip?"

"What do you mean?" he said belligerantly.

"You know what I mean. She's saying things around the village, terrible things. That all this trouble is Alyce's fault. That my own sister casts spells, and that this kind of thing happened in Scotland and again on the ship and everywhere that Alyce goes. It's all lies. There was none of this kind of trouble when we were in New York. We lived very happily and contentedly—"

"In Fall MacDairmid's house."

"Yes, but that had nothing to do with it. It's just an

407

unfortunate set of circumstances. These things could happen to anyone at anytime."

"My cow dying like that? The rain ruining the crops? Farmer Bennett's horse—"

"And the malaria and the fire, don't forget those too," Claire said with some belligerance.

"I've been asking you to marry me since you walked into this house," Alan replied. "You haven't been in any hurry. Why all of a sudden now must we run to the kirk? I don't like it."

Claire threw up her hands. "Oh, be honest, Alan. You don't like the idea of taking Alyce in your family. Surely you aren't afraid of that sweet, good child. Surely you can't believe these evil rumors!"

To her amazement Alan only shrugged. "There are more mysterious things in heaven and earth than we know of. I don't feel like taking chances. I've done so well since coming here. Can you imagine my neighbors thinking it's my family causing their troubles and running me out? I'd have to start over again building up everything. That's a frightening thought, Claire."

"I suppose I ought to feel sympathy for you but I cannot. I know Alyce is a good Christian girl and all her life I've seen her dogged by these vicious accusations. Tell me, Alan. Do they burn witches here in New York? Do I have to fear that she'll be dragged away some night and strung up on a gibbet?"

"Come now, you're letting your imagination run away with you. This is not Scotland, after all."

"Ah, but Nell told me it happened in one of the other provinces. And those woman were hanged. They had a trial, of course, but they died all the same. Is that what we have to look forward to here?"

"That's ridiculous. There hasn't been an accusation

of witchcraft in New York since an old woman was run out of East Chester back in the seventies. Stop it, Claire."

Yet she could see something in his face—a questioning, an apprehension. With a shudder she realized that he did not fully believe his own words. A cold finger seemed to streak her spine and a breath, familiar and horrible, blew across her cheek. Claire found herself shaking so strongly that she had to sit down on the nearest bench. Impulsively she reached out and grasped Alan's hands.

"Marry me, Alan. Now, this week, next week. Please. If I am your wife, they won't dare accuse Alyce. And Esther surely will stop this attempt to separate us. I know I've been slow to agree to set a date and I'm sorry that I did that to you. But I'm ready now. The sooner the better. Please, Alan."

He looked deeply into her eyes, but there was no smile or warmth in the look he gave her. Slowly he shook his head.

"Maybe it would be wise to wait just a while longer. Until the weather clears at least."

A terrible sorrow engulfed Claire. It was as though something hopeless and threatening that had been stalking her for years was breathing closely down her neck and she was powerless to escape it. She dropped Alan's hands and turned away, fighting to hold back the tears in her eyes.

"All right then," she said listlessly. "When the rain clears, of course."

The very next day Caleb came home in the early afternoon with larges bruises on his face and one eye swollen shut. After the usual admonitions from Nell and Alan about drinking and carousing, Claire—who had remained strangely silent—pulled him aside and around the back of the house.

"All right. Tell me what really happened. I don't believe that business about fighting over Pope and Protestant for a minute."

Caleb looked a trifle sheepish. "The part about lazy Johansen in the grog shop at the crossroads was true enough. He's always there, swilling away his time and looking for an argument. I just gave him one finally, that's all."

"It was about Alyce, wasn't it?"

"Now why should you think that?"

"Caleb, I know the kind of things that are being said. And I know you. Johansen might get into a fistfight over something as unimportant to you as religious prejudices but you never would. Tell me the truth, please."

Caleb looked around, satisfying himself that there was no one in the nearby fields. "You're right, of course. That ne'er-do-well was spouting off a lot of nonsense about Alyce being a witch and being the cause of all the trouble that's happening around here. I told him to shut his mouth or I'd shut it for him. That was all he needed."

"Oh, Caleb. You could have been badly hurt—even worse than you are. I've seen Johansen. He's a big, strapping fellow with a jaw like iron."

"It's mostly beer flab, though he's heavy, I'll grant you that. But I gave him as good as I got. It seemed important that the villagers know somebody is willing to stand up for that little girl."

Carefully Claire leaned forward and kissed his cheek between the bruises. "You're a dear and I thank you for it. To tell you the truth, Caleb, I'm terribly

410

worried. It's beginning to sound just like back home. Every accident, every unfortunate event, every sickness — all are blamed on Alyce, and with less reason ever than in Ben Brogain. She hasn't been here long, she seldom goes into the village, she's hardly had any contact with the people there and with none of the children. I don't understand it."

"These things never make a lot of sense. Someone talks and all the irrational fear of the dark and the unknown that men live with begins to grow and thicken, blotting out reason. That's all it takes, you know. Bad things will happen no matter what. They are part of life. It's easy to make one poor unfortunate girl the instigator, especially when she's different from everyone else."

"But she's not. She has only that one terrible mark on her face and that's not anything she can be blamed for. I don't understand people!"

There was little Caleb could say. He did not tell Claire that Johansen's had been only one of several tongues wagging about Alyce, though certainly his had been the loudest. He did not want her to know how worried he was too.

When Claire reentered the house she saw Alyce sitting beside the fireplace, staring up at her, the unblemished part of her face as pale as death and her eyes large and dark with anxiety. Claire's gaze flew to the open window to the side of the hearth.

"You heard?"

Alyce nodded. "I was shelling peas by the window. I didn't mean to listen, Claire, but I heard my name . . ."

She sagged forward and Claire flew across the room and clasped her in her arms. "Here, let me get you something to drink. It'll be all right, Alyce, I

411

promise you."

The girl was too frightened to cry. She gripped Claire's arm, unwilling to let her go even as far away as the jug of milk on the sideboard. "It's not all right. It's all starting again. And why, Claire? I haven't done anything, I swear to you I haven't."

Claire smoothed the strands of hair back from Alyce's forehead. "Think just for a moment, Alyce. You haven't spoken to anyone about hearing voices, have you?"

"No, not since we left Scotland. And who would I speak to here? I never see anyone from the village or talk to them."

"I know, I know." Claire's blood chilled at a sudden thought. "Alyce, you didn't bring that tree with you up here, did you? Any part of it—branches, berries . . . ?"

"No, no. I was so ill when we left New York I couldn't do anything. As far as I know, it is still growing back in Fall's garden."

"Then there is nothing they can use against you except wild rumors and coincidences. Don't worry, dear child, please. We'll take care of you, I promise."

Alyce hid her face in the folds of Claire's skirt. "I wish Fall were here," she murmured on a sob.

"Alan will protect you," Claire answered with more conviction than she felt.

"No, Alan doesn't really like me very much. Sometimes I think—I think he is even a little afraid of me."

"Now that's not true. Alan is going to be your brother when we marry. He will care for you just as he would any member of his family."

Alyce did not answer, she simply held tightly to Claire, taking strength from her strong body. Claire bent over her, comforting her and wishing she was as certain about Alan as she sounded. She remembered for the first time in weeks how Fall had stood by Alyce on the *Selkirk*, protecting her from the fears and wrath of the passengers. It made her heart hurt to think of it but she mentally echoed Alyce's words. How she wished he were here now.

Three days later Alan was called to a meeting in the Dutch church near the mill. Claire knew nothing about it until Nell accidentally let it slip that Alan would be late for supper. She stood silently by the table, looking at Nell with such a mixture of apprehension and doubt that the woman thought she must have taken suddenly ill. Behind her Alyce too had frozen in her place.

"Are you certain that's where he went? What was it about?"

"Why, he didn't say. Van Corlear's boy came right after noon, looking for Alan and saying it was urgent that he be at the church at evening. I thought it must be about some — see here, Claire! Where are you going at this hour of the night?"

Claire was already out the door, swinging her cloak around her shoulders. It was not more than a mile or two to the stone church near the river and she knew the way now like a native. Though the woods were darkening and shadows played on the path, she was not afraid. The people who lived here were not given much to violence and the wild animals of the forest seldom strayed this close to settled land. Besides, she was too concerned about the subject of the meeting to care. Her intuition told her it was about Alyce. If she was wrong, she would apologize and leave quietly, more relieved than embarrassed. But if she was right . . .

She knew she had been right even before she stepped to the open door at the back of the church. The tenor of the remarks—more accusation than conversation, the argumentative tone—the way Alan stood facing a circle of men and a sprinkling of women too, his face in a stubborn, angry set was enough to convince her. When he looked up and saw her, he went white. The utter fury of his look gave Claire her first indication of how much he had not wanted her there. She slipped inside and leaned against the back wall, quietly contemplating the group. Alan shook his head ever so slightly at her, warning her off and for a moment she acquiesced. He seemed relieved to realize it.

"We're not saying she should be run out of town, just that she should leave quietlike. Go live somewhere else and leave us God-fearing folk alone."

It was Jan van Corlear's voice, Claire noted. Officious, kindly, patient as he gently consigned Alyce to a life of wandering in a strange country among strange people.

"A witch ought to be hanged!" came a woman's voice. It was not Esther's and indeed, looking around, Claire could not see Esther at all. The comment was said softly as though the woman feared making such a demand openly, but it caused a stir among the others.

"Now, now," van Corlear said again loudly. "There's no call for that kind of thing. This is not Massachussetts!"

Another angry voice drowned him out. "Althea's right. A tool of the devil has to be rooted out or you never know any peace."

"She don't have to be hanged," came a man's voice

414

from the other side of the room. "What about just putting her in gaol, keeping her from contamination with good folks?"

"That won't stop a witch. She can work her evil from inside prison just as easy as out."

"Now wait a moment," Alan cried, seeing that Claire was about to throw herself into the discussion. "Just wait. You have nothing against this girl but the mark on her face."

"That's all we need."

"She's a gentle girl who never harms anyone. She can't help that birthmark."

"So you say, Alan Morehead. And how do you explain my best stallion having to be shot when he broke his leg in a simple rabbit hole. As sure-footed an animal as ever was."

"Or Goody Maitland's little son dying of scarlet fever after only two days."

"Any animal can suffer an accident," Alan said. "And it's not uncommon for young children to die. We lose several that way every year."

"But the fire in your own field. And all this rain . . ."

"Yes, and there's Indians been seen. No savages been around here for twenty years and now, all of a sudden, they're lurking about the woods. I saw one of them myself yesterday."

"That's all we need, the savages bearing down on us."

"That's nonsense!" Alan yelled over the cries of the crowd. "Indians haven't bothered anyone in this area since the last massacre forty years ago. You're letting your fears run away with you."

"You only say that, Alan Morehead, 'cause she's related to that girl you plan to marry. She's not your family yet and you'll be wise never to let her be. A marked girl like that is nothing but trouble and always will be."

Over the heads of the crowd, Alan's eyes locked with Claire's. She had stood, frozen, saying nothing, allowing him to defend her sister. Now the look in his eyes betrayed what he really felt.

He isn't sure, Claire thought with a sickening pain in her chest. He wants to defend Alyce, but he isn't sure they are not right. Maybe she is a witch and he would be marrying a witch's sister.

For a long minute she held his gaze while the noise of the crowd increased around them. Then, pulling her cloak around her, she fled from the room and into the darkness.

Eighteen

There were only a few scattered graves around the church, and Claire was well past them before Alan caught up with her. Grabbing her arm, he whirled her around jerking her savagely.

"What the devil do you think you're doing! You can't walk back to the farm now. It's dark."

Claire tried to yank her arm away but his grip was fierce. "Let me go. I walked down here and I can walk back."

"I told you to stay home. What do you mean by disobeying me like this and walking into a meeting where you're not wanted? I won't have a wife that disobeys me, Claire. We might as well get that settled now."

With a furious yank of her arm Claire broke free. "I'm not your wife! And who has more right to be at a meeting such as this one than I? It's my sister they're talking about."

"I can take care of Alyce," Alan said somewhat more gently.

"Oh, yes. You were doing wonderfully well defending her. 'She can't help her birthmark!' For God's sake, Alan, they were calling her a witch. They were talking about throwing her in gaol or even hanging her!"

"Calm down, Claire. They don't mean it. They're not the kind of people who would do such things. They're only frightened of things they don't understand, that's all."

"Well, I'm frightened too. For Alyce."

He took her elbow, turning her back toward the church. "Come on. You can't walk back. You can ride postillion with me on old Job."

"Hadn't you better go back to your friends?" Claire said coolly. "Who knows what measures they might come up with next to save themselves from the terrible demon if you're not there to stop them."

Alan ignored her sarcasm. "I told them they'd better not do anything until I returned. They'll do that much for me."

She bit back another biting comment and allowed him to lead her to where his horse was munching the grass. The ride home was uncomfortable and made in stony silence. It was very late when they arrived but Claire could not even think of stretching out on her bed. Every nerve seemed alive and throbbing. Finally she slipped out of the house and made her way to the barn where Caleb usually slept. It was difficult to wake him. Claire had to shake him violently before he groaned and rolled over, peering at her with blurry eyes from over the covers.

"Caleb, get up! You've got to do something for me."

"Mistress Claire," he mumbled, struggling to sit up. "What's the matter? It's the middle of the night."

Claire leaned toward him, whispering. "I know it's late but you're my only hope. You've got to go to New York, Caleb, and find Fall. We need him desperately."

"Go to —! My God, Miss Claire, that's a long way. And to start in the middle of the night—"

"I know, I know. I wouldn't ask it of you except that it is so urgent. I don't even want to summon Fall but I have no one else to turn to. Please, Caleb."

Something in her manner stopped him. "Is it . . . ?"

"Yes, Alyce. Please hurry."

It was all he needed. He threw off the covers and began pulling on his breeches over his long shirt. "I'll go to the river and see if I can get aboard a sloop. That would be the fastest route."

It was not much to pin her hopes on—the trip down and back took so long—yet Claire had nothing else. She watched Caleb loping down the path to be swallowed by the darkness, then went back to the house. She was surprised to see her father up and sitting in a chair near the hearth. Alan had stretched out on a mattress on the far side of the room, still fully dressed. As she walked over to Tom, she saw Nell peering down from the loft above, her face a tiny circle in the center of a huge nightcap.

"What's all the commotion?" she asked sleepily and, when Claire didn't answer, came padding down the steps to the kitchen, a large shawl draped over her nightrobe. Claire gave her a look that said she could not explain now and pulled up a chair opposite her father.

Tom did not even look up. He had become so withdrawn and quiet these last few days that Claire had little hope of even helping him to see the danger Alyce was in, much less to count on his help. But she had to try. She reached out and laid a hand on his arm and he looked up at her with absent eyes.

"Papa, we may have to leave this place. Soon."

"Leave. But didn't we just arrive?"

"Yes. But something has—come up."

"Does Alan wish to go? Is he sending us away? I've offended him somehow?"

"No, Papa. You haven't done anything. And Alan is not sending us away. But Alyce may be in some danger and I don't think we should linger here."

Nell broke in, turning quickly from the hearth. "Not that old business again?"

Claire nodded. "Papa, can you stand another journey so soon?"

To her amazement Tom's eyes flared into life, showing more vitality than any time since he left gaol. "They've started again, haven't they? Followed us from Ben Brogain, I'll wager. She's a good girl. Not a witch!"

"Papa, be quiet, she'll hear you."

Tom had risen from his chair and began to shout. "Foul lies, that's all they ever were! And her mother the sweetest lady ever to walk this earth and—"

"Papa!" Claire cried, trying to pull him back into the chair. "You'll wake her. You'll frighten her."

"No harm can come to that angel while I live. I swore it . . ."

To Claire's distress she heard movement above, Alyce's steps, followed by her face, peered from the loft down the ladder hole.

"Go back to bed, Alyce. He's not himself."

Alyce disappeared and Claire hoped she had obeyed her. A moment later she saw her coming down the ladder, having drawn on her overskirt and bodice over her chemise.

"Well, we might as well have a party," Alan said from his cot. "It appears there's going to be little sleep this night."

"Now calm down, everybody," Nell said in her best motherly tone. "I'll just make us a little toddy and then we'll all go back to bed to sleep soundly. Might as well make good use of the time since we're all awake anyway."

Nell fussed at the embers, fanning them into life, then began stirring things in a pot hanging on a chain over the fire. As she worked, Claire tried to make some excuse to Alyce as to why she was awake and so nervous. It was a poor attempt and the girl saw through it right away. "I'm not afraid," she said, trying to sound brave. Claire put her to work pulling up the table and benches and was about to take a seat there herself when the door burst open and Caleb came staggering in.

"Lord, have mercy," Nell cried, looking as though she had seen a ghost emerge from the darkness.

"Caleb, I thought you'd be halfway to the river by now."

He stood gripping the edge of the table and gasping for breath. "Indians!" he cried. "All around the house. I stumbled right into the middle of them. They chased me here—"

Alan was on his feet immediately. "Indians? Here?"

"Surrounding your farm, as near as I could guess. My God, I thought I was going to lose my hair for sure."

"But surely they wouldn't—"

Claire's cry was stopped by a sharp swish not ten inches from her face. An arrow, the end still quivering, was embedded in the wall behind her. She stifled a scream as pandemonium broke loose. Alyce began to scream as Claire rushed to her side. Nell stood, bleating like a sheep, too frozen to move, with the hot poker still clutched in her hand.

Alan was the first to gain control of himself. "Close the shutters," he cried, rushing around the room. "Quick, Claire, get my flintlock and powder. Caleb, can you use one of these things?"

"No," Caleb answered, grabbing up a long iron peel that stood beside the fireplace. "But I'll break the head of the one that gets nearest to me."

"That's no help now." Alan reached around the outside of the window and yanked the shutter closed. Another arrow flew past him through the room, followed by another and another. The air was filled with them. Claire ducked to the floor, dragging Alyce and her father to their knees and under the table. She yelled at Nell to join them, then crawled to the window opposite Alan to pull the shutter closed.

"Oh my God! Alan, the hay!"

Alan looked over his shoulder long enough to see the tall yellow bonfire that had been his hayrick. With a groan, he reached out and closed the other shutter, then ducked down to the floor. "They'll burn the barn next and then the house, but we can't get out of here, or they'll kill us in the yard."

There was a pain in his voice that went far beyond fear. Yet the danger was too great for Claire to think about it now. Outside they could hear the high-pitched caterwauling that Indians used for a battle cry. It sent a cold shiver up her spine. As she pulled the second shutter shut, she caught a glimpse of the barn, already licked by yellow tongues of flame. Alan was going to lose everything. All he had worked for so hard and so long.

She crawled across the floor to where Alan had the long barrel of the gun poking through a narrow slit between the shutters and began passing him the powder and shot. It was a slow business, punctuated by the thud of arrows in the wooden shutters. There was so little they could do and the inhuman cries of the savages were growing closer. All at once one of the shutters was pulled away and an arm thrust through, followed by a painted mask of a face. Claire screamed and Alan, using the end of his musket, shoved the Indian back into the yard. A second savage followed, his face a twisted grimace of hate. There wasn't time to load. Alan raised the butt to strike but the Indian grabbed it and yanked it from his hands, then swiftly swept a tomahawk down, and it thudded against Alan's skull. He dropped to his knees while Claire scrambling back to the table, reaching for Alyce. Something in Nell gave way to hysteria and she stood up in full view of the braves swarming through the window and doors screaming like a banshee.

"Get down, woman," Caleb yelled. A sharp brilliant flash streaked across the room and Nell collapsed in a white heap.

Claire could stand no more. Death running away was better than death waiting in terror. Pulling Alyce behind her, she raced to the door, stumbling over one of the painted braves but regaining her balance. Somehow they got through the door though she had no memory of throwing the latch. The darkness of the fields was broken by the flaring light of the hayricks burning furiously now but Claire hardly saw them. Pulling Alyce, she dashed across the yard toward the forest, desperate to reach the safety of the trees. At any minute she expected to be cut down, but she dared not look around for fear the savages would be reaching long arms to drag her to the ground.

Only a little farther! The Indians must be so busy with the carnage in the house that they hadn't realized the girls had fled. Perhaps there was a chance after all.

She had reached the shelter of the trees when two men stepped in front of her—two massive, black shapes with long grasping arms. No savage cries, no war paint. Claire went reeling back against a tree, the breath knocked out of her. She felt Alyce torn from her arms and, screaming and clutching, struggled to keep hold of her. She could hear Alyce screaming hysterically. There was a jumbled melange of images—Alyce being dragged away, a man, black as a huge raven, pulling Alyce up on a horse, then thundering away into the darkness. Claire, clutching her heaving chest cried out and tried to run after them. She was brought abruptly to a stop by two sinewy arms, gripping her in a vise like iron.

And there was something familiar about that grip, the pungent unpleasant smell of this person, the low chuckles as he toyed with her struggling body, watching her wail as Alyce was hauled away.

These were not Indians. No paint, no offensive savage odors, no wild cries. Too late recognition came, and she stared in utter horror into the triumphant, spiteful eyes of Jimmy Cole.

Claire gasped as she was pushed flat against a tree trunk. "I don't believe it," she breathed.

"Thought you'd done for me, didn't you?" Jimmy smiled, leering into her face. She tried to turn her head away from his hot and offensive breath, but he dug his fingers into her chin and forced her face upward. "I've got you now though, and you'll not get away this time."

Fear like a cold wash swept through her. She was horribly aware of images and sounds—the yelping of the savages in the distance, the pitch blackness of the forest just beyond, a wavering yellow thread of light glimpsed between the trees near the house.

Cole wrapped one steel arm around her and began dragging her deeper into the forest and away from the house. Her arms were pinned beneath his grip, but she dug her heels into the soft leaves that covered the ground in an effort to hamper him.

"Alan! Alan!" she screamed over and over until in an abrupt gesture, Jimmy swung back his free arm and hit her a brutal blow on the side of her head. It all but knocked her out. For a moment everything went black and Claire slumped in his grip. When she realized he was having trouble dragging her further, she went even limper, sinking almost to the ground.

"Get up, you bitch," he yelled in a paroxysm of fury. "Yer Alan won't help you, he's too busy with them Indians. Walk or, so help me, I'll kill you here on the spot."

"Do it then," Claire screamed back. "I'd rather be dead than with you."

He raised his arm a second time, then thought better of it. Using both hands, he hauled her to her feet and pulled her along the path. Deliberately Claire caught her foot around the narrow trunk of a half-grown ash and clung for dear life. Her hampering drove Jimmy to a rage beyond all reason. Loosening his grip, he reached down for a thick branch lying at the base of the tree and raised it over her head.

"Damn you, if it's death you want, I'll give it to you."

He swung the staff and Claire threw up her hands to ward off the blow. There was a deadly swish and she ducked, trying to protect her head with her arms and cowering against the tree.

But the blow never came. Everything stopped, suspended for an instant. Then Jimmy Cole came pitching forward against her. Horrified, Claire scrambled from underneath his body. The dim light caught a brief reflection of the glint of metal just visible through his shirt, quickly becoming swallowed under the seepage of blood.

Clare stood transfixed, watching the limp body. She heard a noise off to the side and looked quickly up, expecting to see more Indians pounding toward her, caterwauling in triumph. Instead a dark form stepped out of the shadows, reaching for her as her knees gave way and she began to sink to the ground.

"Fall!"

"It seems I'm always having to rescue you at the last minute from this creature."

"But how? When? How did you know—"

His arms went around her, pulling her against his warm, strong body. Gladly Claire fell against him, her head buried in his chest, her arms encircling his waist. His hands stroked her hair gently and she could feel his cheek against her head.

"I don't know. I didn't expect to see this wretch again, but he's finished this time. He'll never bother you again."

"Fall, something terrible has happened. Indians—they attacked Alan's farm, burned it, killed Nell, and abducted Alyce." She began to cry with the accumulation of all the horrors she had witnessed. "I have to get her back, Fall. Can we go after her? Help me, please."

He gripped her shoulders and looked sternly into her eyes. "Listen to me, Claire. It wasn't Indians who took Alyce. I was not far away when you ran into those two men and I saw enough of the other one to recognize him. It was my brother, Edgar."

"But what on earth would he want with Alyce? Will he protect her then until the Indians are gone?"

"I doubt that. Edgar never does anything so selfless. No, he took her away for some reason. I don't know yet what it is. Nor do I understand it."

Frantically Claire gripped his coat, tugging at the lapels. "Then we have to go after them, right now.

426

She was terrified, Fall. She must be doubly so now. Let's find them—"

"Listen to me, Claire. Edgar was mounted. He took off through the woods on a horse. Even though it's night and the roads are little more than paths, it would be impossible to catch him on foot. We'll have to wait at least until dawn when we can try to pick up his trail."

Claire covered her face with her hands. She was still trembling from shock and fear. When she thought what Alyce must be feeling, it made her sick inside as well.

"Listen. It's become quiet. The Indians have gone."

Claire raised her head to the abrupt silence that had replaced the frightening yells of the savages.

"Let's go back to the house and see what we can do. Can you make it?"

She nodded and, with Fall's arm around her, stepped around the path to avoid Cole's body, then let him lead her back to the clearing. As they got closer, they could see Alan beating at the flames of the barn with a blanket of some sort. The fire had only caught in one place and had not spread to engulf the entire building. With a little luck they might be able to prevent it from spreading. They both hurried to help him, fearing to see what the quiet house held. Working furiously, the three of them managed to beat the flames down far enough so there was no danger of losing the barn. The hayricks were beyond help, but the house had hardly been touched. Not so bad, really, Claire thought. Not nearly so devastating as other raids she had heard about.

Leaving Fall and Alan to wet down the damaged area of the barn, Claire hurried to the house. She hesitated on the threshold, afraid to enter, then pushed open the door. Nell was sitting in a chair,

427

huddled over, still in her nightdress. Caleb was bent over her, putting a damp cloth to her forehead.

"Nell, did they hurt you?" Claire cried, running across the room.

"Praise God," the woman said when she saw her. "I thought they must have carried you both away."

"The fire?" Caleb asked her, nodding toward the barn.

"It's under control, but they might need your help. Go on. I'll stay with Nell."

Caleb did not move off at once. "Claire, you'd better see to your pa," he said gently.

Claire had assumed he was asleep. "But Nell—"

"Nell's all right. She only fainted. It's your pa. I laid him out on the bed but there wasn't much I could do beyond that."

"Papa!" Claire cried, as she realized what Caleb was trying to tell her. Leaving Nell, she flew to the cot and knelt beside Tom. He was as pale as the coverlet beneath his head. Caleb had laid a thin blanket over him which was already stained in several places with blood from several wounds. Claire lifted it just long enough to see the massive injuries to his chest and throat.

"Oh, Papa," she cried. Tom stirred and she realized he was still alive. "Nell, quickly. Bring me that basin and some water. Maybe there's something we can do yet."

Feebly Tom moved his hand to stop her. "No," he whispered. "Don't want . . ."

Hearing a noise at the door, Claire looked up to see that Fall had entered. Her anguished look brought him to her side at once where he knelt down beside her.

Tom moved his head just enough to see and recognize Fall bending over him. Suddenly he was galva-

428

nized into new life. He struggled up off the pillow, reaching out grasping fingers for Fall's coat.

"Papa, you must be still and quiet," Claire started to say but Tom's croaking voice interrupted her.

"Listen," Tom said in a voice that was barely more than a whisper.

Fall looked quizzically at Claire, then back to Tom. He found it difficult to believe that Tom wanted to speak to him. "What is it, old man?"

Tom's fingers grasped Fall's coat and pulled him toward him. "Listen. Morgan . . ."

He fell silent. At his father's name, Fall suddenly realized that whatever Tom had to say to him would bear listening to. He leaned closer to the dying man, taking his frantic hand to still it. "What of Morgan? I'm listening. Speak slowly and carefully."

It seemed to reassure Tom and he lay back, looking up at Fall and forming the words very carefully. "Alyce—I took her. The laird, he gave me commission to care for her. He didn't want—want to expose her, to let her die."

"Alyce? But why? Why should my father care about a little marked foundling?"

"No foundling. No foundling!" His lips worked soundlessly and his chin worked back and forth. "Your mother, she died giving birth! Morgan was crazy with grief, out of his mind. When he saw . . ."

The hand that gripped Fall's was so tight he realized his own fingers were growing numb. He waited, holding his breath. When Tom's eyes began to close, he was overcome with panic.

Don't die now, he thought. Not yet.

"What did my father see?" he said in a level voice.

"When he saw the mark—the devil's mark, he wanted no part of her. He sent me to . . ."

"My God, Tom," Fall said, reaching out suddenly

429

and jerking the dying man's head up. "Are you telling me Alyce was my mother's child? That she's my sister?"

Tom nodded, his head wobbling back and forth. "Yes, yes," he breathed on a long sigh. "Finally, to tell you . . ."

Catching himself, Fall gently laid the old man's head back on the cot. "But why? Why give away his own child? How could he do such a thing?"

"He was crazy, I tell you. Crazy that your mother had died from this little marked girl. I think he . . . I think he was sorry later but he'd never go back. But he made sure she was took care of. Morgan . . . Morgan was a fine man. As fine a man as . . ."

Fall sat back, suddenly very weary. Beside him, Claire took the basin Nell had brought and dipped a cloth to dampen it. Gently she separated the two men's hands, laying her father's alongside his body.

"Is that all you wanted to tell me?" Fall asked, leaning close to Tom's face one last time.

He nodded, imperceptibly and his lips formed the words that his voice no longer could. "Kept . . . my word. Ful . . . filled my commission . . ."

Fall laid a hand on Tom's shoulder. "Yes. You took good care of Alyce. You did more than just protect her. You loved her and kept her safe. You've been a good servant, Tom."

He had the satisfaction of seeing the old man try to smile. "Tell . . . Morgan . . ."

Of course he wouldn't know that Morgan was dead. "I will," Fall said. "I promise."

Tom's eyes closed on a second long sigh. With one last look at Claire, Fall moved away and left her to minister to her father for the short time that was left. He moved to the table and sat down heavily on one of the benches, trying to make some sense of this

430

astounding revelation.

So Alyce was his sister. Gentle, marked Alyce. All at once other things fell into place — the protectiveness he had sometimes felt toward the girl; the look about her that he could never quite place. It was his mother's portrait, of course. Now that he knew, the resemblance was striking.

And Edgar. He looked up suddenly. Now there was some kind of reasoning behind Edgar's abduction of Alyce. He didn't yet know what it was but he could make a pretty good guess. Morgan must have regretted his decision to cut off his only daughter and when he knew he was dying, he left part of his inheritance to her. It had to be that. That would be the only thing to drive Edgar to such lengths to reclaim her.

Within half an hour Tom was dead. By then Alan had returned, exhausted, his face blackened by his bout with the fire. No one felt like trying to sleep. Nell made some hot broth, then helped Claire wrap Tom's body for burial. After that was done, there was nothing left but to wait for dawn.

They grouped around the table sipping the hot broth liberally laced with some of the brandy Alan had set aside for his wedding. Conversation was labored and centered mostly on trying to make some sense of the evening's horrors. Two of Alan's neighbors arrived to help with the fire. They sat nursing their tankards with long faces.

"This is only the beginning. Those savages must be burning farms all up and down the river. That's how they work, you know, when they go on the warpath. Strike everywhere, quick and hard."

"But why me?" Alan groaned. "I've never had trouble with the natives. And I didn't notice any fires anywhere else in the valley."

"You cannot explain the mind of a savage."

"We'll have to get everyone together. Maybe move into the mill house. It's a good strong stone house and they wouldn't be able to burn it."

Caleb made scoffing noise with his tongue. "Are you so certain the tribes have gone to war? Maybe this was just an isolated incident."

The three farmers all spoke at once. "Indians don't work that way."

"I seen it coming for a long time now. The more settlers move in—".

"We have to protect our farms, our wives, and children. They're nothing but butchers, these savages."

For the first time Fall spoke up. "Caleb is right. Think for a moment, gentlemen. How many Indians were there all together?"

Caleb studied his hands. "I'd guess maybe six or seven. More like six, now I think on it. Though they made enough noise for three times that number."

"Claire?"

She tried to picture the house just before grabbing Alyce's hand and running from the room. "Maybe five. But there could have been more. I was too frightened to count."

"Nell?"

"One was enough. I blacked out after I saw that painted face and that knife."

"So, at the most, say six, maybe seven," Fall went on. "That's a small number for a war party bent on starting a whole new war."

"But they don't need many," Meinheer van Tanner interrupted.

"Yes, but there's also this to consider. If they had really intended to burn Alan's farm, they would have done it. There was nothing to stop them. As it was, they destroyed the hayricks, got the barn going just enough to keep us busy, and did not hurt the house at all. And did they attack any of you? Did they attempt to scalp you, Nell, after you fainted? Did they run after you and Alyce, Claire?"

"By God," Alan exclaimed, "I wondered why that brave who came through the window didn't finish me off with his tomahawk. He had every chance when I dropped my musket."

"But Papa—" Claire started.

"Exactly," Fall said, looking only at her. "I believe this was an isolated party of young braves out for revenge on Tom for the capture of Lace's killer. If they had known I was in the neighborhood, they might have hacked me to death too."

He turned to the others. "Of course you'll want to take precautions, but I'll wager none of you will be bothered again. I saw some of the remains of Indian raids up around Fort Orange and, believe me, they don't do things halfway as was done here. You would all be missing your hair and lying in the charred ruins of this house if that's what they wanted."

Nell gave a shudder. "Halfway was close enough, thank you! I never want to get any closer!"

Though only half-convinced, Alan's neighbors took themselves off to their own homes. Claire dozed near the fire until the first light began to break and the sounds of spades on stone outside woke her. They buried Tom with only a few hasty prayers before taking a quick breakfast, and then Fall was in the woods trying to pick up Edgar's trail with Claire close behind.

"I'll find them sooner without you tagging along," he said as he bent to study the crushed leaves on the path.

"I'm staying with you. If we find Alyce, she'll need

433

me. And besides . . ."

She shrugged and he gave her no further argument. Reaching for her hand, he gave it a quick squeeze that seemed to say he understood her need to be close to him and that he felt the same way himself.

"It may be difficult keeping up," he warned.

"I'll manage."

"Come on, then."

Nineteen

The horse had proved to be a bad idea. It had enabled them to get away quickly and probably had prevented their being followed. But Edgar had gone only a short way when he realized he would have to abandon the animal and carry on on foot.

The trouble was he didn't know this country at all. And never had he seen such thick underbrush and overarching trees. It was too lush, too dark, and far too hazardous to hack one's way through in the middle of the night alone, much less when one was hampered by a reluctant, unwilling girl.

Yet the girl was his reason for being here, and he kept a tight grip on her thin arm, half-pulling her through the woods with only a sense of traveling west toward the river. He should have taken more time to scout out the lay of the land before attempting this abduction, but that would have run the risk of being noticed. Claire Montcrieff had run away from him once already. He wasn't anxious to lose her trail again.

Beside him, Alyce plodded, half-dragging her weary feet. It seemed they had been walking for hours, crashing through thick thickets and brush that

435

reached grasping thorny fingers to scrape her face and tear at her skirts. Dawn was more a sense of imminent expectation than an actual light. The terror that had numbed her body was giving way to an overwhelming weariness, yet still she was pulled and thrust by the stern fingers on her arm. She had no idea who held her, forcing her onward, only that he was like some huge black bird, threatening her with destruction — a vulture on human legs. She was alone and afraid and in the merciless grip of a monster, and all she could do was fight down the trembling that consumed her body, mumble soundless prayers, and keep dragging her feet along the forest trail.

With the first rays of dawn she began to make out that they had reached a tiny stream that cut a small ravine through the woods. They had been traveling along its upper banks where the brush was not so thick and she had heard its murmuring motion without realizing what it was.

She grasped the trunk of the next tree that brushed her free arm and mumbled, "water . . . "

Edgar stopped and looked back at the sorry sight of the girl, leaning on the tree and gasping for breath. They had gone far enough now that he supposed they could afford a short rest. "All right," he answered and let go of her arm. "But only for a few minutes."

Alyce scurried down the bank and knelt beside the stream, cupping its clear, icy waters in her hand. After she had drunk as much as she wanted, she sat back on the bank and leaned her head on her arms. She felt the movement beside her as Edgar sat down near enough to reach for her if she tried to bolt.

"Who are you?" Alyce asked softly without looking up.

"Don't you remember?"

The voice brought a memory surging back. She looked quickly up, shielding the marked side of her face with her hand and squinting at Edgar in the gray light.

"I see you do," he said with a thin smile. "You needn't try to hide your face. I'm quite familiar with it." Reaching out quickly he pulled away her hand, gripped her chin, and turned her face up to the light, examining it coldly. Alyce cringed under his blatant examination, and the red mark on her cheek turned vivid scarlet.

"It's really quite appalling, isn't it?" Edgar said with utter insensitivity. "How you got such a thing from this family, I'll never know. It must have come from the McFalls."

"What do you mean?"

"Of course. You don't know, do you? I have some interesting news for you, child. Your father was Morgan MacDairmid, the Laird of Ben Brogain."

Alyce's light eyes glinted in the dawning light. "No. My father is Tom."

"Tom raised you but he did not breed you. That honor fell to my own sire. Yes, now I know it, I can see something of the look of my mother about you. No doubt it was the sight of such a daughter that killed her."

"Mother? What do you mean?"

"Tell me something," Edgar went on without hearing her. "They have always said you are a witch. Are you a witch?"

From some deep well within her, Alyce could feel her fear dying under a thin, cold anger. She looked Edgar straight in the eye for the first time. "Yes," she

437

answered. She herself did not know why she said such a thing. It seemed to be a voice beyond her reasoning, but it had its effect. Edgar held her chin a moment longer, studying her eyes, then abruptly dropped his hand, and turned away.

"Nonsense!" he muttered.

"Why do you want me?" Alyce said, sounding like a little girl again. "I want to go home. I want Claire and Papa."

"You must forget the Montcrieffs. You will never see them again. We're going back to Scotland, you and I, and you are going to take your rightful place in Ben Brogain—the daughter and heiress of the laird."

"I don't know what you are talking about. I don't want to go back to Scotland. I want to go home."

He gripped her arm again and pulled her to her feet. "Come on. No more talking. No more rest."

"Please—"

In a sudden fury Edgar turned on her. "You foolish girl! You're rich, don't you understand? Your father left you everything except that which I had already taken as mine. You're coming back with me whether you want to or not!"

Alyce pulled away from him, her arm searing with pain at his grip. "No, no!" she cried. "I won't. I'll put a spell on you!"

There was only the merest flicker in Edgar's eyes, but she saw that he was afraid of her. Beyond thinking, she cried, "You are an evil man and I will make you pay for your evil ways." Frantically she dredged up every incantation she had ever heard. "May the blood be turned to water in your veins. May your insides rot to feed the creatures of the earth . . . "

438

Furiously Edgar lashed out and struck her across the mouth. "I don't believe in curses. You'll do as I say if I have to tie you and drag you every step of the way to Scotland."

An unreasoning panic swelled within her, carrying her along its wild torrent. She was hardly aware of what she was saying or doing as she lashed out at him, struggling out of his grip and flailing her arms against him in a fury of motion. Edgar thrashed back at her, trying to grip her flying hands.

"Damn you! Be still!"

"May your—"

She was screaming at him now, and crying, out of her mind with fear. He backed away, tottering for a moment on the ledge of the bank. Then he lost his balance and flailed the air with his arms as he struggled to regain his footing. Thrusting her hands against his chest, Alyce gave him a shove backward and saw him fall, then turned to scramble in the opposite direction. She was sure he would be on her heels and had gone several feet before the unaccustomed silence of the forest brought her to a stop. Looking around, she saw she was alone. The monster was gone.

Or had her spirits stepped in to save her after all? Edging her way quietly, she retraced her steps to the bank, listening all the time for any sound that would mean Edgar roaring down on her again. When she reached the bank she knelt, crept forward, and peered over the edge.

He lay there, face down in the stream, unmoving. The water whispered and bubbled around him, staining the blackness of his doublet. Why, she wondered? Had the spirit of the stream struck him down for the evil thing he was? Had the forest closed around him to suffocate him in its effort to save her from his wrath?

She silently gave thanks to all the spirits who had acted on her behalf. Sitting on the bank, she studied Edgar's body long enough to accept the fact that he was either unconscious or dead and would bother her no more. Then she turned her face to the sun filtering between the trees and sought to hear her voices telling her what she should do.

She wanted to go home, to be with Tom and Claire and Jamie again, to be safe and well loved.

But no. She only brought trouble on those she loved. It was her fault they were sent from Scotland. She had brought them trouble on the ship, and surely it was her doing that forced the Indians to attack them last evening. If she went back to them now, the people who were Alan's neighbors would blame her for the coming of the Indians and that would make life difficult for Claire and Papa. She couldn't go back. Never again.

But where then? Alyce listened, straining to hear words in the soft sloughing of the wind among the leaves.

Caleb had said the Indians honored people with a mark like hers. They did not consider it evil at all. They thought it meant she was touched by God. Perhaps . . .

Why not? Hadn't Caleb said, too, that there was a village to the north along the river? Last night those savages had not tried to harm her. If she found their village now, maybe they would take her in and let her live with them in peace. And if they didn't . . . well, she had nowhere else to go anyway so what did it matter?

Carefully Alyce studied the position of the newly risen sun. She would head west toward the river and, when she reached it, she would turn northward. She must be careful to avoid any farms she might come across or any people like herself. Surely, her spirits would show her the way to go and help her to find berries and roots to eat until she reached the Indian village.

With one last look at the black form lying in the river bed, she turned away, forcing her weary feet forward but filled with a new hope.

The trail was not difficult to follow as long as Edgar had used his horse but, once that animal had been abandoned, it grew very confusing. Fall expected it to veer south in the direction of New York for he was certain Edgar intended to carry Alyce back to Scotland. What other reason would he have for taking the girl in the first place? With Claire close behind he searched the woods, making a large circular inspection when he lost the direction and always surprised to see it pick up again moving ever northward.

It was nearing noon when they passed close enough to a farm to see smoke rising from its chimney. They veered off their course long enough to beg some buttermilk and learned that the body of a stranger had been discovered that morning lying face down in the Pocantico creek.

"Are you certain it was a stranger?" Fall asked, trying not to let his hopes rise.

" 'Twas no one that any of the folks hereabout had

441

ever seen before. Tall and thin, fancy clothes — not dressed a'tall for walking in the woods — with a black beard. Haven't seen anyone with a beard like that since the days of the old king."

Fall and Claire exchanged glances. "A long beard?"

"No, no. One of those fancy little things, comes to a point."

Fall was already on his feet, thanking the good wife for the drink and out the door. It was two miles to the Ricketts farm and when they got there Claire was gasping from hurrying to keep up with Fall's long strides.

Edgar's body had been laid out in the shade near the root cellar. There was a clean cloth laid over it, and it took Fall only a moment when he lifted the edge to know it was his brother.

"I suppose I ought to be sorry but somehow I don't feel anything," he said softly to Claire. They were out of earshot of Gilbert Ricketts and his two sons who were rather proud of the notoriety finding the body had brought them.

"Will you tell them he's . . . "

Fall laid a finger to his lips and looked over toward the farmer. "No. I'll make sure he's decently buried but that's all."

"Fall, with Edgar dead, where would Alyce have gone? They obviously haven't seen her or they'd tell us. They know her by her mark."

"You know her better than I. What might she do? Would she head back to Alan's farm, assuming she knew the way?"

"I think she could find the way. At the very least she would stop at one of the farms and ask. But no one seems to have seen her."

442

"All the same I think we'd better go back to Alan's before trying to search any farther." Reaching inside his coat pocket he took out a small cloth purse and removed two large brass coins, laying them cautiously over his brother's eyes.

"That should ensure a proper burial," he muttered and replaced the cloth.

Claire nodded, knowing it was as much as Fall wished to do for a brother he despised. She could not even bring herself to look at the wretched face.

By the time they returned to Alan's farm the afternoon sun was beginning its long descent toward the horizon. Claire was buoyed up nearing the house by the hope that Alyce would be there, afraid and shaken but safe. When she stepped inside the small room and saw both Nell and Caleb look up at them with expectant faces, her hopes slipped away. Alyce had not returned and they had no idea where she might have gone.

Nell set out a meal for them and they gathered around the table to discuss what to do next. Even Alan came to join them once he saw they had returned.

"We'll have to go on searching," Claire said after she had appeased the worst of her hunger. The long days' trek, following a night of little sleep, had her mind so numbed she could hardly think.

Nell poured some more ale into her glass. "The poor bairn. She'll be getting hungry by now. I hope she finds some berries or roots."

"I wouldn't worry too much," Alan said in his casual way. "This time of year the woods are full of food."

"If one is familiar with them and knows where to

look," Fall answered impatiently. "What does Alyce know of surviving in the woods alone?"

Alan was offended by his impatient tone. "I only meant that she probably won't starve."

Claire set down her spoon and laid her hands over her face. "But it will soon be night. All I can think of is how frightened and alone she is. What might happen to her. What animals . . . " Her voice broke on a sob. "We've got to find her, Fall. We've got to. Maybe we could all take a different direction in the morning, at first light. Between us—"

"Hold a moment," Alan said. "I've too much to do, Claire. I can't go traipsing through the woods looking for a girl who probably has powers to help herself anyway."

"What do you mean!"

The look on her face gave Alan pause. "Just that she's not so helpless as you think. She'll be all right. She's bound to stumble on someone sooner or later who will help her find her way."

"If they don't throw her into gaol first! You don't want her back, do you? You're glad you she's gone. It relieves you of an embarrassing problem."

"Now I didn't say that."

"But it's what you mean. Well, I won't let her die out there alone. I'll find her if I have to search all these woods by myself."

Gently Fall laid a hand on Claire's, calming her just by his touch. "Sit down, Claire. She's my sister, remember? I won't abandon her. And you certainly won't have to find her alone."

Claire stared at him for a moment. She had already forgotten the strange new relationship he shared with Alyce. Slowly she sank back into her chair. "If only I wasn't so tired."

For the first time Caleb looked up from where he had been studying his hands. "You know," he said, "I have a strange idea I may know where Alyce went. She should have come back here of course, but it may be that she decided that having already gone part of the way, she would go ahead and have a look at that Algonquin village I told her about."

"What village?"

"Well, it seems there is a large Indian village farther north on the river. It was told to me down in New York, and she used to ask me questions about it all the time. She was intrigued because the savages thought a mark like hers was a sign of the Great Spirit's approval."

Alan made a scoffing noise. "Ignorant savages!"

Caleb gave him a long scathing look. "Maybe but you can see how a girl like Alyce, whose birthmark has brought her so much pain, might be taken with the notion of a different kind of attitude. Anyway, she asked me to take her there and, when I said I couldn't, she bothered me about just where it was. She knows it's north on the river. Maybe, just maybe, she decided to find it."

They eagerly picked up on Caleb's idea and discussed it at some length. Finally Fall decided the matter for everyone. They would rest that night, then get an early start the next morning. He and Claire — who insisted she be allowed to go — would take a boat up river to search for the village. Nell, Caleb, and Alan would make a last search of the woods and alert all the neighbors that Alyce was missing. His plan seemed a sensible one to everyone but Alan. He stood up, laying his broad hands on the table and looking directly at Claire.

"I haven't much time to give to searching for a foolish young girl who should have had the sense to make her way back home, not go looking for a bunch of savages. And I don't think it at all proper that you should go off with this man without a chaperone. We're supposed to be betrothed, remember?"

Claire was too astounded to speak. Fall broke in before she could form an answer.

"If you think it's not proper for me to go, then you take Claire and I'll search the woods."

"You know I can't do that. I have a farm to tend, and one that's been ravaged at that."

Claire found her voice. "We may be betrothed but we're not yet married, Alan Morehead, and I'll go with whomever I want and wherever I want. You don't care anything about Alyce, but Fall and I do. Besides, Fall is a married man."

"It's still not proper," Alan cried, his voice rising.

"Really, you two," Fall began, "I can—"

"No!" Alan shouted and turned back to Claire. "This whole business is insane. I tell you now if you go off with that man tomorrow, that will be the end of us. I wash my hands of you."

Deliberately Claire looked at Fall. "You will please wake me at first light." Then, pulling her skirts away from the chair, she stalked to the ladder and climbed to the loft. Alan watched her go with burning eyes. He turned his glare on Fall and started for the door.

"Really, Master Morehead," Fall said in his level voice. "Claire is very tired and upset. You ought not to let this bother you so. I'll take good care of her."

Alan reached for his blanket piled near the door. "I'll just bet you will," he snapped and stalked out the

446

door, making for the barn.

"Tsk, tsk," Nell clucked her tongue. "Ah well, he's not the right man for her anyway. I always thought so."

They left before dawn the next morning. By the time the gray light of sunrise had diffused into the green-shrouded hills, they were on the river, propped on the prow of a round-bottomed sloop on its way north. The master thought he had an approximate idea where the old Indian village was located and agreed to put them ashore as near it as possible, then pick them up again on his way down.

For all her mixed emotions, Claire was entranced by the beauty of the river as the light grew, tinging its clear waters with blue and silver and giving depth to the dark-green slopes on either side. They were on a wide bay here that narrowed farther up into a ribboned channel. The gently sloping fields and woods grew higher as they traveled, and in the distance she could see the sharp crescents of low mountains. Overhead they were accompanied by a cacophony of sea gulls and small black-and-white terns. In the river dolphins played around the prow of the boat and she got an occasional glimpse of a sturgeon ten feet long or more. The abundance of life in the crystal waters was astounding—thick schools of fish, bass, whitefish, carp, sturgeon; turtles sunning themselves on the rocky shore; and the banks encrusted with oysters and clamshells littering the shore like tiny white pebbles. After the tumultuous events of the past days there was a delicious peace on the river as though all concerns of the land had been left behind. Only the quiet sloughing of the sail in the gentle wind and the smooth dipping of the prow in the waters broke the silence once the birds moved off.

"You're not sorry you came?" Fall asked. It was the first time he had spoken to her since they climbed aboard. She turned from her perusal of the water and studied his face, serious for once.

"No. I'm not sorry. It was good of Alan to offer us a home, but I knew a long time ago it would never work. I think he was afraid of Alyce in some way."

Fall's face was close to hers. It had been such a long time since she had seen him so near and it struck a dear, remembered chord. She longed to reach out and lay her palm along the side of his cheek, to stroke the lovely curve of his lip but she dared not.

"You could never love any man who wouldn't care for your sister, could you?"

"No. I decided that a long time ago. If I can just find her, if only she's safe and well, then . . . well, then I'll figure out something. I don't know what it will be, but something."

Fall laid an arm on his knee and looked up at the sail. "You needn't worry about that. I've decided for you. I'll take care of you both."

"That's not necessary."

"But it is. Alyce is my sister and now I have a responsibility toward her."

"I accept that but what about me? Do you think I'm going to be content to live in your house, waiting on your wealthy widow, and be grateful for her handouts? I suppose you'd want me to slip down the stairs into your bed at night too."

He laughed and laid an arm around her shoulders. "I wouldn't mind that."

"No, but I have a feeling she would. And your Immetje is not the woman to put up with such dalliances!"

Fall grew more serious. "She's not my Immetje."

"But you said . . ."

"You foolish girl. Do you really think I'd wed a woman and then go gallivanting off to rescue the next? Would I be here at all if I was Meinheer Strycker? For God's sake, Claire. Worrying over your sister and your father has made you soft in the head."

She pulled away and stared at him. "Fall! Are you saying you did not go through with that wedding?"

The twinkle in his eye was infectious. "That's right."

"But you let me think . . . you let Alan think . . ."

"No, I did not. You jumped to the conclusion that I was married and said so to everyone within hearing. I just didn't correct you, that's all. I was afraid, if Alan knew I wasn't tied to another woman, he would have never let you go off with me."

"But your fine?"

Fall frowned and looked quickly away. "I don't know what I'm going to do about that yet. The governor gave me a generous extension to attempt to find an answer, but I got a little sidetracked."

"That reminds me. How *did* you know I needed you, Fall? It was so—so providential, your stepping in the way you did just at the right moment."

Fall gave a short laugh. "I'd like to say I could feel you calling me but it was much more prosaic than that. I was tailing Edgar and Cole. I knew they were up to something the minute I saw them together in New York, but I wasn't sure what or why. They lost me several times, especially when they joined up with those Indians, but I managed not to get too far away. I still did not understand what they planned when the Indians attacked the house, but, when I saw them make off with you and Alyce, it began to make sense. It was difficult to know who to go after for a moment — Edgar or Cole — but I had a feeling of the two, Cole would be up to the worst mischief. And I was right."

"Thank heaven," Claire breathed. She gave a small shudder. "I still can barely think of that horrible man's hands on my body."

He glanced at her sideways, his eyes full of meaning. "We shall have to see what we can do about replacing those memories with something more pleasant."

Claire hesitated for only a moment, then moved into the strong circle of his arms, leaning gratefully against him.

"Oh, Fall," she whispered, "I'm so glad you're here. Alan would never have gone looking for Alyce, and I don't know how I would have managed alone."

Gently he stroked back her hair from her face and bent to kiss her warm, full lips. "We do seem to do everything better together, don't we?"

Claire snuggled against him. The future was still a dark emptiness which she could make no sense of at all, but she would worry about that later. For now she was content.

The master set them ashore with some misgivings after urging them to stay with him. Claire refused — she would never be content until she had proved to her satisfaction that Alyce had not made her way here. Promising to pick them up on the next change of tide, the little sloop wobbled off up river.

Though the woods were raucous with the sounds of creatures—birds, squirrels, and insects—the village itself lay moribund and dead. It had been a large one once. There were huge mounds of crushed oyster and clam shells piled along the shore. The houses had been pulled up but it was obvious where they had stood by the decaying fire stones. Litter was everywhere, rotting and old.

"They haven't lived here for a long time," Claire said softly as though afraid to disturb the forlorn peace of the place.

"It's not surprising, really. This is too close to civilization. The tribe must have moved up river as more settlers poured into the valley. There is a trading post a little farther north and to the south van Cortlandt has his summer hunting lodge. With all these white men moving in, they must have resigned themselves to finding a new home up country."

Claire pushed aside a few twigs of half-charred sticks with her foot. "There hasn't been a fire here for a long time. Oh, Fall. Do you suppose Alyce never came here at all?"

Fall studied the ground looking for recent disturbances. "There is no evidence of a recent visitor but it would be difficult to tell. The ground is so dry and there are so many shells."

Discouraged, they nevertheless had a careful look around, straining to find any sign of a recent intruder. When the village itself proved fruitless, they began circling the woods that surrounded the small town like an amphitheater. The ground sloped steeply upward only a few feet away from the shore and soon the vegetation was so thick they gave up the search and turned back. After another hour's intensive inspection of the less heavily wooded area, they ended up back on the shore sitting by the silver water. Claire leaned her arms on her knees and put her head in her hands. When she thought about the possibility of Alyce lying injured or dead somewhere in these desolate woods, it filled her heart with despair.

"What will I do, Fall? If she didn't make her way back to Alan's and she didn't come here, where can I look next? I have this horrible presentiment that she wants to die. She heard me talking to Alan the night of the meeting. Suppose she made up her mind that there was no place where she could be safe. It would be just like her."

"Now Claire, you don't know that. You're letting yourself get carried away."

Claire ran her fingers through her hair in an attempt to brush away the wetness from her eyes without Fall noticing. "It's just the idea of her being hurt and alone somewhere with no one to help or to comfort her. She could even die without ever knowing how much we love her!"

Fall laid an arm around Claire's shoulders and pulled her to him. "She knows. She had a lifetime of concern and care from you and Tom."

They stayed by the river for a long time more from not knowing what to do next than from a need to spot the orange sail of the returning sloop. The day was beginning to wear away as Claire studied the river, noting how it altered its moods with the changing hours. It was pewter gray now, the high hills on the far side darkening to black. She could see the smooth current flowing south now, and soon the little sail would appear between the hills on the horizon.

She nestled her head in the warm curve of Fall's shoulder and tipped her face up to the warm, comforting light.

And then she saw it. How many times had she glanced at that hill behind them that afternoon without spotting the flash of red twinkling like firelight. The afternoon sun caught it fully now, high on a ridge far above the area they had searched earlier.

Claire sat up and put her hand over her eyes, squinting at the crescent of the hill. "Fall, are those berries?"

He glanced up at the direction she was watching so intently. "Where?"

"Up there," she pointed. "Near the top of that hill."

"Oh. I suppose they are. What of it?"

Claire was on her feet. "I don't know why I didn't notice them before," she cried, her excitement growing.

"It's only some kind of bush."

"No, it's tree, covered with those clumps of berries I've seen so many times at home. It's a rowan tree, Fall. They don't call it by that name here but it's the same thing. Caleb told me about it."

"But I don't see—"

Claire grasped his arm, pulling him toward the fringe of woods. "It's just possible that if Alyce was here and she saw that tree she would have headed straight for it. It's so familiar."

"Claire, that's a very unlikely possibility. She may not have even been here."

"But suppose she was, and she found the village empty. There would be no place left for her to go. That tree might be the only link with home left in her world. Let's look, Fall. Please!"

He pulled her back, shaking his head. "Do you realize how difficult a climb that is. And we might miss the sloop."

"I don't care." She was already hurrying toward the trees. "I'll get up there somehow. You don't have to come, but I will not be satisfied until I know she's not there. I have to try."

He was right behind her. "You're not going without me. You'll never make it alone."

Though Claire did not even look back, she was soon grateful he had followed her. She tried to keep her rekindled hopes from rising too far, knowing how disappointed she would be to get all the way up the hill only to find nothing but overgrown thickets. She was even grateful that the difficulty of the climb soon took most of her concentration. At times the thickets were so dense they lost sight of the red berries and moved more by instinct than landmarks. The steepness of the hill was like a wall in places and often Fall had to pull up on a precarious ledge in order to reach down and hand Claire up. As they climbed higher, Claire could see the river below them spread out in silver splendor as it twined its way between the high hills. She had no time, however, to stop and admire the view. The sun was descending across the river, the shadows beneath the thick trees were growing ever darker, and her breath hurt as she labored for air. Perspiration dampened the back of her dress and her skirts caught on the clinging claws of the thickets, dragging her back, but the top of the hill was drawing closer. Through the trees she spotted the sun-drenched red berries of the mountain ash, now almost directly across the ridge to her left. In losing sight of it, they had climbed too far to one side and had to make their way back across. It was easier going as the ground leveled somewhat.

It was a larger tree than it had seemed from below, its lacy leaves nearly obliterated by clusters of red berries littered over its surface. Pushing the grasping arms of the thick bushes aside, she forced her way toward it, glimpsing the narrow trunk. And below that, curled up on the ground at its roots, a glimmer of blue cloth.

"Fall!" she cried. "I think . . ."

She began to run, not caring if her skirts tore on the thorn bushes. When she cleared the overgrowth and broke into a tiny clearing surrounding the ash, she gave a cry, part triumph, part horror. It brought Fall running on her heels.

Claire was kneeling beside a small blue bundle curved around the trunk. She reached to lift the inert form and Fall glimpsed Alyce's face white against the shadows. As Claire cradled the girl in her arms, he knelt beside them.

"She's unconscious but she's breathing. Oh, Fall, we found her! We found her!"

The tears ran unashamedly down Claire's scratched cheeks as she kissed her sister's impassive face. There was a long inflamed tear down the flushed part of Alyce's cheek, and Claire thought she looked more gaunt than ever before.

"Did she fall? Is anything broken?" Gently Fall felt her thin arms and ankles. Alyce moaned and turned her head, flickering her eyes open briefly, long enough to recognize Claire. She reached up and touched her sister's face, trying to speak before blacking out once more.

455

"I think she's just weak and worn out. Poor dear! She must be starved. How are we going to get her down to the shore?"

"I'll carry her." It felt strange to cradle the girl's wispy body in his arms. He stood up, amazed at how little she weighed. "She's nothing but skin and bones. She must not have eaten since Edgar hauled her away."

Claire could see that across the river on the western shore the sun was a cerise globe poised above the now black hills. The climb down was long and steep but her heart was so eased by their success that she barely felt it. Though Fall was forced to stop and rest several times, they made it down much faster than going up, even with the burden of an unconscious Alyce. By the time they scrambled to the landing, the orange sail was about to put in to shore, and they could see the dark outline of the master, waving his arms at them.

Twenty

Claire saw the carriage pull up in front of the house as she was arranging a bowl of dried flowers on the wide ledge. Pulling back the striped silk curtain she made certain it really was Sir Francis Murray stepping down before going to call Fall. With some trepidation she opened the door and stood waiting while the elegantly clad gentleman walked up the path, all businesslike and serious. When he spotted her, he removed his hat from his elaborate periwig.

"Mistress Montcrieff?"

Though Claire had never formally been introduced, she remembered Sir Francis from the market day at Drummond so long ago. She gave him a curtsy and her warmest smile.

"You are welcome, Sir Francis."

He stepped into the room and was immediately swept up in Fall's affectionate embrace. Pumping his friend's hand, Fall greeted him effusively, trying to say how glad he was to see his old friend again.

"And you look as though you've prospered," he added with a wink.

"Thanks to your friend, Mister Philipse. He's a good fellow to do business with."

"It has made him one of New York's wealthiest citizens. Come, she's in the garden out back."

Sir Francis hesitated. "The girl?"

"Yes, my sister. You must meet her."

Claire relieved Sir Francis of his hat and cane and watched as the two men moved through the kitchen and into the garden. At the far end Alyce was barely visible sitting in a chair with a robe over her lap. She looked up as they approached, Claire noted, without covering her marked cheek. She sighed as she saw Sir Francis bend over the girl's hand.

Hours later, after Murray had left and Nell had helped Alyce up to bed, Claire and Fall walked down the road to the old sheep walk and sat on the boulder that overlooked the river. The sounds of the city were soft in the distance, intermingling with the pastoral complaint of a cow and the bleating of several sheep being driven home. Above them a hawk made one last swoop at the water before heading back to his nest.

Claire leaned back against Fall and rested against him, savoring the light touch of his fingers wandering over her throat.

"So it is really true. Alyce is your true sister."

"That's right. Sir Francis confirmed everything old Tom told us. My father must have been suffering pangs of guilt and remorse over disowning his only daughter for a long time now. Before he died, he decided to make amends and wrote a new will leaving everything that did not already belong to Edgar to her. That will was the first Sir Francis knew about Alyce's relationship to us."

"I wonder what Edgar must have thought when he learned of it."

"Whatever he thought about having a sister, it was obvious enough what he did about it. Once Sir

Francis learned that Edgar had sailed for New York, he decided to go after him just to make certain no harm came to the girl. Sir Francis had a soft spot for my mother, and he figured he owed it to her to protect her only daughter. Of course, he's a man of business too, and this gave him the perfect opportunity to talk with Philipse face to face."

"But, Fall, does that mean Alyce is rich?"

"Not rich but wealthy enough to pay my fine — which she insists on doing."

Claire looked up in surprise. "How good of her. And how typical. That frees you of that problem, then." She smiled up at him, her eyes twinkling with mischief. "Though it also means you'll have to find some other way of making your fortune than to marry a wealthy widow."

He refused to rise to the bait. Very seriously he said, "Caleb told me today that he intends to marry Nell. Isn't that astounding?"

"No, I expected it. He pretends that he hates her, but I noticed that, when those Indians came through Alan's window, it was Nell he rushed to help. And he never left her for a moment."

Abruptly Fall pulled away, grasping Claire by her shoulders and looking directly into her eyes. "Listen to me, Claire. I don't want any more wealthy widows. I don't want anyone but you. I've had my fill of this unsettled life, and I've made up my mind. I want us to be married. Alyce, you, Caleb, and Nell — you are all my family now, the only family I have in the world. I don't want to lose you."

Claire was too astounded to speak at first. He couldn't mean it. It was so unlike him. "But Ben Brogain? You're the eldest son now. Don't you want to go back? Doesn't Alyce want to go back?"

"She has no love for Ben Brogain. How could she

when my family all but drove her away. Her only need is to be close to those she loves. She is delighted that she has the money to help us and she wants to use it for our good."

"Then we'll make our life here in this new country. It gives me a strange feeling to think it, sad but happy too."

"I don't hear you saying 'yes.' Don't you want to marry me?"

Claire hesitated a moment as if she was thinking it over. Then abruptly she threw herself against him, pinning him back on the stone, his arms around her waist, her body stretched the length of his. Her blood went surging. It had been a long time.

A chuckle, starting deep in her throat bubbled to the surface, breaking into a laugh on the waves of sheer delight that swept through her.

"Just try to get away!"

ROMANCE IN THE OLD WEST
by Cassie Edwards

SAVAGE PARADISE   (1985, $3.95)
When a virile Chippewa brave saved Mariana's life, she
never wanted to leave the wilderness of the unsettled Min-
nesota Territory which she had once detested. Lone Hawk
cursed his weakness for the hated paleface, but for now he
would take her time and again to glory in their *Savage Paradise*.

EUGENIA'S EMBRACE   (1880, $3.95)
At sixteen, Eugenia Marie Scott was ill prepared for the
harsh life she was thrust into: the rough, coarse gold min-
ing town of Cripple Creek. There she was drawn to Drew,
an exciting man of adventure. Drew made Eugenia a
woman, and she fell under a spell she would never break
for the rest of her life.

PASSION'S FIRE   (1872, $3.95)
At first sight, Samantha thought Troy was a cad, but after
one brief kiss, one tender caress, he awakened an unfamiliar stirring from deep within her soul. Troy knew he would
be the one to unleash her passions, and he swore to find
her again . . . . to make her burn with *Passion's Fire*.

SAVAGE TORMENT   (1739, $3.95)
Judith should have been afraid of the red-skinned warrior,
but those fears turned to desire as her blue eyes travelled
upward to meet his. She had found her destiny—bound by
his forbidden kiss.